ASHES

A NOVEL

Sharon Gloger Friedman

outskirts
press

Outskirts Press, Inc.
http://www.outskirtspress.com

ISBN: 978-1-4787-6947-7

Library of Congress Control Number: 2018907940

Outskirts Press and the "OP" logo are trademarks belonging to Outskirts Press, Inc.

PRINTED IN THE UNITED STATES OF AMERICA

For George
My husband. My best friend. My for-always love.

"The phoenix hope, can wing her way through the desert skies, and still defying fortune's spite; revive from ashes and rise."

Miguel de Cervantes

PART I

CHAPTER 1

The chill of the waning days of March seeped into the old stone house on Gostinnii Street. In no hurry to leave the warmth of her bed, thirteen-year-old Miriam burrowed deep into the covers. The clanging of pots and pans and the smell of simmering chicken soup from the kitchen below could only mean that her mother had been up for hours preparing the house for Passover.

Miriam groaned at the thought of all that had to be done. The pots and dishes the family used the rest of the year had to be put away. The plates and utensils used just for Passover had to be washed and made ready for the eight-day holiday. All *chametz*, leavened food not kosher for Passover, had to be removed from the house and burned. And despite Mama's head start, they would be cooking and baking all day in preparation for the first Seder tonight.

Half awake, Miriam rolled to her side and tried to reclaim a few more minutes of sleep.

As if she had read Miriam's mind, her mother called up the stairs, "Miriam, get up, you lazy child."

Miriam pulled a pillow over her head and closed her eyes. It was so unfair that her brother Eli could go to school and was not expected to do anything in the house while she had to spend the day cooking and cleaning with Mama.

"Miriam, get up this instant," said her mother in a voice that sent Miriam scrambling out of bed. Shivering, she washed her face in the blue enamel basin on the bedside table, dressed quickly, and put her unruly red curls into a thick braid before she scurried downstairs.

"Look who has blessed me with her presence," said Sadie, her smooth face flushed from the heat of the kitchen. Beads of sweat dotted her forehead, the dark hair peeking out from her head scarf damp with perspiration. When she hugged and kissed Miriam, the matzah flour clinging to the front of her apron sprayed yellow powder into the air.

Sullen and still sleepy, Miriam wriggled from her mother's embrace and drew closer to the warmth of the brick oven.

Sadie studied her spirited daughter. Why hadn't she noticed before how tall Miriam had become or the soft curves that were changing her slender body? When had her round face been replaced with high cheekbones and the small dimple in her chin become more prominent?

Conscious of her mother's stare, Miriam smoothed away the loose curls that had escaped her braid and stared back in defiance, tiny freckles dancing brightly on her cheeks.

"Don't give me that look. I know you are mad at me for getting you up early, but there is much to be done, and I need your help. Uncle Reuben, Aunt Gitel, and the girls will be joining us for the first and second Seders. They'll be staying here both nights. And no arguments; Bina and Riva are going to sleep in your room."

Miriam's blue eyes flashed in anger. "Mama, they are spoiled brats. All Bina talks about are her fancy clothes and the boys in her class. Riva does nothing but whine. And how come Bina and Riva can go to school, and I can't?"

There it was: Miriam's greatest disappointment and Sadie's greatest heartache. Bright and curious and so eager to learn, Miriam desperately wanted to go to school like her brother.

"I am sorry, Miriam, but you know there's not enough money to send both you and Eli to the Jewish school. Papa will continue to teach you at home."

"But, Mama, Uncle Reuben owns a general store just like Papa does. Why don't we have as much money as they do?"

Sadie's face hardened. "Miriam, my brother inherited the store from your grandfather. You know your father started with nothing and made his way on his own. Meyer Raisky is a respected member of this community. You should care less about how much money we have and more about what a good man your father is."

Ashamed, Miriam looked down so Sadie could not see the tears welling in her eyes.

"Now, eat some breakfast and then let's get to work. Papa and Yuri will be home at lunchtime to burn the *chametz*."

The mention of Yuri's name made Miriam smile. A childhood friend of her father's, Yuri Ameniv worked in the store with Meyer. Unmarried and with no living family, he doted on Miriam and Eli, and she could not remember a time when "Uncle" Yuri had not been part of their lives.

Still unhappy about having to help her mother and furious at the thought of sharing her bed with her cousins, Miriam spent the morning doing her chores. By the time she had polished her great-grandmother's silver holiday candlesticks, trimmed the wicks on the glass-bowl kerosene lamps, and washed and dried the Passover dishes, Meyer was making his way up the dirt path to the house.

Sadie greeted her husband with a kiss, touching his cold cheek with her warm hand, inhaling the familiar smell of pipe tobacco that clung to him. "Where's Yuri? I made enough potato soup for both of you."

"There is so much to do at the store before the holiday; he decided to stay," said Meyer, shaking his head slightly and sending his wife a look that clearly meant he would explain everything to her later. "I should get back too; with *Pesach* coming, there were a lot of people in the store when I left."

Sadie did not question him further and handed Meyer the bag of *chametz*.

Clouds the color of a stormy sea cast a chilling darkness over the day. Pulling up the collar of his long black coat to ward off the biting cold, Meyer placed the bag of leavened foods in a metal barrel in the yard behind the house, making sure not to trample the purple blooms just beginning to poke through the soil in Sadie's garden.

As he lit the fire, he found unexpected comfort in reciting the traditional prayer uttered by centuries of Jews before him as they prepared for Passover: "Blessed are You, Lord our God, King of the universe, who has sanctified us by His commandments, and commanded us to remove the leaven."

Meyer moved closer to the fire for warmth and watched as the flames caught and quickly consumed the *chametz*. A sudden gust of wind stirred the ashes, sending them swirling upward like a swarm of blackened butterflies. As the embers popped and sparked, Meyer's thoughts drifted back to his life before Sadie and the children, when he called Kiev home.

Life for Jews in Kiev had always been difficult, but in 1881, after Tsar Alexander II was assassinated and rumors began to circulate that Jews were responsible, it became intolerable. Bad economic conditions only heightened lingering anti-Jewish hatred. Even his friend Yuri, who was not Jewish, was harassed because of his friendship with Meyer.

Fueled by false reports of Jewish aggression in the press, the simmering anti-Semitism boiled over, and within a month of the Tsar's death, the pogroms began. While the police and government officials stood by, bands of rampaging townspeople burned Jewish homes, looted Jewish-owned businesses, desecrated synagogues, and turned their wrath on the people of the Jewish community.

At school when the worst violence broke out, sixteen-year-old Meyer ran toward his home as news of the rioting spread. Fear rose in his throat as billowing clouds of black smoke filled the horizon and darkened the sky. His heart pounding, he crested the hill that led to his home and stared in horror as his house was engulfed in flames.

"Mama! Papa!" he screamed, running blindly toward the inferno.

Choking on the acrid smoke that clogged the air, Meyer raced toward the still-standing barn, praying his parents were safe and hiding inside. Hands shaking so badly he was unable to gain entrance, he kicked the door until it splintered open. Inside, their cow and horses were gone, and the eerie quiet sent a surge of dread through Meyer.

Frantic to find his parents, he was only a few steps into the barn when he saw his father's body lying face down in a pile of blood-soaked hay. Meyer's mouth went dry, and he felt as if all the air had gone out of his lungs. His legs felt disconnected from his body, and he stumbled to where his father lay. Taking his father's limp body in his arms, Meyer looked down to see he had been bludgeoned so brutally he no longer had a face. Drenched in his father's blood, Meyer slipped into a pool of blackness.

When he woke, the first face Meyer saw was Yuri's. He grabbed his friend's hand and sobbed, "My father is dead. I couldn't find my mother."

Mikhail Ameniv, Yuri's father, sat down on the bed. "Meyer, there was rioting against the Jews. People from town ...." He stopped, unable to tell the weeping boy more. "As soon as we heard what was happening, we rode to your house, but we were too late."

"My mother?"

Mikhail shook his head and rested his hand on Meyer's shoulder. "I'm so sorry, son; we found her body in the charred ruins."

The sound of laughter coming from the house brought Meyer back from his terror.

Now there were rumors circulating that the same organized violence against Jewish businesses and homes was being planned for Kishinev within the week. Meyer shuddered as memories of the horrors of the Kiev pogrom overwhelmed him: The smell of burning flesh, the ashes that rained down on the scorched earth, the unbearable anguish of burying the battered and burned bodies of his parents.

Gazing into the kitchen, he could see Sadie and Miriam laughing and wiping matzah flour from each other's cheeks. "I will not let it happen again," he said to no one. "I will not lose someone I love again."

CHAPTER 2

March 30, 1903, Sunday Afternoon

Eli was working at the counter with Yuri when Meyer got back to the store. He smiled as he watched his son finish waiting on a customer. At sixteen, Eli was gangly and thin, all arms and legs and almost as tall as Meyer. Dark-haired and brown-eyed like his mother, his height appeared to be the only trait he inherited from his red-headed father.

A good boy, Meyer thought, always coming straight from school to help out in the store. And so quickly becoming a man.

Sensing his father's gaze, Eli signaled that he wanted to talk to Meyer in the back office.

"Papa, I heard some strange talk in school today. Yankel and some of the other boys said there was going to be trouble for the Jews this week. They said it had to do with a boy being killed in Dubossary and something called a blood libel. What is that? I asked Uncle Yuri, and he said to talk to you."

Meyer sat down, tentacles of fear spreading through his body.

"Eli, this is a false legend that has haunted Jews for centuries. It's the foolish belief that Jews need the blood of a young person to make matzah. The boy in Dubossary was killed by a cousin who wanted his share of their grandparents' inheritance, but the newspapers published the rumor that the boy's body was full of holes used to drain his blood. The papers eventually printed a retraction, but because Passover starts tonight, and we eat matzah, the harm is already done. It looks as if your friend may be right about the possibility of trouble."

"Even if the papers say it's not true?"

"People believe what they want to believe. They are saying the retraction was printed under pressure from wealthy Jews."

Eli looked frightened. Meyer wanted desperately to take his son in his arms and tell him everything would be all right. But he was almost a man now, and he needed to be prepared for what might be coming.

"Yuri has been keeping me informed of what is being said outside the Jewish sections. Hopefully, we will be able to stop this before it starts. Still, do not mention what we've discussed to Mama and Miriam. I don't want to worry them."

Eli nodded, but there was no hiding the fear in his eyes.

Meyer and Eli arrived home to find Reuben, Gitel, and the girls making themselves comfortable in the parlor. They were not surprised that Sadie and Miriam were busy putting the final touches on dinner while Gitel managed to stay as far from the kitchen as possible.

Smoothing his dark-blue brocaded vest over his ample stomach, Reuben rose to greet Meyer with a handshake. "*Chag Semeach*, happy holiday," he said. "And can this be Eli? He has grown so tall. Soon he will be taller than you. And do I see some dark fuzz on his face?" laughed Reuben, patting Eli on the back.

Eli thought he could feel the heat of a blush spread across his face. When his cousins started to giggle, he was sure his face was a bright red. Trying to regain his composure, he was surprised when his aunt pulled him into a hug, crushing him against her generous bosom. The strong smell of her perfume tickled his nose, and the beads on her silk dress scratched his cheek.

"You remember Bina and Riva, don't you? Bina is eleven years old now, and Riva is eight," his aunt said, pointing toward her daughters.

The girls, wearing identical white dresses with black sashes and big black bows in their perfectly curled hair, stared dumbly at Eli.

Eli nodded in their direction and shoved his hands into his pockets to make sure he did not have to hug his cousins. "I need to get changed," he mumbled, seizing on an excuse to leave.

"Me too," chimed in Meyer, ducking into the kitchen on his way upstairs. "It smells delicious in here," Meyer said, hugging his wife and daughter and forcing an air of good cheer.

"Go quickly and wash up so we can start the Seder before sundown," said Sadie. "And again, I see Yuri isn't here. Where is he this time?"

"He'll be here. He's closing the store for me, and then he wanted to go home and change. He knows we have to complete most of the Seder before we can eat. I assure you he will be here in time for dinner. When has he ever missed a chance to enjoy your cooking?"

The long wooden table in the dining room was covered with an embroidered cloth and set with the blue-rimmed Passover dishes that belonged to Sadie's mother. The Seder plate with its symbolic foods was placed in the center, and the candles in the newly polished holder cast a warm glow over the room. As they took their places, Miriam looked at her family with a sudden rush of pride and love. Despite how plain their dark-colored clothes seemed compared with the colorful attire of her visiting relatives, Papa looked especially handsome tonight, his red hair and beard neatly combed. Mama's face was rosy from the heat in the kitchen, and her smile and sparkling brown eyes enhanced her natural beauty. Even Eli had managed to tame his unruly hair for the occasion.

With Meyer at the head of the table, the two families raised the first of four cups of wine that were part of the Seder and recited the prayer that begins the meal: "Blessed are You, God, our Lord, King of the universe, Creator of the fruit of the vine. Blessed are You, God, our Lord, King of the Universe, who has granted us life, sustained us, and enabled us to reach this occasion."

The irony of the holiday they were about to observe did not escape Meyer. The celebration of the Jews' liberation by God from slavery in Egypt, Passover commemorates their freedom as a nation. We no longer wander in the desert, Meyer thought, but we have not escaped the oppression of those who hate us.

Heavy-hearted, Meyer washed his hands as the Seder required, and began the service. Guided by the *Haggadah*, the text that relates the story of the Jews' exodus from Egypt in a set order, Meyer led the families through the Seder. After explaining the symbolism of the foods in the Seder plate; after listening to Riva, the youngest child at the table, recite the four questions that focus on why this night is different from all other nights; and after consuming the third cup of wine, it was at last time for the meal. And just as Meyer had predicted, Yuri arrived as the steaming dinner of matzah ball soup, roasted chicken, potato kugel, and stewed carrots was placed on the table.

His fair skin flushed from the cold and his blond hair tousled from the wind, Yuri greeted everyone and kissed Sadie on the cheek. "I can see that I got here just in time," he said, breathing in the enticing aromas. "Everything looks delicious."

"You do have a talent for showing up when there is food on the table," said Sadie, her eyes revealing the great affection she had for this man who was more like Meyer's brother than a friend. Yuri's family had given Meyer a home after his parents had been killed, despite the danger of having a Jew in their household. Meyer told her many times that he would have been lost without the kindness and love of Yuri and his family. Yes, Yuri liked to gamble and drink at the taverns, and his resistance to settling down had left a trail of broken-hearted women who had succumbed to his charm, but Sadie loved Yuri as much as Meyer did.

Taking the yarmulke Meyer offered him, Yuri took his place at the table next to Miriam. Unlike Meyer and Reuben, who wore uncut beards, Yuri kept his face clean-shaven, except for his neatly trimmed mustache. Miriam kissed his smooth cheek and secretly thought he was even more handsome than Papa.

Catching Yuri's eye, Meyer raised his eyebrows in a silent question. Yuri slowly shook his head and Meyer could feel his heart sink.

When at last the table had been cleared and the dishes washed, and the girls were in bed, Sadie and Gitel excused themselves for the evening. The three men and Eli, sated by the meal and four cups of wine, settled into the overstuffed sofa and high-backed chairs in the parlor. Meyer lit his pipe, inhaling deeply; stretching his six-foot frame, he stared into the flames and crackling logs in the fireplace.

"I didn't want to say anything in front of the women and the girls, but some of my customers have heard rumors that there is going to be violence this week in Kishinev," said Reuben, disturbing Meyer's reverie.

"We have heard the same rumors," said Meyer, leaning forward in his chair. "Yuri, did you learn anything new tonight?"

"I did, and it's worse than we thought. I stopped by the tavern on

Aleksandrov Street and heard some of the men bragging about how they were going to be rich by Easter Sunday. Boris, the one who works in the grain mills, said he'd heard that the Tsar had issued a secret decree allowing people to attack and plunder Jewish homes and businesses without interference from the authorities."

Yuri reached into his pocket and produced a folded paper. "These are starting to appear in the taverns and other places where workers meet."

Meyer took the handbill and read it out loud. "Jews kill our children to get their blood! Jews are stealing from us! Take revenge against the Jewish exploiters in the name of the Tsar!"

The room became quiet, each man alone with his fear. It was Eli who broke the silence.

"Papa, can't we do something? Go to the police? Surely, they won't let this happen."

Meyer and Yuri exchanged glances. Unable to wash away memories of the Kiev atrocities, they knew all too well about the apathy of the authorities and the horrific acts riled-up and hate-filled men were capable of.

"This has been brewing for months now. That anti-Semite Krushevan has been using *Bessarabets,* his newspaper, to stir up trouble. Now these fliers. I plan to meet with the rabbi and members of the committee at the synagogue to put together a delegation to approach the authorities, but I suspect the government is involved," said Meyer.

"From what I've been hearing, I have to agree," Yuri said. "You might also try to talk to the bishop of the Orthodox Church, though I am not sure he will listen."

Meyer turned to his brother-in-law. "Reuben, I know you planned to stay for the second Seder tomorrow night, but under the circumstances, I think you and Gitel and the girls should leave for Oreheyev first thing in the morning. I do not know what the next few days will bring."

Reuben rose to embrace Meyer. "I agree we should go, but I am frightened for all of you. If you think things will be as bad as they appear, come and stay with us."

Sadie was awake when Meyer came into their bedroom. She waited until he was in bed and had slipped under the covers before she spoke.

"You were downstairs for a long time. I saw the look on Yuri's face when he came in, and I know something is wrong. What is happening?"

Meyer took her in his arms. "It's the old troubles. The rumor about the boy who was killed in Dubossary is spreading throughout the city, made worse by false accusations and reports in *Bessarabets*. Yuri has been mixing with the townspeople and he says there is talk of violence against Jews on Easter Sunday."

Sadie clung to Meyer and began to cry.

Meyer gently wiped away her tears as they spilled down her cheeks. "I told Reuben to take Gitel and the girls and leave for home tomorrow just in case things get bad before Sunday. I think you and the children should go with them."

Sadie pulled away from Meyer's embrace. "I will not leave you. Nor will I allow the children to be apart from us."

"You are being unreasonable. Think of the children's safety."

"I am," Sadie insisted, her face set in defiance. "How do we know things will be any better in Oreheyev? This is our home, and who can protect Miriam and Eli better than we can? The people here know you. You've been good to Jews and Gentiles alike. Why would they harm us?"

Because deep down, they resent us, thought Meyer. Because they blame us for all their problems. Because they are being told by the government and a handful of local anti-Semites that it is acceptable to steal from and harm Jews.

Sadie laid her head on Meyer's chest. With images of his dead parents and his Kiev home in ashes carved into his memory, it was hours before he drifted into a fitful sleep.

CHAPTER 3

March 31, 1903, Monday Morning

It was the cold that woke Miriam. Her muscles aching from sleeping curled up and uncovered in the corner of her bed, she eyed her sleeping cousins and immediately recognized the source of her discomfort. Bina was rolled up in the covers on one side of the bed, and Riva, arms and legs spread wide apart, occupied the rest of the mattress.

"Selfish brats," Miriam muttered under her breath. She dressed quickly, taking no care to be quiet. Much to her disappointment, the girls did not stir.

Downstairs, Miriam was surprised to find Eli sitting by himself in the kitchen, a bowl of untouched porridge in front of him. Ladling a bowlful of the hot potato-based cereal from a pot atop the brick oven, Miriam joined him at the table.

Eli looked up as if realizing for the first time that she was downstairs. "You are up early, Miri," he said, calling her by the pet name only he used.

"That's because our cousins have taken over all the covers and my bed. And Bina snores. Loudly. So much for her fancy ways."

"Poor Miri," he laughed.

"Where is everyone? I thought I heard Mama and Papa talking. And why aren't you getting ready for school?"

Eli hesitated. "Papa doesn't want me going to school today. Miri, I'm not supposed to tell you this, but there may be trouble for the Jews this week, and we have to be alert. Uncle Reuben, Aunt Gitel, and the girls are going home today instead of staying for the second Seder, just in case something happens."

Miriam was silent for a moment, trying to absorb all Eli said. "The kind of trouble – the pogroms – that killed Papa's parents?"

Eli hated the look of fear on her face. There was so much more he wanted to tell her. That he loved her and that he would protect her from the violence he knew was coming. Instead, he squeezed her hand. "Everything will be all right, I promise."

When everyone was downstairs for breakfast, Miriam immediately sensed the distance between her parents. Her suspicions were heightened when Uncle Reuben and Papa talked in low tones behind the closed doors of the parlor.

Miriam thought she would be glad to see her relatives leave but found herself feeling oddly sad when she had to tell them goodbye. She was frightened by the way Mama and Uncle Reuben clung to each other. When they finally separated, Uncle Reuben turned to her father. "You know you are all welcome to stay with us. Just don't wait too long to decide."

It was at that moment that Miriam feared Eli would not be able to keep his promise.

CHAPTER 4

March 31, 1903, Monday Afternoon

Meyer and two other men who represented the Jewish community in Kishinev gathered in the rabbi's study. The rumors were all over the city now, and the tension in the room was palpable as they waited in silence for the rabbi to join them.

Lost in thought, Meyer watched specks of dust dancing in the shaft of light from the room's only window. He began to pace, unable to contain his anxiety. So many books, he thought, scanning the tomes on the crowded shelves that lined the study. All the wisdom of our faith, but no answers for what lies ahead for the Jews of Kishinev.

It was then that Rabbi Moses Zirelber joined the group. He was a small man, stooped by age and years spent studying his beloved Torah. His countenance calm as usual, he greeted the men and took a seat behind the large table that served as his desk.

"I have been talking to other members of the synagogue, and I am as concerned as you are about the possible violence," said Rabbi Zirelber, folding his hands, spotted and ribboned with blue veins, in front of him.

"Meyer has suggested, and I agree, that we should send a delegation to talk to Governor von Raaben and ask him to provide protection if mobs gather and become violent. We also discussed seeking out Bishop Iakov and asking him and his clergy to denounce the blood libel murder ritual as untrue and to urge their followers not to harm Jews or their property."

Simon Zecter, who owned a tobacco store in the center of town, shook his head. "Governor von Raaben has shown himself to be sympathetic to Jews, but he spends most of his time gambling and going to dinner parties. Besides, he delegates most of his decisions to Vice Governor Ustrogov, and he is definitely not sympathetic to us. I am not sure how much help we will get from them. I'm also not sure how open Bishop Iakov will be to any request to act on behalf of Jews."

"I don't see why we have to go begging for help from the authorities," said Aaron Fridlander angrily. "I say we arm ourselves and resist. If they want to come after us, we will be ready."

"And what will we fight them with?" asked Meyer. "Rakes? Hoes?"

"Some of us have guns," Aaron said defiantly.

"Enough talk of fighting violence with violence," said the rabbi in a rare show of temper. Smoothing his gray beard to calm himself, he looked from man to man. "We will go to see the governor and the bishop. They are reasonable men and will listen to us."

"It's a waste of time. I have better things to do," said Aaron, storming out of the study.

It took two days to arrange a meeting with the governor. After waiting half an hour to be seen, Meyer and Simon were ushered into the governor's office, richly decorated with deep carpets, inlaid tables, and red velvet-covered chairs. The room's opulence made the men feel uneasy, but it was the prominently displayed portrait of Tsar Nicholas II staring down on them that left them particularly anxious.

Governor von Raaben rose from behind his intricately carved desk and greeted the men warmly. "I understand why you are here," he said with seeming sympathy.

"Then you are aware of the threat of violence against Jews on Easter Sunday," said Meyer. "We ask that you do whatever you can to put a stop to this before it starts."

The governor walked around to the front of his desk. "It is hard to control rumors. I am of the opinion that there won't be violence on Sunday," said von Raaben, "but I will order a police presence in town for extra protection." He offered additional reassurances and walked Meyer and Simon to the door of his office, putting an end to the meeting.

"I am of the opinion there won't be violence," mocked Simon as they left the governor's office. "I am of the opinion that he doesn't know what he's talking about."

The meeting the next day with Bishop Iakov was even less encouraging. The cleric swept into the room in haste, the silk of his long black cassock rustling as he approached Simon and Meyer. Signaling his impatience with the meeting, he fingered the gold cross and image of Christ that hung from the heavy gold chains around his neck. Even as they described the rumors, it quickly became apparent to Meyer and Simon that the bishop knew little of Jewish religious practices. Worse, he showed no inclination to deny the blood libel legend or address his flock on behalf of the Jewish townspeople.

Leaving the massive white church fronted by six Doric columns, the men were disheartened. "We won't get any help from the bishop. I think he believes the blood libel legend is true," said Meyer. "Aaron was right; it was a waste of time."

CHAPTER 5

April 5, 1903, Saturday Night

Miriam's days following the first Seder were filled with confusion. The house felt cold and foreign to her, the comfort and rhythm of their day-to-day lives overshadowed by the tension that hung in the air like a slowly spreading poison.

Rumors of the impending violence in the Jewish sectors of the city continued to mount. Yuri, who as a Christian could easily blend in with the workers at the taverns and cafés scattered around Aleksandrov Street, became Meyer's eyes and ears, appearing at their door late at night to report any news.

It became Miriam's habit in the days leading up to Easter to stay awake and listen for Yuri's voice. Slipping out of bed, she would sit at the top of the stairs, listening to the two men talk. Usually, the message was the same: The police were aware of the rumors, but nothing was being done to dispel them.

But the night before Easter Sunday, Yuri brought disturbing news.

"It's getting worse," reported Yuri. "Outsiders are appearing in the city – Albanians, Turks, and Rumanians – and they are encouraging violence. The Jewish community is fearful, and there is a new rumor spreading about a young Russian girl who worked as a housemaid for a Jewish doctor. I have heard that she poisoned herself, but the story that's circulating is that there were deep wounds all over her body and that the blood had been drained from her remains. There is a lot of hate boiling over. Tomorrow is the last day of Passover, and I think that is adding to the anger out there."

Meyer began pacing the room. His shoulders were bowed, his face furrowed in worry. "I am not sure the governor will be true to his word and provide police for protection. We've asked for soldiers from the garrison outside the city, but we don't know if they will be ordered to protect Jewish homes and property," he said.

Yuri studied the man he considered his brother. Theirs was a friendship that defied all odds, a meeting of opposites in so many ways, begun in a schoolyard when Meyer scared off a classmate who was bullying eleven-year-old Yuri. He smiled at the memory.

"What are you smiling at? There is nothing amusing about what's happening here," said Meyer.

"I was just remembering the first time we met. That pimply-faced Vasily Kalikoff had me down on the ground, punching me, and out of nowhere comes this big red-headed kid I'd never seen before and pulls him off of me."

Meyer nodded. "He was doing a pretty good job of rearranging your face."

"You did a pretty good job of scaring the hell out of him. Actually, you scared the hell out of me. You were breathing so hard and your face was so red, I thought you were waiting your turn to beat me up too. But then you just stared at Vasily, and one look at your fists sent him running."

Meyer laughed. "He did take off pretty quickly."

"It took a lot of courage to stand up to Vasily. We were all afraid of him."

"I was new to the school; I didn't know any better."

"But he never bullied me again and neither did the others. Your friendship protected me."

"It also hurt you. Yuri, don't you think I knew how much abuse you and your family took for taking me in? And now I'm afraid I must prevail upon our friendship once again. If anything happens to me, please look after my family."

"You are talking nonsense. What do you expect will happen to you? The governor will order the police into the city."

"Yuri, we lived through this before. The police looked the other way then, and I fear they will do the same now. In spite of what I have been telling Sadie and the children, I do not have a lot of faith in the authorities' ability or inclination to stop the violence. I have a bad feeling about how things will go, and I need you to promise me you will care for them if I am not around," said Meyer, grasping Yuri's arm.

Sensing Meyer's panic, Yuri faced his friend. "You know I will."

Meyer embraced him. "Do you remember Sadie's older sister Malka? She went to America."

"I do. She lives in New York, right?"

Meyer nodded. "If I am gone, I want Sadie and the children to go live with her. I know it is easier if they go to live with Reuben, but I don't think any place in Russia is going to be safe for Jews. Will you promise me you will get them to America?"

Yuri studied his friend and saw tears in his eyes. "If it gives you peace of mind, yes, I promise."

Still crouching at the top of the stairs, her arms wrapped around her knees for warmth, Miriam could feel her world caving in. Until this very moment, she had not been afraid. She was certain that they were in no danger, that Papa would protect them and keep them safe.

Frightened and bewildered by what she'd heard, Miriam crept silently down the hall to Eli's room. Knocking quietly, she was surprised when he immediately opened the door and appeared wide awake.

He held his finger to his lips and pulled her into his room. "Can't sleep either?" he asked.

Miriam looked away, embarrassed to admit she had been eavesdropping on Papa and Yuri. "I haven't been to sleep yet. I was listening to Papa and Yuri talk," she confessed, and told Eli everything she'd heard.

"I'm scared," she said when she had finished.

Eli wrapped his arm around his sister and felt her shivering. "You're cold, Miri. Let's get you into bed," he said, leading her back to her bedroom.

"Will you stay with me until I fall asleep?"

"Of course I will," he said, pulling the covers over his sister and sitting beside her on the bed.

It took only minutes for an exhausted Miriam to fall asleep. Listening to the steady rise and fall of Miriam's breathing, Eli kissed her forehead and whispered, "I'm scared too."

Despite the weariness that clung to his body, Meyer knew he would not get much sleep this night.

Sadie was having trouble sleeping too, and Meyer found her sitting up in bed when he entered their bedroom. "I'm sorry I'm so late. I hoped you'd be asleep," he said as he undressed.

"I was waiting for you. Yuri's visit this late at night can only mean that the rumors are true and there will be trouble tomorrow. I don't want you to go to the store."

"Sadie, I need to be there. I will not let our livelihood be destroyed. Please, let's not argue about this. We'll talk about it in the morning," said Meyer as he got into bed. "Get some sleep. Tomorrow is going to be a long day."

Instead of curling around his body as she usually did, Sadie rolled away from Meyer in a rare fit of anger.

Meyer sighed and stared at the ceiling, his mind wandering to the first time he saw Sadie. It was in Oreheyev at his cousin Nachum's wedding. Surrounded by jubilant guests, he watched as the bride and groom were lifted up on chairs and carried joyously around the room. Overcome by sadness and loneliness, he retreated from the gaiety of the wedding and stepped outside.

Breathing in the cool night air, he found the solitude beneath the stars comforting. He was thinking about his parents and how much he missed them at times like these, when he heard someone crying.

Peering into the shadows cast by light from the wedding celebration, Meyer saw a young girl weeping into her shawl.

"Are you all right?"

The girl startled and quickly wiped the tears from her face.

"I'm sorry, I didn't mean to frighten you," said Meyer.

The girl stepped into the light. "I tore my new dress," she said, pointing to the hem where a rip had created a streamer of dangling cloth. "I can't go back in there with it looking like this."

Unable to speak at first, Meyer realized this was not a girl, but a young woman, a very beautiful young woman, with dark hair and large brown eyes. Traces of tears remained on her high cheekbones, and he had to work hard to resist the temptation to brush them away.

"I don't think your dress looks bad, but if you don't want to return to the wedding, I would be happy for the company. My name is Meyer Raisky."

"I am Sadie Belitrov."

"Nice to meet you, Sadie Belitrov."

They talked until Sadie's parents came looking for her. She told him she was seventeen and that she and her sister Malka helped out in her father's store, along with her brother Reuben. He told her about his parents, how much he missed them and how he was helping Yuri's parents on their farm. When she left, he knew that he would return to Oreheyev often.

They married the year Sadie turned eighteen. Under the guidance of his father-in-law, Meyer worked in the family general store, learning how to please the customers and balance the ledgers. When Sadie's father died and the store went to Reuben, Meyer knew it was time to make a move on his own.

It took years of hard work to build up his trade in Kishinev. Even when Yuri joined him after his parents' deaths, it took long hours in the store to get where they were today. How could Sadie not understand that he wanted to protect what he had worked so hard for, that everything he did was for her and the children?

Meyer reached out and touched Sadie. She stirred briefly, and when he was finally sure she was in a deep sleep, he kissed her gently, rose from the bed, and dressed in the dark.

Slipping out of the house, his path lit by a sliver of moonlight shining through a cover of gray, ghost-like clouds, Meyer made his way to his store on Chuflinskii Square.

CHAPTER 6

April 6, 1903, Easter Sunday Morning

The sound of a key turning in the lock of the store's front door woke Meyer with a start. Confused to find himself asleep in a chair, and blinded by the sun coming through the large window with "Raisky's General Store" painted in gold letters, he stared at the looming shape hovering above him. His heart racing, he was relieved to see it was Yuri.

"You scared the hell out of me. What are you doing here?" he asked, rubbing his eyes and shaking away the fog of sleep.

"I was about to ask you the same thing."

"I am not going to let everything I've built here be taken from me. If there is going to be trouble, I need to be here."

"And how are you going to stop it?" asked Yuri, looking around the store. "By throwing vegetables at them?"

"I just want to be here to protect what's mine, and I have this," he said, holding up the axe handle he kept under the front counter. "How would you stop them?"

"With this," said Yuri, pulling a rifle from under his long coat.

Meyer leapt to his feet. "Put that thing away before you kill both of us. We don't even know for sure anything is going to happen."

"Last night you were begging me to take care of your family. Now you're saying nothing will happen. Who are you kidding? Meyer, it's going to happen. Coming here I passed houses and stores that have crosses painted on their doors. That can only mean one thing—they want to make sure they aren't mistaken for Jews."

"But we've been good to these people. They are our neighbors. I've given some of them credit when no one else would so they could put food on the table for their families."

"All true, but they've been fed all kinds of false stories by that bastard Krushevan in his newspaper. They are past being rational. Meyer, we know how this will go. You should be home with Sadie and the children. I can take care of the store. Everyone knows I'm not Jewish."

"And everyone knows you are part of my family," said Meyer, eyeing the weapon in Yuri's hand. "Where did you get the rifle?"

"It was my father's. It's old, but it still works."

Meyer sighed. "Show me how to use it."

Sadie awoke with a start. Breathing hard and covered in sweat, she told herself it was just a dream—men from town breaking into the house, torches in their hands, evil on their faces, chasing her. She tried to run, but her legs wouldn't move; she tried to scream, but there was no sound. She blinked to erase the visons of her terror and slowed her breathing. "Just a dream," she said, trying to ignore a creeping sense of dread.

Reaching for Meyer, she was surprised to find his side of the bed empty. Bewildered at first by his absence, the sudden realization of what day it was made her gasp. Sadie wrapped herself in her robe, and hurried downstairs to the kitchen where Eli and Miriam were finishing breakfast.

"Where's Papa?"

Shocked to see her mother still in her robe, hair uncombed, wild-eyed, Miriam stammered, "We thought he was upstairs with you."

The color drained from Sadie's face. "Oh God, he went to the store."

"I thought the store was closed today," said Eli jumping up from his chair. "I'll get my coat and go in too."

"No, you won't," said Sadie, her voice rising in near hysteria. "You will stay here."

"But Papa will need help if there is trouble."

"I'm sure Yuri will be there. I am going to need you here. We need to gather all the valuables and hide them in the attic. No, maybe the cellar will be better."

Miriam and Eli exchanged looks and stared at their mother in alarm.

Realizing how much she'd frightened her children, Sadie softened her face and tried to reassure them. "It's probably nothing, but just in case, we need to be prepared. I'm sure Papa will be home shortly. He probably just went to check on things," she said, and turned quickly to go upstairs so they wouldn't see her cry.

Miriam grabbed Eli's hand. "What's wrong with Mama? Is Papa in danger?"

"Don't be afraid, Miri. Papa is all right," said Eli, looking around the kitchen to see what they could use to defend themselves.

CHAPTER 7

Easter Sunday, Early Afternoon

Easter Sunday, the holiest day for the Christian citizens of Kishinev, was unusually mild. By midday, when church services had ended, townspeople were strolling along the town's boulevards, enjoying the weather. By late afternoon, large crowds had gathered in Chuflinskii Square, drawn there by the shops and merry-go-round at its center.

Meyer and Yuri were surprised by the calm of the morning. Although they'd opened early, only a few of their Jewish customers had entered the store. Now, as more of the townspeople began to assemble in the square, they watched as a growing number of youth congregated near the store, jostling one another and laughing at passers-by. When a policeman appeared and dispersed the boisterous group, Meyer relaxed a bit, surprised to discover his hands were balled into fists.

"Maybe the authorities will do their job after all," said Yuri.

Meyer shook his head and kept his eyes on the square, watching as Isaac Gabinsky, an elderly Jew who frequented the store, walked across the square. Just as he reached its center, he was surrounded by the same group of young men who had been loitering near the shop. Their playfulness quickly turned vicious, as they began pulling on the old man's beard, pushing him from one to the other, shouting, "Beat the Yid."

The frightened old man struggled with the men and managed to pull himself free of the laughing mob, losing his black fur hat in the scuffle.

Taunting the Jew as he fled, the group turned their wrath on the other Jews in the square, pulling at their coats and chasing them from the street. The cry, "Beat the Yids," turned into a chant as the younger members of the mob were joined by drunken adults.

As Meyer started to leave the store to help his neighbors, Yuri grabbed him by his jacket. "Do not go out there. They're harassing Jews, but not hurting them. You will only make it worse."

It did not take long for the chanting to give way to violence. With no interference from the police or onlookers, the rioters began to throw rocks at Jewish-owned stores. They quickly broke into smaller groups and began to spread throughout the streets of the city, breaking windows as they went.

"Look how they are forming groups, and how they are only attacking Jewish stores," said Meyer. "It looks like it's been planned. And the police are just standing there, letting it happen."

Before Yuri could respond, Meyer stepped out of the store and called to the police to stop the vandalism. The sudden sound of the exploding front window was deafening. Shards of glass showered down on Meyer, and only after he tasted the blood running down his face did he realize he had been injured.

Yuri pulled Meyer back into the store and pressed a handkerchief to the bleeding wound. "Are you crazy? What were you thinking?" Taking the cloth from Meyer's forehead, Yuri was relieved to see that the cut was not deep, and that the bleeding was subsiding. "It doesn't look too bad. Are you all right?"

"I'm fine," said Meyer, as he bent to pick up a brick sitting on top of the mound of broken glass at his feet.

Outside, the sound of shouting signaled the return of the rampaging crowds and the two men watched as the small mobs—no longer content to vandalize the stores of Jews—began looting and destroying anything they could not carry out of nearby shops.

"You'd better load your gun. I think this will work for me," said Meyer reaching for the axe handle.

Miriam and Eli spent most of the day helping Sadie search the house for anything she thought was of value. Their great-grandmother's silver candlestick holder, the silverware that Miriam had spent hours polishing just days before, the few pieces of jewelry Sadie had inherited from her mother, and the small silver brooch Meyer had given her on their wedding day were all wrapped in clean cloths and buried in the cellar. Eli placed a large, half-full barrel of potatoes over the spot to hide the disturbed dirt. Sadie removed the family photos hanging on the wall in the parlor and hid them in the attic. The telltale dark squares on the faded wallpaper mocked her effort.

When Sadie was finally convinced that everything of value had been hidden, they sat down for a late lunch of borscht and boiled potatoes. No one spoke, and the only sound was of Eli slurping the beet soup.

Sadie left her lunch untouched and stared blankly at the front door. "He should be home by now," she said more to herself than to Miriam and Eli.

Eli looked across the table at his mother. Her face was a mask of fear.

"I am going to the store to get Papa. It has been quiet here all day. It'll be fine."

This time, Sadie made no effort to stop him.

CHAPTER 8

Easter Sunday, Late Afternoon

Meyer, stationed on one side of the store's entry with Yuri at the other, made sure they were visible to the looters on the street. At first, their presence appeared to ward off the mob, and the initial onslaught of thugs moved on.

Just when Meyer was beginning to think they had escaped the worst of it, a rock glanced off of Yuri's head. Stunned and bleeding, he fell backwards into the store. Meyer crouched down and crawled into the shop as a hail of rocks and bricks flew over his head.

Emboldened by their success at pushing the two men back from their positions at the door, and armed with clubs, machetes, and knives, the drunken mob rushed the store. Struggling to regain his footing, Meyer was kicked and pushed back by the rampaging rioters. Everywhere Meyer looked, he saw the destruction of his life's work. The mob pulled down bolts of cloth that lined the store, tearing and trampling on them in a frenzy of hate. They hurled jars of candy against the walls, overturned bins of notions and small items, and demolished shelves, sending cans of food cascading across the floor. They smashed the cash register and fought with each other like jackals as they grabbed for the bills and coins that spilled from its drawer.

Enraged as men he considered his neighbors made off with whatever they could carry, Meyer grabbed the axe handle he'd dropped and began swinging it in wild circles. "Get out of my store," he screamed, as the sound of crunched bone and a howling cry of pain told Meyer he had hit his mark. Spotting a customer he had given credit to, he screamed, "Maxim, I helped you when you had no money. You would not have been able to feed your family if it wasn't for me. This is how you repay me?"

The brawny leather worker known for his love of whiskey and brawling glared at Meyer. "You are a fucking Yid and I owe you nothing," he said, pulling a knife from his belt and moving toward Meyer in full fury.

"I wouldn't do that if I were you," said Yuri, standing behind Meyer. Blood running from the gash on the side of his head, he pointed his rifle at the charging hulk. "If you think I won't shoot you, you're wrong, you piece of shit. Back off and put down the knife."

Maxim eyed the rifle aimed at his heart. All around him, the vandals froze and watched wordlessly as their leader dropped the knife and backed toward the door, his hands in the air.

Humiliated in front of the other men, Maxim threatened, "I am not done with you, Meyer. Or you either, Jew-lover."

"Just get out of here," shouted Yuri, and turning his gun on the other looters, warned, "and that goes for all of you too. Take nothing, and get the hell out of here before I decide to use this."

Dropping the stolen goods, the looters rushed the door, careening off of one another in their attempt to flee.

"You are making a habit out of saving my life," said a shaken Meyer.

They were picking through the damage when they heard the sound of crunching glass behind them. Yuri whirled around, rifle raised.

"Don't shoot. It's me, Eli," cried the terrified boy.

"Dear God, I could have killed you," said Yuri, his mouth suddenly dry, his heart beating wildly.

Meyer grabbed his son and hugged him. "What are you doing here?"

"We waited all day for you to come home. Mama is crazy with worry. I just wanted to make sure you were all right."

"How did you get here? There are rioting mobs everywhere," said Meyer, his voice rising in panic at the thought of the danger outside.

"I tried to stay off the main roads, and when I saw the mobs, I stuck to the alleys. But when I was crossing Dumbarskya Street, I almost ran right into a group of men. I was so scared, and then an old lady who lived in a house with a cross on the door pulled me into her home. I don't know her name or recognize her from the store, but Papa, she saved my life. I tried to thank her, but as soon as she saw that the men were gone, she shoved me back onto the street."

Eli was breathing hard now, fighting back tears. "There were men ripping up Torah scrolls, stomping and spitting on them in front of the synagogue. Then I saw the Orthodox bishop on the street. He was riding in his carriage and I couldn't believe what he did. He blessed the rioters as he passed them. When I got here and saw the rubble and the store window smashed in I thought you and Yuri were dead," said Eli, giving in to his tears.

Meyer pulled his son to him, holding him tight in his arms. Eli buried his face in his father's chest and sobbed.

The orgy of destruction and looting—unimpeded by the authorities—continued into the night. When the rioters finally tired of ransacking and destroying Jewish-owned stores, Chuflinskii Square looked like a battlefield. Doors hung off their hinges, slapping against their frames with each gust of wind. Bricks and rocks were strewn throughout. The street was covered in glass and littered with pieces of clothing and rotting food. Sacks of spilled flour and salt were everywhere, blanketing the street in white powder. A black pot-belly stove with a gaping hole where its door had been stood like a lone sentinel in the center of the square, an obscene reminder of the senselessness of the violence.

Meyer slipped out of the store to survey the damage and was sickened by the devastation before him. Alone in the square, he found the silence as unsettling as the deafening noise of the rioters just hours before. Still unable to comprehend the viciousness of the day, he stepped into the rubble, and had walked a few feet into the square when his foot hit what appeared to be a small arm. Thinking it was a doll, he pushed away the debris and stared in terror into the empty eyes of an infant encircled in the protective arms of its bloodied mother.

Meyer fell backwards, his legs churning, propelling him away from the corpses. Fear rose in his throat, and he vomited in a paroxysm of horror.

Half crawling, half running, Meyer made his way to the store, panting and covered in sweat, the taste of terror still in his mouth.

"You look awful," said Yuri. "What happened?"

"Where's Eli?"

"He's sleeping over there," said Yuri, nodding toward the boy curled up on a pile of clothes in the corner. "He's exhausted."

In a shaky whisper, Meyer told Yuri about the bodies in the square. "They are doing more than pillaging; they are killing. I am going to take Eli back to the house where it's safer. I think you will be all right here for a couple of hours. I will be back as soon as I can."

"Stay with your family. I will be fine."

"They are targeting stores, not homes. I am coming back."

Meyer and Eli moved silently in the darkness, sticking to alleys whenever possible. Gripping in one hand the knife that Maxim had left behind, Meyer kept his other hand on Eli's shoulder as they walked. When they neared home and had to walk out in the open, they came upon a man, reeking of alcohol and barely able to stand. Meyer tightened his grip on Eli.

Eyeing Meyer and the large knife in his hand, the drunk muttered something unintelligible and disappeared into the shadows. When Meyer was sure the man was gone, he realized Eli was shaking.

"It's all right. We're almost home," he said, pulling Eli close.

They arrived home sometime after midnight. Expecting the house to be dark, Meyer was surprised to see light coming from the parlor window. Unlocking the door and entering quietly, they found Sadie asleep in a chair, her sewing in her lap.

"I am going back to the store," he whispered to Eli. "You will stay here. Under no circumstances are you to come back into town. I need you to be here for Mama and Miriam. Do you understand?"

Eli nodded. "But Papa, what if they come back to the store?"

"Yuri and I took care of the mobs before; we can do it again. Besides, there really isn't much left to take. I will be home tomorrow, I promise." Meyer hugged his son and kissed his forehead. "Now go to bed."

Eli started upstairs and looked back at his father. "I love you, Papa."

"I love you too, son," said Meyer, his voice catching.

Meyer turned and watched Sadie sleep for a few minutes before he woke her with a kiss on her cheek. Her eyes opened slowly. She smiled sleepily when she saw him, and then fully awake, flew into his arms.

"I was so worried about you. Where is Eli? Is he safe?"

"He is fine. I told him to go to bed. He's exhausted. We had to wait for things to quiet down in town before we could leave. I'm so sorry we worried you. Is Miriam all right?"

"She's good, just frightened for you and Eli," said Sadie. She reached up to brush a loose curl of hair from Meyer's face and saw the cut on his forehead.

"What's this?" she gasped.

"It's nothing; a brick came through the front window and I got hit with a piece of glass. It hardly bled at all."

Holding her hand in his, Meyer told her all that had happened, withholding details about the dead mother and child in the square. "Sadie, I have to go back. Yuri is alone in the store, and I should be there too."

"What about us? What if the violence comes here?"

"You are safe in the house. The mobs are only interested in looting the stores. They got some things from us, but I am afraid they will come back. Sadie, if we lose any more, we will have nothing."

"You are not taking Eli with you," said Sadie defiantly. "You will not take our son."

"Eli will stay here with you and Miriam." He reached for her, but she turned away, anger blazing in her eyes.

"Go," she spat. "Go to your store."

Yuri sat in the doorway of the store, his rifle across his lap. His finger moved instinctively to the weapon's trigger as he watched the large figure moving across the square toward him. Standing, ready to aim, he relaxed as Meyer emerged from of the darkness.

"I was hoping you had decided to stay with Sadie and the children."

"This is where I need to be," said Meyer quietly, Sadie's last words still stinging his heart.

"While you were gone, I rounded up some of the other shopkeepers and we brought the bodies of the dead woman and her child to the Jewish Hospital. It was Tovah, Dov Zuskin's wife, and their daughter Zina. He is in Kiev on business."

"My God—he doesn't know his family is dead," said Meyer, his voice heavy with sorrow.

"I spoke to some of the men, and they are furious that the police did not intervene," said Yuri. "They told me they are going to band together in the square early in the morning to defend against the looters if they return."

"Then we will be with them," said Meyer, unable to erase the image of the dead mother and child from his memory.

CHAPTER 9

Easter Monday Morning

Sleep eluded Sadie after Meyer left. Worried and frightened, and angry at Meyer, she was still sitting in the chair when the first light of day glinted off the parlor window, painting the room in a pink glow. The screeching of a hawk drew her attention, and she looked out the window just as the predator swooped down and snatched a small rabbit nibbling on the sparse blades of grass. The reddish-brown bird spread its massive wings, and casting its shadow over the yard, soared upward, the rabbit struggling mightily in its talons.

Sadie shuddered. A bad omen, she thought, remembering her mother's unnatural fear of large birds. "The little ones are sweet to look at, but the big ones that kill their food are treacherous. They perch high up ready to pounce and their eyes see everything. They are evil," she once told ten-year-old Sadie.

Unsettled by the memory, Sadie was startled to hear "Mama." At first, she thought she had called to her mother out loud, but looked up to see Miriam standing at the foot of the stairs.

"Mama," Miriam said again. "Where are Papa and Eli? Are they home?"

"Eli is asleep upstairs. Papa brought him home during the night and then went back to the store," snapped Sadie.

Miriam stared at her mother, stunned by her tone. "What did I do? Are you mad at me?"

"No, of course not," said Sadie, instantly regretting her impatience with Miriam. "I am just tired and worried about Papa."

"He's safe, right? I mean, Easter Sunday is over, so there should be no more trouble. Right?"

"He's with Yuri. They'll be fine," said Sadie, as much to convince herself as Miriam.

As darkness gave way to early-morning light, Meyer and Yuri joined the nearly one hundred Jewish men armed with canes and stakes who had assembled near Chuflinskii Square to defend their property against the marauders. As they waited for the violence to begin, a palpable tension gripped the merchants, craftsman, and laborers who made up the corps of Jews.

"They are afraid," said Meyer.

"They should be. Look at what they are armed with," said Yuri, touching his rifle hidden under his coat. "I just hope they will be able to protect themselves if they have to. They are more comfortable with their books than they are with weapons."

"Looks like we are going to find out," said Meyer pointing at the first small bands of men assembling on the corners of the streets surrounding the square.

Once again taking up the chant "Beat the Yids" and raising their weapons, several groups of men moved toward the contingent of Jews.

Meyer and Yuri stood side by side with their friends and neighbors. Wielding their primitive weapons, the Jews were able to drive back the first groups of men who advanced on them. Encouraged by their initial success at warding off the rioters, they spread out and began to attack their attackers.

It was then that the same police who stood idly by a day earlier as stores and lives were destroyed, descended on the Jews, breaking up their efforts to defend themselves and arresting anyone who resisted.

After the police had scattered the men, rumors that Jews were attacking Christians spread rapidly throughout the city. The mobs grew larger as outsiders fell in with the townspeople. Once again, they broke into smaller groups and fanned out across the city.

"Let's get out of here," said Meyer, grabbing Yuri by his coat and leading him toward a side alley off New Marketplace.

Making their way back to the store, they witnessed a world gone mad.

Led by teenage boys who no longer confined their fury to stores, the mobs focused their hate on Jewish residences. Breaking apartment windows and doors, they boldly entered homes. As the helpless residents hid cowering in fear, the looters smashed glass and china and shredded so many pillows and mattresses that feathers picked up by a slight wind covered the streets and buildings like new-fallen snow.

On a rampage, the angry crowd tore apart furniture, tossing broken cabinets, sofas, dressers, and tables out on the street to be scavenged by the rioters. Like rabid dogs, men and women fell on clothing and coats that were thrown onto the cobblestones, leaving the scene wearing any garments that fit them.

After the crowd had expended its hate on Jewish properties, the looting and destruction quickly turned into a bloody and savage frenzy of vicious attacks on the Jewish men, women, and children of Kishinev. Ransacked homes and stores became fertile hunting grounds for the bloodthirsty mob. Jews discovered in lofts, closets, under beds, and in outdoor sheds were pulled from their hiding places and brutally beaten. An elderly woman fleeing for her life was beaten in the courtyard of her home and left to die in a pool of blood. A young boy, blind in one eye, was stabbed in his other eye. Crowbars and clubs found their targets with terrifying accuracy, leaving a trail of cracked skulls, broken bones, and death. Four men and women found hiding in an attic were thrown from the roof of their home and beaten by the rioters below.

Witnessing the mayhem as they retreated to the store, Yuri urged Meyer to go home. "You are not needed here. You should be with your family. It won't be long before these animals make their way to Gostinnii Street."

Worried now about Sadie and the children, Meyer offered no argument for staying. "Come with me. Let them have the store."

"No, I will not give in to this madness. Now go home. And take this," he said, handing Meyer his rifle. "It's loaded and ready to use. Just pull the trigger."

"I can't take this. How will you protect yourself?"

"With the revolver I have at the store."

Meyer shook his head. "What else have you been keeping from me?"

Yuri smiled and embraced his friend. "Please, go home to your wife and children. I will join you as soon as things quiet down in town."

CHAPTER 10

Easter Monday Afternoon

Sadie's resolve to remain calm quickly gave way to anxiety as the hours passed and Meyer did not return home. Alternately pacing and looking out the window, she could not rid her memory of the hawk swooping down on the rabbit.

"A bad omen," she mumbled to herself, and made a spitting sound between two fingers to ward off the evil spirits.

Watching their mother engage in this old superstition, Miriam and Eli felt their own fear intensify. Eli went to his mother and put his arm around her.

"I am sorry," she said, fighting back tears. "I am so worried that something has happened to Papa. He should be home by now."

"Mama, I think it may be hard to get past the mobs. I know we had to wait it out until things quieted down so we could come home last night."

"Mama, come, we haven't eaten all day. Let's make some lunch," said Miriam. "We'll all feel better if we eat."

A crashing noise made them jump. Eli rushed to the parlor window and peered outside. "Oh God," he whispered.

Miriam and Sadie joined him and watched in horror as a group of ten to fifteen men and women armed with clubs and machetes made their way up Gostinnii Street. As they approached the first house on the corner, a group of five broke off and began throwing rocks at the windows.

Frozen in fear, Miriam and Sadie clung to each other. Eli quickly locked the doors and windows. Grabbing a knife from the kitchen, he pushed his mother and sister toward the cellar door.

"Quick, down here," he said, lighting a lamp to direct their way and bolting the door behind them.

Sadie pulled at her son. "We must protect Miriam from the men," she said staring into Eli's eyes to make sure he understood.

Confused at first, he shuddered in comprehension. Looking around for a safe place to hide his sister, he spotted the barrel of potatoes. He looked at his mother and she nodded.

Emptying the barrel, he called to Miriam. "Get in."

She looked at him as if he had gone mad. "No, it's filthy."

"Miri, get in the barrel now. I am going to cover you with the potatoes and no matter what you hear or what you see, you are not to make a sound. Do not leave this barrel until there is no one here but us. Do you understand?"

She stared dumbly at her brother.

Eli shook her and shouted, "Do you understand?"

Frightened by his anger, she nodded and climbed into the barrel. "Remember, not a sound, and only come out if we are the only ones here," said Eli as he carefully piled the potatoes on top of Miriam.

"Mama, get under the stairs and hide against the far wall. I'm going to wedge myself in the corner opposite Miri."

Sadie nodded and crawled under the wooden stairs. Eli waited for her to position herself in the shadows and blew out the lamp.

With the rifle hidden under his coat, Meyer skirted the main streets and used the alleys to slowly make his way home. Haunted by Sadie's words— *"What about us? What if the violence comes here?"*—he prayed that he would get to his house before the mobs.

His thoughts flew in all directions. How could people he had known for years, people he had helped, turn so murderous? Where were the police? The soldiers from the nearby garrison? Was Yuri safe?

Yuri. "Please, God, keep him from harm," he said aloud.

"Prayers won't help you now, Jew."

A man stepped out of a doorway in the alley, smacking a club against the palm of his hand. Shorter than Meyer, he was solidly built, with long greasy hair, and smelled of sweat and beer. A jagged scar ran from the top of his nose to the corner of his mouth, his eyes hooded and dark. Meyer did not recognize the man or his accent.

The stranger took a step toward Meyer, who fought off his fear and held his ground.

"Where are you going, Jew?"

"Wherever I want, pig," Meyer said slowly slipping his hand around the rifle under his coat.

The man's eyes grew wide at Meyer's boldness, and he laughed. "You think you can get past me, you pissant Jew? Give me your money, and I might let you live."

"If you want my money, you will have to come and get it, because I'm not giving it to you."

As the robber stepped toward him, Meyer brought the rifle out from under his coat. Swinging the weapon with all his might, he struck the surprised attacker across his ribs. Gasping for breath, the man grabbed his side and fell to his knees

"When you wake up in the gutter, remember this Jew got past you," said Meyer bringing the butt of the rifle down on the man's head. "With his money."

Blending in with the marauding mobs and moving from one group to another, Yuri slowly made his way back to the store. Sickened by the bloodshed, he was infuriated to see members of the police force standing idly in the streets as the mobs unleashed their terror in a convulsion of savage violence.

At the store at last, Yuri looked around and breathed a sigh of relief. When he gave Meyer his rifle, he'd left himself unarmed. He smiled at the ease with which he had convinced Meyer he had a gun hidden in the shop. He entered the store cautiously and stared at the havoc inside. While he and Meyer were away, looters had returned, overturning the counters and stealing or destroying what stock remained.

He bent down and picked up a piece of a smashed dish. Meyer will never be able to recover from this, he thought. Absently fingering the point of the shard of china in his hand, he heard a noise behind him. Spinning around, he found himself face to face with Stefan Kosloff, Maxim's younger brother.

Bigger and brawnier than Maxim, Stefan poked a gun in Yuri's chest. "I heard you pulled a gun on my brother," he growled. "How does it feel to be on the firing end of one?"

"Actually, it was a rifle. And your brother was threatening Meyer with a knife," said Yuri, taking a step back. "He's lucky I didn't shoot him," said Yuri with a smile.

"You think this is funny, Jew-lover?"

"I think it's funny that Maxim had to send his little brother to fight his battles."

"Don't spend so much time thinking about Maxim. He is finishing off the other half of this battle."

Yuri felt the blood roaring in his brain. "If anything happens to Meyer and his family, I will hunt down every person you love and butcher them all," he said.

"You forget who has the gun," sneered Stefan.

"But I have this," said Yuri, driving the shard of china into Stefan's stomach. Charging at the bloodied intruder, Yuri fought to wrestle the gun from Stefan's hand. Despite his injury, the big man's strength was overpowering, and as they grappled for the gun, he slammed Yuri to the ground, falling on top of him in the struggle.

Breathing hard, Yuri punched Stefan in the stomach, sending blood spurting from his wound. Kosloff screamed but did not loosen his grip on the gun. Using his knees, Yuri pushed the big man off of him and scrambled to his feet. He advanced on Stefan and in what seemed like a far-off sound, he heard a gunshot.

Looking down in disbelief, Yuri watched a red stain slowly spread across the front of his shirt. His eyes fluttered, and Stefan's face seemed to dissolve into darkness. His last thoughts were of his promise to Meyer to keep Sadie and the children safe.

With a faint beam of light coming through the small cellar window, it did not take long for Eli's eyes to adjust to the darkness. He focused on the barrel, willing Miriam to remain quiet. He could hear his mother shift her weight against the wall and hoped she would find a comfortable spot and be still.

Crouched in a corner and drenched in sweat despite the room's chill,

Eli could no longer ignore the nagging fear that something had happened to his father. Otherwise, he knew he would be here with them. He felt the grip of rising panic as the noise of the mobs got closer, and touched his waistband to reassure himself that the kitchen knife was there.

"Eli, I can't stand it in here. It stinks. I'm hungry, and I have to go to the bathroom. And I am scared," said Miriam in a loud whisper.

"I know, but you have to stay there, and you have to be absolutely quiet. Try to think of something that makes you happy."

"How can I when I am stuffed in a barrel and covered in dirty, smelly potatoes?"

"Miriam, for heaven's sake, hush," hissed Sadie.

The silence of the dark cellar was broken by the chilling sound of the house's front door crashing down on the floor above. Shouting, groaning floorboards from heavy footsteps, and the clattering of broken glass and furniture announced the arrival of the angry mob.

Miriam whimpered, and Sadie forced her fist into her mouth to keep from screaming. Eli pulled the knife from his waistband. Fear rippled across every nerve in his body.

The invasion upstairs seemed to be never-ending, the sounds of destruction moving from room to room. There was a loud crash right above them, and then the cellar door splintered open. Light poured into the cellar, and footsteps pounded down the stairs.

Sadie saw him first and gasped. The man turned toward the sound and Eli instantly recognized Maxim, the customer his father had so often given credit to.

Peering through the barrel staves, Miriam saw him too. Her body shaking, she felt the warm trickle of urine running down her leg as her bladder released. She stuffed the sleeve of her blouse into her mouth to keep from screaming and shut her eyes.

Drawing his gun, Maxim moved quickly under the stairs and pulled Sadie out into the open, dragging her by the neck. "Where's Meyer?"

Eyes wide in fear, she shook her head. "I don't know. He hasn't been home for days."

"Don't lie to me, woman," he growled, tightening his grip on her throat and shaking her.

Anger overtook her fear, and fully aware this man was going to kill them all, Sadie lashed out at Maxim's face, leaving deep, bloody scratches down his cheeks.

"Bitch," growled Maxim in wild fury. Slapping Sadie across the face, he shoved her to the ground and forced her legs apart.

Sadie screamed, and kicking furiously at her attacker, pushed herself away from Maxim, as Eli flew from his hiding place. "Don't touch her," he roared, charging at Maxim with his knife.

Ignoring Sadie's futile attempts to fight him off, Maxim turned and fired at the boy.

Eli felt the bullet fly by his head. His heart pounding, he lunged at the big man, driving his knife deep into his thigh.

Enraged and howling in pain, Maxim pulled the knife from his leg and raised his weapon. Sadie leapt at him, gouging at his eyes, desperately reaching for the gun. Tossing Sadie aside as if she was weightless, Maxim took aim at Eli and fired.

Walking through backstreets and alleys, Meyer made his way home, ducking into doorways when the mobs were nearby. At every turn, he witnessed unspeakable acts of violence. With each step that drew him nearer to Sadie and the children, he was filled with dread at what he might find.

When he turned onto Gostinnii Street, his heart nearly stopped at the sight of the destruction left in the wake of the lawless mobs. A house was on fire, the smoke pouring from every window. Broken furniture and bedding were strewn everywhere in yards and in the street, as the looters continued to rampage from house to house. Hearing shots, he tightened his grip on the rifle and watched in terror as his neighbor's limp body was thrown out of a window, landing with a sickening thud in the front courtyard.

Running now, Meyer was oblivious to the danger around him. Within minutes, he was standing in front of his house watching strangers stream out the door with his family's belongings. In a blind rage, he fired the rifle into the air as the looters continued to take whatever they wanted.

"Get out of my house," he bellowed, throwing the bolt on the rifle and firing again. This time the men and women scavenging his house fled, scattering like a pack of feral dogs.

Bolting the rifle again, Meyer rushed into the house. "Sadie! Children!" he shouted, frantic to find his family. Spying the open cellar door, he started toward it when a gunshot pierced the air.

"No!" he cried, flying down the stairs to the cellar. It took only seconds for him to take in the savagery that had occurred in the sanctity of his home.

Eli looked up at his father, his eyes dull, his hands clasping his chest. "Papa," he mouthed as a foamy bubble of blood formed on his lips.

Maxim clutched Sadie to him as she clawed at his hands and tried desperately to loosen his grip.

"Let her go now," screamed Meyer, his rifle pointed at Maxim.

Ignoring the throbbing pain in his leg, Maxim turned and faced Meyer. "I told you I wasn't done with you. And I'm not done with your family, either," he said running his hand over Sadie's breasts and pointing the gun at her head. A leering grin flashed across his face. "Go ahead. See if you can shoot me before I kill your precious wife."

Her eyes darting from Meyer to her bleeding son, Sadie sank her teeth into Maxim's arm. His grin turned to fury and he flung Sadie to the ground.

Meyer fired. The bullet ripped through Maxim's head in a shower of blood and bone.

The smell of gunpowder and death filled the room. Meyer started to shake as the reality of the scene before him began to sink in.

"Miriam? Where's Miriam?" he cried out in a sudden panic.

Sadie pointed to the barrel and crawled to Eli. Taking her son in her arms, she gently brushed the matted hair from his forehead. Kissing his ashen face, she crooned soft words in his ear, as his every breath rattled in his chest.

Meyer could hear Miriam crying in the barrel as he tore at the potatoes. When her hand shot up to reach him, his knees nearly buckled in relief. Pulling his child to him, he rocked to her as she cried in his arms.

"I knew you would come back to protect us. Eli said...." She stopped and stared, aware for the first time of the carnage in the cellar. "No! Please, God, no," she wailed spying Eli in her mother's arms.

At the sound of Miriam's voice, Eli turned in her direction. Weak and moaning in pain, he reached for his father and sister.

"I'm sorry I couldn't stop him, Papa," he said in a barely audible whisper. Focusing on his mother's face and clinging to Miriam's hand, he drew in a long breath of air. A gasp escaped his lips and he was gone.

Sadie closed her son's eyes and in a spasm of grief, flew at Meyer, slapping him across the face. "You should have been here. You said we would be safe, and now Eli is dead. You killed him just as much as Maxim did," she yelled, collapsing in tears.

Sadie's words were a knife in Meyer's heart. He should never have left them alone and unprotected. Weeping, he tried to comfort his wife, but she pushed him away. His face contorted in grief and shock, he implored Sadie to forgive him.

"I can't stand to look at you," she cried. "Do not touch me."

"Stop it!" shrieked Miriam. "Eli would hate this. He was so brave and thought only of protecting his family and now you are tearing us apart. You make his death mean nothing."

Stunned, Sadie grew quiet. Meyer approached her slowly, and she allowed herself to be enfolded into his arms. Pulling Miriam into his embrace, Meyer wept for the death of his son and prayed that God would forgive him for taking a man's life.

CHAPTER 11

Easter Monday Evening

While Sadie and Miriam remained with Eli's body, Meyer took his rifle and went upstairs to be sure no looters lurked in the house. Going from room to room, opening closet doors and searching the shadows, he assured himself they were safe, but the destruction in his home overwhelmed him. Everywhere he turned, he saw pieces of his life with Sadie and the children destroyed. What could not be carried off had been demolished. Furniture that belonged to Sadie's parents had been axed to kindling. Their beds were ripped to shreds, feathers coating the floor in a carpet of down. Broken dishes and glasses crunched under his feet as he walked through the kitchen.

Picking his way through the broken furniture downstairs, Meyer found the dining room table overturned but undamaged. Setting it upright, he rummaged through the house looking for anything he could use to wash Eli's body and prepare him for burial.

Returning to the cellar, Meyer found Sadie cradling Eli in her arms, covered in his blood, her eyes hollow pits of blackness. Miriam sat unmoving, coated in dust from the barrel, her tears leaving tracks on her dirt-caked cheeks.

"You know what we must do," he said quietly, trying to pry Sadie's arms from around their son.

She began to weep. "Just let me hold him a little longer. Look how peaceful he looks," she said kissing his face. "Remember how he would sleep with his thumb in mouth, all curled up in a ball like a little kitten?" She smiled at the memory and then quickly gave way to tears.

"Please, Sadie. We can't delay much longer. Somehow the mob missed the linens hanging on the clothesline. I laid out everything we need."

Sadie nodded, but did not move. It was Miriam who rose first and led her mother out of the cellar.

Meyer lifted Eli's lifeless body and carried him upstairs. He placed the boy on the table in the dining room and amid the chaos left by the mobs, he removed Eli's clothes, gasping at the sight of the gaping wound in his son's chest.

After Eli's body had been thoroughly washed, Meyer wrapped Eli in a white linen shroud in accordance with Jewish law. Sadie brought him the tallis Eli wore for the first time at his Bar Mitzvah, his rite of passage into manhood.

"I hid this with some other valuables in the attic," she said, her voice cracking with emotion, her eyes red and raw from crying.

According to Jewish custom, Meyer cut a corner of the prayer shawl's fringes and draped it around the shroud. He then lit candles and, because Jewish law dictated that a body never be left alone, Sadie and Miriam took up the vigil.

His heart heavy, Meyer retreated to the cellar to deal with the other body in his house. He stared at what was left of Maxim's bloodied face. Discovery of his body in the cellar would mean certain death for all of them, he knew. He had to get rid of it, and he had to do it quickly while it was still dark.

Relieved to find that the looters had not gotten to the shed in the garden, Meyer found the old wooden cart he was looking for. Once used for carrying goods to and from the store, it was big enough to transport Maxim's body.

Dragging Maxim by the legs, Meyer struggled to get him up the stairs to the main floor and out the back door. Leaving the body hidden in the bushes, Meyer returned to the house and scrubbed off all traces of Maxim's blood.

As the night grew darker, Meyer retrieved Maxim's body. Checking the street to be sure the mobs were gone, he worked his way toward a nearby stream that emptied into the Dnester River. Sweating beneath his coat, Meyer flinched in fear when an owl landed on a branch above his head. When he was convinced no one was near, he uttered a prayer of forgiveness and overturned the cart. Only when he heard the splash of Maxim's body entering the water did his breathing return to normal.

Rabbi Zirelber was waiting for Meyer when he returned home. Surprised by the clergy's presence, he thought he had come to discuss the funeral arrangements. "Rabbi, how did you hear about Eli?"

The older man embraced Meyer. "I only just learned what happened here. May God console you among the other mourners of Zion and Jerusalem," he said. "I know your loss is great, but I am afraid I came here to bring you more tragic news. The police finally stepped in to stop the rioting and looting this evening. They discovered Yuri's body inside your store and the body of Stefan Kosloff in the doorway. They assumed Yuri was Jewish and took him to the morgue at the Jewish Hospital. Morris Belekov recognized him and alerted me. I am so sorry."

Meyer stared at the rabbi in disbelief. He covered his face and wept for his son, his friend, and for the decisions he'd made that could never be undone.

Rabbi Zirelber placed his hands on Meyer's heaving shoulders. "You have to be strong for Sadie and Miriam. I will send some men from the burial committee to keep vigil over Eli so you can all get some sleep."

CHAPTER 12

When the sun rose on Kishinev the morning after the pogrom, for-ty-nine Jews had been killed, five hundred people wounded, and thirteen hundred homes and stores had been destroyed. The corpses of the Jewish men, women, and children were placed side-by-side in the court-yard of the Jewish Hospital, waiting to be identified by grieving friends and relatives. Amid the bodies with broken skulls, missing limbs, and gaping wounds, doctors worked feverishly to save the injured.

Meyer looked for Yuri among the rows of dirt-caked, blood-soaked bodies. His heart clutched as he recognized some of his customers. He fought back tears at the sight of the battered body of a boy of three or four and wondered if the child's parents had been killed in the massacre too.

Meyer continued down the rows of corpses and was almost near the end when he spied the body of his friend. Yuri's chest was covered in dried blood, his face frozen in a look of surprise. Shaking, Meyer knelt beside the body and numbed by grief, closed his eyes. He had no idea how long he'd been sitting there, when he felt a hand on his shoulder.

"Meyer, you found Yuri," said Rabbi Zirelber in a near whisper. The pi-ous man appeared to have grown ancient overnight. There were dark circles under his eyes and deep lines etched his normally serene face. His black coat was splattered with dirt, and his hands had a tremor that Meyer could not recall noticing before. The anguished role of consoling and counseling the mourners of so many dead had clearly left its mark on this man so beloved by the Jews of Kishinev.

"Rabbi, I need to speak to you about Yuri. I know as a non-Jew he is not allowed to be buried in our cemetery, but he has been family to me since we were boys. Please, is there any way we can bury him in our plot?"

The old man looked up at the sky as if searching for a divine answer. Sighing, he touched Meyer's arm. "Go home to your family and prepare for Eli's funeral. We will take care of Yuri. Nothing according to God's laws happened here. He will understand."

It seemed to Miriam as if all she heard in the days following the pogrom were the sounds of mourning. Crying, wailing, screaming filled the air, and in her most desperate hours, she added her lamentations to the others. They attended funeral after funeral as neighbors and friends buried their loved ones. It seemed like every family they knew was sitting *shiva*, the required seven-day mourning period following burial.

Because there were so many funerals, Eli and Yuri were buried on the third day following the pogrom instead of within the customary twenty-four hours. The day held a chill, and as they left the house to go to the cemetery, the sun retreated behind a growing bank of gray clouds.

The rabbi and men from the synagogue were already at the grave sites when they arrived. Looking exhausted and defeated, Rabbi Zirelber conducted a short service. Eli and Yuri were laid to rest beside the tiny graves of Daniel and Isaac, the twin boys who were born before Miriam and who died in their first month.

When the rabbi signaled it was time, Meyer, Sadie, and Miriam took turns shoveling dirt over the plain wooden coffins, joined one by one by the other mourners. After the burial was completed and the rabbi and other mourners left to attend to another funeral, the grieving family lingered in silence at the grave, unable to relinquish Eli and Yuri to the dead.

The sky darkened, and the clouds turned the color of anger. A wind from the north moved in, tugging at their clothes as if signaling that it was time to go. With his arms around Miriam and Sadie, Meyer gently led them away from the graves. They were just outside the cemetery gate when a pelting rain began to fall, as if even God could no longer hold back His tears.

CHAPTER 13

May 1903

In the days and weeks following the funeral, Miriam became a silent observer of the simmering strain between her parents. After the seven days of *shiva* ended and members of the synagogue no longer came to pay their respects, a disturbing stillness found its way into every corner of the house.

Miriam watched for the gentle touches and loving looks that once passed between her mother and father and saw none. Instead, she sensed a gulf between them that seemed to grow wider with each passing day. Their lives, once so intertwined that Miriam had come to think one could not exist without the other, were now being torn apart by guilt and resentment. Miriam's sadness remained an ache that could not be soothed, and like her parents, she was lost in a well of grief for her brother and beloved Uncle Yuri.

Eli was there in her thoughts when she awoke in the morning. His face would suddenly appear as she worked to clean the rubble out of the house. Sometimes she thought she could hear him calling her name, and when she turned to respond, she felt his presence in the movement of the air around her. The hardest moments to bear were when he came to her in her dreams, calling her Miri and telling her to take care of Mama and Papa.

Meyer spent every day at the synagogue, searching for solace in God's word and finding none. His remorse over the deaths of Eli and Yuri battled daily with his fear that his hand in killing Maxim would be discovered, and he would be taken from his family. He grew gaunt, taking his meals alone, often leaving them untouched.

He could feel the seams of their marriage slowly unraveling. Sadie remained distraught and distant. Every time she looked at him, her face revealed what she would not say aloud: *You failed us. Eli would still be alive if you hadn't left us to go to the store.* He spent his nights downstairs, sleep eluding him. When slumber finally overtook him, he had nightmares of vacant eyes staring back at him and of bloodied bodies floating in the Dnester River. He cried out in his sleep and would wake in a panic, drenched in sweat and drowning in guilt.

When Meyer finally mustered the courage to return to the store, he found there was nothing left to salvage. Like the other Jewish-owned stores on Chuflinskii Square, his shop had been vandalized and emptied of its contents. Sections of the main room had been torched, and piles of ashes were the only trace of what had once been shelves and barrels. "Die Yid" and "Jews burn in hell" were scrawled in black soot on the walls. But it was the sight of Yuri's blood staining the floor red that broke his spirit and his heart. He boarded up the door and front window and turned his back on the very thing he told Sadie he needed to protect. He would not rebuild. He would not stay. Kishinev was no longer his home.

Sorrow swallowed Sadie. She was consumed by the grief that circled her heart. It came in waves, crashing over her, pulling her under and filling her lungs so she could not breathe. It left her empty and disconnected, unable to focus on anything but the sharp pangs of sadness that crushed her heart. The days melted one into another, most finding her unable to leave her bed and the slumber that offered her an escape from despair. Unlike the dreams that left Meyer thrashing in his sleep, Sadie's brought her peace, for in them Eli was still alive.

In the days when she was able to rouse herself, Sadie sat alone in the parlor staring out the window. In those quiet moments memories of Eli as a child would weave their way into her thoughts: His easy smile and his first steps. The sound of his laughter. The way his hair would never stay combed. How handsome he looked at his Bar Mitzvah. As day turned to evening and shadows danced on the bare walls, Sadie would lapse into a desolate reverie.

CHAPTER 14

Spring gave way to summer, and with the warmer weather came a gradual thawing of the tension that hung over the house on Gostinnii Street. Sadie and Meyer were talking to each other again, and though Meyer still slept downstairs, he began to take his meals with his wife and daughter. It was at dinner one night that he announced his plans for them to leave Kishinev and go to America.

Stunned, Sadie stared at him. "I will not leave. This is our home. This is where Eli and the twins are buried."

"And so is Yuri, but we cannot live for the dead," responded Meyer, rising angrily from the table. "Everywhere I look here I see Eli and Yuri, and that's precisely why I want to leave," he said, pacing around the room. "And we have to be realistic. The store is a complete loss and we will soon run out of money."

Sadie folded her arms across her chest and straightened her shoulders. Her face was stone. "I don't want to go," she said, not looking at Meyer.

"Sadie, I killed a man. I pray every day that God will forgive me for what I've done. I live in fear that Maxim's disappearance will be traced to me and that I will be taken away by the police. I heard talk in town that his family has been badgering the police for an investigation into his disappearance."

Sadie looked up, and there was fear in her eyes. She had been a fool not to recognize there could be consequences for Maxim's death. "You know how hard it is for Jews to leave Russia. We will need passports from the government. How would we get out? Where would we go?"

Meyer sat down again. "There is a man who can smuggle us across the border into Germany. He has to be paid, of course, and border guards have to be bribed, but he can arrange for passage to Hamburg and get us steamship tickets to go from there to America. We could go to your sister Malka in New York."

Miriam was shocked into silence as she listened to her parents talk. Frightened at the thought of leaving friends and the only home she'd ever known, she was also excited at the prospect of going to a new country. She waited for her mother to say something, unsure of what she wanted to hear.

Meyer took Sadie's hands in his. "I know this is hard for you to believe now, but I am only thinking about what is best for you and Miriam. There is real danger here. This pogrom is only the beginning. The hatred out there is not going away. We are not safe here anymore."

Sadie closed her hand around Meyer's. "It's just so hard to think of us living anywhere else." She rose and wordlessly walked through the house. Although order had been restored, the looters had destroyed or carried off most of their furniture, and the rooms were bare and cold. Empty walls stared back at her, happy memories replaced by the horror of the Easter Monday pogrom. She still could not walk past the cellar door and doubted she would ever be able to go down there again. Her house, she realized, was no longer her home. She went to Meyer and put her arm around his waist.

"I have to let Malka know we are coming," she said.

That night, Meyer returned to the bedroom upstairs, and after he and Sadie made love for the first time in months, they wept in each other's arms. No words were spoken, but forgiveness was asked, and forgiveness was given.

CHAPTER 15

December 1903

The ensuing months were taken up with preparations for their departure. Letters between Sadie and Malka went back and forth, and at last,
arrangements had been made for their arrival in New York. They would
stay with her sister until they were able to find work and a place to live.

Even though most of their belongings had been destroyed by the looters, Sadie agonized over what to leave behind. Meyer reminded her daily that they should take only what they needed or could use in their new
home.

It took some time for Meyer to make contact with the man who would
get them into Germany. He quickly discovered that leaving Russia without
a passport was not only risky, it was also expensive. When Meyer balked at
the price, the "agent," as the man was known, shrugged.

"You want to leave Russia without government permission, you have to
pay a lot of people to look the other way. If you want to save money, go by
yourself and send for your family once you are established in America. Most
of the people I help do it that way."

Meyer clenched his jaw, and a muscle twitched in his cheek. "I will not
leave my family behind. We will find a way for all of us to travel together."

It didn't take long for Meyer to confirm that they did not have enough
cash to pay for all the expenses of the trip. Little by little, to avoid drawing
attention to their plans to leave, he sold off the valuables Sadie had hidden

in the cellar, keeping only the silver candlestick holder that belonged to her grandmother and the few pieces of jewelry she sewed into the hems of their coats for safekeeping. Meyer quickly dismissed the idea of selling the house. Though the money was needed, he was fearful of alerting the authorities or the townspeople they were fleeing Kishinev.

On the day they were to begin their journey, Sadie walked through the empty house for the last time. Looking out on the courtyard at everything that was so familiar to her, she grew cold and fearful. They were leaving behind all they knew and facing unknown dangers to go to a country where they didn't speak the language. She'd heard stories of the fierce Atlantic Ocean storms that tossed ships and their passengers around like sticks in a whirlwind, and of the terrible conditions on the ship. She worried that they would not be allowed to enter America because they didn't have the proper papers or that they would be separated from each other. "Please God," she prayed softly, "watch over us."

Miriam spent her last day in Kishinev in her room. Her parents had been tense and squabbling all day, and she welcomed the silence of the upstairs. In the quiet, she turned her thoughts to Eli. As she had done almost since the day he died, she talked to him, telling him that they were finally going to America. She reassured him that leaving Kishinev did not mean he was being left behind. No matter where they were, she told him, he would always be with her. Sitting in the late afternoon sun that warmed her room, she bowed her head and longed for her brother.

Hours before they were to meet the emigrant agent, Meyer slipped out of the house and made his way to the synagogue. Sitting near the back of the empty sanctuary, he was lost in his prayers when Rabbi Zirelber sat down beside him.

"Meyer, I am glad to see you here, but services don't start for a few hours. Are you all right?"

"Rabbi, I wanted to be here to pray for one last time. I also came to say goodbye. We are leaving Kishinev today. What happened here haunts me every day. I am afraid to leave Sadie and Miriam alone for too long. I cannot look at the people I thought were my friends and neighbors without wanting to harm them. My son, Yuri...." Meyer's voice trailed off in sorrow, tears streaming down his cheeks. "I just can't stay here any longer."

The rabbi waited for Meyer to compose himself. "I understand. I have sensed your pain for months and hoped that time would help you cope with your loss. You are a good man, Meyer, and you will be missed by many here."

"Am I a good man, Rabbi? I put my store before the safety of my family. I killed a man."

"You did what you thought was right at the time. And while I cannot condone taking a life, you did what you needed to do to save your family," said the pious old man. "I will keep you, Sadie, and Miriam in my prayers. I hope you will find the peace you seek in your new home. *Zay gezunt*, travel with health, my dear friend."

PART II

CHAPTER 16

January 25, 1904

Twenty days after leaving Kishinev, Meyer, Sadie, and Miriam arrived in America. Their journey to the Land of Opportunity had taken them across risky borders where guards eyed them contemptuously and demanded more money than the agreed-upon bribes to let them pass. They endured a cold and filthy train ride to Hamburg, where they waited four days in crowded, bug-infested barracks for their ship to reach port. They subsisted on meager meals of cold potatoes and bread as their savings rapidly diminished. Miriam's fourteenth birthday passed unnoticed on their last night in Hamburg.

As eager as they were to leave the unsanitary conditions of the barracks, their elation at the ship's arrival was quickly dashed when they were escorted below decks to the steerage compartment of the ship. Along with hundreds of other passengers desperate for a better life, they spent twelve misery-filled days breathing the fetid air in a large area that used to be a cargo hold. They slept in bunks piled so closely together they could not sit up, leaving Miriam anxious and battling harrowing memories of being confined in the dark barrel in the cellar. Rough seas, the stench of unwashed bodies, open toilet facilities and the vomit of seasick passengers overpowered their senses. Trips to the upper decks for fresh air were infrequent, and as steerage passengers they were only allowed access to the deck adjacent to a dirt-belching smokestack. Yet even the soot, constant cold wind, and biting saltwater spray did not dull their delight at escaping the suffocating conditions below.

When at last the ship entered New York Harbor, the sight of the Statue of Liberty brought Sadie to tears. Exhausted and covered in grime, she was relieved that the voyage was at its end, but terrified of what was to come. During the endless days of the trip, she'd listened to the other steerage passengers exchanging stories about what could happen when they passed through the gates of Ellis Island. They spoke of the nightmarish experiences of family and friends who had traveled before them: physical and mental examinations; children separated from their parents; passengers with diseases refused entry and sent back across the sea; instances where one spouse was allowed to enter, but the other was denied. There was a reason, they said, that it was called the Island of Tears. Suddenly, it seemed to Sadie that arriving at their destination was as perilous as all they had endured to reach it.

Sharing Sadie's anxieties, Miriam gazed out on the water as tugboats guided the ship into the harbor. She could not dismiss the terrifying tales she'd heard while lying in her bunk. What if she was separated from Mama and Papa? What if she had a sickness she didn't know about? What if she answered a question wrong and wasn't allowed to stay in America? As they waited for the barge that would take them from the ship to Ellis Island, she was overwhelmed by a stream of what-ifs. She clung to Meyer's arm, her lips trembling, tears in her eyes.

"Papa, I am so frightened. We've come so far; what if they turn us back?"

Standing on the deck in the cold wind and gazing out on the stately Statue of Liberty, Meyer put his arms around Miriam and Sadie. "It's going to be all right. We are healthy, we have the papers the agent gave us, and Aunt Malka will be waiting for us."

"The way we look and smell, I doubt she will want to claim us," said Sadie, forcing a smile.

Stepping off the barge, they were surprised to find it was difficult to walk. Swaying with each step until they grew accustomed to being on land after so many days at sea, Meyer and Sadie linked arms with Miriam to steady themselves.

When they entered the ground floor of the Great Hall, they were assailed by the roar of hundreds of frightened people speaking dozens of different languages. In the press of so many people, Miriam fought off a rising panic. Just ahead of them, an old woman became separated from her husband and was hysterical, screaming his name as she searched the crowd. Miriam let out a small cry of fear and looked as if she was about to dissolve in tears. Sadie instinctively took her hand. "You must look strong and alert," she whispered. "Do not give them any reason to think you are weak or afraid."

A short, plump woman with a halo of gray hair and a kind face approached them. After determining that they spoke Yiddish, she escorted them up the steep stairway that marked the beginning of the end of their journey.

Hours later, after passing physical and eye examinations and mental and intelligence assessments, they were granted entry into their new home. With landing cards pinned to their clothes and carrying their luggage, they made their way to the first floor of the building where they were to meet Sadie's sister.

"It's been almost twelve years since Malka came to America. I'm not even sure what she looks like now," said Sadie, as she scanned the crowd of people waiting for their loved ones behind a metal barrier.

She searched in vain for the thin, dark-haired older sister she remembered. In a panic, she clutched Meyer's arm. "I don't see her. Do you? What if they never got our last message? What if they're not coming?"

Meyer touched her arm and pointed to a heavyset woman pushing her way to the front of the throng. "Is that her?"

Sadie studied the tired-looking woman for a moment and found no traces of her sister. Their eyes met, and it was only when the woman smiled that Sadie recognized Malka. Just three years older than Sadie, Malka's dark hair now had touches of gray, and her once-high cheekbones had disappeared under the flesh of her fuller face.

"Sadie," cried Malka, breaking free of the crowd as Sadie ran toward her. Caught up in the crush of surging people, the two sisters fell into each other's arms. "My little sister," said Malka, kissing Sadie's face over and over. "I have been so worried about you, and now that you are here, I almost can't believe it."

"I can't believe it either," said Sadie, as she reached out to caress her sister's face. "I'd forgotten how much you look like Mama," she said, her eyes moist with tears.

Still standing with her arms around Malka, Sadie was suddenly aware of a tall teenage boy waiting nearby. He had the same dark curly hair and brown eyes as his mother, but it was the dimples in his cheeks that she remembered in the little five-year-old boy she had last seen when Malka, her husband Lazar, and two-year-old Sonia left Oreheyev for America.

"Can this be Avrum?" she gasped.

Malka turned and smiled proudly at her son. "Come, Avrum," she said in accented English, "and say hello to your Aunt Sadie."

Smiling shyly, the seventeen-year-old came forward and hugged Sadie. "I am glad you are here," he said in perfect Yiddish.

Sadie hugged him tightly and introduced him to Meyer and Miriam, who'd made their way through the swarm of other travelers to join them.

Avrum shook hands with Meyer and hesitating at first, gave Sadie an awkward hug. "Papa is at the store, and my sister Sonia is watching my brother and sister, so Mama and I will escort you into America," he said, so solemnly that they looked at each other and laughed for the first time in weeks.

CHAPTER 17

Their introduction to New York's Lower East Side was an assault on their senses. The noise, the jumble of people and pushcarts, the store signs in Yiddish and a language they did not recognize, and the smell of rotting food and horse manure in the streets left them dizzy. By the time they reached Malka's cramped apartment above Lazar's small delicatessen on Canal Street, they were stunned into silence. The living quarters were dark and cold and permeated by an odor they could not identify. The furniture was threadbare. Drying laundry hung from a rope strung across the kitchen where a table and four unmatched chairs were crammed into a corner. A flat iron sat at the edge of the stove, waiting to be heated.

"I am sorry the apartment is so small. I hope you will be comfortable here," said Malka, as they entered the front room, where a sewing machine occupied the center of the parlor next to a pile of white shirts. She pointed to an alcove where a curtain hung across its opening. "You and Meyer can sleep in there. Miriam can sleep with the girls in the bedroom they share with Avrum and Ira. We hung a sheet between the two beds for privacy."

Ignoring Miriam's look of dismay, Sadie hugged her sister. "It will be fine. We cannot tell you how much it means to us that we are together. We could not have gotten here without your help."

While the tired travelers washed up, Malka sent Avrum downstairs to help his father in the store and to tell the other children to come home from the nearby park. They soon heard the thumping of small feet on the stairs.

Three rosy-cheeked children in worn, ill-fitting coats burst into the room and stopped short at the sight of their newly arrived relatives.

Malka laughed and scooped her youngest daughter into her arms. "This is Rebecca. She's three. Sonia is fourteen years old and Ira is twelve. Children, this is your Aunt Sadie, your Uncle Meyer and your cousin Miriam. Come say hello. They are going to stay with us for a little while."

Sonia and Ira looked down at their shoes, too shy to come forward. Squirming in her mother's arms, Rebecca leaned forward and reached out to Miriam.

Her face lighting up with delight, Miriam took the curly haired toddler in her arms and twirled her around; the child's sweet laughter brightening the dark room.

While they waited for Lazar to close the delicatessen and come upstairs, Sadie and Malka worked together in the kitchen preparing dinner. Malka moved so quickly that Sadie could not keep up with her. "What's the hurry?" she asked.

"Lazar likes to have dinner on the table as soon as he gets home. He eats first and then I feed the children. Tonight, I will give him dinner and then we will eat."

Sadie was silent for a moment and then said, "That's fine."

Malka kept her eyes down as she talked. "He is a good man, just set in his ways."

Sadie remembered the last time Malka said Lazar Abkin was a good man. She was sixteen years old when Malka married him against their father's better instincts. Unable to hold a job for very long, Lazar was a brute of a man, tall and muscular and with a reputation for having a quick temper and quicker fists. His nose flattened from his many brawls, his face was set in a perpetual scowl with piercing eyes that flashed in anger at the slightest provocation, violence always simmering just below the surface.

A frequent customer at their father's store, Lazar showered Malka with attention and courted her with unwavering persistence. And much to everyone's surprise, the shy young woman was drawn to him. Despite the family's many reservations, and worn down by Malka's pleas, their father finally gave his permission for them to marry.

But marriage did not keep Lazar from making the rounds of the local taverns, and stories of his drunken brawls were gossiped throughout the Jewish community. Deeply ashamed of their son-in-law's behavior, the Belitrovs were frantic over Malka's safety. She rarely visited, and when she did it was always without Lazar. Even Sadie noticed her sister looked tired and thin, her always meticulously cared-for hair unkempt, her clothes rumpled and soiled. Once, while they were washing dishes after lunch, Sadie noticed bruises in the shape of fingers on Malka's arm.

"What are these?" she asked, grabbing her sister's wrist. "Did he do this to you?"

Malka did not answer at first. Tears filled her eyes. "Please don't tell Mama and Papa. He got mad at me because I forgot the bread was in the oven and it was ruined. When he calmed down, he said he was sorry. He promised not to do it again."

"Malka, come home and stay with us," pleaded Sadie. "It would make Mama and Papa so happy. They are worried about you, and so am I."

"You don't know him," she said. "He's a good man; he just gets angry sometimes."

And hurts you, thought Sadie.

Three months after their wedding, Malka was pregnant. Morning sickness left her weak and in bed most of the day. Angry that she wasn't able to cook his meals and clean the house, Lazar began staying out late, some nights not coming home at all. Near the end of her pregnancy Malka moved back in with her parents. When Avrum was born, it took two days to find Lazar and tell him he had a son.

It did not take long for Sadie and Meyer to see that Lazar had not mellowed over the years. It was clear that Malka and the children feared him. Any happy sounds in the apartment disappeared as soon as Lazar came upstairs. The air was thick with tension and Lazar did nothing to hide his displeasure at his in-laws' presence in his home. What troubled Meyer and Sadie most was that he took his anger out on Malka and the children. He yelled at Malka for anything that displeased him, and he was quick to use his hands when the children disobeyed or annoyed him.

Miriam felt sorry for her cousins. Avrum and Ira worked all day in the delicatessen with Lazar, while Sonia spent her days watching Rebecca and helping her mother with the piecework she did, sewing sleeves onto shirts for a contractor who dropped off and picked up the goods.

"Why don't you go to school?" Miriam asked one morning when Sonia was dressing Rebecca to go the park.

"Papa doesn't think it's important for girls to go to school. Avrum and Ira only went to school until the sixth grade. Papa said that was all the education they needed, and then they had to work in the store. Besides, he wants me to help Mama bring in extra money."

"Do you want to go to school?"

Sonia shrugged and combed Rebecca's unruly hair. "We speak Yiddish in the house, but Avrum is teaching me to read and write English. Sometimes he is too tired from the store to read with me."

Miriam nodded. As much as she loved being with her cousins, she was frightened of Lazar. She barely spoke to him, terrified she would become the object of his anger.

Meyer was desperate to have enough money to allow them to move into an apartment of their own. "We can't stay here much longer. I cannot stand to watch the way Lazar treats Malka and the children. I am sure that being here makes it worse for them," Meyer said in low tones to make sure his words didn't carry through the paper-thin walls.

"I was a fool for thinking that things were better for Malka here in America," whispered Sadie. "If anything, they are worse, and I agree our presence is making Lazar even angrier."

"We have some money left from the voyage, but not enough to move into an apartment and have anything left over to live off of," said Meyer. "I've been watching the pushcart peddlers. It doesn't look that much different from running the store."

Sadie looked doubtful.

"Do you want to leave here?"

"You know I do."

"Then I have to try. I will buy what I need from Lazar. I am counting on him wanting to get rid of us badly enough that he will let me buy on credit until I can pay him back."

CHAPTER 18

Rising at dawn, Meyer dressed, kissed still-sleeping Sadie goodbye, and walked to a nearby stable where he rented a pushcart for ten cents a day. Loading the cart with the knishes, potatoes, pickles, and bread he got from Lazar, he trudged to Hester Street and jockeyed for space on a sidewalk teeming with other peddlers selling everything from fish to used clothing to dented pots and pans. Any thought that his experience running his own store would help him peddle his goods disappeared within minutes of setting up amid the tumult of the men hawking their wares in a chorus of different languages. A mixture of Yiddish, Italian, Polish, and Russian assaulted his ears. Customers haggled loudly over every transaction, always arguing they could get the item cheaper somewhere else. Young boys with dirty faces and in torn clothes stole potatoes from his pushcart. The stink of horse manure hovered over the market, made worse by a biting wind that always seemed to blow in his direction.

"Whoever said the streets of America are paved with gold was wrong. They are paved with horse dung. I cannot rid myself of the smell. It's taken up permanent residence in my nose," Meyer complained to Sadie after his first day. "It was so cold that I couldn't feel my hands and feet most of the time."

Meyer shivered and wrapped his hands around the cup of hot tea Sadie brought him "The worst of it is I am not even sure I made back my expenses," he said lowering his voice. "Judging by the prices the other peddlers were charging for goods like mine, I don't think Lazar is giving me such a good deal."

"Maybe this is just a bad idea," said Sadie.

"I have to give it some more time. I need to find a way to draw more people to my cart. If I have to, I'll find a new supplier."

Exhausted, but unable to sleep, Meyer listened to the sounds of the city outside. The clopping hooves of a horse drawing a dairy wagon echoed off the walls of the tenements. Two men argued on the street below. As he always did when he could not sleep, he thought of Eli and Yuri, and how much he missed them. On this night, however, memories of his lost son and friend were quickly shoved aside by the nagging fear that he would not be able to provide for Sadie and Miriam in their new country. Meyer turned to his side and wrapped his body around Sadie's for warmth. All I can do is to return to the market and try again, he thought as he fell into a restless sleep.

The next morning Meyer got to Hester Street early and found a spot next to a peddler already set up and ready to begin his day. The old man's cart was filled with coats, gloves, and hats. Meyer nodded at him and began piling up the foods Lazar had given him the night before onto his pushcart.

"You need to make sure everything looks appetizing," said the dry-goods peddler in Yiddish.

Meyer turned and faced the man. Short and white-haired, with gentle brown eyes and a full, flowing beard that reached the top of his chest, the peddler extended his hand. "I am Oscar Gershunoff. You are new to peddling, aren't you?"

"Meyer Raisky," said Meyer, shaking the older man's hand. "Is it that obvious?"

"Well, you aren't displaying your wares in a way that makes people want to buy them, let alone stop and look at them. Don't pile them up like that. Spread them out so people can see what you have to offer. And frankly," he said, looking like he had swallowed something vile-tasting, "the knishes don't look so good."

"They are left over from yesterday. I didn't make enough money to buy more," admitted Meyer.

"Probably not a good idea to sell stale goods. You will get a bad reputation. If you really want to get rid of them, admit they are a day old and sell them for half price. Better than not selling them at all."

The older man eyed Meyer's thin coat. "Here, take this," he said, handing Meyer a coat from a large pile. "You can pay me when you have the money. You need to wear two coats out here, or you'll freeze to death on the streets."

"I can't take this," said Meyer, giving the coat back to him. "I don't know when I will be able to pay you for it."

Oscar shook his head and thrust the garment into Meyer's hand. "You look honest. I trust you."

More peddlers were arriving with their pushcarts, and women were already starting to survey their goods. Before the cacophony of languages and raised voices began, Meyer thanked Oscar for his advice and the coat and spread out his stock of potatoes, pickles, and bread. He placed the knishes to the back, telling each person who stopped at his cart they were a day old, but half the price. By mid-morning, the knishes were gone.

Each morning, Meyer got to the pushcart market in time to set up next to Oscar. The coat merchant was friendly, and they talked as they prepared for the day. He told Meyer he had been a tailor in Minsk. After his wife died three years ago, he immigrated to America to be with his son, daughter-in-law, and two grandchildren.

"I thought I would have an easier life here, but as you can see, money is scarce," Oscar said nodding toward his pushcart. "Still, I'd rather live here than under the rule of the Tsar."

Meyer's face clouded, and he looked off in the distance.

"Did I say something wrong? I am sorry if I offended you."

"No, not at all," replied Meyer. "We fled Kishinev because of the anti-Semitism sanctioned by the Russian government. Our son Eli was killed in a pogrom. So was my friend, a man who was like a brother to me."

"I am sorry for your loss. I read about what happened in Kishinev in the Jewish papers. I can't even imagine…" he said, looking away from Meyer's obvious grief.

"Thank you. And thank you for all your advice and friendship."

Oscar patted Meyer's shoulder and returned to setting out his wares.

Meyer watched how the old peddler placed his goods, separating coats by men's, women's, and children's sizes, and providing a hand mirror to customers so they could see how they looked in their new purchases. As Oscar suggested, Meyer displayed his wares in arrangements that invited people to survey the items for sale. He quickly fell into the rhythm of selling to the demanding and savvy Hester Street crowd and became adept at negotiating with his customers. Over time, as word spread that the day-old knishes Lazar happily unloaded on him could be had for half off, he developed a steady stream of customers; customers who bought more than just knishes.

Sadie rose early in the morning so she could have a few minutes alone with Meyer before he left to begin his day. She knew he would not return until everything on his cart had been sold, and she worried about the long hours he spent standing in the cold. Some nights he was too tired to eat and went straight to bed.

Shivering in her robe, Sadie slipped into the kitchen and stoked the dying embers in the stove, the apartment's only source of heat. She added more coal from the nearby scuttle and poked the small black lumps until they caught. When the coals finally glowed red, she placed a pot of coffee on top of the stove to warm.

Not yet accustomed to the noise of city streets and the activities of a house full of children, Sadie relished this time when she was alone and the house was quiet. Solitude suited her these days, a luxury that allowed her time to think. Most days, after Lazar and the boys went downstairs to the store, she helped Malka sew the piecework that the contractor delivered each morning. While Rebecca napped, Sonia and Miriam joined them, and they chatted happily as they sewed sleeves onto men's shirts.

Like Meyer, Sadie was horrified by Lazar's treatment of Malka and the children. In the two weeks they had spent living with her sister, Sadie had grown increasingly concerned about their welfare. All the joy was gone from Malka's eyes. Instead, Sadie saw only sadness, and worse, fear. Malka cowered in Lazar's presence, and the children were clearly afraid of him. The night before, Lazar slapped Ira across the face for dropping and breaking a glass. As tears ran down the mortified boy's cheeks, Lazar mocked him, calling him weak and a crybaby. Asthmatic, Ira began to wheeze and gulp for air. When Avrum tried to comfort his brother and calm him down, Lazar slapped him too and told him not to interfere. Sadie looked at her sister in disbelief. Her eyes moist, Malka shook her head and looked away.

And to Sadie's horror, the apartment's thin walls did nothing to muffle the sounds of Lazar's almost nightly demands on Malka and his savage disregard for her protests. When the rhythmic creaking of their bed finally stopped and Lazar's snoring echoed off the walls, Sadie listened to her sister's sobs.

Clutching a cup of coffee to warm her hands and breathing in its dark aroma, Sadie knew that if she were to be honest with herself, it was more than Lazar's behavior that was driving her to want a place of their own. She could not look at Avrum without thinking of Eli. His devotion to his brother and sisters; the way he treated the customers at his father's store; and his gentle, protective nature reminded her so much of Eli that she could feel the cracks in her heart grow wider every time he was near.

Eli still came to her in her dreams. Some nights he seemed lost, searching for her, his face contorted in fear, and she would wake up drenched in sweat. Other nights, he was her handsome son, happy and laughing, and she would awaken distraught because her dream was over and he was gone. It was in those waking moments that she allowed herself to wonder what Eli would have looked like as a man. Would he have become the teacher he wanted to be? Would he have married and had children? The ache would not leave her; the hollow place in her soul would not close.

Wedged between Sonia and Rebecca in a bed too small to accommodate three people, Miriam ignored her fear of closed-in spaces and was glad to have their body heat for warmth. Despite her extra nightgown and the pair of Meyer's socks on her feet, she could not escape the bone-chilling cold. Kishinev mornings were frigid, she thought, but here the freezing temperatures leaked through the walls into every corner of the apartment. She wanted to bring her legs up to her chest for additional warmth but knew any movement would catapult Sonia or Rebecca onto the floor.

She heard Avrum and Ira stirring on the other side of the sheet that separated their sleeping quarters. She smiled as she listened to them yawning and coming awake in the early morning darkness. Her cousins were the best part of their stay here, and in just a short time she had come to love them all. She especially looked forward to the evenings when Avrum and Sonia helped her learn to speak and read English. Little Rebecca followed Miriam around every chance she got. Only Ira remained shy around her. Thin and small for his age, his frequent asthma attacks provoked angry reactions from Lazar, especially if he was too sick to work in the delicatessen. If Aunt Malka let Ira stay in bed to rest, Uncle Lazar would scream at her and say she was babying him.

Miriam cringed when she recalled her uncle's treatment of Ira and Avrum over a broken glass. Later that night, when Avrum was helping her with English, he apologized for his father's behavior.

"I'm sorry you had to see that. He just gets angry and loses his temper. It was nothing," he said, the pained expression on his face belying his words.

Not sure what to say and embarrassed for her cousin, Miriam looked away. "I understand," she mumbled.

But the truth was that her uncle frightened her, and she looked for any excuse to avoid him. Papa never spoke to Mama the way Lazar spoke to Aunt Malka, she thought, and he never raised a hand to me or Eli.

She missed her brother more than ever and could not believe that he had been gone nearly nine months. In her mind, he was looking down on them and he knew they were no longer in Kishinev. She hoped that he and Yuri were together. She wondered if he was glad they were in America. "I miss you," she whispered as the first rays of the morning sun filtered into the cold room.

CHAPTER 19

Pulling his coat tightly around his body to ward off the icy wind, Meyer returned his pushcart to the stable and began the three-block walk back to the apartment. He was in a good mood. It had been a successful day on the street, and he had even been able to take a small break and share a pleasant lunch with Oscar. A few more weeks of selling and he would have enough money to move his family into a place of their own. And the sooner the better, he thought. Lazar's obvious annoyance with the presence of his in-laws in his home grew daily and his temper was so volatile that Meyer was desperate to move Sadie and Miriam out of the apartment and away from his explosive outbursts.

Meyer's good mood disappeared as soon as he climbed the stairs to the apartment and heard Lazar's voice raised in anger. The sound of something smashing against a wall made his heart race. Bursting through the door, he was shocked by the chaotic scene before him. Pieces of a plate and food covered the floor and what looked like most of Lazar's dinner ran down the wall in obscene streaks of green and brown. Fists clenched, Lazar was advancing toward Avrum as the boy shielded Sonia and Ira behind his back. Ira was pale, wheezing and gulping for air. Rebecca was screaming in Malka's arms, and Sadie and Miriam sat on the bed in the alcove clinging to each other, fear etched on their faces.

Meyer went to Sadie and Miriam and put his arms around them. Malka was rocking Rebecca to soothe her, and as she kissed the crying child's forehead Meyer saw a bruise starting to form on his sister-in-law's cheek.

"What's going on here?" he demanded.

Lazar whirled and seeing the contempt in Meyer's eyes, snarled "it's none of your damn business. Stay out of it." Breathing hard, his nostrils flared in fury, he glared at Meyer and took a step toward him.

"Don't," screamed Malka.

Lazar stared angrily at Malka, the cords of his neck straining against his skin. "Bitch," he growled, and grabbing his coat, stormed out of the apartment.

After Lazar left, it felt as if the air had returned to the room. Ira's rattled breathing slowly settled back to normal. Rebecca's wailing stopped, and wiping the tears from her mother's face with her tiny hands, she kissed Malka's cheek where the bruise was turning hues of purple and blue.

"Did my kiss make you feel better?" she asked in a tremulous voice.

Malka smiled. "It did, my *shayna maideleh*, my beautiful little girl. Everything is fine. Papa just gets angry sometimes, but he loves us. He won't be so mad tomorrow. Now let Sonia put you to bed."

The toddler nodded sleepily and held out her arms to her visibly shaken sister.

"I'll help too," said Miriam, eager to escape the horror of the altercation and the look of utter humiliation on Avrum's face.

Sadie went to Malka and took her in her arms. Burrowing into Sadie's shoulder, she could no longer hold back her tears. "I am so sorry you had to see him that way. He must have had a bad day."

Sadie wondered how bad a day he had to have to make it all right to abuse his family. Barely containing her rage at Lazar, Sadie was glad that her sister could not see the look of disgust on her face. She brushed back Malka's hair from her forehead and tenderly touched her cheek. "Meyer and the boys will clean everything up. I'm going to get a cold cloth to put on your cheek, and then you should get into bed. I will stay with you for a while if you want."

Avrum kissed his mother good night. As she turned to go to her bedroom, he grabbed her arm.

Sensing what he was about to say, Malka held up her hand to silence him. "You will not speak badly of your father. I forbid it."

Avrum looked away, his face flushed, his hatred for his father festering red-hot and ready to erupt.

Seeking a private place to talk, Meyer and Sadie wrapped themselves in blankets and retreated to the landing outside the apartment's front door.

"What happened?" Meyer asked in a low voice.

Sadie had to fold her hands in her lap to keep them from shaking. "It was awful. You know how Malka always has Lazar's dinner on the table for him when he comes home? She made his meal first and put it on the table. It got late, so she started to make dinner for the children. When he did come home, it was obvious he was in a foul mood. He didn't say a word about why he was late and just sat down to eat. But the food was cold. He started to scream at Malka about how hard he works and that he expected a hot meal to be waiting for him. When Malka tried to explain that it was cold because he was late, he hit her and threw the plate against the wall."

"What kind of man strikes his wife? And in front of his children?"

"It's worse. When Avrum screamed at him to stop, Lazar got this look of pure rage on his face and started toward him. Thank God, that's when you came in. I think he would have beaten his own son bloody. I am afraid for all of them. I hate that Malka stays with him, but I don't see how she and the children could manage on their own. And Meyer, he yelled at Malka for spending so much time with me. As much as I hate to leave my sister, I can see now that we are making things worse for her. We need to go."

Meyer sighed. "I'll start looking for an apartment tomorrow."

Rebecca fell into a deep sleep almost as soon as Sonia put her in the bed. Looking at her sister's serene face, Sonia wondered how much the child would remember of the horrific evening. Her father had hit her mother before, but she had never seen him turn his wrath toward Avrum the way he did tonight. She could hear Ira crying from the other side of the sheet and worried that he would have another asthma attack. And it all happened in front of Miriam. What must she think of us?

Sensing her cousin's despair, Miriam touched Sonia's shoulder. "It will be better in the morning."

A sudden noise behind her made Miriam jump, her eyes wide in fear. Avrum had pulled the sheet that divided the room aside with such force that the rod that held it up wobbled and nearly came down. Staring at Miriam, he hissed, "You've seen what he is like. It will never get better unless the son of a bitch dies. I swear I will kill him if he ever hits Mama again."

Sonia gasped. "Don't say that, Avrum. You know you don't mean it. You are just upset from tonight."

In a calm voice that frightened Miriam more than his anger, Avrum said "I do mean it. I'm going to bed. I have to get up early to open the delicatessen. I doubt we will see Papa for a couple of days."

Avrum's prediction turned out to be accurate. Lazar did not come home the following morning or the day after, and no one, not even Malka, seemed to be overly concerned. Sonia confided in Miriam that it was not an unusual occurrence. Ira and Avrum kept things running in the delicatessen and the sounds of laughter once again echoed through the apartment.

Lazar returned to the apartment on the morning of the third day, wearing the same clothes he wore when he left and reeking of cheap whiskey and sweat. His eyes were bloodshot and there was a cut caked with dried blood on his forehead. He spoke not a word and went directly into the bedroom where he slept the day away. Malka shushed the children at the slightest sound, and joylessness returned to the rooms above the delicatessen.

CHAPTER 20

After estimating what it would cost to buy even the barest minimum of furniture and kitchen needs, Meyer's hopes of finding a decent place to live quickly devolved into finding any place they could afford. The older, low-rent tenements were coated in filth, had outside water pumps for cooking and bathing, and rows of wooden outhouses for bathroom use. Unwilling to move his family into such squalor, he settled on a three-room, fourth-floor apartment on Hester Street. Although it lacked heat, it did have a toilet in the hallway and a tap in the kitchen, so they wouldn't have to haul pails of water upstairs from a downstairs pump. It was less than he had hoped for, and they would be sharing the bathroom with three other families, but at least they would be free of Lazar.

Sadie was determined not to let her disappointment show when Meyer brought her to see the apartment. After trudging up four flights of stairs and navigating their way down a long, dark hallway that smelled of urine, Meyer led her to the last unit on the right. He hesitated before unlocking the door, and she knew he was anxious about her reaction.

"I hope you like it," he said, turning the key over in his hand. "It needs some cleaning up, but I am hoping it will be temporary and we will be able to move into something nicer in a short while."

"I'm sure it will be fine," she said, trying to sound convincing.

They entered through the kitchen and the first thing Sadie noticed when they stepped into the dark apartment was the smell. The odors of years of cooked meals combined with the stink of mildew, creating a sickening stench. Covering her nose and mouth to keep from gagging, she looked for a window to open and found none in the kitchen.

"Where's the window?" she asked, the apartment's vile smell filling her nose and stinging her throat.

"There's one in the front room," said Meyer, leading her to the next room where a narrow shaft of light cut through a torn and yellowed shade. When Sadie pulled the shade to open the window, it ripped and came off in her hand, providing a view of a fire escape and another tenement less than three feet away. Lines of laundry billowing in the cold wind were strung between the two buildings.

Meyer showed her the windowless bedroom and looked around the apartment in despair. Viewing the grime-streaked walls of the airless rooms through Sadie's eyes for the first time, he felt as if he'd failed her. "I am so sorry, Sadie. I wanted to find a nicer place, but this is all we can afford."

Sadie took his face in her hands and kissed him. "Once we clean it up and air it out, it will be fine. We will make it our home."

Kissing her back, Meyer said, "I promise you, this is temporary. I won't be a pushcart peddler forever."

Sadie waited until she was alone in the kitchen with Malka to tell her they were moving to the apartment on Hester Street. Malka turned away from her sister and stirred a pot of potato soup on the stove. "I was hoping you would stay longer, but I am not surprised. I understand that you need to be in a place of your own, and I know Lazar does not make you feel welcome."

"We just think things will be better for you if we leave. We've intruded enough." Hesitating for a moment, Sadie gave voice to her fears. "I don't mean to interfere, but Lazar's temper grows shorter each day, and I am very worried about how he treats you and the children."

Malka wiped her hands on her apron and looked at Sadie, her eyes misting. "I've thought about leaving him so many times. Two years ago, he hit me and pushed me down. I was three months pregnant, and I lost the baby. When I told him I was taking the children and leaving, he said he would find us and kill us all. I believed him, and in truth, we had no place to go."

Stunned, Sadie could feel her knees weaken, and she had to hold on to the kitchen sink to keep her balance. "Malka, as soon as we can afford a bigger apartment, I want you and the children to come live with us. I am afraid he really will kill you one of these days."

"You will have to get a very big apartment," Malka said ruefully. "I think I am pregnant again. I missed my monthly and I have been feeling nauseous."

Sadie stared at her sister. "Does Lazar know?"

"I haven't told him yet. I've been waiting for him to be in a good mood." Her mouth formed a crooked smile. She shook her head and broke into a bitter laugh at the absurdity of Lazar being in a good mood.

Miriam didn't know how to feel about the move. Mama had taken her aside and told her that they would have to make the best of the apartment they would be living in. She didn't understand what that meant until she saw it. Even smaller than Aunt Malka's apartment, the odor and filth made her sick to her stomach. Her face fell as Sadie walked her through the rooms. "Where will I sleep?"

"In the front room. At least you will have a bed to yourself again," answered Sadie, trying to dull her daughter's obvious disappointment in the apartment.

"Where is the bathroom?"

Sadie could see this wasn't going to be easy. "In the hallway. We will be sharing it with three other families, just like we shared one with Aunt Malka and her family."

Miriam frowned. "It's not the same. They are our family. I don't want to go to the bathroom where strangers go. Why can't we stay at Aunt Malka's?"

Sadie's patience with her daughter disappeared and her voice grew stern. "Your father has been working long hours so we can be a family in our own home. This is the best we can do, and you will not let him see your disappointment."

"Yes, Mama," said Miriam, tight-lipped and trying not to cry. "Even though I will have a bed of my own, I will still miss my cousins."

"Please, Miriam, don't make this harder than it already is. It's not as if you are never going to see them again. We only live a few blocks away. Now, we're going to go back to Aunt Malka's and get a bucket and soap and turn this mess into a decent place to live."

Happy to have his in-laws move out, Lazar gave Avrum and Ira time off from the delicatessen to help Meyer load the meager furniture he had purchased onto his pushcart and bring it into the apartment. Leaving Ira downstairs to guard the cart, Meyer and Avrum made three trips to the fourth floor. The two bed frames, mattresses, table, and three wooden chairs Meyer had bargained for from a fellow peddler grew heavier as they climbed each flight of the dark stairway.

By the time Meyer and Avrum cleared the final landing with the last of the furniture, Sadie and Miriam had washed the dirt off the walls, scrubbed the floors and hung the plain white curtain Malka made from an old sheet on the window in the front room. They were putting away the few dishes, utensils, pots, and pans they'd brought with them from Kishinev when Meyer, exhausted and sweating despite the frigid mid-February temperature, collapsed into a chair. "Those stairs got steeper and the furniture heavier with every trip," he groaned.

"Only for you, Uncle," teased Avrum. "I can help you set up the beds, and then if you want, Ira and I can return the pushcart. We pass right by the stable on the way home. And it will give us a little more time away from the store," he added, flashing a sly smile.

Miriam went downstairs to keep Ira company while Avrum and Meyer put the bed frames together. Her younger cousin was stamping his feet and blowing into his hands to stay warm. Ira's wrists poked out from the sleeves of his too-small coat and the holes in the black stockings poking below his knickers left his pale skin exposed to the frigid temperature. Worried about his asthma, Miriam felt terrible that he had been left out in the cold.

"I'll stay with the cart if you want to go upstairs and get warm," she offered.

"I can wait," said Ira, cramming his gloveless hands into the pockets of his coat. "Do you like your apartment?"

Miriam shrugged. "It's all right. It's small, but Mama says we will fix it up and make it nicer."

"I wish you were still staying with us," Ira said. "Mama is sad to see you go, and so am I."

Me too, thought Miriam. Me too.

Their first night in the apartment turned out to be the coldest of the winter. With the stove the only source of heat, they moved Miriam's bed into the kitchen. Dressed in layers of clothing, they huddled together under the blankets waiting for their bodies to provide some additional warmth. Exhausted, but too cold to fall asleep, they listened to the snow and sleet pelting the window in the front room while every wall seemed to channel cold air into the apartment.

"I am trying to think of warm things," said Miriam, her teeth chattering. "Hot chicken soup. Freshly baked bread. Mama's stew."

"Now you're making me hungry," said Meyer laughing. "How about a nice roaring fire in the fireplace? Or a summer day with the sun beating down?"

"Or sitting in a tub full of hot water," added Sadie wistfully.

"I know this is hard," sighed Meyer, "but we are safe here and things will get better, I promise."

CHAPTER 21

It had been nearly a week since Sadie had seen Malka. Worried about her sister, she suggested to Miriam that they take a break from their housework and walk down to the delicatessen. Delighted to be able to see her cousins and escape the tiny apartment, Miriam grabbed her coat and was waiting impatiently at the door before Sadie had finished getting dressed.

The slate-gray sky threatened snow. Sadie and Miriam walked with their heads down, struggling to stay on their feet as they were buffeted by a bitter February wind. The frigid air filled their lungs and made their eyes water, their tears freezing on their cheeks. Propelled by the fierce gusts of wind and eager to get out of the cold, they hastened their steps.

"Can we stop into the delicatessen first to see Avrum and Ira before we go upstairs to see Aunt Malka and the girls?"

"Let's see how busy they are," said Sadie, fearful of angering Lazar with their presence.

Peering into the store, Sadie was relieved to see there was only one customer at the counter and that Lazar was not there.

A blast of cold air announced their entrance. Avrum looked up and broke into a wide smile. Coming from behind the counter to greet them, he hugged them both.

"It's so good to see you. Mama will be so glad you are here. Ira," he called to his brother, "give Miriam some soup to warm her up."

Ira beckoned Miriam over. When Miriam stepped to the counter,

Avrum lowered his voice. "I am really glad you are here, Aunt Sadie. Mama is not feeling well. She is having trouble keeping her food down."

Sadie nodded, unsure if Avrum knew that his mother was pregnant. "I will go upstairs to see her. Tell Miriam to come up after she's finished her soup."

When Malka answered the door, Sadie was alarmed by her appearance. There were dark circles under her eyes, made more obvious by the pallor of her skin. A weak smile crossed Malka's face as she kissed and hugged her sister.

"Malka, you don't look well. Why didn't you send one of the children to come get me? Where are Sonia and Rebecca?"

Malka started to speak, and suddenly bolted for the kitchen. Her whole body convulsed as she emptied her stomach into a bucket, the smell of bile filling the room. Sadie brought Malka a glass of water and smoothed the hair away from her sweaty forehead.

"I'm sorry," said Malka, slowly sipping the water. "This started about a week ago, and it's not just in the morning. I was never this sick with the other children, not even Avrum."

"Does Lazar know yet?"

"After this week, yes. He ranted about another mouth to feed, as if it was my fault."

"Have you told the children yet?"

"I think Avrum suspects. He is old enough to remember I was sick in the mornings with the baby I lost. The others don't know yet, but I will have to tell them soon." Malka rose and washed her face in the sink. "He wants me to end the pregnancy."

Sadie gasped, remembering stories of women in Kishinev who had tried to abort their babies and died. "Please tell me you are not considering doing this."

Malka shook her head. "I don't care what he wants; I am having this baby."

"What will you do if Lazar insists? Malka, he is dangerous when he gets angry. I worry about you and the children all the time."

Malka went quiet. She studied her hands, twisting the thin gold band that circled her finger. When she finally spoke, her voice was filled with resolve. "I will do whatever is necessary to appease him, but I will have this baby."

CHAPTER 22

March, 1904

Determined to improve their living conditions, Meyer rose before dawn each morning to get to the Washington Market, where he purchased wholesale fruit and vegetables to add to the food items he was still buying from Lazar. He set up every morning next to Oscar and remained at his pushcart until darkness fell and people scurried home. His business was picking up, and many of his customers returned to his cart each day to buy their produce. Still, when he finished counting the money he took in at the end of the day, he was only earning enough to make do. After buying stock for the pushcart, paying for coal for the stove, gas to light the apartment, food and rent, there was not much left over. It bothered him that Sadie was now doing piecework like Malka to bring in extra money.

"I don't mind," she told him after her first week of sewing sleeves onto men's shirts. "It keeps me busy, and if we can save the little bit I earn, we have a chance to get ahead."

Meyer had to admit it helped, and he knew that Sadie was as eager as he was to move into a nicer apartment. They were managing despite the less than ideal conditions, but Miriam missed having her own room and complained daily about the lack of bathroom privacy.

"People are so rude," she grumbled the day after they'd moved into the apartment. "Someone kept pounding on the door while I was using the toilet. I was going as fast as I could. Did they think all that noise would make me go faster? And it stinks in there," she said, her face twisted in revulsion.

Meyer felt a pang of guilt as he recalled Miriam's look of disgust. It hurt him to see his daughter so unhappy. She desperately wanted to go to school, but she had to be fluent in English. Avrum was helping her, but not on a regular basis, and her progress was slow. Oscar told him about free classes where newly arrived immigrant children were taught to speak and read English. Once they mastered the language, Oscar said they could transfer to a public school. Meyer mulled over this information for days, unsure of what to do, paralyzed by an irrational fear for Miriam's safety.

The last days of winter brought a raging snowstorm to the city. Waking before dawn, Meyer looked outside the window and could barely see the tenement across the way as the wind sent swirls of snow beating against the buildings. Spear-like icicles hung from the eaves. Cursing a day of lost income, Meyer returned to the warmth of his bed and Sadie's body. Slipping between the covers, he drew Sadie to him. She turned toward him, smiling sleepily. "Don't you have to set up your cart?"

"There's a blinding snowstorm out there and you are here, nice and warm," Meyer whispered, reaching under her nightgown and cupping her breasts. Responding to his touch, Sadie pressed her body against his and covered his mouth with deep kisses. Instantly aroused, Meyer's hands slowly traveled down to her hips, his lips finding the hollow of her neck. Sadie moaned low in her throat and rolled to her back, pulling Meyer with her. Wrapping her legs around him, she gasped in pleasure when he entered her.

Shivering under her blanket, Miriam was surprised when Meyer made his way to the kitchen to add coal to the stove. "Is something wrong? Why aren't you at your pushcart?" she asked in alarm.

"Go look outside," he said.

Miriam wrapped herself in her blanket and peered out the window. Falling in large, wet flakes, snow billowed like gauzy clouds, blurring images of the empty street below. Frowning, she moved in front of the stove for warmth.

"Why the sad face? Aren't you happy to have me home today?"

"I was hoping to go see my cousins today, but now it looks like I'll be cooped up in the apartment all day."

"Why is that so bad?" asked Sadie, joining them in the kitchen, her face still flushed from their morning of love making. She smiled shyly at Meyer and kissed Miriam on the cheek.

"Because no matter how many layers of clothing I put on, it's still freezing in here. And I feel like the walls of the apartment are closing in on me. There's no room to move here."

Miriam's unhappiness tugged at Meyer's heart. His once cheerful daughter had become sullen and unreachable. She often cried out in her sleep, and he knew that as they approached the first anniversary of Eli's death, memories of the events in the cellar haunted her. He could see how lonely she was. He had fallen into a comforting routine of work and going to the synagogue Friday nights and Saturdays, and while Miriam helped Sadie with her sewing, the only activity she looked forward to was her infrequent English lessons with Avrum. Despite his fears of outside influences on Miriam, he could see that her spirit was being crushed by his compulsion to protect his remaining child. She was fourteen and beginning to assert her independence. As much as it pained him to admit it, he knew that he could no longer shelter his willful daughter.

CHAPTER 23

April 1904

Passover began on the first day of April. Sadie and Miriam removed all *chametz* in the apartment and switched to the few Passover dishes they brought with them from Kishinev, but memories of the pogrom and Eli's death cast a pall over the holiday. Any hope of sharing the first Seder with Malka and her family was dashed by Malka's relentless nausea. Instead of a celebration surrounded by family and friends, their Seder was haunted by the faces of the loved ones who weren't there.

The end of the eight-day holiday marked the *yahrzeit*—the anniversary—of Eli's death. As the day approached, Sadie became more remote, and Miriam frequently found her mother sitting with her sewing in her lap, staring into space.

For Miriam, the memories of last Passover and all that happened remained so vivid she could not fathom that a year had passed since Eli's death. He was still so much a part of her—always in her thoughts, present most nights in her dreams—that she could not accept the finality of his first *yahrzeit* even as Meyer recited the mourner's *Kaddish* and lit the *yahrzeit* candle. Staring into the flame as wisps of gray smoke curled toward the ceiling, Miriam began to cry. Looking to her parents for comfort, she saw instead the utter pain of Eli's loss on their faces.

In the days that followed, Miriam's time was spent helping Sadie with her sewing. Only occasional visits to see her cousins broke the tedium of her days. She stopped complaining about the apartment, but her unhappiness was so evident that Meyer suppressed his fears and enrolled Miriam in the English course.

A smile lit Miriam's face for the first time in weeks when Meyer told her about the class. "When you finish this class, you will be able to attend public school," he said, delighted to see his daughter so happy.

"Papa, thank you. I promise I will study hard, and I will still help Mama with the shirts."

Meyer touched Miriam's face and kissed her. "Don't worry about the shirts. Just learn English so you can teach it to me and Mama," he said.

Along with twenty other students whose native languages included Yiddish, Italian, Polish, and Russian, Miriam spent her days in a classroom where only English was spoken. Waking early each morning so she could practice what she'd learned the day before, she would read the words to Sadie and Meyer and they would repeat them back to her. To Miriam's delight, her parents' English vocabulary was expanding along with hers.

The English basics Miriam learned from Avrum helped her to move swiftly through her classroom lessons. Her quick mind and eagerness to learn did not go unnoticed by her teacher, Miss Jacobs. "You are doing so well," said the petite instructor during the third week of class. "I'm afraid some of our reading material is going to be too easy for you. I have some books that are a little more advanced. If you like, you can borrow them and read them at home."

Her teacher's praise made Miriam blush. "I would love to have books to read at home."

"Well then, I will bring you some tomorrow. But you must promise to tell me if there is anything you can't read or don't understand, so I can help you."

"I promise," she said, wanting more than ever to please her teacher. Everything about Miss Jacobs fascinated Miriam. She admired how the slim young woman wore her dark hair piled in a neat knot in the style of the day. She noted how she was always perfectly dressed in long skirts and puffy-sleeved blouses with a small bow at her neck. But what gave Miriam the most hope was the idea that with an education, she could be a teacher just like Miss Jacobs.

Miriam devoured the books Miss Jacobs gave her and made so much progress that her teacher asked her if she would help Rivka Feltman, a Yiddish-speaking student who was falling behind the rest of the students. "I'm not sure why she isn't progressing. Perhaps she will respond better to someone closer to her own age than she does to me," Miss Jacobs said.

Painfully shy, Rivka sat quietly at the back of the class, her shoulders hunched and her head down as if she wanted to make herself disappear. Unlike the other students who were eager to show off their new-found English skills, Rivka spoke only when called upon. When asked to read out loud, she stumbled over words and her heavily accented English made her hard to understand. Miss Jacobs tried to draw her out, but Rivka seemed to wither under the teacher's attention. Miriam could tell how nervous she was because she would blink furiously when she was asked to read.

As they were leaving for the day, Miriam caught up with Rivka and introduced herself. "Miss Jacobs thought it would be good if we worked together on our lessons," she said in Yiddish.

"You mean Miss Jacobs wants you to help the class dummy," she snapped, her round face turning red.

Surprised by Rivka's anger, Miriam tried to soothe the girl's feelings. "No, you've got it all wrong. It will help me too. I have much to learn, and I think we can help each other."

"You're not fooling me. I know the other students laugh at the way I pronounce the words," said Rivka, her brown, deep-set eyes blinking rapidly as she pulled her sweater tighter around her full-figured body as if to fend off Miriam's offer of help.

"I honestly don't know what you're talking about. I only know it would benefit both of us to practice our English together. I really want to be able to master the language so I can go to public school. Don't you see that you would be helping me?"

Rivka grew quiet. She twirled a lock of brown hair that had escaped her bun. The blinking began to slow. "I cannot hear what the teacher is saying," Rivka said softly, lowering her eyes.

"Why don't you ask to sit up front, closer to Miss Jacobs? Or ask her to speak louder?"

"Because I am afraid she will call on me more, and I don't want to embarrass myself."

Suddenly realizing how self-conscious Rivka was, Miriam softened her tone. "Please, give it a chance. You can come home with me after class and we can go over each day's lesson. We can start tomorrow, if you like."

Still not looking directly at Miriam, Rivka shrugged and said, "I am willing to try, but I cannot stay too long. I have to cook dinner for my father."

After two weeks of meeting with Miriam after school, Rivka's reading and speaking skills were at the same level as the rest of the class. And as the two young women became friends, they discovered they lived within a block of each other. Fifteen-year-old Rivka told Miriam about her family, that her mother died when she was thirteen years old. They left Kiev the next year, coming to New York to be with cousins. Her father worked in the garment industry and as soon as her English improved so she could get a better job, she would go to work in the needle trades too. As they walked home together one blustery afternoon, Rivka confessed to Miriam that she didn't hear well because she was partially deaf in her left ear, the result of an infection when she was an infant.

"It's been a problem my whole life. I am shy, so I don't tell people I can't hear them, and then they think I am stupid."

"Well, I know you're not stupid, and I think it's time to show everyone else how smart you really are."

At Miriam's urging, Rivka requested a desk at the front of the class. No longer afraid to speak up, she began to participate in class and thrived on Miss Jacobs' encouragement. More than anything, the friendship that blossomed between Rivka and Miriam transformed the lonely girl.

Seven weeks after she started classes, Miriam was the first in her group to successfully complete all that was required to begin her public-school education.

"I really do hate to see you leave," Miss Jacobs said on Miriam's last day in class. "I have enjoyed having you as a student and I am so grateful to you for all you did to help Rivka. For very selfish reasons, I wish you could stay longer."

Miriam could feel the heat of embarrassment creep up her neck to her face. "I loved being in this class. I have learned so much."

Miss Jacobs beamed. "Will you continue to help Rivka? She is doing so well; I would hate to see her fall behind again."

"Of course. She's really quite smart. Plus, I would miss not seeing her every day."

"I'm glad to hear it. She only needs a few more weeks before she will be done too. And you should do very well when school starts in the fall. I hope you will come by to see us. I want to know how you are doing," said Miss Jacobs, giving Miriam a warm hug.

"Thank you for everything," said Miriam, her voice husky with emotion.

CHAPTER 24

Summer 1904

Her classes at an end, Miriam helped Sadie with her sewing, pulling out basting stitches, cutting threads and inspecting the finished work to make sure the final stitching was straight and tight. She was glad to relieve Sadie of some of her duties and relished the quiet time alone with her mother. While they worked, Sadie would tell her stories of growing up in Kiev with Aunt Malka and Uncle Reuben. Miriam never tired of hearing how her parents met or how Uncle Yuri came to be a member of their family. She covered her face and giggled when her mother reminded her of her escapade as a three-year-old when she decided it would be a good idea to turn their gray cat white and covered him in flour.

After a day of sewing, both Sadie and Miriam looked forward to Rivka's late afternoon visit for her daily lesson. Sadie took an instant liking to Miriam's new friend, and at Rivka's prompting, joined the girls at the kitchen table when Miriam went over their vocabulary and spelling lessons.

"K-nee," said Rivka, looking at a picture of a knee with the word spelled out beside it. Peering over her shoulder, Sadie nodded and repeated, "K-nee."

"It's pronounced 'nee,'" said Miriam. "The K is silent, so you don't have to say it."

"If you don't have to say it, why is it there?" asked Sadie, exasperation spilling into her voice.

"I don't know. It's just like the word 'knife.' You just don't say the K," responded Miriam.

Rivka and Sadie stared at her in total bewilderment. The look on their faces was so unexpected that Miriam began to laugh. "I'm sorry. I'm not laughing at you, but you should see your faces," she said, laughing harder.

"This language is nonsense," said Sadie, throwing her hands up in frustration. "Letters that are there but aren't said. No wonder the words refuse to listen to my tongue." She looked at both girls and burst into laughter.

June quickly turned to July and the summer's heat and humidity caused as much discomfort as the cold of winter. With little circulating air, the apartment was stifling by noon. Drenched in sweat, Sadie and Miriam had to repeatedly sponge themselves with cool water to continue sewing.

Meyer fared no better on the street. He found himself longing for the cold as the sun beat down in a relentless assault and the concrete beneath his feet radiated scorching heat through his shoes. Nighttime offered little relief. Most evenings Meyer carried their mattresses to the roof, where they joined their neighbors in search of fresh air and a restful night's sleep.

The July heat was especially hard on Malka. In the seventh month of her pregnancy, her hands and feet swelled. Going up and down the stairs had become so difficult she rarely left the apartment. Sonia tended to Rebecca and Sadie and Miriam made frequent visits, often accompanied by Rivka, to help with meals. On their last visit, Sadie became alarmed when she found her sister padding around in bedroom slippers, her feet so swollen she was unable to put on shoes.

"Malka, you've got to stay off your feet and put them up so the swelling will go down. I don't know how you are able to walk," exclaimed Sadie, putting a cold compress on the back of her sister's neck to help her cool off.

"I know, but Sonia is busy with Rebecca and Lazar gets angry if the apartment isn't clean and his dinner isn't ready when he gets home. I am not doing contract work anymore. It's just too hot to sit over the sewing machine."

Sadie sighed. Things would never change. Malka would always put Lazar's needs before her own. "What are you going to do when the baby comes?"

"What I always do. Try not to make him angry."

Leaving Malka and Sadie to talk, Miriam and Sonia took Rebecca outside to escape the heat of the apartment. Passing the delicatessen on their way out, they waved at Avrum and Ira, who were stocking shelves while Lazar waited on a customer.

The girls settled themselves on a shaded stoop where they could watch Rebecca playing with a group of neighborhood children as they ran through the spray from an open fire hydrant. Turning her face to catch a light breeze that fluttered through an adjacent alley, Miriam spotted Avrum walking quickly toward them.

"I just came out to say hello," he said, still wearing his long white apron. "Where's Rivka?"

Sonia nudged Miriam. "I told you he had a crush on her."

Avrum's cheeks went from pink to scarlet at the mention of Rivka's name. "I do not have a crush on her. I was just wondering where she was."

"She's at home. Her father isn't feeling well, and she is taking care of him," said Miriam, unable to hide her smile at Avrum's obvious discomfort.

"Okay, I was just wondering. Anyway, I'd better get back before Papa realizes I am gone. Ira was really mad that I left and stuck him with stocking the shelves."

As soon as Avrum was out of sight, the girls began to giggle. "I guess I'd better make sure Rivka comes with us the next time we come over," Miriam said. "But I don't think she has any idea how he feels about her."

"I know I teased him, but I am glad to see him taking some interest in a social life. He works hard all day in the store, and now with Mama so big and swollen from the baby, he does what he can to help her around the apartment when he is home."

"You must be excited about the baby."

Sonia stared at the children playing on the street, before answering. "I would be if Mama wasn't so uncomfortable and unhappy. And I don't think Papa wants the baby. He yells at Mama more than usual. It's like she can't do anything right. And I am really worried about Avrum. I am afraid that one of these days he is going to really lose his temper and strike out at Papa."

Remembering Avrum's anger the night her uncle hit her aunt, Miriam agreed Sonia had reason to worry.

August brought with it more intense heat. Rivka finished her English class and to celebrate her success, Sadie baked a chocolate-filled babka. Even the oppressive temperature in the apartment could not dampen their festive mood, and they laughed when the melted chocolate smeared around their lips as they ate the butter-laden cake topped with cinnamon streusel.

"Mrs. Raisky, this is delicious. I haven't had babka since we left Russia. I remember my mother baking it and how good the house would smell for hours after it came out of the oven. Thank you so much for making this day so special."

"How could we not celebrate my fellow classmate's achievements in English? We are so proud of you. And now I will have two teachers to help me speak this unpronounceable language," said Sadie, smiling in pleasure at Rivka's radiant face. "Will you be going to school in the fall like Miriam?"

Rivka shook her head. "I am going to work at the Triangle Shirtwaist Factory. I start next week. My father is a cutter at another factory, but he knew someone at the Triangle and got me a job as a floor girl, keeping count of the spools of thread the seamstresses use. I will make four dollars a week. I'm hoping to be able to work on a sewing machine after I've been there for a while. I like to sew, and the pay is much better."

Miriam frowned. "I was hoping we would be able to spend more time together before you started working."

"Me too," said Rivka. "But my father said I should take the job while they had the opening." Her eyes began their rapid blinking. "We need the extra money."

Sadie squeezed Rivka's hand. "You will do well at whatever you do." She rose to wrap up slices of babka for Rivka's father when a pounding on the door made them all jump.

Avrum stood sweating and panting in the hall. "Aunt Sadie, we need you. Mama is having the baby and we don't know what to do. She said it's taking too long for the baby to come. Mrs. Goldberg from next door was supposed to help, but she's not at home. Papa said to get you."

Sadie was out the door before Avrum finished speaking. Barely catching his breath, Avrum turned and followed his aunt with Miriam and Rivka trailing behind him.

The sound of a newborn's wail greeted them as they ran up the stairs.

So out of breath that none of them could speak, they stood in the bedroom doorway gawking as Mrs. Goldberg handed a clean, pink, and hungry infant to Malka. Looking up through thick, round glasses, she made a clucking noise with her tongue and ordered everyone but Sadie out of the room. "Too many people are not good for the baby," she said in a gravelly voice that did not fit her petite frame. Pursing her wrinkled lips and pointing to the door, she bellowed, "Out!"

"Wait," protested Avrum. "Is it a boy or a girl?"

"You have a new sister," said Malka, her voice weak, sweat-soaked hair plastered to her face. "Her name is Esther, in memory of Eli," she added, looking directly at Sadie.

Sadie went to her sister and watching her new niece latch on so eagerly to Malka's breast, felt a sudden rush of love for the tiny newborn. "Esther," she said out loud, testing the sound of the baby's name. It was only when she tasted the salt of her tears that she realized she was crying.

Mrs. Goldberg finished tending to Malka and waited for Esther to sate herself at Malka's breast and fall asleep. Placing the sleeping baby in a cradle beside the bed, the old midwife beckoned to Sadie. "Your sister needs to get a lot of rest. Thank God Sonia went looking for me and found me. Lazar is useless, and Malka was having a hard time. The baby was facing forward. Once I turned her, Malka pushed her out easily. The baby looks healthy, but Malka said she was about three weeks early, so make sure she gets plenty of milk. I'll look in on your sister tomorrow."

Sadie hugged Mrs. Goldberg. "Thank you. I feel like you saved Malka and the baby. I wouldn't have known what to do."

Mrs. Goldberg patted her on the arm. "*Mazel tov*. You have a beautiful niece."

As soon as Sadie left the bedroom she was accosted by Avrum and Sonia, anxious to know how their mother and sister were. "They are both fine, and they are both asleep. Your mother is going to need to rest a lot. Sonia, I am afraid you are going to have your hands full."

"It's all right. I don't mind. Rebecca is easy to look after, and I told her she is a big sister now, so she will have to help with the baby."

"I can help too," Avrum said. "I'm just so glad they are all right. I could tell how frightened Mama was."

"You both did all the right things, and your mother is going to be fine, just tired for a while. Where are Miriam and Rivka?" she asked, looking past them.

"They went down to the store to tell Papa and Ira that the baby was a girl. Papa is not going to be happy. He kept telling Mama that she better have a boy," answered Avrum, his face twisted in anger.

CHAPTER 25

Miriam was dressed and ready for her first day of school so early she was able to join Meyer for breakfast before he left for the day. She stood before him and twirled around so that her dark-blue skirt flared out around her ankles. "How do I look?"

Meyer beamed when he looked at his daughter's happy face. "Lovely," he said, kissing the top of her head.

Miriam adjusted a button on her white blouse and inspected her newly polished shoes. "I was too excited to sleep. Miss Jacobs said that I would be put in a sixth-grade class, so I will probably be older than the other students. Still, I just hope I can keep up with them."

"Of course you will. Look how fast you finished the English class."

Miriam kissed her father's cheek. "Thank you. I know you and Mama are working hard so I can go to school. I promise to make both of you proud of me."

Meyer left the apartment a happy man. For the first time since their arrival in New York, he felt things were going well. His business was picking up and with what Sadie's sewing brought in, they would soon be able to move to a nicer apartment. He'd paid Lazar back for the initial credit he'd extended to help him get started. Malka was doing well following Esther's birth, and the tiny baby was thriving, growing fatter and pinker with each passing day. But what made Meyer's heart soar was the change in Miriam.

The morose, brooding fourteen-year-old was gone, replaced by the sweet, smiling child he missed so much. Meyer could finally see a future for them in America.

Navigating the halls to her classroom, Miriam could hear loud voices before she reached its door. Stepping inside, she was taken aback by the sheer number of students packed into the small room. Standing at the front, a plump woman with gray hair and an annoyed look on her face was trying to achieve some semblance of order. Miriam stood frozen, uncertain of what to do.

The older woman finally glanced her way. "Are you supposed to be in the sixth grade?" she barked.

"Yes. I'm Miriam Raisky," Miriam said in her best English, the tremor in her voice betraying her fear.

"Oh, Miss Jacobs told me about you. Welcome. I am Mrs. Cullen, your teacher," she said, her face and voice softening. "As you can see, we have more students than desks, so you will have to share one. There's a desk with only one student," she said, pointing to one in the rear of the room that was occupied by a sullen, dark-haired girl.

"My name is Miriam. Mrs. Cullen said we were to share a desk," she said, as she squeezed into the seat next to the girl, trying not to bump her.

The girl stared dully at Miriam and turned away, giving Miriam reason to wonder if perhaps her English was not as good as she thought it was. She was about to ask the girl her name, when Mrs. Cullen banged a ruler on the front desk and in a loud voice, called the class to order.

The girl beside Miriam sat mute and motionless. Miriam looked around the room to see if she recognized any faces from Miss Jacobs' class and was disappointed to find none. Instead, there were nearly sixty other students of varying ages and sizes squirming uncertainly under the teacher's hard gaze.

Hands on her hips, Mrs. Cullen surveyed her students and sighed. They were mostly immigrant children, and she was in despair wondering how she was going to give them the attention they needed when there were so many of them. Yet, even knowing that the large class meant less learning would take place, it pained her that one-third of them would drop out by the end of the term because their families needed them to contribute an income.

Clearing her throat, Mrs. Cullen began class by asking each student to stand and state his or her name. Miriam's seatmate surprised her by having a voice. Her name was Fiona.

That night at dinner, Meyer and Sadie wanted to know everything about her first day of class. Miriam did not want to tell them how disappointed she was to have spent most of the day waiting her turn to be called up to Mrs. Cullen's desk for an evaluation of her reading skills. While she waited, she was supposed to get to know her seatmate better, but Fiona did not seem interested in making friends and other than saying she was from Ireland, offered no other information.

"I share a desk with a girl name Fiona from Ireland," Miriam told her parents. "I guess she is shy, because she didn't talk much, but she did say when she first saw me that she thought I was Irish because of my red hair. That changed as soon as she heard my accent," laughed Miriam.

In bed that night, Sadie and Meyer held hands and talked in whispers. "If business continues the way it has, we should be able to move to a bigger apartment in a couple of months. And I am so proud of Miriam, though I always thought it would be Eli who would be the scholar in the family," said Meyer, staring into the darkness.

"Hmm," murmured Sadie. "But Miriam has always wanted to go to school. Remember how angry she was that we could not afford to send her to school with Eli. And she is so bright and determined."

"Stubborn is more like it," laughed Meyer. "But you know, her stubbornness may be a good thing. She will always go after what she wants. And I am starting to believe that in this country it is possible for her to succeed and for us to have a better future than we would have had in Russia."

"Tu, tu," said Sadie, making a spitting sound between two fingers to ward off the evil spirits. "Don't tempt the fates by talking about good things to come," she said, kissing Meyer goodnight.

Meyer rolled to his side and was asleep almost immediately. Listening to his slow, even breathing, Sadie wished sleep would find her so readily. She closed her eyes but knew sleep would not come. Too many thoughts filled her head; too many memories tugged at her heart; too many fears clouded her thinking. She knew how easily loved ones can be snatched away; how quickly things change. Don't plan for the future, she told herself. God is listening.

CHAPTER 26

January 1905

Wind-driven sleet pelted Meyer's face stinging like hundreds of tiny pinpricks as he set up his cart in his usual space. Oscar was not there yet, but he knew his friend would not miss a day like this when even the hardiest New Yorkers could not go without gloves and hats. He only hoped that Oscar's customers would also want to warm themselves with his hot potatoes or knishes. He eyed the sky for any signs that his misery would soon end. "No such luck," he said aloud, as heavy gray clouds hovered overhead.

"So, you are talking to yourself now, are you?" said Oscar, his eyes sparkling with mischief.

"Good morning, or should I say afternoon," replied Meyer. "It's so late, I thought you'd decided to use a little sleet as reason to stay in bed."

"What, an old man is five minutes late and you think he's ready for retirement? And you're the one who is always complaining about the weather. 'It's too hot. It's too cold,'" said Oscar in such a perfect imitation of Meyer's grousing that he could not help but smile.

Their banter was interrupted when a well-dressed customer approached Oscar in search of a pair of warm gloves. As the man walked away from Oscar's cart wearing his purchase, he nearly slipped on a patch of ice.

"Be careful; you don't want to get those new gloves dirty," Oscar cried out to the red-faced man. "I know today is going to be a bad one, but I am going to stay out here as long as I have customers," said Oscar, turning up the collar of his coat and facing away from the wind. "You?"

"I'll stay as long as I can, but I have a feeling that if this keeps up all morning, no one will be out."

"Where's that famous Raisky optimism?" joked Oscar.

"Back at the apartment with my warm bed," said Meyer, pulling his hat down over his reddened ears.

The afternoon sky turned black, the wind gaining a new fury as it whipped down alleyways and sent goods from pushcarts flying onto the street. The sleet that had fallen earlier had changed to rain, then back to sleet, and a thin layer of ice coated the ground, making walking treacherous. Only a few intrepid shoppers were daring enough to come out in the weather, and they weren't stopping at Meyer's cart.

"I'm going to close up," Meyer told Oscar. "I am wet and freezing. I haven't had a sale in over an hour, and it doesn't look like there will be any soon. I am going home to a bowl of Sadie's chicken soup. Why don't you join me?"

Oscar watched as Meyer began packing up his cart and considered taking Meyer up on his invitation. "You are as delicate as a baby," he said, falling into their habit of good-natured ribbing.

Meyer was about to return Oscar's needling when the sounds of a commotion grabbed his attention. Turning in the direction of the noise, Meyer watched in horror as a driverless, horse-drawn carriage careened down the street. Snorting in fear, its breath forming clouds of steam, the horse became panicked when a blowing newspaper landed across its face. Running blind and dragging the overturned carriage, the terrified horse suddenly veered to the right and was bearing down on Oscar and Meyer.

Before Oscar could react, Meyer leapt from behind his cart and pushed his friend out of the path of the galloping horse. Landing on his back, Oscar gasped when he saw the carriage break loose from the horse's harness and fall on Meyer, the chassis covering his body, a spinning wheel striking him in the head.

Lying among the ruins of his pushcart, blood running down his face, Meyer was barely conscious. There was a ringing in his ears, and though he could hear Oscar calling his name from far away, he could not move under the weight of the twisted carriage.

Other pushcart peddlers and bystanders rushed to help Oscar lift the carriage off Meyer. "Thank God you are alive," said Oscar, pushing aside the debris that left Meyer coated in dust and food from his cart. "I thought you were a dead man when I saw the carriage land on you. Your head is bleeding. We have to get you to the hospital."

Meyer touched the wound on his scalp and winced in pain. "No hospital. Please take me home. The apartment is just up the block."

Oscar carefully helped him to his feet. Pain jolted up Meyer's right leg when he put his weight on it. Dizzy and having trouble focusing his eyes, Meyer grew suddenly nauseous and vomited. Unsteady on his feet and seeing flashes of light before his eyes, he suffered further indignity when he had to lean on his friend to keep from falling as they made their way down the slippery sidewalk.

Climbing the four flights of stairs to the apartment proved to be more of a challenge than navigating the icy sidewalks. The two men had to stop to rest at each landing. Gasping for breath and his head pounding, Meyer fought off waves of nausea. Oscar was faring no better, his face pale and shiny with sweat, his breath coming in short bursts.

"At this rate, we will make it to your apartment in time for next year's Passover Seder," said Oscar, panting.

"We're halfway there. I think we will make it in time for Rosh Hashanah this year."

"You're making jokes," said Oscar, putting his arm around Meyer and starting up the next flight of stairs. "A good sign."

Blocks away, Miriam stepped carefully on the ice-coated sidewalks. Slowly making her way home after school, her mind turned to the day's lessons. Recognizing Miriam's potential, Mrs. Cullen had begun giving her extra assignments to help her advance more rapidly to the next grade. Today she'd studied world geography, and her head was filled with images of far-away places.

The stinging cold turned her thoughts to the hot cup of tea Mama would have waiting for her. It was Friday and *Shabbat* started tonight at sundown. Miriam looked forward to helping Mama with cooking the meal for the Sabbath. She loved the rituals of this special night. Mama would light the *Shabbat* candles in her grandmother's candlesticks and they would sit down to a delicious dinner. Tomorrow Papa would spend the morning at the synagogue praying, and they would go for a walk in the park in the afternoon. Miriam was hoping to see Rivka on Sunday. Her friend worked six days a week, twelve, sometimes fourteen hours a day, and Sunday was her only day off. They did not see each other often now and although Rivka never complained, she was always tired-looking when they met. Miriam knew how much Rivka's father depended on her income, and it made her feel guilty that she was able to continue to go to school while her friend had to work.

Turning the corner onto Hester Street, Miriam was surprised at how glad she was to see the old red-brick apartment building. She hurried up the stairs and entering the apartment, she was shocked to see a white-haired man standing in their kitchen.

"Mama, are you all right?" Miriam stopped short when she saw Meyer sitting in a chair, a blood-stained bandage wrapped around his head. "Oh my God, what happened?"

"It's all right," said Sadie, putting her arms around Miriam. "This is Oscar, Papa's friend. There was an accident at the pushcarts. Oscar brought Papa home."

Oscar stepped forward. "Your papa saved my life. A runaway horse and carriage were coming right at me and your papa pushed me out of the way. The carriage came loose and fell on him." Tears filled his eyes.

"I am just banged up a bit," said Meyer weakly. "I will be back at my pushcart tomorrow. Avrum, my nephew, can take it back to the stable for me."

Oscar looked away, surprised that Meyer did not remember that his cart had been destroyed in the crash. "I will take care of it," he said. "You just take care of yourself."

Sadie walked Oscar to the door. "I am so grateful to you for looking after Meyer and bringing him home."

Emotion filling his voice, Oscar said, "He pushed me out of the way with no thought to his own safety. I will never forget that." His forehead furrowed. He started to say more and then hesitated.

Seeing the concern on his face, Sadie asked, "Is there something you're not telling me?"

"Perhaps it's just confusion about what happened during the accident, but Meyer does not seem to remember that his cart was smashed to pieces by the horse. I am worried that his injury may be worse than it appears."

Sadie brought her hand to her mouth, her eyes growing wide.

"I'm sorry. I did not mean to upset you. I just think that you might want to encourage him to take his time coming back to work. I will settle things with the stable about the damaged cart. Do you have a doctor?"

Sadie shook her head.

"There is a doctor who sees my son's family. Dr. Cohen. I will send him to check on Meyer. I think the wound on his head needs stitches."

Sadie sent Miriam to Malka's apartment to tell them what happened and then slowly guided Meyer to the bedroom to make him more comfortable. Unsteady on his feet and his head pounding, he moaned with each step he took.

"Wait for me to get undressed. I am going to heat some water on the stove so we can get you cleaned up."

Returning with a basin of warm water, Sadie helped Meyer remove his clothes. He grimaced in pain as each item of clothing came off. When he was fully undressed, Sadie was shocked by the bruises on his torso and legs.

"Don't tell me it's worse than it looks," she said, her legs shaking as she realized how close he came to being crushed to death.

"I am so tired," he said, staring dully at Sadie. "My head feels like it is the size of a melon, and everything looks blurry."

The doctor arrived just as Sadie finished getting Meyer washed and into his night clothes. A short man with dark hair and large green eyes, he offered Sadie a calming smile. "Mrs. Raisky, I am Ephraim Cohen. Oscar Gershunoff told me about your husband."

"Thank you for coming so quickly," she said, leading him into the bedroom, where Meyer sat propped up in bed, his eyes fluttering as he struggled to stay awake. "He's in a lot of pain and he keeps saying everything looks blurry." She touched Meyer's arm. "Meyer, this is Dr. Cohen. He is here to look at your head."

Meyer opened his eyes slowly. "Tell Eli he has to help Yuri at the store. I should be able to go back to work tomorrow."

Sadie's face drained of all color. She caught the doctor's eye and shook her head, the fear on her face telling him all he needed to know.

After examining Meyer for any other injuries, Dr. Cohen stitched the deep gash in his scalp and tested Meyer's physical and mental responses. When he was done, he signaled Sadie to step into the front room.

"Considering a carriage fell on him, it's a miracle that he has no broken bones. The wound on his head is deep, but it will heal, as will the bruises. What concerns me is his confusion, though it is not unusual immediately following a blow to the head. I take it there is no store to go to tomorrow."

Sadie's eye grew moist. "Eli is our son and Yuri is my husband's best friend. They were killed in a pogrom more than a year ago. It's why we left Russia and came here."

The doctor's lips formed a thin line. "I am sorry for your loss," he said. "I don't want you to worry. I am hopeful that your husband's confusion and blurred vision are temporary, but it may take a few weeks for his brain to recover from the injury. I left some headache powder for his pain. He can have a packet every four hours if he needs it. He should sleep, but I want you to wake him every hour or so for the next few hours just to make sure he can be roused. I will look in on him tomorrow."

"I don't know how we can thank you for all you have done. Please, what is your fee?"

"Oscar has taken care of it. He told me to tell you it was the least he could do."

CHAPTER 27

In the weeks following the accident, Meyer's head wound healed and his bruises disappeared, but the debilitating after effects lingered. His headaches remained, and his eyes improved only slightly, leaving his world a series of blurry images. He could not remember the facts of the accident and had difficulty recalling recent events. Frustrated by his limitations, he was easily irritated and grew restless at home.

"I am going crazy cooped up in the house. It's no wonder I can't think straight," he told Sadie after a month away from the pushcart market. "I want to go back to my pushcart."

"I think you should wait another week or so. Dr. Cohen said you need more time to heal."

"What I need to do is get back to work."

Meyer set out the next morning to stock his pushcart. Avrum helped him with his purchases from the delicatessen. "Uncle, maybe you don't go the Washington Market. Why don't you see how things go today before you take on extra goods," he said after Meyer had trouble remembering his usual order.

"I think you are right. Sadie said to take it slow, too. Thank you."

Meyer's return to his pushcart was overwhelming. The noise on the street reverberated in his head, pounding like a sledge hammer. He had trouble keeping track of his sales and what the customers wanted. Near the end of the day he mistakenly shortchanged a man who became so irate he would have overturned Meyer's cart had Oscar not stepped in to stop him.

"You need to go home, my friend," Oscar said gently. "Perhaps you just need a few more weeks before you come back."

Meyer was near tears, ashamed that his friend had seen him so helpless.

At dinner that night, Meyer ate his meal in silence. Wary of his recent mood swings, Sadie and Miriam made no attempt to draw him into conversation. It was only after Miriam was in bed that Sadie questioned him about his day.

"You were right," he said. "It was too soon to go back. It felt like my brain was too big for my skull. There was so much noise my head throbbed, and I couldn't think. I made mistakes with the customers. I had trouble making change." He cradled his head in his hands. "What will we do if I cannot return to work?"

"You just need to give yourself more time to heal."

"You keep saying that, but I don't feel any better. The headaches and nausea are still there. I am tired all the time, and I keep forgetting things. Walking back to the apartment today, I went the wrong way. I had to ask someone on the street for directions to my own home." Meyer lowered his head and began to sob.

Shaken by this admission, Sadie put her arms around Meyer. "We will be all right," she said, trying to reassure him. "I will take in more piece work."

"You know it won't be enough. We are already eating into what little we saved." Growing more agitated, he began to pace around the bedroom. "I promised you and Miriam a better apartment. Now I am afraid we won't be able to afford this one." He was yelling now, his hands balled into fists.

"Meyer, please settle down. You'll wake Miriam."

At the mention of Miriam's name, Meyer grew quiet. "Please don't tell her I got lost today," he pleaded, his face a map of shame.

In the dark room adjacent to her parents' bedroom, Miriam lay awake, the apartment's thin walls doing nothing to mute their conversation. She had spent weeks trying to convince herself that Papa would get better with time. She watched in vain for signs that he was becoming himself again. Listening to the despair in her father's voice, she lost all hope for a return to things as they had been.

The next Sunday, Miriam met Rivka at the park. The sun was bright in a cloudless sky, making the late March day warm enough to be outdoors. Walking arm in arm, they chatted easily, catching up on each other's week. When Rivka inquired about Meyer, Miriam guided Rivka to a bench so they could talk in private.

"Papa is not doing well. He hasn't been able to work at his pushcart since the accident. Mama is taking in extra piece work, and though she can make more working in a factory, she is afraid to leave Papa alone. He is easily distracted now and forgets things. Yesterday he was boiling water for tea and forgot what he was doing. The water boiled out and the bottom of the pot got scorched. Mama is afraid next time it will be something that could catch fire."

"I am so sorry. It must be very hard for you and your mother to see him this way."

Miriam took her friend's hand in hers. "I have a huge favor to ask you. I want to leave school and go to work. Do you think you could find me a job at the Triangle Shirtwaist Factory?"

Rivka was silent for a moment. "There are usually openings for the lower-level jobs, but the hours are long and the pay is terrible. Are you sure you want to leave school?"

"I don't have a choice. I overheard my parents talking, and we are going to run out of money soon. I know they sold a piece of Mama's jewelry, so things must be getting bad. Whatever I would make is better than nothing. I can use a sewing machine. I will do piece work. I'm willing to do anything."

It was two weeks before Rivka got back to Miriam. "I have been given a new job sewing fronts of shirts to the backs. I told Mr. Salutsky, the foreman, about you and he said you could have my job as a floor girl. I am not sure what they will pay you, but I was making four dollars a week."

"Rivka, you have no idea how much I appreciate this."

"He said you can start work on Monday morning. You have to be there by seven-thirty. And bring a lunch, though I am not sure if there will be time to eat it."

"I cannot thank you enough," said Miriam, hugging her friend.

"I hope you still feel that way after you've begun working there. Miriam, the work is tedious, and the hours are grueling. Plus, you need to watch out for Salutsky. His hands wander, if you know what I mean."

Miriam worried all day about telling Mrs. Cullen that she could no longer attend school. As the other students filed out of the room, she lingered by the teacher's desk

Looking up from her papers, Mrs. Cullen studied her favorite student for a moment before speaking. "Miriam, are you feeling all right? You look pale."

"Mrs. Cullen, I am so sorry, but I am going to have to leave school. My father was injured in an accident and he can't work."

Her teacher sighed. No matter how many times she'd had this conversation with other students, it always upset her when family circumstances worked to deprive young minds of an education. And in Miriam's case, she viewed it as a tragedy. The child was so bright and had such a hunger to learn.

"Is there no way you can remain in school? You have been doing so well and are nearly ready to move up a grade."

Miriam stared out the window, too embarrassed to admit that her family was in desperate need of money. "I am needed at home," she said, biting her lower lip.

"I hope that your situation is temporary and that you will be able to return to school soon," said Mrs. Cullen, giving Miriam a long hug. Miriam pulled away from her teacher and without another word, headed out the classroom door and down the hall for the last time.

Miriam waited until after they had finished their *Shabbat* dinner to tell Sadie and Meyer that she was leaving school to take a job at the Triangle factory.

"I will be working with Rivka," she said, forcing excitement into her voice. "She is going to be working on a sewing machine and I am taking her job as a floor girl. I start Monday. Rivka said she was paid four dollars a week for her work."

Stunned, neither Sadie nor Meyer could speak at first.

"You should have talked to us about this," sputtered Meyer, his face florid, his eyes bulging in anger.

Miriam was frightened by his rage. "Why are you so mad, Papa? I just want to help. This way you have time to get better and when you do, I can go back to school." Turning to Sadie, she implored, "Mama, you understand, don't you?"

"I agree with your father," said Sadie. "This is a decision we should have made as a family."

Seeing she would get no support from her mother, Miriam remained defiant. "I didn't tell you because I knew you would object. I am fifteen; I am not a child anymore, and I did this for us. You taught me that family helps family."

Meyer stood so abruptly he knocked his chair to the floor. "I can take care of my family," he said, storming into the bedroom and slamming the door.

"Mama, I am only trying to help," said Miriam, tears streaming down her face. "I know four dollars a week is not a lot, but it will help."

Sadie reached across the table and wiped the tears from Miriam's cheeks, her hand lingering in a gentle caress. Her headstrong daughter could not know how much she had hurt Meyer's pride.

"Miriam, I know you mean well and are only thinking of what you can do to help, but your father is a proud man. He is ashamed that he cannot work. Your leaving school to go to work makes him feel like he cannot provide for us."

Miriam's face caved. "I never meant to hurt him. But I cannot stay in school knowing how bad things are. I know you sold a piece of your jewelry. And don't look so shocked; these walls hide nothing. Mama, how are we going to manage if Papa cannot go back to work? Where will we go if we cannot pay the rent? We can't go back to Aunt Malka's, and I can tell you are already making less for our meals to save money. Please let me do this. I want to do this."

Sadie stood and looked out the window, gazing into the darkness. The money she'd gotten for the necklace she'd sold to the old jeweler on Houston Street was almost gone. The rent was paid for this week, and there was money for next week, but after that she was unsure if they would have enough to avoid eviction. Suddenly the apartment they so desperately wanted to leave seemed a palace when she considered the alternative. With Miriam's salary added to what she made sewing at home, they could manage here.

Miriam joined her at the window. "Mama, please talk to Papa and make him understand that I only want to do what is best for us as a family. I can't bear to think that I hurt him, and I don't want to go against his wishes, but

I will be at the factory Monday morning."

Sadie found Meyer lying on the bed, staring at the ceiling. "Are you all right?"

"My head hurts," he said, not looking at her.

Sadie sat down beside him and began to gently massage his temples.

"That feels good. Your hands are magic." He sighed and propped himself up on a pillow. "I should not have lost my temper with Miriam. She is a good girl and means well, but she belongs in school. We can manage until I can return to work."

"Meyer, I don't think we can. You know how the landlord is about paying on time. He evicted a family downstairs because they missed a week's rent. We are close to running out of money. Even if Miriam earns four dollars a week, I may have to sell another piece of jewelry to keep us going. I agree she belongs in school, but we really don't have a choice. And she is determined to work at the Triangle factory. She desperately wants your approval. She is miserable over the idea of defying you."

Meyer's shoulders sagged in defeat. "I will talk to her in the morning. But I want to be clear that this is only until I can go back to work." He closed his eyes and was asleep in minutes.

Sadie drew the covers over Meyer and turned down the gas lights. Sitting in the semi-darkness, she gave in to her fears that Miriam would never be able to return to school and wept.

PART III

CHAPTER 28

April 1905

Unable to sleep the night before her first day at the Triangle factory, Miriam was grateful for the small shaft of pink light peeking through the window in the front room. Slipping silently out of the apartment to use the bathroom in the hall, she smiled when she realized that the early hour meant no one would be banging on the door, screaming at her to hurry up.

Returning to the apartment, Miriam was surprised to find Meyer in the kitchen. "You are up so early," he said, cutting thick slices of bread and pouring the hot water he'd set to boil into their cups for tea.

"I am too excited to sleep," she said, unwilling to admit to her father that she was also nervous. "Why are you up?"

Meyer blew on his tea to cool it and took a sip before speaking. "I don't sleep so well these days. The headaches come and go, and this morning one made an early arrival." He smiled, but Miriam could see the pain on his face.

"Papa, I know you are worried about me, but I will be fine."

"It is my job as your father to worry about you. I know you are not a little girl anymore, but you will always be *my* little girl. I want more for you than to work in a garment factory. You should be back in school."

Miriam felt her throat tighten. "When you are feeling better I will go back, I promise."

Meyer stared into his cup of tea and wondered if he would ever be well enough to provide for his family again. "I plan to hold you to your promise," he said, hoping he sounded more confident than he felt.

Miriam looked at the small clock by the sink and quickly finished her bread and tea. "I'm meeting Rivka on the corner so we can walk to the factory together," she said, picking up the lunch Sadie had prepared for her the night before.

Meyer reached into the pocket of his robe and gave Miriam two nickels. "It will be dark when you come home. Use this so you and Rivka can come back on the trolley."

When Miriam kissed her father goodbye, he pulled her into a tight hug. "Just be safe," he said.

Rivka was waiting at the corner, her arms folded around her body to keep warm. "It's colder out here than I thought it would be. Are you ready for your first day?"

"I think so. I am a little scared."

"You will be fine. You will be working on the ninth floor with me, and I promise to keep an eye on you. But I have to tell you, I don't know what you will be doing. Salutsky gave the floor-girl job to Dora, one of his favorites. She is always smiling at him. Some of the girls say that they are friendly, if you know what I mean. But don't worry, the other girls are all very nice."

"It's not the girls I am worried about."

"Just do your job, and keep your eyes down when Salutsky is around. He's always looking for a reason to scream at someone, so don't talk while you are working. Don't drink too much water, either, because you only get one bathroom break, and he'll dock your pay if you take too long. He likes to brush up against the girls, so keep your distance from him if you can."

Rivka's words did nothing to reassure Miriam, and they walked in silence until they reached the Asch Building where the Triangle Shirtwaist Factory occupied the top three floors. Located on the corner of Greene Street and Washington Place near Washington Square, the tan brick ten-story building seemed to Miriam to reach the sky.

Rivka guided Miriam to the Greene street entrance where the freight elevator was located. "We aren't allowed to use the passenger elevators in the lobby," she said.

Miriam could feel a rising panic. "I don't like to be in closed-in places," she stammered as they waited for the elevator to descend to the ground floor.

Rivka looked at her oddly. Seeing how pale her friend had become, she tried to quell Miriam's fears. "The freight elevator is much bigger than the passenger elevator. It won't be so bad."

A group of chatty young women joined them at the grated elevator door. Determined not to betray her fear in front of the others, Miriam nodded and said no more.

When the wooden freight elevator finally arrived, the operator, a young man neatly dressed in a white shirt and brown slacks, his dark hair combed back from his forehead, opened the grate. "Step in carefully, ladies," he said, bowing and making a sweeping gesture with his hand. "Riding with Gino always guarantees a smooth trip."

Laughing, Rivka and the other young women filed into the car. Miriam hesitated, cold sweat coating her body. Reluctantly, she stepped into the crowded space next to Rivka and closed her eyes. When the grate clanged shut, Miriam grabbed Rivka's hand and held it tightly until they stopped at the ninth floor. The few seconds it took for Gino to open the grate seemed an eternity to her.

Stepping out of the elevator, Miriam was overwhelmed by the scene before her. Rows of sewing machines were lined up one after another, the narrow aisles between them jammed with baskets piled high with cloth. Paper patterns hung from clothes lines strung around the work area. Bins with scraps of cloth and boxes filled with muslin, cards of lace, and tissue paper were stacked on shelves and against the walls throughout the room. The buzz of voices in English, Italian, and Yiddish grew louder as the women from the elevator joined their friends.

Taking Miriam by the hand, Rivka showed her where to put her coat and pocketbook and acquainted her with several of the women who worked on the sewing machines. At precisely seven-thirty, Herman Salutsky appeared on the floor. Everyone scurried to their work stations and the room was quickly filled with the whirring of more than two hundred electric-powered sewing machines. Rivka introduced Miriam to the foreman and hurried to her work space.

Miriam was immediately repelled by the large man who would control her every moment at the factory. Well over six feet tall, with muscular arms thick with dark hair extending from his rolled-up shirt sleeves, Salutsky was intimidating and knew it.

"So, you are Miriam Raisky," he said, openly appraising her body, his dark beady eyes lingering on her breasts. "How old are you?"

Miriam kept her eyes lowered. "Fifteen."

His thin lips curled into a smile, revealing crooked, tobacco-stained teeth. "Ah, you speak English. That's good." He dug his thick fingers into his vest pocket and retrieved a cheap pocket watch attached to a chain stretched taut by his protruding belly. "You should have been at work five minutes ago. Follow me and we will get you started."

Salutsky led Miriam to an area where a group of younger girls were working on cutting threads off of finished garments. "Angie will show you what to do," he said nodding toward a pretty, dark-haired girl. "She speaks English too."

Sixteen-year-old Angie Galissi rose quickly and barely looking at Salutsky, greeted Miriam. Tall and slender, long black lashes setting off her deep brown eyes, she offered Miriam a welcoming smile.

"This is the new girl, Miriam Raisky. Just show her what we want done and don't take a lot of time talking," growled Salutsky, leaving abruptly to bark orders at a young man chatting with a pretty young woman in the sewing area.

Angie rolled her eyes and whispered, "Try to stay out of his way. He is a mean bastard."

"So I've heard," Miriam whispered back.

Miriam hardly needed instructions for her job. Joining Angie and three other girls in what was called the "kindergarten" because they were among the youngest employees, she spent eleven hours snipping the threads off the finished high-necked blouses. She was allowed one bathroom break, and barely made it to the toilet and back in time.

As they quickly downed lunch in their work area, Angie introduced Miriam to the other girls who toiled as "cleaners." Two of the girls—twelve-year-old Celia and fourteen-year-old Rosalie—were Italian like Angie, and spoke very little English. The third girl, fourteen-year-old Osna Babich, spoke only Yiddish. When Miriam said hello in her native language, the quiet girl's face lit up. "At last I have someone I can talk to," she said, smiling.

When the day ended at seven o'clock, the men and women on the ninth floor wasted no time in scooping up their belongings and heading for the freight elevator. Rivka was waiting for Miriam where they had left their things, her friend's pocketbook and coat in her hands. "Here," she said. "Let's get out of here."

Putting on her coat, Miriam followed Rivka and the other women through a door to a hallway so narrow they had to walk single file. Trailing behind Rivka, Miriam fought off her dread of closed-in spaces, even as she could feel the sweat dripping down her sides.

Turning to Miriam, Rivka told her she would have to open her pocketbook for inspection. "They want to make sure you aren't stealing anything."

Miriam laughed in spite of her fears. "What can I steal, the loose threads off the shirtwaists?" she said under her breath.

"Don't even joke about it," warned Rivka. "Just open your purse and let them look through it. Mr. Blanck and Mr. Harris have fired girls who wouldn't let the bosses inspect their purses. They even lock the only other way out—the door to the Washington Place exit—to make sure you have to leave through this door."

"Who are Mr. Blanck and Mr. Harris?"

"Max Blanck and Isaac Harris. They are the owners. Just open your purse so we can get out of here," hissed Rivka.

With so many people leaving the building at once, they had to wait their turn for the freight elevator to take them down to the Greene Street exit. Miriam's anxiety increased each time the car ascended and the workers piled in. When they were finally able to board the car, Miriam could feel her heart thumping, her breath becoming more rapid.

"Close your eyes like you did this morning," said Rivka quietly as she took Miriam's hand. "Think about something soothing."

Miriam closed her eyes and tried to picture her mother's garden in Kishinev, but dark images of the cellar and the potato barrel flooded her thoughts. When they were out of the building into the dark April evening, Miriam finally felt her heart slow and her breathing return to normal.

"I'm sorry to behave like such a baby, but I have a terrible fear of small spaces. I don't like to talk about it, but there was pogrom where we lived in Kishinev. My brother Eli hid me in a barrel and covered me with potatoes to keep me safe. Ever since then, I get panicky in closed-in spaces."

"That must have been terrifying for you. I don't blame you for being afraid." Rivka stopped for a moment and faced her friend. "I didn't know you have a brother."

"Had. He was killed in the pogrom. So was my father's best friend."

Unable to find the words to convey her sorrow, Rivka slipped her arm through Miriam's, and the girls walked in silence toward the trolley stop.

Her neck and back muscles aching and her fingers sore from eleven hours of cutting threads, Miriam forced her body to climb the four flights of stairs to the apartment. She knew her parents would be waiting to hear everything about her day. Setting her mouth in a smile, she opened the door.

As Miriam expected, Sadie and Meyer peppered her with questions as soon as she entered the apartment. "Do you like your job? Are the people nice? Are you hungry?"

"Yes, yes, and yes. So let's eat, and I will tell you everything," said Miriam, who longed for her bed but knew her parents needed assurance that her first day had gone well.

The smell of stew simmering on the stove made Miriam's mouth water, reminding her she really was hungry. Sadie and Meyer waited patiently for her to finish her meal before questioning her again.

"So, how was it? What did you do?" asked Meyer.

Miriam had already decided not to tell her parents how disappointing her first day was. "It was a long day, but the girls I work with are nice. Rivka is on the same floor, so that's good. Today, I worked cutting threads from finished blouses, but I will only be doing that until I learn how to do more complicated work on the shirtwaists."

"I thought you were going to take Rivka's job as a floor girl," said Meyer, his voice rising in anger.

"It's all right, Papa. They gave the job to another girl. But it's fine. I just have to wait for another opening." Before they could question her further, and afraid to upset her father even more, Miriam rose from the kitchen table. "I was too excited to sleep last night, and I am really tired. I'm going to wash up and go to bed. Mama, the stew was delicious. I love you both," she said, kissing her parents good night.

Meyer and Sadie lay awake talking in the darkness of their bedroom. "It's not right that they did not give Rivka's old job to Miriam," said Meyer, his agitation returning. "Oscar told me about that place. He said they don't treat the girls well. He also heard it's not safe because the owners ignore the fire safety laws and refuse to install sprinklers. Does she even know what they are paying her for cutting threads? It better be enough to make it worth her while to work in that damn sweatshop." Lines of pain appeared around his eyes and he began to rub his forehead.

Sadie sat up and gently messaged his temples. "Don't get so excited. I know you are worried about her, but she is smart enough and capable enough to look out for herself. Let's give her time to sort things out."

Meyer closed his eyes as Sadie's fingers eased the stabbing pain in his head. "She'd better sort it out soon," he said, sleep starting to overtake him. "I don't like her working there."

CHAPTER 29

Despite Meyer's efforts to be quiet, Miriam could hear him moving around in the kitchen. Dreading a repeat of last night's barrage of questions, she stayed still, hoping he would retreat back into the bedroom before she had to get up. The scraping of his chair as he sat at the table convinced her that there was no hiding from the inevitable.

"Good morning, Papa," she said, as she pushed back the covers. "I hope you slept well."

Meyer glanced up as Miriam stretched and yawned, her hair tousled about her face, an image of her as a small, sleepy-eyed child suddenly appearing before him. He smiled at the memory.

"I slept as well as I do," he said, shrugging. "Go wash up and get ready for work. I'll make you some breakfast."

When Miriam returned to the kitchen she found a cup of hot tea and a buttered roll waiting for her and she felt in instant surge of guilt. How could she have wanted to avoid her father?

"Papa, I am sorry I upset you last night. I know you just want what's best for me, but I am going to be fine at work. I admit I am disappointed to be cutting threads, but I will show them I am a good worker, and I will get a better position. Please don't worry about me."

Meyer wanted to say so many things to her but knew nothing would change his strong-willed daughter's mind about working. He placed his hand over hers and nodded.

"What are you going to do today?" asked Miriam, eager to change the subject.

"What I do every day. I will walk down the block to see Oscar and the other peddlers while Mama buys what she needs for dinner. We don't stay too long. All the noise on the street makes my head throb."

It hurt Miriam to think of her father as he was now. There had been some improvement in his eyes and he no longer complained that everything was blurry. He had even started reading his prayer book again. But the headaches and mood swings persisted, and he still had memory lapses. Last week at the synagogue he asked for Rabbi Zirelber, the rabbi in Kishinev. When no one knew who he was talking about, his frustration quickly turned to anger. He began to yell and bang his head with his fists. It was Oscar who calmed him down and brought him home.

Miriam shoved aside all thoughts of the effects of Meyer's accident. "I have to go, Papa. Say hello to Oscar for me."

"I will," he said. "Don't forget, tonight we light a *yahrzeit* candle for Eli."

Miriam grew solemn. "I cannot believe he has been gone two years now. I miss him so much."

Meyer felt his throat tighten and looked away. "I think about him every day. Does anyone visit his grave and leave stones to show his time on earth is remembered? I wonder if anyone but us knows how good and brave he was." His eyes glistened with tears. "And what of Yuri? No one is there to pay his memory the respect he deserves."

Miriam hugged her father until he pulled away from her. "Go, I don't want you to be late," he said clearing his throat. He dug two nickels from his pocket. "Take this money so you and Rivka can ride the trolley home."

Miriam shook her head. "We can walk home. The streets are well lit."

Meyer touched her cheek. "Just be safe."

Miriam waved at Rivka as she approached the corner. Seeing her friend gave her hope that today would be a better day. All first days are difficult, she reasoned, and she was determined not to give in to her fear of the crowded elevator.

"Ready for another day of fun?" asked Rivka, smiling broadly.

"Please tell me it will get better," blurted Miriam. "How long will I have to work cutting threads? It is so boring. The girls in my group are all nice, but I am doing the same work as a twelve-year-old."

"*Oy,* you've only been there one day. Just do your work and don't make any trouble. As soon as they put on more of the younger girls, you will be moved to something else. But Angie is the oldest and been there the longest, so she is probably next in line to leave the kindergarten. That is, unless you want to make nice to Salutsky," Rivka said, leering.

"That's disgusting." Miriam slapped Rivka's arm and both girls began to laugh.

As they neared the Asch Building, Miriam could feel her resolve to overcome her fear of small spaces slipping. "I think I'll take the stairs today instead of the elevator."

"You will be late for work if you try to walk up nine flights. If you are even five minutes late, they will dock you half a day's pay," warned Rivka. "We can try to wait until there aren't too many people getting on the elevator. I will be right there with you."

Entering the building on the Greene Street side, they found a crowd of workers waiting for the elevator. When the doors opened, Miriam and Rivka hung back, allowing the group to flow around them. After the elevator filled and began its ascent, Miriam realized she had been holding her breath.

"We will have to take the next car, or we will be late," said Rivka. "You can do it."

Miriam's mouth became dry and beads of perspiration appeared on her upper lip. "I'll be all right," she said, working up the courage to board the hoist.

The elevator doors opened and only a few stragglers boarded the car. Miriam nodded at Rivka and stepped in. "This is better," she said, taking a deep breath.

CHAPTER 30

Miriam's first days at the factory seemed to last an eternity as the hours slowly ticked by. When Saturday, pay day and the end of the work week, finally arrived, Miriam knew she would have to dig deep to find the strength to return on Monday. She'd worked six eleven-hour days, dragged her aching body home at the end of the day, and then pretended that she was happy at her job. At least tonight she could go home with money to give Papa, she thought.

Rivka joined Miriam and Angie as they walked to get their pay envelopes. A long line had already formed and the sounds of young women laughing and talking about their plans for their day off were all around them.

Miriam's hands were trembling when it was her turn to get her pay envelope. Whether it was from excitement or fatigue, she wasn't sure. Moving aside so Rivka could get her money, Miriam peered into the envelope and thought she would be sick. All that mind-numbing work for two dollars.

Mistaking Miriam's expression for fear, Rivka reminded her they would wait for the crowd to thin before they got on the elevator.

"It's not that," said Miriam, fighting back tears. "I was only paid two dollars for all that work. I thought I was going to make four dollars. This morning I had a fight with Papa because he didn't want me to go to work on *Shabbat*. He will be furious that I made so little money."

Rivka's face dropped. "It's my fault. I told you the pay was four dollars when I thought you were taking my job. They pay less for cutting threads. And if you father was angry that you worked on Saturday, he is going to be really mad when we get to the busy season."

"What do you mean?"

Rivka pointed to a sign above the elevator doors:

If you don't come in on Sunday,
don't come in on Monday.

"When things get really busy, we work on Sunday and unless you do piece work, you don't get paid extra. If you don't come in, you are fired. I am so sorry. I should have prepared you better for the conditions here."

Angie and a few other girls neared the elevator. Miriam took a deep breath. "It's not your fault. It's just been a long week. Let's go. It will be good to get out of this place," said Miriam, so eager to leave that she ignored her fear of the crowded elevator.

The streets were still wet from an earlier downpour. Avoiding puddles as they walked, the girls welcomed the cooler temperatures after a day in the overheated factory.

"It feels good to be outside," said Rivka.

"It does. I can feel myself calming down. We are going to my Aunt Malka's tomorrow afternoon. Why don't you come with us? You could see Avrum," she teased.

Rivka blushed. She hadn't told Miriam yet, but she had been meeting Avrum on her day off for the past few weeks. "Actually, I am seeing Avrum tomorrow. We are going to go down to the park," she said, her old habit of blinking her eyes when nervous returning.

Miriam began to smile. "I knew there was something going on between you two."

"There's nothing going on. At least not yet," added Rivka, her face growing redder.

"You've probably seen my cousin more than I do. How is he?"

"He is crazy about baby Esther. His face gets joyous when he talks about her. It's just that sometimes he seems sad. When I ask him what's wrong, he just says he doesn't want to talk about it."

"He doesn't get along well with his father. Don't tell him I said this, but

I don't blame him. My uncle is hard on my aunt and my cousins."

Reaching the corner of Rivka's street, the girls headed off in different directions. "I'll probably see you tomorrow," called Rivka. "And good luck with your father."

I'll need it, thought Miriam.

Dinner was on the stove by the time Miriam arrived home. Expecting her father to confront her about her day as soon as she walked in the door, she was relieved to see just her mother in the kitchen.

"It smells delicious in here," she said, kissing her mother on her cheek. "Where's Papa?"

"He's lying down. He has had a headache all day. The aspirin powder doesn't seem to be helping him. I'm hoping he will feel better if he eats something," said Sadie, starting toward the bedroom.

"Wait. Mama, I am afraid I am going to upset him again. I got paid today," she said, taking the envelope from her purse and handing it to Sadie. "There are only two dollars in it. I'm sorry. I thought it would be twice as much." Her lower lip began to quiver. "I'm afraid Papa will be mad and not let me go back to work."

Sadie looked at the two singles in the envelope and sighed. Miriam was right; Meyer would be upset. She gave the envelope back to Miriam. "It's two dollars more than we had yesterday, and it does help. If Papa gets mad, I will make him understand that we need the money."

But when Meyer emerged from the bedroom, Miriam could no longer hold back her tears.

"What's wrong?" he asked, looking from Sadie to Miriam.

"She's afraid you will be mad at her," said Sadie. "They are paying her half of what she expected."

Seeing his child so distraught and realizing he was the one causing her distress stung his heart. "Come here," he said, opening his arms to embrace her.

Miriam slipped into his arms and sobbed. "Papa, please don't make me quit the job. I will be making more soon. I will show them I can do more than cut threads."

"Shh, it's all right," Meyer said, looking over Miriam's head to meet Sadie's gaze. "I am not happy that your skills are so undervalued, but I am willing to give you some time to see if things get better."

"Thank you, Papa, I promise they will."

Meyer lifted his daughter's face and kissed it. Don't make promises about things you cannot control, he thought.

Miriam slept late the next morning, happy not to have to rush off to the factory. Awake, but remaining under the covers, she recalled her conversation about Avrum with Rivka the day before and worried that things had gotten worse for her aunt and cousins. When she mentioned it to her mother last night, Sadie closed her eyes for a moment but offered no response. Now, she was more eager than ever to visit her aunt this afternoon. With a soft groan, Miriam gave in to the inevitable, and tossing her covers aside, mentally prepared herself for the unfortunate necessity of having to use the bathroom down the hall.

CHAPTER 31

Sadie and Miriam emerged from the dark tenement into a cloudless day, the endless ribbon of blue sky and brilliant sun instantly lifting their spirits.

"I just realized I haven't seen the sun all week," said Miriam as they walked. "I leave for the factory in the dark and come home in the dark."

Sadie turned her face toward the sun. "It does feel good. I wish Papa had come with us. I don't like leaving him alone."

"Has anything happened? Is something wrong?"

"Not really. It's just that he gets so depressed. He feels guilty for not being able to provide for us. He spends too much time alone thinking about things. About the accident. About Eli and Yuri. He goes to the synagogue, but I can tell he isn't finding peace there."

"I feel bad. I know I am adding to his worries."

They stopped in front of Lazar's delicatessen. An elderly woman wearing a large hat and smelling of too much perfume pushed passed them and entered the store.

"He loves you. He will always worry about you. Now," said Sadie, "let's say hello to Uncle Lazar and the boys so we can go upstairs to see Aunt Malka and the girls."

"I think only Ira is in the store. Rivka said she and Avrum were going to the park."

Sadie's eyebrows arched. "Really? Good for them."

After much hugging and kissing and cooing over nine-month-old Esther, Sadie and Malka settled into the kitchen while Miriam and Sonia took Rebecca outside to play. Sitting with Esther in her lap, Sadie nuzzled her plump niece's neck, making the ticklish baby laugh.

"Such a sweet sound," said Sadie, as Malka ducked under the diapers hanging in the kitchen and poured two cups of tea.

"Not so sweet when she is crying. She's teething and not sleeping well at night. Lazar gets annoyed when she cries, so I pick her up right away. She is getting very spoiled and only falls asleep if I hold her."

Sadie studied her sister and could see how exhausted she was. Her skin had an unhealthy pallor and Sadie wondered when she'd last been outside. As Malka moved around the kitchen Sadie could see that she still carried a lot of the weight she'd gained during her pregnancy.

"Esther is really sweet-natured, but she is crawling and getting into everything," said Malka. "Sonia has been so good about watching the baby and Rebecca while I sew, but it's hard to keep Rebecca occupied and take care of Esther at the same time. Lazar has no patience with the baby. He doesn't even want to hold her, and she gets very clingy when he's around. I am beginning to think she is afraid of him."

"I hoped things would get better," said Sadie as Esther curled into her arms, and with her thumb in her mouth, quickly feel asleep.

Malka lowered her voice. "They are worse. Lazar is always angry about something; I'm too fat, the baby cries too much, I coddle Ira, the house isn't clean enough. He has started staying away a few nights at a time. I don't know if he is seeing another woman or if he just gets drunk and sleeps it off somewhere."

"You don't seem to be very upset that he isn't coming home every night."

"God forgive me, but things are better when he is not here. I don't even care if he is seeing a woman. He can stay away for a week as far as I am concerned. As long as Avrum and Ira are able to keep the store going, we will be all right. Besides, the customers prefer dealing with the boys. One of our regulars told Ira she almost stopped shopping at the store because Lazar was so rude. He was furious when he found out what she said."

"That's what scares me. I've seen Lazar's fury. My constant fear is that he will hurt you and the children."

Sadie was about to say more when Sonia, Miriam, and Rebecca swept into the apartment. Malka put her finger to her lips and pointed to Esther, sleeping contently in Sadie's arms.

"We saw Avrum and Rivka, but Avrum clearly wanted us to go away," whispered Sonia.

Malka smiled, happy at the thought of Avrum enjoying the company of Miriam's pretty friend.

CHAPTER 32

August 1905

The busy season had begun, and the blistering heat of August made the Triangle factory's ninth floor stifling. Sweat oozing from every pore, Miriam had to keep wiping her palms on her skirt to keep the scissors from slipping from her hand. Her misery was intensified by the realization that after months in the kindergarten there were still no openings in any of the other areas. Frustrated by the tedium of her work and the pittance she earned, Miriam fell into despair as first Angie left to operate a sewing machine and then Osna was assigned to hand out lace trimmings to the seamstresses. With her new friends gone, Miriam dreaded each minute she had to spend in the shop. Worse still, Salutsky was always nearby, his eyes lingering on her, a sneer pasted on his face. So endless did her days seem that she buried her fear of the elevator somewhere deep in her being and could not wait to step into the car and leave the factory.

"*Oy*, the look on your face! What's the matter?" asked Rivka as they walked toward Hester Street at the end of a fourteen-hour day.

A warm breeze ruffled Miriam's hair, and she wiped a few stray curls from her face. "I spend the entire day, now seven days a week, cutting threads. Threads! I work all day in heat that only the devil could stand, and I have to endure Salutsky's looks and the disgusting things he says to me and the other girls. Then I go home and pretend to be happy so Mama and Papa won't worry. All for a salary that does little to help my parents pay the bills."

Miriam pressed her fingers to her eyes to hold back the tears. "I'm sorry," she said, embarrassed by her outburst. "I am just tired and frustrated. I was stupid to think it would be any different."

"You don't have to apologize to me. If it makes you feel any better, it's just as bad sitting over a hot sewing machine. And Salutsky may leer at you, but at least you don't have to put up with him leaning over you and touching you. He makes it seem like he is checking my work, but he rubs his lower body against my back every time."

Miriam shuddered. "Is there no one we can complain to?"

Rivka shook her head. "Not if you want to keep your job."

An overnight thunderstorm brought little relief from the sweltering heat. Steam rose from the hot city sidewalks, the air heavy with stultifying humidity. By noon the factory was suffocating. Miriam's blouse was soaked with perspiration. Wiping the sweat from her forehead with her sleeve, she looked up to find Salutsky standing over her.

A thin strand of hair pasted to his glistening scalp, he leaned down and growled, "Make sure you don't sweat on the finished blouses. If you do, you can be sure I will dock your pay."

Miriam nodded and swallowing hard, tried not to gag at the foreman's foul smell. Salutsky opened his mouth to say more when one of the sewing machine operators started to scream. The whirring of sewing machines stopped as the other girls rushed to help Yetta, a young seamstress whose finger was gushing blood.

"Get out of my way," yelled Salutsky, shoving his way toward the commotion. Ignoring the bleeding and hysterical girl, he grabbed frantically at the blouses piled around her machine. Only after he had satisfied himself that there was no blood on the garments did he turn his attention to the injured girl.

"What's going on here?" he demanded. "How did this happen?"

"I was working fast like you told us to and my hand was so sweaty it slipped. The needle went through my finger. It feels like it hit the bone," sobbed Yetta, frightened and in pain.

Salutsky looked at her with contempt. "Get out of here. You are of no use to me now."

"Please, I can work," implored Yetta, wiping away her tears with her un-injured hand. Wrapping her dripping finger in a scrap of cotton material, she held up her damaged hand. "See," she said, "the bleeding is stopping. I beg you, let me stay."

"Just go," screamed Salutsky, a spray of spittle escaping his mouth.

Yetta ran sobbing from the room as the others looked away in silence, aware that they were only an accident away from the same fate.

"The rest of you get back to work," snarled Salutsky. "Damn it! I need to get these garments out of here tonight," he said, kicking a stool and sending it across the room.

Rivka stepped forward, her eyes blinking madly. "Um, Mr. Salutsky," she said, her voice quavering.

"What the hell do you want?"

"If you need someone to take Yetta's place, Miriam can use a sewing machine, and she is fast."

"Who the hell is Miriam?"

"Miriam Raisky. She works in the kindergarten cutting threads," answered Rivka, avoiding Salutsky's glare.

The foreman took a dirty handkerchief from his pocket and blew his nose. The bleating sound made Rivka flinch and she took a step back.

"All right. Go get her and get her started. But I am warning you, she'd better be as good as you say she is or I'll dock you for her mistakes."

"I cannot thank you enough for recommending me," said Miriam, looping her arm through Rivka's as they walked home. "I can't wait to tell Mama and Papa."

"Yeah, well you thanked me when I got you into the Triangle factory, and look how that turned out."

"I know. But at least I will be making more money."

"You understand that it's piece work, right?" asked Rivka. "Salutsky contracts the work to Harris and Blanck. You get paid for the number of pieces you complete. The pieces are delivered to you in bundles, when you finish a bundle you get a ticket. At the end of the week your pay is based on the number of tickets you turn in. The faster you work, the more tickets you get, and the more you get paid, but you also have to be careful. They will take money out of your pay if you make mistakes or ruin a garment. They are also going to dock you for the needles, thread, and electricity you use. And you don't want to wind up like Yetta. I heard she lives with her grandmother and younger brother and works to support them both. I know how much she needed the job."

Miriam's shoulders slumped. "I feel terrible that I got the job because she got hurt."

"Don't feel bad. Accidents happen all the time because we have to work so fast. When it gets really busy, it gets worse. Salutsky is always pushing us to work even faster. Just concentrate on what you are doing, and you will be all right. And another thing. If you see two men dressed in suits on the floor, that's Harris and Blank. Whatever you do, don't look up. Look busy."

CHAPTER 33

It took only a matter of days for Miriam to appreciate Rivka's words of caution. From the moment she took her place behind her sewing machine until she left the factory, her day was filled with an endless stream of sleeves to be sewn onto shirtwaists. As soon as she finished one bundle, another was dropped by her machine. Salutsky was always nearby inspecting her work for errors and appearing disappointed when he found none. Each time he hovered over her, he would run his hands down her back.

Two things fueled Miriam's determination to continue working: anticipation of a larger pay envelope and the instant camaraderie she found among the other machine operators. Angie sat at one side of Miriam and Ida Shalman on the other side. Slightly built, with a heart-shaped face and an abundance of brown hair piled high on her head, Ida smiled at Miriam and welcomed her warmly to the "club," as she called it. "Let me know if you need any help," she whispered kindly.

"The girls are really nice," Miriam told Rivka as they made their way home. "Everyone has been so helpful. I wish we had more time to talk to each other."

"Just make sure you don't talk while you work," advised Rivka. "Salutsky will fine you if he catches you. He'll also fine you if you take too many breaks."

Miriam started to say something, then hesitated.

"What?" asked Rivka.

"Is it my imagination, or do some of the girls not like Ida? I noticed whenever she tries to take part in a conversation during lunch the others pretty much ignore her. I don't understand why. She seems like a very nice person."

Rivka pursed her lips and slowly released her breath. "I don't know if it's true or not, but she has a reputation for being easy. Some of the girls say she gets more work during slow times because she is a favorite of Salutsky's, if you know what I mean."

Miriam's eyes narrowed. "Do you believe the rumors?"

"I don't listen to the talk," said Rivka. "Who am I to judge someone else? I've certainly been judged plenty in my life. I actually like Ida."

Miriam smiled at her friend. "Good, because I like her too."

With a pay envelope containing four dollars and fifty cents in her purse, Miriam took the last flight of apartment stairs two at a time, eager to give her new earnings to her father. The smile on her face as she came through the door quickly faded when she saw her cousin Avrum sitting at the kitchen table with her parents. Her mother's eyes were red and puffy from crying.

"Oh my God, what happened?" gasped Miriam. "Is Aunt Malka all right?"

Avrum looked from his aunt to his uncle. "My father hasn't been home for a week. Last Saturday he just came upstairs from the store, packed some clothes, and left without saying a word."

Miriam's mouth twisted in shock. "Oh, Avrum, I am so sorry."

"Good riddance," he said, his face contorting in anger. "I hope this time he is gone for good."

Meyer put his hand on Avrum's shoulder. "I know you don't mean that."

"I do," he said, his voice filled with hatred. "He is a brute and a bully. Uncle Meyer, you've seen how mean he can get. The slightest thing sets him off. If Esther cries. If Ira has an asthma attack. If Rebecca's toys are on the floor. If sales are slow in the store. And Mama can do nothing right. No matter how hard she tries to please him he finds fault and yells at her. Sometimes worse." His eyes filled with tears.

"The night before he left, he got angry at Ira for leaving the store early because he didn't feel well. Papa was yelling and poking Ira hard in the chest and Ira started to cry. When Mama stepped in to try to calm Papa down he slapped her across the face. He called her a fat cow and then said she had turned Ira into a little sissy. That's when I punched him."

Sadie buried her face in her hands and sobbed.

Avrum stared straight ahead, his fists clenched as if he were reliving the ugly scene. "I think Papa was more surprised than hurt, though his nose was bleeding badly. I thought he would kill me, but he just stared at me and walked into the bedroom and slammed the door."

Avrum wiped the tears from his eyes and rose to leave. "I didn't mean to upset you, Aunt Sadie. I'm sorry."

"No, you did the right thing telling us. I'll come by tomorrow. If you need anything, please let us know."

"I will," said Avrum hugging his aunt and uncle goodbye. He locked eyes with Miriam and pointed his chin toward the door.

"I am going to walk downstairs with Avrum," said Miriam. "I'll be right back."

As soon as they were out of the apartment, Avrum turned to Miriam. "Please tell Rivka I won't be able to see her for a few weeks. I just need to get things under control at the delicatessen. Make sure she understands it's only temporary. I'm afraid she'll think I don't want to see her."

"I doubt that she would think that, but I will explain to her what happened." Miriam took her cousin's hand in hers. "You did the right thing, protecting your mother and Ira. I hope you know that. It's not your fault that he left."

Touched by Miriam's gentleness and compassion, he bent and kissed her on the cheek. "I have to go. I left Ira in charge of the store, and I have been gone too long."

Avrum took a few steps and then looked back at Miriam. "If I am so glad he's gone, why do I feel so guilty about hitting him?"

CHAPTER 34

Rivka did not have time to miss her Sundays with Avrum. The busy season meant working from seven-thirty in the morning to nine o'clock at night, turning out women's shirtwaists to meet the department stores' growing demand for the popular blouses.

At the end of the day, the weary workers lined up and submitted to the prying eyes of the inspectors, who searched their purses and checked under the cuffs of their sleeves to make sure they weren't stealing buttons or lace or scraps of material. The doors to the freight elevator were often locked, and a then a long parade of grumbling women had to walk down nine flights of stairs to exit the building. Only Miriam was glad for the excuse to avoid the elevator.

Too tired to walk home after her first full week of sitting at a sewing machine for fourteen hours, Miriam convinced Rivka they should join a group of girls heading for the trolley stop.

"I can't believe that bastard Salutsky locked the elevator doors again," complained a girl Miriam did not know.

"Yeah, I guess Ida didn't treat him to anything," snickered another in a voice so shrill it could cut glass. One of her friends laughed and obscenely thrust her hips back and forth. Then she cupped her hands in front of her breasts, making the others laugh harder.

Repelled by their cruelty, Miriam and Rivka drew back from the group. The sound of sniffling made them turn, and they were horrified to see Ida standing behind them.

Miriam took a step toward Ida, but the mortified girl held up her hands to ward her off. Before Miriam or Rivka could stop her, she ran off into the darkness.

The next morning, Miriam looked around the room when she got off the elevator and was relieved to see Ida sitting at her sewing machine. Smiling at her friend as she took her seat, Miriam reached over and squeezed her hand. Ida gave her a weak smile and resumed her work.

It wasn't until they were eating lunch at their work area that Miriam was finally able to talk to Ida. "I'm sorry about what you heard last night. It was hurtful and crude and uncalled for."

"You are not the one who should be apologizing," said Ida defiantly. "I know what the others say about me. I am not hurt by their gossip. I am hurt because the girls who talk about me behind my back used to be my friends."

"I hope you know that Rivka and I don't believe a word of what they are saying," said Miriam.

Ida's chin trembled, and she took a deep breath to compose herself. "Thank you. I am not what they say I am. It's a rumor that got started by Daniel, a cutter who used to work here. I went to the movies with him once. When he brought me home he started pawing at me and pushed me up against the wall of my building. When I told him to stop, he just kept pressing against me, and I could feel him get hard. I pushed him to get away from him and he fell backwards onto the sidewalk. He called me a bitch and yelled I would be sorry. When I got to work on Monday, some of the men smirked at me. Daniel had bragged to the other cutters that I was an easy lay and by the end of the day, the whole floor was talking about me."

"Did you tell anyone what really happened?"

"I was too embarrassed and afraid no one would believe me. And I don't know where this business about me and Salutsky came from. He is revolting. He finds excuses to hand me my work instead of just putting it down on the table and always manages to brush up against my breasts. I hate that man, but what can I do?"

Before Miriam could answer, Ida's eyes widened in fear. She quickly shoved aside her lunch and started up her sewing machine. Miriam did not need to turn around to know what had frightened her.

"Get back to work," said Salutsky in a voice so menacing Miriam felt the hair on the back of her neck rise. "Lunch break is over," he said, holding his pocket watch inches from Miriam's face as if to offer proof.

Even though ten minutes of their allotted half an hour remained, Miriam did not protest. Instead, she lowered her eyes and returned to her sewing machine.

"I will dock your pay next time I catch you talking," said Salutsky, sneering at both girls as he walked away.

With the whirring of her machine as cover, Miriam looked over at Ida and said out loud, "I hate him too."

Despite their weariness at the end of the day, Miriam and Rivka agreed they would rather walk home than join the girls who had said such cruel things about Ida.

"After fourteen hours in the factory, it feels good to be outside," said Miriam, breathing in the fresh air. "And now we have some extra time to talk."

"I know. I feel like we have so much to catch up on. How is your father?"

Miriam sighed. "I don't see much progress. He still gets headaches and loud noises bother him. He is also forgetful, so Mama is constantly checking the stove to make sure he hasn't left it lit. He goes with Mama to the pushcarts everyday while she shops so he can see Oscar and talk to him. And Oscar has been so good. He visits Papa at the apartment and looks after him when he is at the synagogue. I think Papa would be a little lost without him."

Finding it hard to talk about her father, Miriam changed the subject and asked about Avrum. "Do you see him at all?"

Rivka's face lit up at the mention of Avrum's name. "He came by one night last week, but it was late and he only stayed a few minutes. His father still hasn't come back, and he thinks he is gone for good this time. He suspects he is staying with a woman."

"Mama told me the same thing. The awful part is that no one in the family is sad to see him go. Except for Avrum, my cousins were all afraid of him, and he was absolutely cruel to my aunt. I think she is relieved that he hasn't come home."

Rivka frowned. "I'm worried about Avrum. He's working hard in the store. He gets up before dawn to go to the market and then gets everything ready to open the store. He said Ira helps and even Sonia comes down to the store when she isn't watching Rebecca and Esther, but I can tell he's struggling to keep the store going and take his father's place as the head of the family."

Miriam grew quiet. She felt like there was no end to the misery that had befallen the people she loved so much. She was worried about Avrum too. And her hopes that her father would be as he once was were slowly slipping away. He was no longer the man of steadfast strength who had always been there to take care of his family, and what hurt Miriam the most was that he knew it.

Rivka touched her shoulder. "Are you all right? You look like you are far away."

"I was just thinking about all that has happened since we left Kishinev. I was so hopeful we would have a better life here. But I'd forgotten how easy it is for life to change in a second."

CHAPTER 35

1906

The early months of 1906 tumbled one after another in a blur of bundles of sleeves and shirt fronts and every day seemed like the one before it to Miriam. With no letup in sight and Salutsky's constant harangues to work faster, Miriam had to force herself to get up in the cold and show up at the factory each morning.

"My body aches all over, and by the time I come home, Mama and Papa are usually asleep," Miriam grumbled to Rivka as they each purchased a hot roll from a pushcart vendor before they set out for the day. "Mama leaves my supper on the kitchen table, but I'm usually too tired to eat it. Some nights I am so exhausted I go to bed in my clothes. I haven't seen my aunt and cousins in months, and I barely see Mama and Papa. I turned sixteen in January and got home too late to celebrate my own birthday. If we didn't walk to work together, we would never have time to talk."

"True, but think about how much more money we are making," said Rivka, stepping around a patch of ice.

"I don't even care that my pay envelope is fatter. I just want this madness to end," wailed Miriam.

"You will be singing a different tune when things slow down and you're bringing home half of what you are making now."

Miriam sighed. "I know you're right. But I'm not sure how much longer I can keep this up. At least you see Avrum every couple of weeks. My whole life is going from home to work and back again."

"Have you been setting aside any money from your pay for yourself?"

"No, I give all my money to Papa. Why?"

"Because when things slow down, we should plan to do something fun. Maybe go to the movies or to Luna Park at Coney Island. And it would give us something to look forward to. I'll start saving a few pennies from my pay each week if you will."

Miriam hesitated for only a second. "Let's do it," she said, her mood lightening at just the thought of such an outing.

The end of March brought no signs of spring. Gloomy clouds blanketed the sky and a cold, relentless wind battered the city. Sadie and Meyer looped their arms to keep from being bowled over as they walked to Malka's apartment.

"I'm glad you decided to come with me," said Sadie. "It's been a while since you've seen Esther. She is adorable and getting so big. And wait until you hear her talk."

Meyer nodded, and stopped for a moment, a perplexed look on his face.

"What's the matter? Is everything okay?"

"I thought the deli was that way," he said, pointing in the opposite direction from Malka's apartment on Canal Street.

"Now I know it's been too long since you've been there," said Sadie trying to make light of Meyer's confusion. "It's this way."

"Oh, right." He paused. "Sadie, I would rather not go into the deli; I don't want to have to talk to Lazar."

Sadie squeezed his arm. "He's not there anymore. Remember, I told you he hasn't been home in months."

"I guess I forgot."

"That's all right. I'd like to forget about him too."

Meyer smiled, and they continued in silence until they reached the delicatessen. "Looks like Avrum is doing a good job. Look how many customers there are," he said. "I knew that boy had a good head on his shoulders."

Spotting his aunt and uncle standing outside the store, Avrum waved at them and turned his attention back to his customer, a small woman wrapped in a long wool coat. Ira darted from the store to hug Sadie and Meyer.

"Mama will be so glad to see you," he said, as the wind sent his merchant's apron flapping around his body. "I have to get back to the store. Mrs. Goldfarb is placing a big order for her husband's birthday dinner, and she wants to taste and smell everything! She's driving us crazy."

Peeking into the store, Sadie could see the round woman sniffing at a slice of meat and shaking her head. Amused by how obvious it was that Avrum was struggling not to betray his annoyance, Sadie laughed. "Go, help your brother. He looks like he is about to strangle Mrs. Goldfarb."

They were greeted with smiles and kisses when Sonia answered the door, Esther in her arms. The nineteen-month-old squealed "Sadie" when she saw her aunt. Her arms outstretched, she lunged toward Sadie, nearly falling from Sonia's grasp.

"That is quite a welcome! Esther gets bigger every time I see her, and you get more beautiful," laughed Sadie, kissing Esther's chubby cheeks and hugging Sonia.

"And where is Rebecca?" asked Meyer, pretending he couldn't see the five-year-old hiding behind the couch.

"Here I am," she exclaimed, rushing to Meyer's open arms. "Uncle Meyer, don't tickle me with your beard," she warned, starting the game they always played.

"Of course I won't," he said, gently rubbing his beard against her face as the child broke into peals of laughter.

"Me too," demanded Esther, her curly hair falling over her face as she wriggled from Sadie's arms to Meyer's.

Smiling at the happy sounds that filled the tiny apartment, Sadie found Malka in the kitchen. Kissing her sister, she was pleased to see that Malka was looking healthier. Her face seemed softer, her brown eyes clearer.

"It's strange, I had a feeling you would be here today," said Malka, wiping her hands on her apron.

"I am glad to see you are looking more rested." Sadie hesitated and then asked, "Have you heard from Lazar?"

"No, but one of our customers told Avrum she saw him working in the fish market. We also heard that he has been seen in bars in the Bowery with different women."

Sadie hated that Lazar's reckless habits were bringing shame to Malka and the children. "I am so sorry," she said, touching her sister's face.

"God forgive me, but we really don't miss him. The children are happier. The tension and fear have disappeared. Ira hasn't had an asthma attack in months, and Avrum is a different person now that all his anger is gone."

"You do look much better. And Sonia has blossomed into a beautiful young woman."

Malka frowned as she watched Sonia and Meyer play with the little ones. "She should be in school and enjoying being with people her own age. I feel bad, but I just wouldn't be able to manage without her. The boys are doing a wonderful job in the store, but I still have to do the contract work and I need Sonia home to look after Esther and Rebecca."

"I am sure she understands."

"She doesn't complain, but I see how she looks at Avrum and Rivka when they are together, and I know she has dreams of her own."

Sadie could feel the taste of bitterness rise in her throat. For young girls who had to stay at home to tend to siblings or who had to work because their father could not, dreams were a curse.

CHAPTER 36

Rivka's warning about a thinner pay envelope when the work slowed down rang in Miriam's ears. The busy season had finally come to an end, and so had her weekly wages of eight dollars.

"A lot less, right?" said Rivka, peering into her pay envelope.

Miriam counted out four dollars and put the money in her purse. "Exactly half. My parents are going to miss the extra money, but they are happy that I am going to be home more."

"I'm not sure my father feels the same way. He's been sending money to my grandparents in Kiev, and now we will have less to send and less to spend. And he is worried about his job. He said the company he works for has already let two cutters go now that things have slowed down."

"That's what's wrong with the garment industry. There is either too much work to do or not enough."

Rivka shrugged. "We'll manage. We've been through this before."

Whenever Miriam considered Rivka's life, she knew that hers was not as bad as she thought. The extra pay she brought in over the last six months meant her parents could save some money. At first, she didn't understand why Mama insisted that they continue to make do on Miriam's smaller salary and whatever her own contract work brought in. Now, listening to Rivka, Miriam saw the wisdom of setting aside half her salary each week. For the first time since they had arrived in America, they had a reserve of cash, stashed safely in a jar at the bottom of Sadie's sewing basket.

The first Sunday Miriam did not have to go the factory, she slept late, waking to the smell of the freshly baked bread Sadie was removing from the oven.

"I see your nose works better than your ears. I am surprised you could sleep through the noise we made in the kitchen," said Sadie, kissing her sleepy-eyed daughter. "Wash up and come to the table. It will be nice to have breakfast together for a change."

"I'll be right back," she said, and wrapping herself in a blanket, she trundled down the hall to the bathroom.

Waiting for Miriam's usual complaints about having to share the bathroom with that "disgusting family across the hall," Meyer and Sadie stared at her when she took her place at the table and wordlessly took a sip of tea.

"What?" she asked, looking at her parents' stunned faces.

"Nothing," said Meyer, laughing. "It's just so nice to all be together for a meal."

And it was. They lingered over their cups of tea and warm buttered bread and talked of the ordinary things that occupied their week: Miriam's work and the new friends she'd made at the factory; Oscar's new grandson who looked just like him, according to Meyer; their visit to see Malka and how big Esther and Rebecca had gotten.

Miriam could not stop smiling. Taking pleasure in the easy conversation around their kitchen table, she realized how much she had missed these quiet family moments.

Mindful of another rapidly approaching busy season, Rivka and Miriam kept their vow to enjoy their one day a week away from the factory. Using what little money they had saved from their pay, they dedicated their Sundays to fun. They window-shopped on Fifth Avenue, marveling at the fashions they could not afford—including shirtwaists that had most likely passed through their hands. They spent hours roaming the tree-lined neighborhoods of the rich, gazing at the great mansions and making up stories about the people who lived in them. They would stop at a corner soda fountain for a dish of ice cream and spend afternoons in Central Park watching crowds strolling in their Sunday finest. They ended each outing with a cold, flavored drink—cherry for Miriam and raspberry for Rivka—at Mr. Wohlman's soda stand.

Ida frequently joined them. After the night at the trolley stop when two of the factory girls had spoken so cruelly about Ida, Miriam and Rivka made sure to include her in their plans. Much to their delight, what had begun as a kindness had grown into genuine friendship.

It was always understood that late Sunday afternoons were Rivka's time to spend with Avrum. On one of their last Sundays off, after Rivka left them to meet Avrum in the park, Ida suggested that they visit a fortune teller.

"There's a woman who lives in my building who reads palms, and she said she would only charge us a nickel each instead of her usual fifteen cents."

"I don't know," said Miriam, unwilling to spend even five cents on what she considered foolishness. "I don't believe in such things. I think it's silly. There was an old lady in Kishinev who said she could see the future. She told my mother that she would live a long and happy life in our village, and we know how that turned out."

"It's not silly. Mrs. Gluskin, the lady in my building, told one of our neighbors that she was going to have a boy. This after she had had three girls, and she was right! Come on, it will be fun."

Miriam wanted to point out that Mrs. Gluskin had a fifty percent chance of guessing right, but the look of expectation on Ida's face changed her mind.

"All right, let's go see Mrs. Gluskin."

Ida led the way down a dimly lit hallway to Mrs. Gluskin's second-floor apartment. The wailing of an infant grew louder as they approached, and they had to knock several times before a girl of six or seven, her blonde stringy hair hanging in her face, let them into the dark, airless front room. Fayga Gluskin, thin and worn-looking, stood in the middle of the overheated room holding a screaming infant in her arms. A skinny toddler, his skin so pale he looked ghost-like, sucked noisily on his thumb. Holding tightly to his mother's leg, he burrowed into the folds of her skirt.

"The baby is hungry. Just let me feed him, and we can sit down and do your fortunes," said the woman, opening the top of her dress and nestling the squalling infant to her breast. "Asher, go to Sarah," she commanded.

Whimpering, the small boy ran from his mother to his sister. Wiping his runny nose in the crook of his arm, he eyed Miriam and Ida suspiciously.

While Ida made funny faces in a vain attempt to get Asher to smile, Miriam struggled against the urge to flee the stifling apartment. Stacks of paper and dirty clothing were littered throughout and a sagging, dirt-stained couch was propped against the far wall. The smell of unwashed bodies was overpowering, and as the infant suckled with surprising ferocity, Miriam detected the distinct odor of a dirty diaper. She was about to suggest to Ida that they leave when Mrs. Gluskin plucked the infant from her breast and handed the startled baby to his sister.

"Come," she said, pointing to a table and two chairs by the apartment's sole window. "Who is going first?"

Miriam pointed to Ida, hoping that by the time it was her turn she would have found a good reason not to sit with the fortune teller.

Ida offered her palm and listened intently as Mrs. Gluskin told her she would soon meet a Jewish man who would ask her to marry him. She predicted that they would have four children, two boys and two girls. Studying Ida's palm a bit more, she told her that good fortune would come to her in the coming year.

The rosy look into her future obviously pleased Ida. She happily dug a nickel from her purse and gave it to Mrs. Gluskin, even as Miriam rolled her eyes and suppressed the urge to laugh at the woman's fake fortune-telling skills.

The baby was crying again, providing, Miriam hoped, a reason to avoid her turn. But the infant's mother ignored her son's insistent howling and beckoned Miriam to take a seat.

Sweat pasting her blouse to her body, Miriam reluctantly placed her hand in Mrs. Gluskin's. The baby's incessant crying jarred her nerves.

"Hmm," said the tiny woman as she ran her bony fingers across Miriam's palm. The expression on her face became grave. She turned Miriam's hand over and then back to her palm. She closed her eyes and sighed.

Miriam had been expecting the same happy nonsense Ida had received. Now she searched Mrs. Gluskin's face for signs of bad news. The fortune teller's disinterested demeanor changed, her eyes seemed kinder, and Miriam felt a jolt of fear. "What do you see?"

"I see fire and death. Have you ever been in a fire? Has someone you love been in a fire?"

Despite the apartment's suffocating heat, Miriam felt a sudden chill. Images of the burned-out homes and stores in the aftermath of the Kishinev pogrom flashed before her. She recalled her father's stories of his mother— the grandmother she never knew—who burned to death in her own house.

Her heart began to pound.

"I haven't been in a fire, but my grandmother was killed in one," she stammered, her face growing ashen.

"I see fire and death," repeated Mrs. Gluskin. "You must be very careful and guard yourself from anything associated with fire."

"Is that all you see?"

"I'm afraid that's all."

Miriam rose unsteadily from the chair. Her hand trembling, she gave Mrs. Gluskin a nickel, and turning to leave, felt the woman's hand on her arm. "My dear, I do not mean to frighten you, but I hope you will trust what I saw. You must be vigilant about the dangers of fire."

Once they were back on the street, Ida tried to calm her shaken friend. "You know I don't believe a word she said, and neither should you. You were right; it's all silly, and I am so sorry I made you come."

Miriam took several deep breaths. "It's all right. You don't have to apologize. Her reading just caught me by surprise," said Miriam, the color returning to her face, her voice growing steadier. "I guess I expected the usual promises of a happy life."

"Then you're not mad at me?"

"Of course not. Let's just forget about it," said Miriam, even as she knew she would never be able to rid her mind of the fortune teller's last words to her.

CHAPTER 37

January 1907

Although New York City was locked in a week-long deep freeze, the Triangle factory held to its seven-day work schedule. Too cold for them to walk to the Asch Building, Miriam and Rivka huddled together for warmth on the trolley.

"You don't seem very happy this morning," said Rivka, her teeth chattering from the cold.

"What's to be happy about? It's as cold as Siberia out, and here we are on our way to work on a Sunday."

What Miriam did not tell Rivka was that today was her seventeenth birthday, and instead of being with her family, she would labor fourteen hours behind a sewing machine. Instead of enjoying the day with friends or a young man—any young man—she would spend it avoiding Salutsky's wanderings hands and the disgusting comments he would direct toward her when he was in her area.

She wondered if she would ever meet someone who cared about her. Mama had already met and fallen in love with Papa at seventeen, and I haven't even talked to a man my age, other than Avrum, she fretted.

Lost in thought, Miriam did not hear Rivka call her name. "Hey, are you there? This is our stop," she said, pulling her sullen friend toward the trolley door.

Covering their faces with the red woolen scarves Sadie had knitted for them as Chanukah gifts, Miriam and Rivka scurried along the empty streets to the factory. Eager to escape the punishing cold, Miriam pushed hard against the door to the Greene Street entrance and jumped back in surprise when she saw Ida, Angie, and Osna waiting for her with a "Happy Birthday" sign written in large red letters.

"Happy Birthday!" said Rivka, hugging her startled friend.

"How did you know it was my birthday?"

"Your mother told me the last time Ida and I were at your apartment. We told her to expect you later tonight, because we are taking you to Schmookayler's to celebrate after work."

Schmookayler's Pharmacy and Soda Fountain was a favorite after-work meeting place of the Triangle workers. Irving Schmookayler, the store owner, took great pride in his store, keeping its black-and-white tiled floor spotless, the fountain spouts gleaming and the long marble counter—fronted by eight tall stools—shining to a high gloss.

As was usual after a long day, Schmookayler's was crowded with factory workers wanting a cup of hot coffee or a bowl of steaming soup and a place to unwind. Rivka entered the store, followed by a blast of cold air that made the customers seated at the counter turn in her direction. Elbowing her way through the crowd to an empty table near the back, she claimed the spot for the group.

Squeezing five around a table for four and sipping cups of steaming coffee, the young women teased each other about potential suitors while lamenting the lack of worthwhile prospects on the ninth floor. They were all surprised when Angie told them that Gino, the elevator operator, had been coming around to see her at her family's apartment.

"Of course," said Angie, "my father will not let us be together in the same room unless one of my sisters, or worse for Gino, one of my brothers, is there to chaperone us."

"And I think mine papa am hard," said Osna, whose English was spotty in spite of her earnest efforts to master the language.

"That's Italian fathers for you," Angie laughed.

Miriam was about to point out that Jewish fathers could be just as protective, when she overheard two men in suits at the next table talking about a factory fire.

"Excuse me," she said to the dark-haired man sitting nearest to her, "I didn't mean to eavesdrop, but did you say there was a fire in a factory?"

"At the Diamond Waist Factory, one of Harris and Blanck's properties. Do you ladies work at the Triangle?"

"We do."

"Well, then you work in the same dangerous conditions they had at the Diamond. The doors leading outside were locked or opened inward and the fabrics piled everywhere went up like tinder. Fortunately, the fire started before business hours, so no one was hurt, but word is Harris and Blanck have torched their own factories before. You can bet those two thieves will collect a nice bundle of cash from the insurance company. They don't call them the 'Shirtwaist Kings' for nothing," he added contemptuously.

"How do you know all this?" asked Ida.

"We're with the ILGWU, the International Ladies Garment Workers Union. The union can help you get better pay and better working conditions. You should come to one of our meetings and find out more about what we can do for you," he said. He reached into his coat pocket and handed her a leaflet listing meeting times and places.

Ida took the sheet of paper but said nothing. She glanced at Miriam, and although they had not spoken about the fortune teller's reading since that Sunday at Mrs. Gluskin's, she could tell her friend was frightened by what she heard. Hoping to reassure Miriam, she said, "We don't have to worry about fire. The Asch Building was built to be fireproof."

The second man, thin-lipped, his blond hair slicked down and parted in the middle, smirked. "Are there locked doors in your work area? Do you have fabric scraps everywhere? Do the sewing machines leak oil on the floor?" Without waiting for an answer, he rose and put on his overcoat. "Believe me," he said, "you should all be worried."

As soon as the two men left, Angie spoke up. "You'll lose your job if Salutsky or the owners even think you are considering joining the union. The ILGWU has been trying to organize the shirtwaist industry for a while. Harris and Blanck are dead set against unions. I've even heard they search our things while we're working to see if any of us holds a union card. Anyone associated with a union is automatically fired."

Ida's eyes became slits. Miriam watched as she folded the union leaflet and tucked it into her purse.

Sadie and Meyer were waiting for Miriam when she entered the apartment. Smiles, hugs, and wishes for a happy birthday were followed by tea and freshly baked babka. Ignoring the late hour, they lingered at the kitchen table, talking and laughing.

It was well after midnight when Miriam finally settled into her bed. Her body cried for sleep, but her mind was racing, filled with fear and longing. As she always did when she was troubled, she sought comfort in thoughts of Eli. At seventeen, she was year older than Eli when he was killed. "What would you have accomplished at seventeen?" she whispered into the darkness. "Certainly more than I have."

Her eyes grew heavy and her thoughts veered to the two young men at Schmookayler's. The dark-haired one was very good-looking, she thought as she drifted to sleep. But dreams of the handsome man with shining dark hair escaped her. Shivering under the blankets, Miriam was terrorized by images of the Asch Building engulfed in towering flames.

CHAPTER 38

Fall 1907

The early signs were there, but the Triangle workers were too busy struggling to exist on their meager wages to take note of the economic crisis looming on the horizon. Two major New York City brokerage firms closed their doors in early October, setting off a nationwide, six-week run on the banks that took the country into a recession. As department store orders for shirtwaists fell off, Harris and Blanck first cut back hours and then laid off workers. By the end of November, normally one of the industry's busiest months, the owners shuttered the factory, contracting out what little work they had.

In the six weeks leading up to the closing, Miriam watched as the work force dwindled around her, silently thanking God that she was still working. Ida and Osna were let go a week before the doors were locked and the remaining workers were told to go home.

"I never thought I would be sorry not to have to work the busy season," grumbled Rivka as they waited in line for their last pay envelopes. "If I can't pick up some contract work, we are going to be in trouble. My father has been without a job for a couple of weeks now. I hope we are called back to work soon."

"Thankfully, my father is working," said Angie, "but we have a big family and a lot of mouths to feed. I need to work."

Miriam opened her pay envelope and drew in her breath. "This is not enough. I worked more hours than I am getting paid for," she exclaimed to the clerk handing out the cash.

"Consider yourself lucky you are getting anything at all," he snarled.

Once they were out of the building, Miriam looked around and lowered her voice. "I am starting to understand why Ida is always talking about joining the union. She keeps saying we would get paid better and work shorter hours in a safer environment if we worked in a unionized shop."

"If you want to be called back when the factory opens again, you better not even think about joining the union," said Angie, looking around to be sure no one overheard their conversation. "I've heard that Salutsky has spies on the ninth floor who tell him everything that goes on. You do not want to be associated with unionizing the Triangle."

Aware of the slowdown occurring at the Triangle factory, Sadie had been doing extra contract work for weeks. When Miriam arrived home in the late afternoon, her face drawn and cheerless, Sadie knew the factory had finally closed.

Miriam handed her pay envelope to her mother. "Mama, what are we going to do? There is half of what I should have been paid in there, and I have no idea when the factory will reopen."

"We've known this has been coming for a few weeks now. We can manage if you will do contract work with me."

"Of course I will. I will do whatever work we can get, but it still isn't going to replace what I make at the factory."

"I know, but Papa can help too. He didn't want me to tell you, but he has been doing odd jobs at the synagogue. You know, fixing things, keeping the sanctuary clean. What little money he brings in also helps."

Miriam slumped in her chair and closed her eyes. How must Papa, once a store owner and a respected member of the community, feel having to sweep floors for pennies a day? "What about the money we set aside from my busy-season pay? Can't we use some of that?" she asked.

"We do not touch that unless we absolutely have to," said Sadie so adamantly that Miriam flinched.

Without another word, she rose and went to the pile of sleeves next to Sadie's sewing machine. "What do you need me to do?" she asked.

The shutdown dragged on for months. With so many garment industry workers desperate for work, the contractors were paying less per piece than they did before. To make up the difference, Miriam and Sadie took on as much work as they could get, frequently sewing late into the night to fill the contractor's orders.

The long days stretched into long nights, and Miriam grew desperate to escape the gloom that had settled over the apartment. The constant anxiety about money wore them down, but the day-to-day stress and uncertainty affected Meyer the most. Withdrawn and depressed, his headaches were coming more frequently. Some days they were so painful he could not get out of bed. His moods became unpredictable and the slightest frustration would send him into fits of rage. When Rivka stopped by to tell her their factory friends were getting together at Ida's apartment Saturday night, she felt as if she had been thrown a life line.

By the time Miriam arrived at the second-floor apartment Ida shared with her aunt, Angie, Osna, and Rivka were already there. The three girls were sitting together on a worn-looking couch that also served as Ida's bed, laughing so hard that tears were streaming down their cheeks.

"What did I miss? What's so funny?" asked Miriam, adding her coat to the pile on a nearby chair.

"They laugh at mine talking," said Osna, good naturedly. "I think mine talking am pretty fine."

Miriam could not contain a smile. Her small friend with the big blue eyes was always such a good sport when teased about her English. In truth, her gentleness and sweet nature made her everyone's favorite.

"You are doing better than pretty fine; you are doing great," said Miriam.

Osna beamed. "See," she said turning to the others proudly. "Mine talking am doing great."

There was beat of silence and then a convulsion of laughter, Osna laughing as hard as her friends.

"Okay," said Ida, clapping her hands. "My Aunt Molly is in New Jersey visiting her son and daughter-in-law, the princess who is too good to come here to see her, so let's party." She arched her eyebrows and smiled. "That means I'll boil some water for the tea to go with the cookies my aunt baked before she left."

The hot tea and sugar cookies mellowed the group, and it did not take long for their conversation to drift to the Triangle shutdown.

"I hope we go back to work soon," said Rivka. "If not, we won't be able to pay our rent. I've been picking up some contract sewing but it's not steady; just whenever there is enough work to dole out."

"I'm pretty much doing the same thing," said Angie. "I guess we're lucky because Papa is still working, but some days we don't eat a lot."

Ida took a sip of tea and eyed the group, unsure of how they would receive her news. "I've been doing a little bit of contract work too, but I have also been going to ILGWU meetings."

Angie froze, her cup of tea hovering halfway to her mouth. "Ida, are you crazy? Do you want to get fired?"

"I don't want to get fired, but I don't want to work almost a hundred hours a week for pennies an hour, either. I know it's risky, but unless we stand up for ourselves, nothing will change. Harris and Blanck will get richer on our sweat. The work conditions—the locked doors, the searches, the ridiculous fines, the way Salutsky talks to us and touches our bodies with his filthy hands—will never stop," she said, slamming her hand on the table, rattling the dishes, sending tea splashing over the rims of their cups. Breathing hard, her face flushed with anger, Ida sank back in her chair.

The girls stared at their friend in stunned silence.

"I'm sorry. I didn't mean to go on like that, but I see no other way to make things better at the factory. There is strength in numbers, and with the union behind us, we can get the owners to meet our demands."

Angie stood. "Everything you say is true. But we all know Harris and Blanck don't care about our demands and will never give in to them. If they find out we even talked about the ILGWU, we could all be fired. Ida, you are my friend, but please don't bring up the union again." She grabbed her coat. "I'd better get going. My father will be waiting up for me."

"I make to go too," said Osna. Her eyes lowered, she followed Angie out the door.

"Well, I certainly know how to ruin an evening," sighed Ida as she cleared the dishes.

Miriam moved to the sink and began washing the cups and saucers while Rivka stood towel in hand, ready to dry. Searching for the right words, Miriam finally spoke.

"I don't think any of us disagrees with what you said, but you have to understand that not everyone has the courage you do to set aside the needs they have now for something better in the future. We know that the Triangle bosses don't care what happens to their workers. All they care about is how much money they make."

"That's exactly my point!" exclaimed Ida. "Things will never get better. They will get worse because we let them treat us the way we do. We're not human beings to them."

Rivka wiped her hands on the towel and hung it to dry on the line strung above the sink. "Ida, please be careful at the factory. Salutsky and the owners have eyes and ears everywhere. If they can burn down their own factories, who knows what else they are capable of?"

Touched by Rivka's concern, Ida hugged her friend. "Please don't worry about me. I'll be fine. And before I forget, I have a message for Miriam."

"For me? Who would send me a message?"

"Jacob Zadkin."

"Who is Jacob Zadkin?"

"Remember the two men sitting next to us at Schmookayler's the night of your birthday? Jacob was the one with the dark hair. He is an organizer for the ILGWU and he's always asking me about my redheaded friend. He told me to invite you to our next meeting."

Miriam became flustered. Her face felt hot. "He is awfully cocky."

"And very handsome," said Ida.

Rivka could not resist the urge to tease Miriam. "Sounds like you have an admirer."

"An admirer I'll never meet. The last place you'll find me is at a union gathering."

CHAPTER 39

1908

By February, the economy was on the rebound, and the Triangle factory resumed full production. It was the busy season again and even with the return of the seven-day work schedule, Miriam and the others were relieved to be back at work.

"If the shutdown had gone on for another week, we probably would have been evicted from our apartment," Rivka told Miriam as they waited for the freight elevator. "We are two weeks behind in our rent, and I had to beg the landlord to give us another week until I get paid. We'll still owe him, just not as much."

Miriam was only half listening to Rivka. After months of not riding the elevator, the old fear of confined spaces had returned. Sweat dripped down the front of her blouse and her mouth felt dry. When the car arrived and Gino slid the grate open with a clang, she jumped.

Rivka took her hand. "You know you can do this. Just close your eyes," she whispered.

"You'd think I'd be over this by now," she said, stepping into the elevator. Her eyes clamped shut, she held tightly to Rivka's hand and did not let go until they reached the ninth floor.

Salutsky stood waiting at the elevator, pocket watch in hand. "Put your things away and get right to work," he barked. "You should all be glad you still have a job."

Rivka's eyes widened. "And nothing changes, does it?" she said under her breath.

Ida walked up behind her and whispered, "No it doesn't."

A month into the busy season, Miriam's joy at being back at work was replaced by utter exhaustion. The fifteen-hour days to meet the pent-up demand for shirtwaists were made worse by Salutsky's constant harangues to work faster. Injuries increased along with the pace, and for each girl who sewed her finger instead of cloth and was unable to work, another was ready to take her place.

"That we can be replaced so easily just shows you how little we are valued as workers," said Ida as they waited in line to have their purses checked. "We are like cattle to them."

"Shh," whispered Rivka. "Someone will hear you. It's dangerous to talk that way."

Ida frowned and moved toward the front of the line where Salutsky stood waiting to search for stolen goods. Miriam and Rivka lowered their eyes as the foreman rifled through their things. When he signaled they could go, Ida handed Salutsky her purse, defiantly meeting his gaze.

Holding Ida's stare, Salutsky took everything out of her handbag, slowly examining each item. He paused when he withdrew a handkerchief with tiny pink flowers embroidered along the edges. Smiling, he brought it to his face and blew his nose before placing the damp cloth back in her handbag.

Her eyes pools of undisguised rage, Ida refused to let Salutsky humiliate her in front of the others. "Here," she said, holding the offensive handkerchief by a corner, "you seem to need this more than I do." Without looking back, she strode out the door.

"Damn it, damn it, damn it," spit Ida once she was outside. "That handkerchief was a gift from my aunt."

"What are you talking about? Are you all right?" asked Miriam.

"I just made things worse with Salutsky." Shaking with anger, Ida recounted her run-in with the foreman.

"Oh my God, what have you done?" cried Rivka.

Word of Ida's confrontation with Salutsky had already spread throughout the ninth floor by the time Rivka and Miriam emerged from the freight elevator the next morning. Whispers circulated the room as the cutters and seamstresses speculated whether Ida would show up for work. When Gino slid open the metal grate and she was part of the crowd that stepped out of the elevator, the chatter ceased.

Staring straight ahead, Ida walked confidently to her sewing machine. Her face was unreadable, and if she was surprised by the subtle nods of approval from the girls who had once gossiped so viciously about her, she did not show it. Nor did she acknowledge the palpable tension that swallowed the room when Salutsky entered.

Dead silence replaced the normal hum of the machines, and every eye focused on the stony-faced foreman as he walked down the aisle toward Ida. Standing in front of her, his eyes were slits of fury, his thin lips pulled back in a snarl.

"Get your things and get out of here. You're done," thundered Salutsky.

When Ida did not budge, the girls seated around her rose suddenly and scampered to the other side of the room.

"Did you hear me, you little whore? I said you're done. Now get the hell out of here." A muscle in Salutsky's jaw began to twitch convulsively, and he took a menacing step toward her.

"I will only go if you ask me nicely, Her-man," she said, drawing out his name, taunting him with her contempt.

Enraged by her defiance, Salutsky grabbed Ida by the shoulders and yanked her over the table, sending her and the sewing machine crashing to the floor.

Ida staggered to her feet, blood trickling from a cut on her forehead. Leaning on a table to steady herself, her hand found a pair of scissors. "Touch me again," she said, brandishing the shears like a knife, "and I will be last girl you ever put your filthy hands on."

Salutsky screamed in blind fury, the veins on his neck bulging wildly, spittle flying from his mouth like a rabid dog. He sprang at her, his hands nearly finding her throat when two of the cutters grabbed him from behind and wrestled him to the floor.

"You fucking bitch. You don't know who you are dealing with," shouted Salutsky, his face purple with rage. "You will never work in this industry again."

Ida glared at her attacker. "Don't worry, Her-man. You'll see me around. I'm not done making your life miserable."

Salutsky pulled away from the two men and kicked wildly at Ida, narrowly missing her legs. Two more cutters joined the fray and dragged the cursing Salutsky into the elevator.

As soon as the elevator doors closed, Ida's knees gave way. Sinking to the floor, her body shook uncontrollably.

Miriam rushed to help her to her feet. "Are you okay? You're bleeding."

Ida touched her head and winced. "That bastard. I should have stabbed him."

"Don't say that. You should be afraid of his threats. He is not someone you want as an enemy," warned Rivka.

Miriam handed Ida her things. "You'd better get out of here before Salutsky comes back. Angie sent word to Gino to delay bringing him back up, but I am not sure how long he'll be able to hold him off."

Ida nodded and grimaced in a jolt of pain. As she turned to leave, the sound of clapping made her pause. Slow at first, it became a deafening chorus of respect as she walked past the men and women of the ninth floor toward the stairs.

It took less than an hour for news of Ida's defiant stand against Salutsky to spread throughout the factory. Workers retold the incident over and over until it took on mythic overtones. The version Salutsky told the bosses on the tenth floor was somewhat more ominous. The gutsy seamstress the workers spoke of was portrayed as a union-loving troublemaker.

The very idea of a unionist in their shop sent Harris and Blanck into a frenzy of paranoia. Anyone associated with the union, they declared, was to be fired on the spot.

Armed with his bosses' decree and still smarting from the humiliation he'd suffered in front of the nearly two hundred fifty workers on the ninth floor, Salutsky unleashed a campaign of vengeance on the operators. He prowled the floor like a bloodthirsty predator, leaning over the women as they worked, his hands brushing against their breasts, the stink of his breath hot on the back of their necks. He demanded they work faster and then purposely slowed them down by stopping their work to inspect the garments, ripping out stitches and ordering they be done over. Fines were levied for failure to meet his quota, talking, or taking too long in the bathroom. He locked the elevators every night, so the girls had to walk down nine flights of stairs to leave the building. Searches of personal property for any signs of union activity increased. When a copy of the *Jewish Daily Forward*, considered a socialist union newspaper, was found in the pocket of a seamstress' coat, she was fired, despite her protests that she only bought the paper to read the advice column to help her find a husband.

Salutsky's one-man war of intimidation finally came to an end when Harris and Blanck noticed the sharp plunge in production on the ninth floor. Orders counted. Salutsky's wounded pride did not.

CHAPTER 40

Winter would not relinquish its hold on the city, dashing all hopes for signs of spring. Traces of snow black with dirt still coated the streets, soiling the shoes of unwary New Yorkers. On Fifth Avenue, wealthy matrons picked their way around dirty puddles, lifting the hems of their embroidered skirts as they crossed slush-covered roads. In the dark tenements of the Lower East Side, families huddled around stoves to ward off the cold.

The gloom of lingering winter matched the prevailing mood of the Triangle workers. By the time the busy season ended, morale was low, their unrest festering like an open wound.

Seizing on the turmoil among the workers, Ida found a way to make good on her promise to create trouble for Salutsky. When word of the way she stood up to the foreman came to the attention of the executives at the International Ladies Garment Workers Union, she was quickly enlisted to help organize the Triangle factory.

Ida approached Miriam and Rivka for their help in getting the workers to come to union meetings. Miriam agreed readily. Months of Salutsky's mistreatment and his manhandling of Ida had erased any fears she'd had about bringing the ILGWU into the factory.

"You were right," said Miriam. "The owners don't care how we are treated as long as we deliver the shirtwaists they need to fill their orders."

"I'm glad you finally see it for yourself. If we band together and agree to stop working, they will have to meet our demands. The ILGWU helped the workers in the cloak industry last year. They went on strike and after seven weeks they got a fifty-five-hour work week, better pay, better work conditions, and they no longer have to pay for power, needles, and thread."

Rivka's eyes began to blink. "Seven weeks is a long time to go without wages. My father and I are still recovering from the shutdown."

"I know, but the ILGWU helps strikers. They have funds for that." Sensing Rivka's hesitancy, Ida continued, "We are getting ahead of ourselves. First, we need to see if there is any interest in unionizing. That's why I thought we could meet in small groups to let the girls know what the union has to offer."

Miriam looked at Rivka and could see that her friend was unsure of what to do. "I think that doing nothing will get us nothing. I think we should do it."

Rivka's eyes were blinking faster. "I need some time to decide. If the bosses or Salutsky find out what we're doing, we'll be on the street."

"Take as much time as you need. You too, Miriam. And if you change your mind or decide against helping, it's okay. And yes, you do need to be careful." Ida touched the small scar beneath the curls of her bangs. "We know what they are capable of."

On her first Sunday off in months, Miriam fought the urge to stay under the warm covers and got up early so she could join her parents for breakfast.

"As cold as it is, I thought for sure you would sleep late," said Sadie, filling their cups with tea and placing a breakfast of buttered slices of challah on the table.

"I have to admit I was tempted to, but it's been so long since we all had a meal together. I've seen so little of you both it feels like I've been away on a long journey."

Meyer smiled at his daughter, her hair a mass of unruly curls, a faint line on her cheek left by the creased fabric of her pillow. How old was she now? Seventeen? Eighteen? He could not remember. His mind wandered to those early days in Oreheyev when he first met Sadie. Wasn't she about the same age as Miriam is now? Shouldn't she be seeing a young man by now? He would, he decided, ask around the synagogue to see if anyone knew of an eligible young man who would be suitable for his daughter, someone pious and learned. He was mentally making a list of congregants he could ask, when he realized Miriam was talking to him.

"Papa, I said I wanted your opinion on something."

Struggling to focus his thoughts, Meyer took a sip of tea. "Sorry, I didn't hear you. My opinion on what?"

"I've been asked to do something I believe in, but it's something that could cost me my job."

"What could have such serious consequences?"

"Helping Ida bring the union into the Triangle factory. I believe if we do nothing to improve the conditions there, nothing will change. But if the owners find out I am in any way associated with the union, I will be fired."

Meyer clasped his hands in front of him. "I do not know much about unions, but I do know about standing up for what you believe in. I will always wonder if things would have been different if the Jews in Kishinev had been strong enough to fight the years of our so-called neighbors' anti-Semitism instead of ignoring it."

Still unsure about her decision to help recruit girls to come to Ida's union meeting, Miriam was relieved Rivka did not bring up the subject as they made their way to work on Monday morning. Rivka was eager to tell her about her Sunday with Avrum, and Miriam was happy to hear how her aunt and cousins were doing.

"Business at the delicatessen has really picked up. Avrum is thinking about creating an area with a few tables and chairs so people can eat in the shop," said Rivka.

"I feel guilty that I haven't been to see them in months. Did you see Sonia and Ira? How are Rebecca and Esther? My aunt?"

"They're all fine. I didn't see Sonia. Avrum said she was out with some friends she met in the park; other girls who take care of younger children. Ira was in the store. He's gotten so tall and good-looking. Avrum said there is a girl who lives in the building next door who is always coming into the deli to talk to him. Avrum teases him as soon as she leaves."

"Poor Ira. And the girls and my aunt?"

"They're fine. Both girls are getting big. Avrum said Esther follows Rebecca everywhere and wants to do everything she does. Your aunt is doing well, all things considered. I get the impression she doesn't miss your uncle at all."

"Oscar, Papa's friend, told him he heard my uncle was hanging around with a rough crowd in the Bowery. A bunch of gamblers and thieves."

"If Avrum knows he hasn't said anything," said Rivka as they turned the corner onto Greene Street, the Asch Building looming in front of them. A sudden gust of wind nearly blew them off their feet and they grabbed on to each other to keep from falling. Planting her feet, Rivka managed to stay upright, but Miriam hit a patch of ice and she slipped, landing hard on her behind.

"Not a great way to start the day," laughed Miriam, scrambling to her feet and brushing off the back of her skirt. "I hope it gets better."

It did not.

Salutsky was in a foul mood. His bloodshot eyes seemed to dart everywhere in search of any worker who had committed an infraction worthy of his wrath. Spotting a cutter flirting with a secretary down from the tenth floor to deliver a new order, Salutsky stormed over to the two, screaming at the man to get back to work and ordering the terrified young woman to "get your ass upstairs."

Still on a rampage, Salutsky marched up and down the aisles of sewing machines, stopping to inspect a new girl's work. As the terrified operator looked on, he ripped out the stitches from the garment she was working on. "You stupid cow, make this mess again and you're fired," he said, throwing the material in her face. "Do it over," he ordered and mocking the girl's tears, continued his advance on the other seamstresses.

Miriam could hear his approach as he stomped down the aisle. Keeping her eyes down, she carefully guided a sleeve through the bobbing needle.

Salutsky stood in front of her, hands on his hips, staring at her as she sewed. Cold fingers of fear gripped her heart. Had one of his spies told him she'd been talking to Ida about the union?

"You'd better work faster," he warned, "or you will be joining your friend Ida looking for work somewhere else." He leaned down toward her, his paw-like hands planted on the table, his face so close she could smell his cheap pipe tobacco on his breath. His lips curled, he whispered, "If you're nice to me, I will be nicer to you."

Miriam leaned back in her chair, repulsed by his presence and his offer. She returned his stare and remained quiet, hoping he would leave, when someone yelled, "Fire!"

"Damn it!" cursed Salutsky, running toward the pressing area, where a paper pattern hanging from an overhead line was in flames. "Hurry up and throw some water on that thing!" he yelled, even as two of the pressers grabbed a nearby bucket and doused the blazing pattern.

The acrid smell of smoke filled Miriam's nostrils. Her heart nearly bursting from her chest, she rose from her chair, ready to flee Salutsky and the fire.

"Sit down," snapped Angie, keeping her eyes on Salutsky. "It's nothing. A presser must have gotten too close to a pattern with a hot iron. It happens sometimes. See, it's already out."

Miriam sank into her chair, her thoughts racing. Was this the fire the fortune teller had warned her about? Why had Salutsky mentioned Ida?

"He's coming back," whispered Angie. "Get to work."

Her palms moist with sweat, Miriam reached for a sleeve as Salutsky passed her chair. Leering, he ran his hand along her arm and down her back. Burning with resentment and fear, Miriam no longer had doubts about helping Ida.

CHAPTER 41

The first meeting at Ida's apartment was to discuss a strategy for stirring up interest in the ILGWU. Ida told Miriam her aunt was going to the Yiddish theater with some of her friends, so she was surprised when she heard voices coming from her apartment. When Ida opened the door, Miriam could not hide her look of astonishment when she caught sight of the handsome dark-haired young man from Schmookayler's sitting in the front room.

He rose and came forward to meet her. When he smiled, Miriam's breath caught in her throat.

"Miriam, this is Jacob Zadkin. You two met last year, the night of your birthday."

"Hello, Miriam. I didn't realize your gathering that night was a celebration. I hope I didn't ruin your birthday with my enthusiasm for the union."

"No, not at all. It's nice to see you again," sputtered Miriam, smoothing her hair and wishing she had changed her clothes after work.

Amused by Miriam's discomfort, Ida led the way to the kitchen. "Let's sit and have some tea while we talk. We have a lot to figure out."

Miriam found it hard to concentrate while sitting so close to Jacob. She nodded as if she was listening to the conversation, but her thoughts were jumbled, distracted by the faint, spicy smell of his aftershave and the nearness of his leg to hers. Casting sly glances in his direction, she studied his features. He'd grown a mustache since their previous encounter at Schmookayler's. Thick black lashes framed his light-blue eyes, so pale they could easily be mistaken for gray. A small scar curved around his left eye. His hands, she noticed, were smooth, his fingernails clean and neatly trimmed.

"Union headquarters can be intimidating, so, we will start with small group meetings at Ida's apartment," said Jacob, turning to Miriam.

His sudden attention caught her off guard and she struggled to get her bearings. She'd heard almost none of what they had discussed, and Jacob was looking at her so earnestly, waiting for a response.

Miriam's mind raced. "Small meetings do make the most sense. How many people do you anticipate?" she asked, trying to sound fully involved in the plans.

They decided the first gathering of five would take place at Ida's apartment the following Thursday. Miriam was grateful the meeting was a week away, giving her time to have Ida fill her in on the details she'd missed. Jacob showed no signs of wanting to leave, and even though Miriam knew her parents would be waiting up for her, she was glad they lingered over their tea talking about the union. It was only after Ida's aunt arrived home from the theater that they realized how late it had gotten.

Saying their goodbyes, Miriam and Jacob left together. When they reached the street, Jacob asked if he could walk her home.

"I live just three blocks from here on Hester Street," said Miriam. "I don't want to put you to any trouble."

"It's no trouble. It's late for you to be out by yourself, and I am going in that direction anyway." He smiled, and any intention Miriam had of walking home alone vanished.

The night air was brisk enough for them to see their breath. A carpet of dark clouds parted, and the moon cast a thin beam of light as they walked. Crossing the street, Jacob placed his hand on Miriam's elbow, guiding her away from a puddle of blackened slush. She liked the feel of his hand on her arm.

"How long have you worked at the Triangle?" he asked when they'd reached the sidewalk.

"Almost three years now, but it feels like forever."

"The Triangle has a reputation as one of the worst factories to work for. I'm glad you decided to help us."

"To be honest, I was thinking of going back on my promise to help Ida. Even after Salutsky attacked her, I was afraid I would lose my job if the owners found out I was involved with the ILGWU. But Salutsky is out of control, ranting all the time, touching us whenever and wherever he wants. And there was a small fire on the ninth floor that really frightened me. I am just so tired of it. I've finally realized that if we don't do anything, it will only get worse."

They had reached Miriam's apartment and stopped under a gas streetlight, their shadows flickering on the ground around them. "I'd better go in," said Miriam. "My parents will be worrying about where I am. Thank you for walking me home."

"It really was my pleasure. I can come by next Thursday evening and we can walk to the meeting together, if you like."

Miriam felt the blood rush to her cheeks. "I would like that very much."

"See you then," said Jacob, flashing the smile Miriam found so irresistible.

Miriam started up the stairs and turned just as Jacob began walking in the direction from which they'd come. "I thought you said you were walking this way," she shouted.

Grinning, he turned and shouted back, "I lied."

As Miriam expected, Sadie and Meyer were at the kitchen table, cold cups of tea in front of them.

"I am sorry it's so late. Time got away from us."

Meyer's face was stern. "I don't like you out this late or walking home alone at this hour."

"I know it's late, but, Papa, I wasn't alone. Jacob Zadkin, a union representative who was at the meeting, walked me home."

"So, it's all right if a complete stranger walks you home?"

Miriam took a deep breath. She was exhausted and did not want to have this conversation. "Jacob is not a stranger. I met him the night of my birthday at Schmookayler's."

"Oh, so that makes him an old acquaintance? There are plenty of nice young men at the synagogue you could be walking home with instead of this Jacob person."

"Meyer," said Sadie, her voice brittle around the edges. "I am sure Jacob is also a nice person, or Miriam would not have allowed him to escort her home. We are all tired, and I think we should go to bed. Tomorrow night is *Shabbat* and we need to be up early to go to the pushcart market. You can talk to Oscar while I shop."

Meyer grunted, "I still don't like you coming home with strangers." He rose and kissed Miriam and Sadie good night. "Miriam, I don't like this business at all," he said, slamming the bedroom door.

Miriam stared at her mother in bewilderment. "What was that all about?"

"He's had a headache all afternoon, and that always puts him in a bad mood. He was worried about you. The later it got, the more worked up he became. He's been carrying on about how much he hates that you are still working at the factory. He keeps talking about finding a nice young man at the synagogue for you to marry."

Miriam buried her head in her hands, furious at what she considered her father's meddling. "Mama, please stop this before it goes any further. I don't want—I don't *need*—him to find me a husband."

"I know, but I think that's why he was so upset that a man he doesn't know walked home with you. He just wants to make sure you marry someone suitable. Someone who will treat you well."

Her fury mounting, Miriam took a moment to calm herself before she spoke. "This is ridiculous. Why all this talk of marriage? And shouldn't it be up to me to decide who and when I marry?"

Sadie's fingers slowly traced circles on the tablecloth. "You must know that he only wants what's best for you."

"I do know that. But that doesn't mean he can tell me who I should spend the rest of my life with."

CHAPTER 42

The following Thursday Miriam waited impatiently for Rivka to collect her things so they could leave the factory. "Come on, Rivka. Let's go."

"I'm coming. Why the rush?"

Miriam lowered her voice. "I want to get home in time to change my clothes. Remember?"

Puzzled at first, Rivka said, "I don't know what you are ...." She stopped and whispered, "I forgot about your meeting."

Miriam raised her eyebrows in alarm and looked to see if anyone overheard their conversation. Relieved to see that they were alone in the coat room, she pointed toward the elevator.

Once they were some distance from the factory, Miriam finally spoke. "We're meeting at Ida's tonight. Osna said she would come. Angie's cousin, Ambra Nitti, and two women from the eighth floor will also be there. Are you sure you don't want to join us?"

Rivka looked down at her shoes, torn between wanting to help her friends and the fear of losing her job. "I know what you are doing is the right thing, but I cannot put my job in jeopardy."

Miriam understood perfectly. Her parents needed her salary. Papa would always be plagued by the injuries he sustained in the accident. She had finally accepted the fact that he would never be able to return to his pushcart, and if she went without work for any length of time, she did not know how they would pay for rent and food. Her anguish was only diminished by her belief that to stand by and do nothing would be worse.

Miriam studied her image in the mirror in her parents' room and frowned. Her hair seemed to have a mind of its own, and she gave up trying to tame the stray curls that escaped the bun at the nape of her neck. She hated the freckles that dotted her cheeks and wished she'd inherited Mama's shiny chestnut locks, instead of Papa's stubborn red curls. Smoothing the front of her freshly ironed blouse, she attached the small blue brooch Mama had given her to its high collar. She added a trace of rouge to her cheeks and lips and deemed the result satisfactory but not dazzling. She chided herself for being so nervous about seeing Jacob again. "Just don't make a fool of yourself," she told the anxious face staring back at her. She put on the short wool jacket that matched her gray skirt and steeled herself for the questions her parents were sure to ask before she left.

"Where are you going all dressed up?" asked Meyer.

"Papa, we talked about this at dinner. I am going to a union meeting at Ida's."

"I'll walk you there, then."

"Thank you, but there is no need. Jacob is walking with me and he will walk me home." Miriam looked at her mother imploringly, desperately wanting to avoid a confrontation.

"It's all right, Meyer. She will be fine," said Sadie, nodding for Miriam to leave.

Taking her mother's lead—and before her father could say more—Miriam kissed them both and was out the door.

"I don't like this," said Meyer, his voice hoarse with anger. "What do we know about this man? I've heard some of these union guys are roughnecks."

"What we know is that Miriam likes him. She is a smart girl, and we have to trust her judgment."

"What does she know? She is only eighteen."

"I was younger than her when I met you, and I knew," she said, softly caressing his face with her hands.

Jacob was standing at the bottom of the stairs when Miriam emerged from of the building. Dressed in a dark suit and sporting a black bowler hat low on his forehead, he looked especially handsome. Jacob smiled when he saw Miriam, and she had to hold on to the railing, unwilling to trust her wobbling knees to take her safely down the steps.

"You look lovely," said Jacob, offering his arm.

"Thank you," said Miriam, shyly slipping her arm through his.

"How was your day?"

"Over," she exclaimed with a smile. "Tell me about yours."

Jacob laughed. "I should have known better than to ask. I was in meetings most of the day. We are trying to organize a hat factory on Clinton Street. Plans are for the workers to start picketing on Monday." His voice rang with excitement. "I've been working on this one for months and I think we finally have a chance at unionizing the shop. The conditions there are deplorable. I worry about the safety of the workers."

"You really love what you are doing, don't you?"

He nodded. "I like that I can help people, but I don't want to do this forever. I am taking classes at New York University at night. I want to be a lawyer, but at the rate I am going, it will take a while."

"You are lucky to be able to continue your education. I had hoped to be a teacher one day, but my father was injured in an accident and is unable to work. My mother sews at home to bring in some money, but it's not enough. I left school to go to work at the Triangle factory. I don't even think about returning to school anymore."

The first to arrive, Jacob and Miriam were greeted at the door by Ida's Aunt Molly. Dressed in a flowing, pale-green dress and smelling of rose-scented perfume, she embraced Miriam, kissing her on each cheek. She turned to Jacob and after looking him over, cooed, "You must be the union man. Ida is right, you are exceptionally good-looking."

Jacob laughed nervously. Red-faced, he was struggling to collect himself when Ida boomed out from the kitchen, "Don't listen to her. Come on in. I'm just boiling water for tea."

Grateful for a reason to excuse themselves, Miriam and Jacob hastened toward the kitchen.

Shaking her head, Ida set the teapot on the stove. "Sorry about that. She is a big flirt, but she's harmless."

"I heard that," yelled Ida's aunt. "I am leaving, anyway. Morty is taking me dancing. By the way, there's a group of pretty young ladies coming up the stairs."

The nervous-looking girls spilled into the apartment. "We am arrived," announced Osna, her fractured English making them laugh and instantly putting everyone at ease.

Ida served tea and Claire and Rose, the girls who worked on the eighth floor, introduced themselves. After a few minutes of chatter, Jacob shifted the conversation to the reason they were meeting. Leaning forward, his elbows on his knees, he began, "First, I want to thank you for coming tonight. I know you are worried about your jobs, and I promise you this gathering is a secret one. It's why we are here instead of at union headquarters. I am not going to talk for long; I just want you to know that Local 25 of the IL-GWU wants to help you get better working conditions so you don't have to worry about your safety. We'll fight to eliminate piece work so you will get a guaranteed salary. We'll make sure you work shorter hours so you will have time to go to night school if you want," he added, looking directly at Miriam.

Encouraged by her smile, Jacob continued. "The owners don't want the union in their shop because they know they will lose the flexibility they have to cut your wages or extend or shorten your hours at will. If you join the union, we will fight for you. We will make sure you don't have to show up in the slow season and wait for hours for work only to be told to go home without pay for that day. We will limit forced overtime and make sure that the foremen cannot favor one worker over another by giving them work while denying others."

Seventeen-year-old Ambra Nitti, a raven-haired beauty with eyes as black as onyx, spoke up. "What about the way the foremen treat us? Can you help stop the way they talk to us and yell at us and the way … you know?" Embarrassed, her voice trailed off and she lowered her eyes.

Jacob cleared his throat. "Most certainly, yes."

Osna squirmed in her seat. "You can do this how?"

"You already know that you do not matter to the owners," said Jacob. "They know your job can easily be filled by someone else eager to take it. But when you come together with other workers who believe what you do, you have the strength of numbers behind you. The owners cannot function if all of you refuse to work."

"My cousin Angie told me not to come here," said Ambra. "But I am glad I did. I am going to tell her she should come to a meeting. We need to do this."

"I am so encouraged by this meeting," said Jacob as they left Ida's apartment. "I know it was only four girls, but if we can keep getting this level of interest and build on it, we will be able to get the owners to meet our demands and change their practices."

"I hope so. These girls are risking a lot just by coming to the meeting. Salutsky has spies everywhere. We are all terrified of him."

"We know all about him. He is one of the worst," said Jacob as they passed Chumsky's Diner, its front window displaying an array of pastries. The door opened as a customer stepped out and the smell of brewing coffee engulfed them.

Jacob looked at his watch. "It's still early. Please join me for some coffee and one of those delicious-looking Danish."

Miriam hesitated. Meyer would be furious if she was late again.

"Come on. My mouth is watering just looking at those pastries. You won't deprive me of one, will you?" He curled his lips downward into a mock frown, but his eyes were bright and merry.

Miriam could not contain a smile. "Only if you promise to get me home by nine o'clock."

He raised his right hand. "I promise."

There was only one customer seated at the bright-green counter when they entered the diner. Jacob ordered their coffee and two pastries and brought them to a small table near the window.

The hot coffee warmed them, and their small talk turned to more serious topics. Miriam told him about the pogrom and Eli's and Yuri's deaths. She recounted their harrowing journey to New York and life in her aunt's apartment. He listened quietly as she described her father's injury and its life-changing effects.

Jacob, like Miriam, came to America to escape the anti-Semitism of Russia. Unlike Miriam, he came to America alone. Both his parents and only sibling, Sophie, died when an influenza epidemic swept through their small village. Worried about the rampant hatred of Jews or that he would be conscripted into the Russian army, his uncle arranged for then sixteen-year-old Jacob to come to America to live with a great aunt. She died when he was nineteen, and he'd been on his own ever since.

"I was so lucky to have my great-aunt Jenny take me in. She was a widow with no children of her own and she treated me like a son from the minute I appeared at her doorstep," said Jacob, his voice heavy with emotion. "When she died three years ago, she left me a little money and that, plus my ILGWU salary, help me go to the university at night. I share an apartment with my friend Max Astrovski. He goes to law school too. It's a struggle some days, but every time I get discouraged about work or school, I think about my parents and my sister and work harder to honor their memory."

Miriam thought of her father's words about wanting to find a good man for her to marry. Where, she thought, would he ever find a more decent, hard-working man than the one sitting beside her?

CHAPTER 43

1909

The third weekend of the new year ushered in a two-day storm that left the city coated in snow and ice. Saturday's light, fluffy flakes turned to a mixture of sleet and heavy snow on Sunday and the gray, water-laden clouds made the world outside look ominous and unforgiving. Trolley wires collapsed under the weight of encrusted ice and littered the streets. Horse-drawn carriages struggled to navigate the treacherously iced-over roads. Most citizens of the Lower East Side spent the weekend huddled around their stoves to stay warm.

Despite the still-falling snow on Monday, Avrum and Ira were downstairs preparing to open the delicatessen, when a policeman entered the shop. Broad-shouldered, his belly straining against the buttons of his wool coat, the big man removed his hat, revealing a fringe of gray hair. His face bright red from the cold, he brushed the snow from his coat and looked around.

Avrum signaled to Ira and came from behind the counter. "Good morning, sir. Is there something I can help you with? We're not open yet, but I can certainly get you a cup of coffee if you'd like one."

"Thank you, but I'm not here for coffee. I'm Officer Campbell. Are you related to Lazar Abkin?"

Avrum looked at Ira and saw the fear in his eyes. "I am Avrum Abkin, and this is my brother Ira. Lazar Abkin is our father. Is he in trouble?"

The big cop looked away for a moment. He hated this part of the job. "I'm sorry, son, but I have some bad news. We found your father's body this morning in the Bowery. It looks like he wandered out of one of the saloons there and passed out in an alley. It was a mean night to be out in the elements. I'm afraid he froze to death."

Ira gasped. Avrum's face remained expressionless. "How did you know to come here?"

"We've had some run-ins with your father before, mostly drunk-and-disorderly stuff. We knew who he was and one of the men at the precinct connected him to your delicatessen. I'm sorry to put you through this, but someone will have to come to the morgue for positive identification and to make arrangements for the body."

Avrum nodded. "I will take care of it this morning."

Ira sniffled and wiped the tears from his cheeks. "We have to tell Mama and the girls," he said, his voice cracking.

The policeman put his hand on Avrum's shoulder. "Do you want me to talk to your mother?"

"Thank you, Officer Campbell, but I think I'd better be the one to tell her."

Avrum hung the "Closed" sign on the door and putting his arm around Ira, guided him upstairs. "You have to pull yourself together. Take Rebecca and Esther into the bedroom so I can tell Mama and Sonia."

Ira stood before the door to the apartment but didn't move. "I hated him. Now I can't believe he is dead and that we'll never see him again."

Avrum scowled. He wanted to remind Ira that they hadn't seen their father in over a year when he was alive but kept that thought to himself. "Just be careful not to upset Rebecca. Esther probably doesn't even remember him."

Sonia was coming out of the kitchen when they entered the apartment. One look at Ira and she knew something was wrong. "It's Uncle Meyer, isn't it?" she said in a shaky voice.

Avrum shook his head. "He's fine. Come into the front room. I need to talk to you and Mama. Ira will watch the girls."

Malka twisted the gold wedding ring she still wore as Avrum told her what he knew about Lazar's death. Sonia began to cry, but Malka sat rigidly, staring off into space. Avrum had prepared himself for some outward signs of grief. He waited for the tears to come and was bewildered when she shed none.

"Mama, are you all right?"

"How will we find the money to bury him?" she asked, her eyes dull, her voice flat.

"They can bury the bastard in Potter's Field, for all I care," snapped Avrum.

Malka's eyes flared in anger. "He is your father. I will not allow you to speak so disrespectfully of him."

Stung by her words, Avrum rose. "How can I respect him when I am ashamed to be his son? I'm going to the morgue to identify his body. That's the most respect he will get from me," he spat, storming out of the apartment and slamming the door behind him.

Sonia was sobbing now. He does not deserve your tears, thought Malka, taking her daughter into her arms.

The snow had stopped but the penetrating cold lingered. Stomping his feet and blowing into his hands, Avrum waited on a corner for Rivka and Miriam to come out of the Asch Building. Their heads down to shield their faces from the biting wind, they would have walked past him if he had not called out to them.

Spying Avrum, Miriam began to shake with fear and calmed down only when he assured her that Meyer and Sadie were all right. Relieved, Miriam studied his face. "Something must be wrong, or you wouldn't be here."

Rivka took his hand. "Avrum, what is it?"

"My father is dead," he blurted, his voice hard and ragged. "The police think he was drunk and passed out in an alley in the Bowery and froze to death. A fitting end for a no-good drunk, don't you think?"

Rivka and Miriam looked at each other, unsure of what to say. Avrum had never made a secret about his feelings for his father, but the hate in his voice shocked them.

"I'm so sorry, Avrum. How is Aunt Malka? Ira and Sonia? Is anyone with them?"

"I went by your place and told your parents. They are at our apartment now. I told them I would bring you there."

Rivka stepped closer to him. "Are you okay?"

Avrum nodded but did not meet her gaze. "We should go."

He linked arms with Rivka and Miriam so they wouldn't slip as they slowly trudged through the icy streets. The sounds of the city were muted by mounds of snow, and they walked in silence as the wind and cold buffeted their bodies. When they finally reached the delicatessen, Miriam rushed upstairs to the apartment, leaving Rivka and Avrum alone.

Still unable to find the words that would help Avrum come to terms with his father's death, Rivka put her arms around him. She could feel the thudding of his heart and wondered if there was any part of him that would ever forgive his father for all he had put the family through.

"I hate him, and I am so angry at him for the way he treated us," he said as if he'd entered her thoughts. "I don't ever remember loving him. Even when I was little he frightened me. I don't know why my mother continues to defend him. He abused her, and when he left us he brought shame to our family. She knows how I feel about him. She said I was being disrespectful. I know she is right, and I feel guilty for feeling this way, but I cannot help it. He was a tyrant. He was always taunting Ira and screaming at my sisters, even the little ones. God forgive me, but I am glad he is dead."

Her heart ached for him. He tried so hard to do what was right for his mother and the children. "You have every right to feel the way you do," she said in a quiet voice. "But perhaps time will allow you to remember him differently."

"Time will make no difference," he said bitterly.

Malka was sitting at the kitchen table with Sadie and Meyer when Avrum returned to the apartment. Ashamed of the way he'd spoken to his mother earlier, he went to her and sinking to his knees, hugged her tightly. "Mama, I am so sorry. I shouldn't have said those things to you. Please forgive me."

"Shh," said Malka, stroking his hair. "There is nothing to forgive. We were both upset."

His mother's words eased the heaviness he'd carried in his heart all day. He stood and hugged his aunt and uncle, then went into the front room where Miriam and Sonia were playing with Esther and Rebecca.

Sonia looked up at him, her eyes still red from crying. Of all of them, he knew she was the most forgiving of their father's failings. He sat down beside her and drew her into his arms. "He is at peace," he said to comfort his sister, though his words sounded hollow to his ears.

As unpleasant as it was, one important decision remained and Avrum returned to the kitchen. "Mama, the morgue will hold Papa's body for only a couple of days. What are we going to do about burying him?"

Meyer touched his arm. "My friend Oscar spoke to the rabbi at our synagogue. The Hebrew Free Burial Association is going to take care of the arrangements. He can be buried tomorrow according to Jewish law."

The funeral was held graveside with only the family and Rivka present. A cold January wind whipped through the cemetery and the small group shivered under a steel-gray sky as the rabbi intoned the service. When the rabbi signaled it was time to fill the grave, Avrum waited while one at a time the mourners placed a shovel of dirt on the casket. Taking the shovel from Ira, he stood looking down into his father's grave. Feeling no sadness and acknowledging a deep sense of relief, he fulfilled his duty as a son and threw a shovelful of dirt on the plain pine box. Nodding to the rabbi and the workmen waiting to complete the burial, Avrum turned and walked toward his family.

The stove had been untended all afternoon, and the apartment was cold when they returned from the funeral. While Sadie worked to light the coals, Meyer went next door to Mrs. Goldberg's to retrieve Esther and Rebecca.

Loud voices brought Sadie out of the kitchen and she found Malka and Avrum in a heated discussion about observing the week of mourning.

"Of course you will sit *shiva*," exclaimed Malka. "He was your father!"

"Mama, please, let's not have this conversation again," implored Avrum. "I am not being disrespectful. I just see no point to it. It's supposed be a time to mourn Papa's loss and dwell on the good memories of him. Well, I don't have good memories of him. You want to know what I remember? His drunken rages. Being slapped around. The bruises on your face and arms. How he picked on Ira. He left us, Mama. *He. Left. Us.*" His rage spent, Avrum sank into a chair and buried his face in his hands. His voice brimming with despair, he said, "Mama, the store has been closed for two days. We cannot afford to close it for seven more. Customers have already found new places to shop. We will be out of business if I don't open up."

Malka's shoulders sagged. He was right. Keeping the store closed for a week would ruin them.

"If Ira wants to sit *shiva*, I can manage the store by myself," Avrum said quietly.

Sadie put her arm around her sister. "Meyer and I will be here every day, so Sonia can sit *shiva* too. We can watch Esther and Rebecca."

Too tired to argue and distressed by her own mixed feelings about Lazar's death, Malka relented. "Keep the store open."

Avrum walked downstairs with Miriam and her parents. "I can't thank you enough for all you have done for us these past few days. We could not have gotten through this without you. And I apologize if I upset you tonight. I hope you will not think less of me because of the way I feel about my father."

Sadie touched his face. "We could never think less of you. You were the man of the house long before your father left. The best thing you can do now is to help your mother and be the kind of person that will teach Ira and the girls how a good man acts."

"I will, Aunt Sadie. I promise." Hugging each of them, he clung to Sadie for a moment before pulling away.

CHAPTER 44

Miriam tugged at Rivka's sleeve and urged her to hurry, so they could leave the factory. In the months following Lazar's death, Rivka had been spending all her free time with Avrum while Miriam had become increasingly more involved in union activities. Other than walking to and from work, they had spent little time together, and tonight had been planned as an evening of girl talk.

"Okay, okay, I'm coming. What's the big rush?"

"I promised Mama and Papa I wouldn't be late tonight, and I want us to have plenty of time to talk," said Miriam.

"Well, then—let's go. Why do I always have to wait for you?" asked Rivka, her voice dripping with mock exasperation.

They walked passed Schmookayler's and stopped at a small delicatessen off Washington Place. Their finances limited their selection, and they bought rolls and coffee before settling into one of the two small tables squeezed into the corner of the store.

"I feel like a traitor eating at any deli other than Avrum's" said Rivka, looking around so she could tell him what the owner's business was like.

"I'm sure Avrum will forgive you. From what I can tell, he would forgive you just about anything."

Rivka smiled but then grew reflective. "I am worried about him. He hasn't been himself since his father died. He won't admit it, but I know he feels guilty that he does not mourn his father's loss. The problem is he won't talk about it; he keeps it all inside him."

Miriam took a sip of coffee. "When we first came to America, we stayed with my aunt and uncle. Lazar terrified me. He had a real mean streak and was always screaming at my aunt. When he came upstairs from the deli, the kids would get quiet and stay out of his way, because it didn't take much to set him off. But not Avrum. He would stand up to him. He was my cousins' protector. Especially Ira. Uncle Lazar was always making fun of him. After one really ugly fight, Avrum said he wished his father was dead, and he meant it."

Rivka brought her hands together, her fingertips touching as if in prayer. "I just want him to be at peace with himself. Avrum may think he hates his father, but I wonder if what is really bothering him is that he wanted to love his father but never could."

"He shouldn't have any feelings of guilt. Lazar was a hard man to love."

Rivka grew thoughtful and shook her head. "How are you and Jacob doing?"

Miriam smiled. "Most of the time we spend together revolves around planning the union meetings. He is so passionate about improving the working and safety conditions in the garment factories."

"You said you and Jacob spend 'most of the time' working on union affairs. What do you do the rest of the time?"

Miriam's smile turned to laughter. "Well, we are getting to know each other better. We go out for coffee or ice cream after the meetings and talk. He is so charming and polite and funny. He's going to law school at night so he can continue to help working people."

"And you seem quite taken with him."

"I am crazy about him."

Rivka and Miriam parted at the corner where they usually met.

"See you in the morning," Miriam called out as she turned toward Hester Street. She walked slowly, enjoying the crisp night air, her head filled with thoughts of Jacob. Voicing her feelings about him to Rivka was the first time she'd said out loud what her heart had been telling her for months. She wondered if he felt the same way about her. He was certainly attentive, but she felt so inexperienced when it came to men she did not know how to interpret his intentions. Confused by her own unanswered questions, she was nearing her building when she heard her name. Startled, she looked around and there was Jacob leaning against the streetlight.

"Jacob, you frightened me. What are you doing here?"

"I'm sorry. I didn't mean to scare you." His eyes searched her face. "I missed you. My class finished early, and I thought I would take a chance on seeing you after you met with Rivka. I hope it's okay."

Miriam's face flushed with pleasure. "I'm glad you did. I hope you weren't waiting too long."

"I just got here a few minutes ago." Jacob pointed toward the apartment stoop. "Do you have time to sit with me for a few minutes?"

"Of course."

Jacob brushed the dirt from the steps and spread out his jacket for Miriam. He waited for her to be seated before he sat down beside her, their shoulders touching.

"I am going to have some time off from law school the next couple of weeks, and if it's all right with you, I'd like us to see more of each other. I know we will be working on the union meetings, but they never leave us much time to be just us."

Miriam could feel her heart flutter. "I would really like that," she said, trying to keep her voice steady.

Jacob's smile broadened. "Will you have dinner with me Sunday? I promise no talk about the ILGWU. That's for tomorrow night's meeting."

"Sunday would be wonderful. And I will hold you to your promise," teased Miriam.

Jacob rose, and taking Miriam's hand, helped her up from the steps. Still holding her hand, he walked her to the door. "I'll see you at Ida's tomorrow." Scooping up his jacket, he waited until Miriam was safely in the building before making his way home.

Sadie was sitting in the front room mending one of Meyer's shirts when Miriam let herself into the apartment. Expecting a lecture from her father, she was alarmed when he wasn't waiting for her.

"Where's Papa? Is he all right?"

"He went to bed early. Nothing serious, just one of those bad days he still has."

"What happened?"

"He forgot he'd made plans to help Oscar at the cart today and then was upset with himself when Oscar got concerned and came to the apartment looking for him. He was irritable and had a headache all day."

"I'm sorry, Mama. If he has a bad day, I know you have a bad day."

"I'm all right," said Sadie, putting down her sewing and patting the seat next to her. "Come, tell me about your evening."

Miriam shared her conversation with Rivka and then told her about Jacob's surprise visit. Sadie smiled, watching how animated Miriam became when she talked about Jacob.

"You like this boy, don't you?"

Miriam picked a loose thread from her sleeve. "Funny, Rivka asked me the same thing. Yes, I like him a lot."

"So, are we going to meet him?"

"He asked me to have dinner with him Sunday night. You will meet him when he comes to the apartment. Just make sure Papa doesn't scare him off," she said, only half-kidding.

"I'll try," said Sadie, only half-laughing.

Jacob and Miriam were barely out the door when they both burst into nervous laughter.

"I am surprised your father didn't ask me what I ate for breakfast. He asked me about every other part of my life."

"I'm so sorry. I should have warned you."

"It's all right. It's pretty clear he loves you very much."

"I know he does, but it's his accident. He doesn't always realize that he says things that he should probably keep to himself."

"You mean like when he asked me how much money I make?"

Mortified, Miriam hid her face in her hands. "Exactly like that."

"I have to say the look of horror on your face and your mother's when he asked was worth the grilling I took from your father," chuckled Jacob.

"I know he was rude, but he can't help it. I hope you aren't angry."

"Angry? No, of course not."

Miriam let out a sigh of relief. "Thank you for understanding."

Shaking his head, Jacob said, "You don't have to thank me. I like your father. Now, let's get some dinner. How about Ratner's?"

Miriam had heard about the restaurant that only served dairy dishes but had never eaten there. "It sounds wonderful."

When they entered the restaurant, the young waiter waved at Jacob and pointed to a table near the front. "Do you know that man?" she asked as Jacob helped her get seated and took the chair opposite her.

"That's Max, my roommate. He usually waits tables here during the day, but he is working extra shifts, so he can pay for the next semester of law school."

Coming up behind them, Max clapped Jacob on the back. "I heard my name, and he'd better be saying good things about me." Tall, with black wavy hair and dark, piercing eyes, Max took Miriam's hand. "I am so glad to finally meet you, though Jacob talks about you so much I feel like I already know you."

Jacob buried his face in a menu. "Guilty as charged."

"Spoken like a true lawyer-to-be," chided Max. "I know Jacob will have the potato *latkes* and coffee, but what can I get you, Miriam."

"Cheese blintzes, please. With sour cream. And a cup of tea."

"Excellent choice. I see *mademoiselle* has a gourmet palate."

While they waited for their order, Miriam and Jacob watched as Max chatted with the other customers. "He certainly is a charmer," said Miriam.

"Oh, indeed he is. There is a long line of heartbroken women to prove it."

"He sounds like my father's friend Yuri." Miriam grew wistful. "The women loved him, and he loved the women, but he never wanted to settle down. I had a mad crush on him. I'd convinced myself that he was waiting for me to grow up so we could marry. Silly, I know." Her voice trailed off and she looked down at her folded hands.

"I don't think it's silly at all. When I was in grade school I had a crush on one of my teachers. When I found out she was married, I was heartbroken."

"She probably had six kids at home too," said Max, who had a talent for suddenly appearing out of nowhere. "I hate to break up this romantic interlude, but here you go," he said, placing their meals on the table. "I wish I could say it was on the house, but ...." He shrugged his shoulders and nodded toward the kitchen.

They ate slowly, enjoying the food and each other's company. They talked of family and exchanged stories about leaving Russia and how bewildering everything was when they first got to America.

"I was seasick almost from the moment I stepped on the ship," said

Jacob, shuddering at the memory. "I really thought I was going to die. A young woman also travelling by herself kept putting cold rags on my head. She must have had a stomach of iron, because she never got sick. She kept telling me I had to get better and be strong or they wouldn't let me into America. I think I was so frightened at the thought of being sent back to Russia that I willed myself better. We left the ship together but when we landed on Ellis Island, we were separated. I only knew her first name was Anna and I never got to thank her for her many kindnesses. Actually, for saving my life."

"I don't know how you made that trip by yourself. It must have been terrifying."

"I wish I could tell you how brave I was, but I was so scared. I started making deals with God: If I live through this I will be a better person. If I live through this I will do good things for others. If I live through this I will be a better Jew. He delivered me to America, and now I am trying to make good on my promises."

They were standing at the door to Miriam's apartment saying goodnight when an elderly man emerged from the apartment across the hall. Wearing a tattered robe that exposed a chest covered with thick gray hair, he brushed by Jacob and headed for the bathroom down the hall.

Miriam cringed. "We really need to find a better place to meet."

Jacob laughed. "It just adds to the romantic atmosphere." He moved closer to Miriam. "I hope you enjoyed the evening as much as I did."

"I did. I'm sorry to see it end."

"Me too." He leaned down and gently pressed his lips to hers.

CHAPTER 45

September 1909

Chumsky's Diner became Jacob and Miriam's regular stop on the way home from the union meetings at Ida's apartment. Spotting the couple as they entered the restaurant, the elderly owner reached into the display case for two cheese Danish. Delighted as always to see the young couple, he smiled as he brought the pastries to their usual table near the window. "Your coffee is coming right up," he said, his ruddy cheeks bright against his pale skin.

Jacob helped Miriam remove her jacket. "Amazing how predictable we are," he said.

"I think it's kind of sweet that he remembers what we order."

"I guess," said Jacob, looking impatiently for Mr. Chumsky and their cups of coffee.

"Something is wrong, isn't it? You have been distracted all evening."

Jacob ran his hand across his face. "Nothing is wrong. I just think we need to move beyond the small meetings to a large gathering. There were only three attendees tonight, and I could see how hesitant they were to commit to joining the union. Coming together with a large group of women with common concerns will help to motivate workers, make them realize there is strength in numbers and an organization willing to help them."

Mr. Chumsky approached the table, and sensing they were deep in a serious conversation, he placed the cups of coffee on the table and left without stopping to chat as he usually did.

Jacob waited until they were alone again and continued. "Last month about fifteen hundred tailors went out on strike and got shorter hours and a twenty percent wage increase. The ILGWU's Waistmaker's Local 25 has conducted successful strikes at some of the smaller shirtwaist factories. There is so much unrest out there, that I think now is time to move things along. I want to have a large meeting, so workers can hear from Clara Lemlich, one of the founders of the local, about what the union can help them accomplish. She works at Leiserson's factory, which is almost as bad as the Triangle, so she's one of them. She is small—only about five feet tall—but she isn't afraid to stand up to the bosses or the authorities."

"Look how excited you are. Should I be jealous of this tiny girl?"

Jacob stared at her in confusion. "No, why should you be?" His eyes widened in recognition. "Oh, you're kidding. Right?"

Miriam broke into a smile. "Of course I'm kidding. It's just that you haven't been this enthusiastic about anything in days."

Shamefaced, Jacob stirred his coffee and took a sip before speaking. "I'm sorry. I know I get carried away. But I really think it's time for the next step."

"I suppose you are right. But don't forget how much these girls risk to attend meetings."

"Believe me, I think about it every day. It can get rough out there. Clara was attacked and beaten last week while picketing Leiserson's. She and some of the other strikers were assaulted by thugs hired by the employers to break up the picket line."

Miriam closed her eyes. It never occurred to her that there could be more at risk than losing her job.

More than one hundred Triangle Shirtwaist workers attended a secret meeting at Beethoven Hall to hear members of ILGWU's Local 25 and the Women's Trade Union League speak about workers' needs and the union's goals. Fearing employer-hired spies, Jacob stood near the entrance watching for anyone who looked out of place, while the shirtwaist workers filed into the vast auditorium.

As the women took their seats, Miriam joined Jacob at the back of the room. "You look worried," she said. "I thought you would be elated. It's a bigger crowd than we expected."

"No, this is good. I just want to be sure that there is no one here who shouldn't be. I don't want to let these women down."

Unsettled by Jacob's concerns, Miriam walked toward the front and scanned the crowd. She caught sight of Ambra and Osna, but it was Rivka's face she was looking for and did not find. Their last conversation about attending the meeting had not gone well. They'd arranged for Avrum and Jacob to meet the previous Sunday. The couples talked easily as they strolled through Washington Square, enjoying the crisp fall day until the discussion turned to the upcoming meeting at Beethoven Hall. Rivka bridled at the mere mention of the union. Hands on her hips, she was quick to tell Jacob the she did not want to be associated with "this folly that will cost us all our jobs." Disappointed, but not surprised by Rivka's absence, Miriam joined Ambra and Osna in the audience as the union representatives took the stage.

The crowd was respectful and listened intently as the speakers described the ways the union could protect them. But it was the diminutive Clara Lemlich who held them rapt. Like them, she had suffered the long hours, poor wages and indignities of the sweatshop. She had been on picket lines that got results. When she'd finished speaking, there was a moment of silence and then thunderous applause filled the hall.

Jacob brought Miriam over to meet Clara after the speeches. Up close, the young woman looked frail, her eyes weary. Miriam could make out a yellow area on her cheek where a bruise was in the final stages of healing. Despite her injuries and fatigue, her passion for the rights of the workers was undeniable.

"I think I should be jealous of Miss Lemlich, after all," Miriam said later, as they walked toward her apartment.

Jubilant over the meeting turnout and the enthusiasm of the crowd, Jacob drew Miriam close and kissed her. "I promise you have no need to be jealous, but she was incredible, wasn't she?"

"She was. I watched the women around me and they were nodding in agreement as she spoke. They could tell she identified with them. Local 25 is one hundred people stronger because of her, I am sure."

Jacob's tone turned somber. "Now we have to hope that word did not get out about the meeting. The crowd was bigger than I expected, and I don't have a lot of faith in a group that size keeping it quiet."

The following morning, after shop-floor spies brought word of the meeting to Harris and Blanck, one hundred fifty workers who had attended the meeting or who were suspected of being union sympathizers were laid off. Salutsky, his face scarlet with rage, seemed to be everywhere, first pushing the terrified workers toward the freight elevator and then screaming at the remaining seamstresses to get to work. Rivka clung to Angie as Miriam, Osna, Ambra, and dozens of girls from the ninth floor were roughly escorted from the building.

As soon as word of trouble at the Triangle factory reached ILGWU's headquarters, Jacob raced to the factory to assure the laid-off workers the union was on their side. As he calmed the anxious and crying young women leaving the building, his eyes swept the crowd for sight of Miriam. He spotted Osna walking in a daze and ran to her.

"More girls am coming in to take our jobs when we am pushed out," she said, bursting into tears.

Jacob put his arm around her. "We will help you get through this, and we are going to get your jobs back, I promise. I need to find Miriam—have you seen her?"

Osna wiped away her tears. "She am coming down on the stairs, not in the elevator."

"Are you okay to go home?"

"I am good. You go to Miriam."

Kissing Osna on the forehead, Jacob made his way to the Greene Street entrance. His body tensed when he spied Miriam bent over and leaning against the building.

"Are you all right? Did they hurt you?" he said, rushing to help her.

"I'm fine. Just out of breath. I couldn't wait to get out of there and took the stairs too fast. I am so glad to see you," she said, as he enveloped her in his arms.

"How bad was it up there?"

"They were waiting for us. I think they knew about the meeting before it was even over. They already have new girls to take our place."

"I know. Osna told me."

"Thank God, Rivka and Angie still have their jobs. I was sure that just being my friend would get them fired. But I am so worried about the others. They need their jobs."

"We are holding a meeting this afternoon. If they are firing out of one door and hiring through another, there is reason to strike the Triangle."

Worried about how her parents would take the news of the lockout, Miriam slowly climbed the stairs to her apartment. She had no idea how long it would last or how long she would go without a salary. The hardships of the factory shutdown two years ago still fresh in her mind, she hesitated before opening the door.

"Thank God you are all right," cried Sadie, holding on to Miriam.

"We heard there was violence at the factory. That it had to do with the union," said Meyer.

Stunned by how fast news of the lockout had traveled, Miriam freed herself from her mother's arms. "I am fine. How did you hear about the trouble at the Triangle?"

"We were at the pushcart market. Papa was talking to Oscar when one of his customers told him her daughter was home because she had been forced to leave the factory for going to the meeting last night. We came right home expecting to find you here. What happened?"

Describing the scene on the ninth floor, Miriam fought back her tears. "It could be a while until I get paid again. The union will provide some funds, but I don't think it will be enough. How will we manage?"

Sadie shrugged and put her arm through Meyer's. "We've managed before, and we will manage again."

CHAPTER 46

October 1909

The Triangle workers gathered at ILGWU headquarters. Some were eager to take to the picket line. Others were so terrified they could not speak. Jacob circulated among them, offering reassurances and instructions.

Their job as picketers, he told them, was to do "sentry duty" before the doors of the Triangle factory opened and again at the end of the day when the workers left. They were there to tell the strikebreakers who entered and left the building that they were striking the Triangle and to ask them to come to union headquarters to find out more about the reasons for the strike.

Standing before the assembled strikers, Jacob made it clear that what was most important was their safety. "Don't walk in groups of more than two or three. Don't stand still in front of the factory. Instead, walk up and down the block. Don't stop the person you want to talk to, rather walk alongside of her as you are talking. Don't put your hand on the person you are talking to or touch anyone's clothing because it could be considered assault. Don't call anyone a scab or use abusive language. Finally, if you are arrested, take down the badge number of the policeman and get the information to the union officers."

The crowd fell silent and Miriam could see the fear on the faces of the young women. "Why would we get arrested?" shouted someone from the back.

Jacob frowned. The image of Clara Lemlich's bruised face clear in his mind. "If you follow my instructions, you should be fine. But I am not going to lie to you. The strikebreakers will try to antagonize you and pull you into an altercation. The police will be there, but they are not there to protect you. They will be looking for reasons to arrest you. Don't fall into their trap."

The following morning, one hundred fifty girls arrived at the Triangle factory well before the factory opened. Dressed in their best clothes and wearing wide-brimmed hats, they took up their picket signs, assembled in groups of two or three, and walked slowly up and down the block, ready and waiting for the work day to begin.

Miriam, Osna, and Ambra fell in behind the other girls and chatted nervously. When a lone worker walked toward the Greene Street entrance, Miriam called out to her, "Triangle workers are striking for shorter hours and increased wages. Come to union headquarters tonight to find out more about what we are doing and how we can help you."

Eyes down, the young woman ignored Miriam and hurried into the building.

"I know her," said Ambra. "She works on the eighth floor. I have no respect for the girls who stay after the way we were treated."

Miriam thought of Rivka and how badly she needed her job. "Some of the girls have families here and back home who depend on them. We should not hold that against them."

Before Ambra could respond, Osna stopped so abruptly, Miriam bumped into her. "Oy, look who am here," she said, pointing at the two chauffeur-driven cars pulling up in front of the Asch Building.

The picketers slowed and watched as Isaac Harris and Max Blanck emerged from the shiny black vehicles. Adjusting his bowler hat and buttoning his wool coat against the fall chill, Blanck paused and surveyed the women with disdain. Harris came up behind him and together they walked slowly toward the building, ignoring the picketing women, smirks pasted on their faces.

"Bastards," cried out one of the strikers. "Rot in hell," yelled another.

Miriam watched as the indignity of their treatment by the owners erased all timidity among the strikers. To her delight, Harris and Blanck's disregard for their workers had energized and emboldened the women instead of frightening them into submission. As workers begin filing into the Greene Street entrance, the picketers called out to them with new intensity.

"Don't go in," they yelled. "There is a strike going on. Let us help you."

Despite their fervor, the women were largely ignored, and the workers passed into the factory without incident. As start time grew nearer, Rivka was among the last group to arrive for work. Making eye contact with Miriam, she shook her head and mouthed, "I'm sorry."

As Rivka passed by her, Miriam reached out and squeezed her hand. It broke her heart to be on the opposite side of the strike from Rivka. She would miss seeing her friend every day and even now, when they were together there was an undercurrent of tension as they skirted any mention of the lockout.

Lost in thought, Miriam failed to notice the two policemen eyeing the picket line from across the street. Ambra nudged her and pointed in their direction. "We've got company."

Casting a glance in their direction, Miriam was struck by what an odd-looking pair they were. The shorter of the two was thin and sported a large black mustache that extended past his lip and curled up at the edges, giving him a sinister look. The other was large, almost giant-like, with a smooth baby face that belied his size. When they crossed the street and approached the picket line, Miriam walked toward them, aware that the other girls were watching her.

"Good morning, officers," she said, forcing a smile. "Can I help you?"

"Good morning, miss," said the tall one, touching his hat, but remaining stony-faced. "We are here to be certain there are no disturbances."

"That's very nice of you to make sure we are protected," said Miriam trying to keep the sarcasm out of her voice.

The shorter policeman—Officer Gallo, according to the nameplate above his badge—smirked and began striking his billy club against his palm. "I'm sure Mr. Harris and Mr. Blanck will find that very funny. Right, Boyle?"

"Yeah, they'll think it's hysterical." One hand on the handle of his gun, he stepped so close to Miriam she could feel his hot breath on her cheek. "Just make sure you whores don't make any trouble."

Miriam stared wide-eyed at the big man. "What did you say?"

"You heard me, lady. No trouble," sneered Boyle, revealing a row of gray, crooked teeth.

Osna grabbed Miriam's arm and pulled her away. "You not want to be making policemens mad. Come, time we am going anyway."

Boyle crossed his arms over his massive chest. "Better listen to your pretty little friend. I would hate to have to drag you off to jail." His hooded eyes narrowed, and his lips curled in a cruel smile.

Shaking with anger and fear, Miriam allowed Osna to lead her away. Taking deep breaths to calm herself, she knew her friend was right. Antagonizing the police would only get her beaten or arrested or both. Gallo and Boyle had as much as admitted they were on Harris and Blanck's payroll and she was certain there would be no justice for the women of Local 25.

The next morning the police were waiting for the striking girls when they arrived at the factory. Gallo and Boyle were joined by two burly men who leered at the young women as they took their places on the picket line. Warned by Jacob the night before that this was a common tactic designed to intimidate and frighten them, they stared straight ahead and marched resolutely in front of the Washington Place and Greene Street entrances.

Keeping an eye on the police, Miriam joined Ambra and Osna on the Greene Street side of the block where groups of familiar faces were streaming into the entrance. Their eyes lowered, the girls rushed to get on the elevator in the hopes of avoiding an encounter with their former co-workers.

"I am not happy to be seeing my friends not wanting to be seeing me," said Osna. "I hope we am doing good here."

Osna's manhandling of the English language always amused Miriam, and she smiled at her young friend. "We are doing good here and what we are doing will help all the girls at the Triangle, even those who aren't with us on the picket line."

"I hope you are right," said Ambra, "because my cousin Angie is not very happy with me. She barely talks to me now."

"I know, and I am sorry." Miriam's voice was drowned out by shouting near the Washington Place entrance.

"Don't touch me!" screamed one of the strikers. Dropping her sign, Miriam ran toward the disturbance, where four women she did not recognize were taunting and laughing at the striking women. As she drew closer, she thought there was something familiar about the thin, dark-haired girl of about twenty, who seemed to be the group's leader. "Can I help you?" Miriam asked her, hoping to ease the tension.

"No, you can't help me," she growled, a heavy Irish accent coating her words. She turned and glared at Miriam.

Miriam stared at the woman's make-up-caked face. "Fiona?" she gasped. "Fiona is that you? I'm Miriam. Miriam Raisky. Remember? From Mrs. Cullen's class."

Sensing that all eyes were on them, Fiona raised her chin in defiance. The nostrils of her sharp nose flared. "Oh, I remember you all right, bitch. You were Mrs. Cullen's little pet. A regular goody-goody," she sneered and spit in Miriam's direction.

Shocked, Miriam looked down at the glob of saliva at her feet and then back at Fiona. "I see that you are well-suited for this work," she said icily.

Taking the sign Ambra handed to her, Miriam reclaimed her place on the picket line. Her face burned with rage as the four women shouted at them and called them whores while the police looked on, grinning obscenely. She slowed her pace, so she could walk beside the others, whispering words of encouragement and urging them to ignore the strikebreakers. She noted with pride that although some had tears in their eyes, all remained on the picket line.

CHAPTER 47

November 1909

Over the next few weeks, the harassment escalated into daily violence. Prostitutes and thugs hired by Harris and Blanck escorted new workers across the picket lines, all under the protection of the New York City police and detectives on the Triangle payroll. Name-calling and jostling gave way to skirmishes and beatings. And while the clashes were provoked by the strikebreakers, only the picketing women were arrested and hauled into court in police wagons. Charged with vagrancy or incitement, they were fined up to ten dollars, more than most earned in a week. Many of the girls were beaten by the arresting officers. Others were made to spend the night in jail, left in cold cells without food or a blanket.

"I'm not sure how much longer we can go on," Miriam told Jacob at the end of a grueling day of picketing in the cold. Unable to control her anger and frustration, Miriam's words tumbled out in a barrage of despair. "The police and the owners' thugs grow more vicious. The girls are tired, and morale is low. They see their families suffering because they are not bringing home a pay envelope. They are called whores and have things thrown at them. We tell them not to fight back, but they are the ones being arrested and beaten. Ambra was hauled in and fined today when one of the scabs pushed her. *She* pushed Ambra! We are out there every day, but we are not seeing any progress."

Jacob pressed his hands to his eyes. "We will make progress, but it will be in small steps at first. The Women's Trade Union League is supporting us now. There are a lot of important women among their members and they are working to bring attention to the terrible conditions in the shirtwaist factories. Their involvement will get the strike into the papers and make the public aware of what we are trying to accomplish."

"I hope you are right. A few of the girls have left the picket line and gone back to work, and I am afraid more will follow."

It was Friday before sundown and they were standing in front of Miriam's apartment. Jacob was joining Miriam and her parents for *Shabbat* dinner for the first time. "I am more worried about dinner with your parents than I am about the success of the strike," said Jacob, hoping to lighten Miriam's mood.

"I can promise you that you won't be called names or arrested, but I can't promise that my father won't hound you with questions again," said Miriam, a smile flickering across her face.

"Seriously, I am looking forward to dinner. I just hope your mother didn't go to too much trouble. I know it's been hard for them since the strike began."

"My mother has been talking about you coming to dinner for days. It won't be anything fancy, but it will be delicious."

Sadie accepted the box of pastries Jacob brought, with a hug. When Meyer gave him a hearty handshake, Jacob felt the tension leave his body. Taking a deep breath, he inhaled the aroma of roasted chicken. "Everything smells so good. It reminds me of my mother's kitchen on *Shabbat* when I was little," he said, taking a yarmulke from his coat pocket and placing it on his head.

Sadie blushed with pleasure and gestured toward the silver candlesticks set out on the small kitchen counter. She covered her head with her shawl and lit the *Shabbat* candles. Holding her hands over her eyes, she recited the ancient prayer that welcomed the peace and sanctity of the Sabbath. "Blessed are you, Lord our God, King of the universe, who has sanctified us with his commandments, and commanded us to kindle the light of the holy *Shabbat*."

Jacob stood transfixed, carried back to his childhood before his parents and sister died. Standing there with Miriam and her family, he felt a deep sadness for all he had lost.

"*Shabbat Shalom*," said Sadie, kissing him on the cheek.

"*Shabbat Shalom*," he responded, his voice laced with emotion.

"Time to eat," proclaimed Meyer. "I'm hungry."

Sadie rolled her eyes and directed everyone to the kitchen table set with a plain white tablecloth and the few good dishes that had journeyed with them from Kishinev. At the center of the table were a freshly baked challah and cups of wine. Meyer said the blessings over each, and after sipping their wine and eating a piece of the bread, Sadie filled their plates with chicken and potatoes and the fresh green beans Avrum brought her from the wholesale market. They sat elbow-to-elbow around the small table, enjoying the meal and conversation. Miriam slipped her hand under the tablecloth and into Jacob's hand as he patiently answered Meyer's many questions about his job at the ILGWU, including those he had forgotten he'd asked him before.

"I agree that the strike is necessary to help the girls get better working conditions," Meyer said. "But I worry about Miriam's safety as well as the other girls'. My friend Oscar told me that there has been violence on the picket line. That some of the girls have been arrested and beaten."

Miriam's eyes darted from her father to Jacob. She could see that Jacob was struggling with what to tell Meyer.

After a long pause, he said, "We are always concerned about the safety of the young women when there is a strike. I can assure you the ILGWU is doing everything it can to protect them."

If Meyer was wise to Jacob's evasive answer, he did not let on. "Just make sure my daughter is safe," he cautioned.

"Mr. Raisky, I am doing everything I can to ensure just that."

"Good, because we have already lost one child."

Eli's sudden presence filled the room. Caught off guard, Miriam could feel her eyes well with tears. Jacob released her hand and lowered his eyes. Sadie swallowed hard and rose from the table while Meyer, his eyes hollow, seemed to retreat to another time and place.

Taking a moment to calm herself, Sadie lit the stove to boil water for tea and placed a plate of the pastries Jacob brought on the table. "Tea will be ready in a few minutes, and then we can have dessert," she said, breaking the heavy silence that engulfed the room.

At the sound of Sadie's voice, the far-away look disappeared from

Meyer's face. Smiling at his wife, he placed a Danish on his plate.

Steering the conversation to a lighter topic, Sadie reminded Miriam that they were going to Malka's Sunday afternoon to celebrate Rebecca's eighth birthday. "Rivka will be there too. Jacob, why don't you join us?"

"I would love to," said Jacob. "It will be good to see Avrum again and meet his family."

Flurries were falling when Miriam and Jacob stepped out onto the steps to her apartment. The moon was hidden behind a veil of thick clouds, and the lightly falling snow was visible in the streetlight's eerie yellow glow. Cupping her hands to catch the tiny flakes, Miriam smiled and nestled into Jacob's arms.

"I like this," he said, breathing in her sweet scent. He brought her face to his and kissed her. "Are you okay? I could see how upset you got when you father mentioned your brother." He brushed away a snowflake that had settled on Miriam's cheek.

"It's funny. I think about him every day, but I still get emotional when we talk about him. It's been five years since he was killed, but it still feels raw. And I still miss him."

Jacob stared silently into the shadows of the dimly lit street. When he finally spoke, his voice was low and raspy. "People say that you stop missing your loved ones after a time. But I don't think it ever goes away. I miss my parents and sister every day, and they have been gone for years. I still see their faces at night before I drift off to sleep. I fear the day will come when I won't remember what they looked like."

Her heart aching for him, Miriam pulled him close. Jacob bent to kiss her, first gently and then, unleashing feelings he had held inside for so long, he kissed her with a hunger that surprised both of them. When he pulled away, he was filled with shame.

"I am so sorry. I shouldn't have done that. Please forgive me."

"Shh," she said, holding her fingertips to his lips. "Kiss me again."

CHAPTER 48

After two days of on-and-off snow, the sun shone brightly, delivering a glorious Sunday in November. Waiting for Miriam and her parents in front of Avrum's deli, Jacob stood in the warming sun, his thoughts lingering on their parting Friday night. He loved her. Now he was certain Miriam loved him too. His happiness spilling over, he laughed out loud and feeling foolish looked around hoping no one heard him. To his embarrassment, he found Avrum grinning back at him.

"What's so funny, my friend?"

Jacob could feel his ears grow hot, a sure sign that he was blushing. "You are looking at a happy man, that's all."

Avrum's grin grew wider. "Does my beautiful cousin have anything to do with that happiness?"

Jacob's grin matched Avrum's. "You are a very perceptive man."

"I just know the feeling." Clapping Jacob on the back, Avrum pointed down the street. "Well, here she comes. How are you doing with my uncle? He is very protective of Miriam."

"I know he is. Miriam told me about the pogrom and her brother's death, so I understand why. She also told me about her father's injury."

"He's a good man. I wish you could have known him before the accident. He was a hard worker, and he was always ready to stand up for what he believed in. It's been difficult for him to accept his limitations and his dependence on Miriam and my aunt. But even with his injury, he is the kind of father I always wished I had."

"Miriam adores him, and that's good enough for me."

"Smart man," said Avrum. As Miriam and her parents approached, he spread his arms to receive the warm embraces of his aunt and uncle. Then, stepping in front of Jacob, he hugged Miriam. "Family first," he laughed.

"Only because you are bigger than me," Jacob said good-naturedly, as he took Miriam's hand.

"Let's go upstairs. Rivka is with Mama and the kids, and Ira will close the deli soon," said Avrum, leading them to the building's side entrance and up the stairs to the apartment.

Stepping into the tiny flat, they were greeted with more hugs and kisses. After meeting the rest of Avrum's family, Jacob remained near the door under the scrutiny of Esther's big brown eyes.

"My name is Esther. What's your name?"

"It's nice to meet you, Esther. My name is Jacob."

The child held up one hand, her fingers spread wide. "I'm this many years old."

"You're five! You are such a big girl, I thought you were older. Can you guess how old I am?"

Studying his face, Esther giggled and held up both her hands.

"Close," said Jacob, his eyes twinkling.

Looking very pleased with herself, Esther took Jacob's hand and led him into the crowded front room to join the others. "This is Jacob and I like him," she announced to ripples of laughter.

"I think Miriam likes him too," Avrum called out and suffered a slap on the arm from Rivka.

Miriam looked across the room at Jacob. He was gazing back at her, his head tilted, his eyes questioning. Miriam smiled and nodded slowly.

Sadie joined Malka in the kitchen and set the table while Malka put candles on the cake she'd baked for Rebecca's birthday. It pleased Sadie to see her sister looking so well. Malka's eyes were clear, and her complexion was a healthy pink. Taking advantage of their few moments alone, they talked easily as they worked.

"I cannot get over how big Esther has gotten. She is adorable. Rebecca too," said Sadie.

"They are really such good girls. Rebecca is like Esther's second mother. Whenever Esther needs comforting, it's Rebecca she runs to."

"I can see that Avrum is happier these days, and he is obviously crazy about Rivka. How are Ira and Sonia?"

"Ira is doing well. He likes being in the deli and interacting with the customers. The young girls certainly seem to like him. Sonia I am not so sure about. Now that Rebecca and Esther are older and don't need to be watched so closely, she is doing more contract work. She's made friends with some of the young women she met in the park and they go out together some evenings. She's nineteen but does not talk about meeting any young men. You and I were already married at her age." Malka paused and lowered her eyes. "Of course, look what happened to me."

"What happened is that you have five wonderful children."

"That was the only good thing Lazar ever did." said Malka, placing the cake in the center of the table a little harder than she intended to. "Speaking of marriage, Jacob seems like a very nice young man."

"I agree, but it's too early to talk about marriage. We are still getting to know him. He seems to be honest and hard-working. Meyer likes him, and he is obviously quite taken with Miriam."

"And from the way Miriam's face lights up every time she looks at him, I'd say she feels the same."

"Did I just hear my name?" asked Miriam as she came into the kitchen.

"You did. I was just telling your mama how much I liked Jacob."

Miriam beamed. "Well, you're not the only one. Esther has not let go of his hand since we got here."

"A man who is that good with children will make a wonderful husband," teased Malka.

"So I've heard," said Miriam gleefully. "I'm going downstairs to get Ira. Rebecca keeps asking for her cake, and I don't think we can hold her off much longer."

A tap on her shoulder made Miriam whirl around into Ira's welcoming arms. "Here I am," he said, hugging his cousin so hard he lifted her off her feet.

"I'm sorry I'm late," said Ira after kissing his mother and aunt. "Mr. Teich came into the store as I was closing up, and along with his usual order, he wanted to talk. He's been so lonely since his wife died I didn't have the heart to rush him out. He wanted to know how you were doing, Mama. Actually, he asked a lot of questions about you."

"Oh no," said Malka, wagging her finger in Ira's face. "Do not encourage him. The last thing I need in my life is another man looking for someone to take care of him."

Ira held his hands up in surrender. "Okay, okay. I promise, no more Mama-talk with Mr. Teich."

While the others enjoyed birthday cake, Miriam and Rivka sought the quiet of the front room to catch up. "I miss you," said Miriam.

"I feel the same way. I can't tell you how hard it is for me to cross the picket line. It hurts me to see you and the other girls out in the cold and being treated so badly. Is it true Ambra was roughed up and arrested?"

"She was. She was scared, but not really hurt. ILGWU lawyers arranged for her fine, so she wasn't in jail for very long. I saw it happen. In fact, I know the girl who pushed her. Fiona, the girl I told you about who sat next to me in Mrs. Cullen's class. I'm told she is a prostitute. I wonder what happened to her that led her to such a life."

"Like a lot of us, she probably found out the hard way that America was not the land of instant riches it was said to be."

"Rivka, please do not feel badly about not joining the strike. I know it's been hard for you with your father out of work."

"But I feel like such a traitor. The other girls must hate me."

Rivka looked so miserable it broke Miriam's heart. "They certainly do not. So how are you and Avrum doing?"

"We are good. We are better than good; we are great! Don't say anything yet, but we are talking about getting married. Avrum is working on his plans to add a small eating area to the deli to increase business. Ira will be his partner. He wants to be able to support us and his mother and sisters too."

Miriam hugged Rivka, a lump forming in her throat. "I am so happy for you. I know I am biased about my cousin, but Avrum is a very special man."

CHAPTER 49

Uncertain if it was her talk with Jacob or mere coincidence that brought the two women to Greene Street on Monday morning, Miriam was nonetheless elated to see Ida and a blonde, well-dressed woman walking near the picket line. The two women stepped off the sidewalk into the street to make their way toward her.

"Ida, whatever brought you here, I am so glad to see you."

Ida hugged her friend and introduced her companion. "Miriam, this is Mary Dreier, president of the Women's Trade Union League. The League is backing us in our strike against the Triangle."

"Thank you so much for coming and for your help. I'm afraid we are not making as much progress as we'd hoped. Harris and Blanck aren't budging."

"Don't get discouraged. You are doing all the right things," she said in heavily accented English. Then, distracted by an approaching worker, she called out to the large woman who pushed her way through the picket line. "We are striking the Triangle factory for better hours and wages. Please don't go to work there."

The strikebreaker made an obscene gesture and calling Mary a bitch, kept walking toward the Greene Street entrance. Within minutes another woman approached the building. This time, Mary stepped forward and urged her not to cross the picket line. The girl's hand balled into a fist and before anyone could react, she hit Mary in the chest, propelling her backwards.

Miriam's shock turned to unease as a policeman crossed the street toward them.

"What's going on here? You wouldn't be interfering with the workers, would you?" he asked Mary, his eyes stormy, his body language broadcasting his eagerness for a confrontation.

"No, Officer, I was merely informing the young lady that we are here to get better working conditions for the employees of the Triangle Shirtwaist Factory," replied Mary, her voice remaining soft and steady. "That's when she took it upon herself to accost me."

The picket line came to a standstill, all eyes on the frail-looking woman in the fancy clothes, and the snarling policeman.

"Not so," sneered the woman, her lips drawn tight in defiance. "The bitch hit me."

"Hit you, did she? Come on, lady, you're coming with me," the policeman said, roughly seizing Mary by the arm.

Ida stepped forward to protest. "Do you know who this is?"

"I don't care if she is the Queen of England. She's taking a ride to the station house and if you're not careful, you can join her."

Holding herself erect, Mary remained calm. "You know what to do," she said to Ida as she was led away to a police wagon.

Miriam pulled Ida back. "We are better able to help her if we stay out of jail."

By the time Mary arrived at the police station, a lawyer representing the Women's Trade Union League was waiting for her. The precinct lieutenant told Mary the arrest was a mistake, a misunderstanding by the arresting officer, and that she was free to go. Mary did not file a complaint against the officer, but she made sure to talk to a reporter for *The New York Times* as she left the building.

The next morning, New Yorkers learned that Mary Elizabeth Dreier, daughter of wealthy business leader Theodore Dreier and the president of the Women's Trade Union League, had been arrested for talking to a strikebreaker in front of the Triangle Shirtwaist Factory. In her interview she recounted the many times that the police—whom she had been saying for months were in the employ of the Triangle owners—had roughed up and arrested the striking women. The article galvanized the wealthy and influential members of the WTUL.

Despite the news coverage, there was no let-up in the violence directed at the striking workers. Arrests continued, and unlike the treatment Mary Dreier received, the immigrant women on the lines were hauled before judges who had little sympathy for the cause. Workers in garment factories all around the city were talking about the treatment of the Triangle strikers and taking notice of the unions' tireless efforts on their behalf.

On November 22, the Women's Trade Union League and Local 25 of the International Ladies Garment Workers Union convened a meeting in the Great Hall of Cooper Union. All garment industry workers had been encouraged to attend, and thousands crowded into the union building, overflowing into the aisles and streaming onto the street. The purpose of the meeting was to vote on a proposal to call an industry-wide strike against the city's nearly five hundred shirtwaist manufacturers.

Miriam and Jacob were joined by Ida, Ambra, and Osna, and over the course of two hours, they listened to speaker after speaker offer support while cautioning against a general strike.

Miriam shifted uncomfortably in her seat. "Is this what you expected?" she whispered to Jacob.

"No, but I'm not exactly surprised, either. They are the union's old guard. There has never been a general strike in the garment industry, and I think the idea terrifies them."

"And they are mostly men," added Ida. "They say they understand our complaints, but I wonder if they really do."

A rumble of voices rose from behind them. Miriam turned to see Clara Lemlich threading her way through the throng of people. Walking determinedly toward the stage, she shouted in Yiddish, "I want to say a few words."

The crowded hall began to cheer as Clara Lemlich approached the podium and spoke to the large crowd from her heart. *"I am a working girl, one of those who are on strike against intolerable conditions. I am tired of listening to speakers who would talk in general terms. What we are here for is to decide whether we shall or shall not strike. I offer a resolution that a general strike be declared—now."*

The response was thunderous. The audience was on its feet, cheering for the small girl with the big voice. The vote for a general strike was unanimous.

The following day, fifteen thousand shirtwaist-makers walked out of

the factories in the New York's garment district, striking for a twenty percent pay raise, a fifty-two-hour work week, safer working conditions, overtime pay and union representation. Meetings were held in English, Italian,
and Yiddish in union halls around the city to make plans for picketing. By
the next day, five thousand more walked off their jobs to become a part of
what became known as "The Uprising of Twenty Thousand."

CHAPTER 50

On the second morning of the general strike, Miriam found Rivka waiting for her at their usual corner. "Aren't you cold standing out here in the wind?" asked Miriam, as if Rivka's presence were no surprise.

"If you'll have me, I am ready to go on the picket line," said Rivka. "I'm sorry it took me so long to join you."

"You do not have to apologize, and of course we'll have you. I want to warn you, though, it gets rough. The scabs are nasty and get physical. They are being paid to pick fights, and the police look the other way."

"If I can put up with Salutsky's temper and wandering hands, I think I can handle the scabs and cops."

"Just don't let them provoke you. The police are looking for any excuse to arrest us. Our first stop is union headquarters to pick up our placards. If we're lucky, we can get a cup of hot coffee too."

They could hear the women on the picket line before they could see them. Marching in front of the Asch Building were hundreds of Triangle strikers, carrying signs and calling out to the owner-hired prostitutes and replacement workers not to work at the Triangle factory. Standing by were dozens of policemen and rough-looking men, waiting to pounce at the first sign of trouble.

"Welcome to the line," said Miriam with a sardonic smile.

Ambra and Osna spotted them as they came toward the picketers. Waving them over, they greeted Rivka with hugs. "We am glad to be seeing you," said Osna. "You am missed."

Rivka smiled, even as her eyes misted over. "I have missed you too," she said, hugging each of them back.

"Here comes Angie," said Ambra pointing down the street. "I wasn't sure she would come. Her parents are not happy about the strike." She called to Angie as she crossed the street in their direction. "It will be so good to be all together again."

After instructing Rivka and Angie about what to do and not to do, they joined the throng of young women carrying placards proclaiming "We Shall Fight Until We Win" and "We Are Striking For Humane Treatment." Others wore sashes that said "Striking Garment Workers" and "Ladies Tailors Strikers."

"Don't forget," said Miriam, "don't let them pull you into a confrontation. Even an exchange of harsh words will get you arrested."

"Just keep walking if one of them starts to bother you, and look straight ahead," added Ambra.

"I not to be saying one word," said Osna. "Those *prostitukes* am making business and meaning it!"

It took only a matter of minutes before the usual harassment escalated. A large group of workers exited the building and began taunting the striking women, calling them whores and pushing them off the sidewalk into the street. One girl fell into a puddle, to the cheers of the strikebreakers. The assembled police quickly moved in for the expected altercation. The young woman rose slowly and inspected the damage to her coat. Steely-eyed, she raised her chin in the direction of her abusers and wordlessly resumed her place on the picket line. The disappointed scabs re-entered the factory, and the police returned to their sentry post, clearly unhappy that there would be no arrests at the Triangle that morning.

As the day wore on, the wind grew stronger, and the temperature dropped to below freezing. By the time the picketers returned for the end-of-day shift, a bank of dark clouds had drifted over the sun, snuffing out its warming rays.

Osna shivered, her thin coat no match for the biting cold. "Tomorrow I to be wearing more sweaters under my coat," she stammered through chattering teeth. "And mittens."

Miriam took the sign from Osna's freezing hands. "Go home. The day is almost over anyway. We'll all be here tomorrow."

Osna snatched the sign back from Miriam and stared at her in defiance. "I not be leaving," she said with such determination that Miriam knew it was useless to argue with her tiny friend. They joined the others just as the scabs and replacement workers began leaving the factory.

"Here we go," said Miriam, as they raised their signs and walked toward the Greene Street exit.

Pacing the sidewalk with Rivka, Miriam watched cautiously for any signs of trouble. Most of the women who crossed the picket line looked away as they left the building, clearly not interested in an encounter. Some hurled vile and insulting names at the striking women, while others pushed and shoved their way through the line, but no altercations took place. Just as Miriam was beginning to think they might finally have a day without an arrest on the Triangle line, she spied Fiona, trailed by two other menacing-looking women, heading their way.

"This is not going to be good," she said to Rivka. "That's Fiona in the red skirt. Don't let her or her friends get to you."

The three women came striding toward Miriam, their faces hard as stone. "Hey, bitch," called Fiona, "you looking for trouble?"

Miriam remained silent. Ambra, Angie, and Osna looked on in fear.

Fiona and her accomplices surrounded Miriam. Drawing so near that Miriam could smell the prostitute's stale sweat and cheap perfume, Fiona poked her in the shoulder. "You and your whore friends will stop this and get back to work if you know what is good for you."

Miriam smiled slowly and remained silent.

"Okay, have it your way," said Fiona, pushing Miriam into one of the strikebreakers standing behind her.

"Help! She pushed me. She attacked me!" shrieked the scab, pointing at Miriam.

"Now who's smiling?" smirked Fiona as a policeman grabbed Miriam by the shoulder and spun her around.

Shaking with anger, Miriam found herself face-to-face with Officer Boyle. The burly cop squinted at her and a smile of recognition crossed his face.

"Well, what do you know? It's the little redhead with the big mouth. I think this time you and me are going to make a trip down to the station."

He seized Miriam by both shoulders and shook her so hard her hat tumbled from her head. Fueled by fury and instinct, Miriam yanked free from his grasp. Enraged, Boyle slapped her across her face. A small cut appeared on her cheek where his ring bit into her flesh. The metallic taste of blood filled her mouth. Ignoring her own counsel not to antagonize the police, she spit in the direction of his feet, leaving tiny red specks clinging to his boots.

In a blind fury, Boyle grabbed her by her hair and yanked her head back, his face scarlet with rage. "You little whore," he bellowed, raising his hand again.

"Leave her alone," screamed Rivka, advancing toward the big cop, despite Ambra's attempts to hold her back.

Miriam gasped and tried to signal Rivka to stay quiet. It was bad enough that she had been so reckless and defied Boyle, but now Rivka would pay the price as well.

"If you love this bitch so much, I am happy to oblige and bring you down to the station too," said Boyle, clutching Rivka's arm in a vise-like grip. "You two are getting a free ride to jail. And you," he said pointing to Fiona and the woman who claimed she was attacked, "need to press charges." As the other strikers watched helplessly, Boyle dragged Miriam and Rivka to the police wagon.

"We need to be getting Jacob," said Osna.

By the time they reached the station, Miriam's left eye was swollen and turning frightening shades of purple and blue. Blood from the cut on her cheek had dripped down her face and clotted. Rivka tried to clean it, but Miriam stopped her.

"Let them see what that bastard cop did to me," she said harshly. Softening her tone, she took Rivka's hand. "That was a very brave, but very dumb thing you did back there." Then she added, "I am terrified, and I am so glad you are here with me. I just hope Jacob can get us out of here quickly."

The police wagon came to a sudden stop. They were roughly hauled out of the vehicle and into the station. Shoved into a dimly lit cell with five other women they instantly knew had not been arrested for picketing, they gagged at the stench of sour sweat, alcohol, and urine that poured from the lockup.

"Better get used to it," growled a precinct cop when Miriam put her hand to her nose. "You are going to be here for a while." Pushing them further into the cell, he slammed the cell door shut, its deafening clang leaving Miriam and Rivka shivering in fear.

"What's a matter, dearies?" said a drunken woman of undeterminable age who sat sprawled across a filthy bench. "Aren't we good enough to share a cell with you?"

"Yeah, you too good for us?" taunted a skinny, hollow-eyed girl of sixteen or seventeen, her face covered in pustules and scabs.

"Everything is fine," said Miriam, trying to ignore the angry stares of the other inhabitants of the cell.

Hungry and cold, Miriam and Rivka huddled together in a corner. The drunken woman snored loudly from her bench. Across the way a man paced in his cell, stopping only to rattle the bars and spew obscenities. Each time he called out, the skinny girl screeched at him to shut up.

The hours dragged by slowly, and they lost all sense of time. Miriam was tormented by thoughts of her parents and how worried they must be. Her head ached and she could barely see out of her left eye. The stale air clogged her lungs, and she felt like she couldn't breathe. Rivka paced an area of the cell, walking in a small circle.

"All that walking ain't gonna get you out of here any the quicker," croaked an old woman, a mass of stringy gray hair sticking out around her wizened face.

"Let her walk," yelled a woman with sunken eyes and sallow skin. "All that movement will scare off the rats." The woman shrieked with laughter, and Rivka moved closer to Miriam.

"Now you've done it," squealed the skinny girl, as the sound of heavy footsteps echoed in the hallway. "The coppers are coming to give us a hell for making noise."

Two policemen stood in front of the cell. After taking each prisoner's name, they unlocked the door and slid it open. "You ladies are lucky. We have so many of them striking bitches coming in, we need the cell. You're on your way to court."

Jacob and Ida were waiting outside the Jefferson Market Courthouse. His relief at seeing Miriam and Rivka among the next group of women being herded before the judge quickly vanished when he saw Miriam's bruised and swollen face. "It's going to be all right," he shouted as they were marched into the crowded courtroom.

One by one, a steady stream of picketers, prostitutes, and thieves were called up to plead their case. Looking tired and bored and in need of a shave, the judge listened to the accusers and the accused, pulling at his bushy eyebrows when he had heard enough. His sentencing habits quickly became apparent: first-time offenders were fined, and repeat offenders were dispatched to the workhouse on Blackwell's Island—or worse, to the dreaded Tombs prison.

When it was finally their turn, Rivka rose, blinking wildly, and Miriam feared her legs would give out before she reached the bench. Boyle and Fiona also came forward.

"Them two accosted workers leaving the Triangle Shirtwaist Factory," said Boyle, his thumbs tucked into the belt that strained against his huge belly.

"That's right, Judge. She hit me and my friend," said Fiona, pointing at Miriam, "and the other one helped her."

"Ah, Miss Quinn, nice to see you again," said the judge. "Where is your friend who was also accosted?"

Fiona offered the judge a coy smile. "She's working tonight."

"I'm sure she is," he answered, as laughter filled the courtroom.

Banging his gavel and calling for order, the judge peered over his glasses at Miriam and Rivka and tugged at eyebrows that looked like thick black caterpillars. "I assume you are both going to deny that you accosted Miss Quinn and her friend, so I am going to save you the trouble of having to speak. You are fined ten dollars each. You are both free to go, but I do not want to see you in my court again." He brought his gavel down with a quick bang. "Next!"

Avrum pulled Rivka and his cousin into his arms. "Let's get out of here. Jacob and Ida will take care of your fines and meet us outside."

"Avrum, I've got to get home," said Miriam. "My parents will be frantic with worry."

Rivka nodded. "My father will be worried too."

"It's okay. Ambra came to the deli to tell me you'd both been arrested. Rivka, I stopped on the way here and told your father what happened. I sent Ira to tell Aunt Sadie and Uncle Meyer where you were but told him not to tell them you'd been beaten." He kissed Miriam's forehead. "You're not going to be able to hide this from your parents. How badly does it hurt?"

"It hurts, but not as bad as I must look."

"You're still beautiful," said Jacob, taking Miriam into his arms. Feeling safe for the first time since Boyle clapped his massive hand on her shoulder, she held tightly to Jacob.

"I'm so sorry I wasn't at the station. There have been so many arrests today; I was at another courthouse, and it took Osna a while to find me." He took Miriam's battered face in his hands. "Is it true Boyle did this to you?"

When she nodded yes, he exploded, "I will get that bastard. He is known for roughing up the girls. He even brags about it, but the judges just keep looking away."

Miriam took deep breaths of cold air to calm herself. "I know I can't hide this from my parents," she said, gesturing toward her face, "but I would like to get cleaned up before I go home."

"We can stop at my apartment first and you can wash up. Ida said she would stay to pay the fines for the next group of girls coming in, so we can go."

"I am going to take Rivka home," said Avrum, hugging Miriam one more time. "Are you sure you are okay?"

"I am now," she said, taking Jacob's hand.

Jacob's apartment was located above a candy store on Grand street. Still holding Miriam's hand, Jacob led her up three flights of stairs. "Max is home," he said, spotting the light coming from under the door. Entering the sparsely furnished front room, Miriam was struck by how neat it was.

"I was wondering where you were," said Max, emerging from the kitchen. "Oh my God, what happened to you," he gasped, stopping short at the sight of Miriam's battered face. "Are you all right?"

"Other than a bad headache and an obviously grotesque face, I'm okay," said Miriam, giving Max a half-smile.

"That bastard Boyle did this to her. The damn judge looked right at her and never uttered a word," said Jacob. "He told Miriam and Rivka he would 'save them the trouble of speaking,' and fined them ten dollars each. I swear the shirtwaist owners have everyone in the city government on their payroll."

Max nodded. "It seems like it is getting worse. And it's not just the police. I heard they are bringing in thugs from all over New York and New Jersey."

"Just what we need—more strong-arming," said Jacob, as he guided Miriam to a chair in the kitchen. Taking a clean towel from a drawer, he ran cold water over it and gently washed the bloody cut on her cheek.

When he finished, Miriam touched her face and winced. "My parents are going to be so upset."

CHAPTER 51

As soon as they reached the fourth-floor landing, the door to Miriam's apartment flew open. Meyer stared in horror at Miriam's face, and Sadie clapped her hands over her mouth to stifle a scream.

"I'm okay. Mama, Papa, please don't be mad."

"Mad?" thundered Meyer. "Whoever did this to you is a dead man."

A door across the hall opened with a bang. "Quiet," snapped Mr. Katz, their elderly neighbor, scrawny legs peeking out beneath his nightshirt. "We are trying to sleep here, for God's sake."

"We're sorry," murmured Miriam, as Sadie urged them inside.

Still incensed at the beating inflicted on Miriam, Meyer vented his anger on Jacob. "I thought the union was taking care of the girls while they picketed. You said you would keep Miriam safe. Where were you? Where were the police?"

"Papa, it's not Jacob's fault. It was a policeman who hit me."

His breath coming in rapid bursts, Meyer stared at Miriam. "What do you mean, a policeman hit you?"

Sadie placed her hand on Meyer's back. "Calm down. Let me get a cold cloth for Miriam's face, and she can tell us what happened."

With the cloth over her throbbing eye, Miriam related the incident. "It felt like the police knew what was going to happen. They watched the strikebreakers approach us and only came over after one of them pushed me and started yelling that I had accosted her."

"We know there are some cops who are mistreating the striking women," said Jacob. "We've talked to people in the mayor's office about doing something to stop it, but so far we're getting nowhere."

Meyer looked from Jacob to his daughter. "Miriam, you will not return to the picket line. I forbid it."

"Papa, you were the one who told me to stand up for what I believed in. You said we should have stood up against the Jew-haters in Kishinev. Don't you see, this is no different? I will not be frightened away by their bullying."

Meyer glared at Miriam. His lips were drawn tight, his eyes hard and cold. "Do what you want," he said, slamming the bedroom door so hard dishes rattled in the kitchen.

Miriam's face crumpled. Salty tears burned her swollen eye. "Mama, I can't stand that he is so angry at me. Please make him understand that I must do this. I believe in this."

"I think I should leave and let you two talk," said Jacob.

Sadie shook her head. "Please stay. I want to apologize to you for Meyer's outburst. I think you already know how much he loves Miriam. He is obsessed with her safety."

"I understand, Mrs. Raisky. Believe me, I do. I am sick over what happened to Miriam," said Jacob, his face a mirror of Miriam's pain. "We are working with the Women's Trade Union League to make things better. The members are wealthy, and they are willing to use their influence and money to help the strikers."

"But will they stop the beatings?" asked Sadie.

"I wish I could promise you that they will, but I can't." His face grim, he picked up his coat. "Good night," he said, and headed for the door.

Sadie nodded toward Miriam. "Go downstairs with Jacob. Don't take too long. We're not done talking yet."

The wind whipped down Hester Street, stinging their faces. Miriam nestled into Jacob's arms for warmth, resting her head on his shoulder.

Jacob tightened his arms around her. "I wanted to kill Boyle when I saw what he did to you. I hate that I cannot keep it from happening again."

"It was my fault. I let Fiona and those awful women get to me. I won't let it happen again."

"I'm afraid for you. I got you into this, and now I worry every minute you are on the picket line. I am beginning to think your father is right; you should stop picketing. I might be able to find a place for you to work for the union in the office."

Miriam pushed Jacob away. "You did not get me into this. I am doing it because I want the respect and pay I deserve as a worker. I won't leave the line and my friends. I will not let Boyle and Fiona and the owners and their hired thugs scare me away." Glaring at Jacob, she sputtered, "I think you'd better leave before we have our first argument."

"Okay," he said. "I promise. No more talk of you leaving the picket line."

"Don't you see that everything that happened tonight just makes me more determined to fight back? The police, the courts, the owners—they treat us like we have no worth."

Jacob's lips gently brushed her swollen eye. "I just need to know you will be safe out there. I am afraid they will go out of their way to taunt you into another confrontation."

Miriam pulled Jacob's face to hers and kissed him. "They don't know who they're dealing with."

Sadie was in the kitchen when Miriam returned to the apartment. The tangy smell of vegetable soup warming on the stove and the gnawing emptiness in her stomach reminded her that she hadn't eaten since breakfast.

"I don't expect you were given any food in jail," said Sadie, cutting a thick slice of dark bread and placing it on the table. "Sit, the soup is ready."

By the time her mother brought the soup to the table, Miriam had devoured the bread. Sadie watched wordlessly as her daughter consumed the thick stock, scraping the bowl to catch every drop. Taking the bowl from Miriam's hands, she refilled it and placed it in front of Miriam.

"This is so good," Miriam said, savoring each spoonful. "Thank you."

Sadie quietly studied her daughter's bruised face.

Miriam grew uneasy under Sadie's stare, her stony silence enveloping her like a shroud.

"Mama, I am so sorry. I know how worried you and Papa must have been."

"Do you?"

"What?"

"I said, 'Do you?' Do you really know how worried about you we were when you didn't come home? Do you know what it was like to sit here and wonder where you were? If you were hurt? If you were lying dead in a gutter somewhere?"

"Mama, I was going crazy thinking about how worried you and Papa must have been."

"Then you should know why your father is so upset and angry. I will talk to him in the morning when he has calmed down, but you have to make your own peace with him. His life has been filled with unbearable losses. That is why he feels the way he does."

The next morning Osna, Ambra and Angie were waiting for Rivka and Miriam at Local 25 headquarters. "I am being very thankful to God that you two am all right, but *oy*, Miriam, your eye," said Osna, hugging her friends.

"You don't think it makes me look better?" said Miriam trying to make light of her bruised face.

"I was afraid it would be worse," said Ambra. "Some of the women who were jailed when I was arrested had broken noses and cracked ribs."

Angie grimaced. "Are you sure you want to go back on the picket line?"

Miriam looked at Rivka. "I am not going to back down now."

Rivka's lips grew tight. "Those bastards treated us like we were dirt under their feet. They called us whores and caged us like animals." Her voice began to tremble. "I am not going to let them wear me down. I'm on the line until we get what we want."

A clapping sound made them turn, and they found Clara Lemlich standing behind them, smiling broadly. "Jacob told me what happened. I'm glad that your time in jail and in our less-than-fair court system hasn't frightened you away," she said. "Make sure you grab a cup of coffee and a roll before you go out to picket. It's going to be a long, cold morning," added Clara, as she hurried off.

By the time the five women reached the Triangle factory, the strikers had already begun picketing. Taking up their accustomed places, they paced in front of the Greene Street entrance under the scornful eye of Officer Boyle and two muscle-bound policemen.

"Hey you, redhead, what happened to your face?" shouted Boyle, laughing along with the other two cops.

Coming up behind Rivka, Miriam hissed, "The morning begins."

Rivka rolled her eyes. "And it's not going to get any better. Here come the scabs."

It was a morning of the pushing, jostling, name-calling, and spitting the picketing women had come to expect from the strikebreakers. And as they did every morning, Harris and Blanck pulled up in their chauffeur-driven cars and walked passed the women, not once looking their way. Still, by the time the last person crossed the line—a young girl who looked so terrified Miriam felt a pang of pity for her—the Triangle strikers reveled in a small but hard-won victory: There had been no arrests that morning.

Weeks on the picket line turned into months during one of New York City's coldest winters, and while many of the small- to mid-sized shirtwaist shops settled with their workers early into the general strike, the large manufacturers would not capitulate. Thousands of striking women walked picket lines in the rain, ice, and snow. Their thin shoes soaked, their coats perpetually damp, they took up their placards and marched sick, cold, and hungry. Between shifts, they stood on blustery street corners selling newspapers provided free by the *New York Call* to raise money to support the strike. They were vilified, beaten bloody, and arrested. Many endured five-day workhouse sentences where they were made to scrub floors and clean toilets.

Some were abandoned by their husbands. Others were kicked out by their families, because they no longer brought home a weekly wage. Many pawned what few valuables they had to help feed their families. Strikers would drag themselves home after long hours on the picket line only to find their families had been evicted, their possessions piled up on the sidewalk like yesterday's trash. When ten thousand striking men and women marched on City Hall to protest police brutality, the mayor promised to look into their complaints but did nothing. By Christmas, seven hundred thirty-two workers had been arrested.

As the strike wore on, the plight of the workers on the line was championed by some of the city's most wealthy and influential women. Dubbed the "Mink Brigade" by the press, women such as Alva Vanderbilt Belmont and Ann Morgan, the daughter of J.P. Morgan, were joined by other upper- and middle-class women who used their social status and influence to raise funds to help pay arrested strikers' fines and provide a small allotment for living costs. The resolute dedication of the girls in the face of so much hard-ship drew the admiration of the people of New York and the tide of public sentiment began to crest in favor of the strikers.

But the owners of the biggest shirtwaist companies would not concede. In late December, as their busy season drew near, the owners offered a set-tlement that met all the striker's demands but two. Their terms included fifty-two-hour workweeks; payment for pins, needles, and power; better wages; and reinstatement of striking workers—but they would not agree to unionize their factories or to provide better shop safety. Their proposal was rejected by a large majority of the workers, and the striking men and wom-en returned to the picket line.

By the beginning of 1910, the busy season was fast approaching and the owners relented. Mid-February—thirteen weeks after it began—the gen-eral strike was declared over. All but one of the manufacturers agreed to the strikers' terms. Triangle workers won higher wages, but Harris and Blanck would not improve factory safety conditions or shorten the workweek to the new industry standard. Instead of working half days on Saturday, they worked a full day. In addition, the owners steadfastly refused to allow the shop to unionize.

Exhausted by months on the picket line, the workers at the Triangle Shirtwaist Factory returned to the top three floors of the Asch Building, dis-heartened but relieved to be bringing home a pay envelope again.

PART IV

CHAPTER 52

Bone-weary after eleven hours at her sewing machine, Miriam longed for nothing more than the comfort of her bed. Straining to muster the strength to climb the four flights to the apartment, she was startled when the door to the building opened with a bang, and her neighbor, Mrs. Katz, stood blinking at her through the thick lenses of her wire-rimmed glasses.

"*Nu*, Miriam? Are you going to your apartment or are you just going to stand there?"

"Mrs. Katz! You frightened me. I was just about to go upstairs."

"Good," said the old woman, looping her arm through Miriam's. "You can help me to my apartment. My feet are killing me."

The perfect ending to an endless day, thought Miriam as they took the steps one at a time, stopping at each landing so Mrs. Katz could catch her breath and complain about her aching feet. When they finally reached the fourth floor, Miriam quickly said good night to her cranky neighbor. Hastening across the hall, she let herself into the apartment and sighed in relief.

"Ah, there she is," said Meyer. "Just in time to watch us finish dinner."

Miriam chose to ignore his sarcasm. "I'm sorry I am so late," she said, kissing both her parents. "Salutsky was in an even fouler mood than usual and kept piling on the work."

Ladling a generous helping of stew into a bowl, she joined them at the kitchen table. "Actually, I would have been home ten minutes sooner, but I was recruited by Mrs. Katz to help her up the stairs. I now know everything there is to know about her feet and why they hurt."

"I know she can be difficult, but she's an old lady and you did a *mitzvah* helping her," said Sadie.

Miriam shrugged. "It didn't feel like a *mitzvah*, just the annoying end to a miserable day."

Meyer eyed his daughter. When he spoke, his voice was so low Miriam had to strain to hear him. "We were at Malka's today. Avrum brought lunch from the deli and spent some time talking with us. He said Rivka is working such long hours they hardly see each other. He wonders if the strike was worth it, and since you work the same long hours as Rivka, so do I."

Miriam pushed aside the steaming bowl of stew and chose her words carefully. "I am disappointed that we didn't get more concessions from the Triangle owners, but overall, the gains the other striking workers won are a huge step forward. Jacob says the union will continue to put pressure on Harris and Blanck. Things will get better at the Triangle."

Meyer peered at his daughter and shook his head. "You know we like Jacob, but I am not sure I share his faith in the union. I don't know a lot about bargaining, but it seems to me that now that the strike is over, Harris and Blanck have the upper hand. They gave up very little and their workers are back in the factory." Rising from the table, he slid the bowl of stew back toward Miriam. "Finish your dinner so you can get to bed."

As exhausted as she was, Miriam could not sleep. Her father's words had stirred up the deeply buried doubts she'd been harboring about the strike; doubts that felt like a betrayal of all she believed they were working for. Now wide awake, she thought about the abuse and arrests, the hours spent shivering on the picket line and the sacrifices made by the families. And for what? She was working harder than ever. Safety conditions were no better. The doors to the outside were still locked. The owners had refused to install a sprinkler system. Even with the increase in pay they'd won, Miriam knew they would never be able to make up the wages they lost while on strike. Though she wouldn't admit it to her father, she was beginning to think it wasn't worth it after all.

Waiting for Miriam on their usual corner, Rivka grew concerned when she saw her friend trudging slowly toward her. "Are you all right? You don't look so good," she said, walking to meet Miriam.

"As tired as I was last night, I couldn't fall asleep. And when I finally did, I had weird dreams. In one Eli was alive and he kept telling me I had to quit my job at the Triangle, but he wouldn't tell me why. In another one I was supposed to meet Jacob, but I couldn't remember where, and I was searching all over the city for him. I'm exhausted."

"Don't take this the wrong way, but you look it."

Rivka's bluntness made Miriam laugh. "I can always count on you to tell me the truth."

"My pleasure," she replied with a smile.

"Good, because I want to ask you something and I want you to be honest with me. It's something that has been bothering me since we went back to work." Miriam wavered for a moment and then blurted out, "Do you think all we went through during the strike was worth it?"

Taken aback by Miriam's question, Rivka hesitated before answering. "Um, I haven't given it much thought. I mean, I wish Harris and Blanck had met more of our demands, but I'm not sorry we went out on strike. And before you ask, none of the others have complained either. We are all proud that we were part of something that brought so much attention to the horrible conditions we work under."

"I must be a terrible person. I'm angry and can't help feeling that we were cheated. Don't get me wrong, I am happy to get more in my pay envelope. It's just that I had such high hopes for bettering the working conditions at the Triangle, and now that we are back at work, what reason do the owners have to bargain with us?" she asked, echoing Meyer's words.

They were standing in front of the Greene Street entrance to the building, other workers swerving around them on their way into the factory. "Does Jacob know you feel this way?" asked Rivka, guiding Miriam to the freight elevator.

"No, and please promise you won't tell him. He feels badly enough about how things turned out for us. That I am so angry makes me feel as if I'm being disloyal to him."

"Jacob shouldn't feel bad, and neither should you. We did something pretty incredible. We were warriors out there, and you were one of our leaders."

Miriam hugged her friend and with the old fear of closed-in places still upon her, stepped into the elevator.

By mid-afternoon, Miriam could barely keep her eyes open. The steady whir of more than two hundred sewing machines droning in her ears, and the fetid air of the ninth floor dulled her senses and made her eyelids feel like they were weighted with lead. She would have dozed off if Angie hadn't poked her just as Salutsky approached.

In a bad mood all day, the foreman stopped and leaned down over Miriam, his arms on either side of her, his face so close to hers she could see the scraggly whiskers his razor missed. Sniffing her hair like a dog snuffling out its prey, he snarled, "I checked how many bundles you've done today, and you are falling behind. If you can't meet your quota, there is a line of girls ready to take your place. Now get to work and pick up your pace." His lips twitching upward, he ran a finger down her cheek before moving on.

Burning with indignation, Miriam started to rise from her seat when she felt a firm tug on her skirt. "Don't do anything you'll regret," hissed Angie. "Remember what happened to Ida."

"I hate that bastard."

"We all do, but unless you want to get fired, you will sit down and get back to work."

Miriam slumped into her chair. Anger-fueled adrenaline left her wide awake and she worked furiously the rest of the afternoon to meet her quota. With a triumphant sense of satisfaction, she turned in her bundle tickets to Salutsky and smiling sweetly, wished him a good night.

"What's going on with you and Salutsky?" asked Rivka when they were out on the street. "I saw him hovering over you."

"More of his usual bullying," she said, filling Rivka in on her encounter with the foreman. "I am just glad the day is over."

"Well, I think it's about to get better," said Rivka, pointing across the street to where Jacob stood waiting on the corner.

The very sight of Jacob made Miriam smile. "I don't know what he is up to, but I like it already," she said, as Jacob waved and crossed the street to join them.

"My law class finished early. It's a beautiful evening, and I could think of nothing that I'd rather do than escort two beautiful women home," said Jacob, offering each an arm.

By the time they reached Rivka's street, the distress and the weariness of Miriam's day had vanished. "How did you know I was miserable and needed to see your face?"

Jacob looked at her quizzically. "I just missed you. What's wrong? "

"I'm okay. I was tired before I even got to work this morning, and that made the day even longer than usual. Salutsky gave me a hard time for falling behind in my bundles, and that didn't make my day any better." She touched his cheek. "I'm just glad you are here."

Jacob took her hand from his face and kissed it. "I'm so sorry. I thought we would make things better at the Triangle. I know how much you and the others sacrificed when you went out on strike."

"You have nothing to be sorry about." Miriam looked away and spoke in a quiet voice. "I have a confession to make. I have been struggling with my feelings about the strike for months. But I've been selfish and know that now. We made a difference." In a sudden and unexpected moment of clarity, she added, "Given a choice, I would do it all over again."

CHAPTER 53

August 1910

After a week of summer thunderstorms, Sunday dawned clear and cloudless, the sky a brilliant swath of blue, wisps of steamy mist rising from the pavement. The rain had cleansed the air, leaving it smelling crisp and fresh, and as the sun climbed higher in the sky, the streets came to life. Vendors took to corners to hawk their wares and cars jockeyed with horse-drawn carriages for space on the uneven patch of asphalt that ran between the sidewalks. A light breeze fluttered between the alleyways as finely dressed New Yorkers eager to enjoy such a beautiful day strolled along the city's tree-lined avenues.

"It's the perfect day for a celebration," said Miriam, walking down Canal Street toward her aunt's apartment with Jacob; her parents following behind at a slower pace.

Dodging a small boy who darted onto the sidewalk, Jacob retrieved the child's runaway ball. "I'm surprised Rivka and Avrum didn't make their engagement official sooner," he said, tossing the ball to its young owner. "Anyone who knows them could tell how much they adore each other."

"I think Avrum waited to make sure the deli was profitable enough to support Rivka and my aunt and cousins as well. He added the small area with tables and chairs so people could eat there, and business has really picked up. He told Papa the delicatessen is finally showing a profit instead of just meeting expenses. With Ira's help, he hopes to open a bigger store with more room for eating in. I don't think they plan to get married until next summer."

They'd stopped in front of the deli waiting for Sadie and Meyer to catch up with them when Miriam heard her name called. Turning, she spotted Oscar coming toward them. Dressed in a suit and tie, his face shiny with perspiration, he waved frantically at Jacob and Miriam and hurried to greet them.

After enfolding Miriam in a bear-like hug, Oscar pumped the hand of a somewhat confused Jacob. "I am Oscar, and you must be Miriam's young man. I am so glad to finally meet you."

"And I you, sir," said Jacob. "Miriam talks about you all the time."

"All good things, I hope," he said, slapping Jacob on the back. "And where are your mama and papa, Miriam? Malka said they would be here too."

Now it was Miriam who was confused. Aunt Malka and Oscar? How? When? Trying with little success to hide her surprise, she said, "They should be here any minute. I didn't realize you knew my aunt."

"Ah, yes. We met when Malka came to my pushcart to thank me for helping arrange for her husband's burial. Such a lovely, kind lady. I am happy to say we have become friends," said Oscar, his face blazing a bright shade of red under his white beard.

Or more than friends? wondered Miriam, throwing her arms around Oscar and kissing his cheek. "And I am happy that you are happy," she laughed.

As soon as Esther saw Jacob, she jumped into his arms, nearly bowling him over. "At least let him get in the door," roared Ira, coming to greet the group as they piled into the tiny apartment above the delicatessen.

The child giggled in delight as Jacob covered her face in kisses. "You know, soon you will be too big for me to carry. How old are you now?"

Esther held up six fingers.

"And how old am I?" asked Jacob.

Esther held up ten fingers in what had become their special game. Jacob rolled his eyes. "Close," he said, sending Esther into peals of laughter.

Malka emerged out of the kitchen, wiping her hands on her apron. "Jacob, I should have known you were here. That child is crazy about you," she said, hugging him.

"Well, don't tell Esther," he said in a loud whisper, "but I am crazy about her too."

Esther's face lit up with joy. "See, Mama, I told you he was my boy-friend."

The uproar of laughter that followed startled the six-year-old. Burying her face in Jacob's shoulder, she began to cry.

"Come on, my little girlfriend, let's go see Rivka and Avrum," said Jacob, kissing her cheeks.

"Miriam, if you don't marry that man, we are going to have a serious problem with Esther," said Malka, hugging Meyer and Sadie as they all made their way to the front room. Glancing back at her aunt, Miriam's heart warmed as she watched Malka and Oscar exchange shy glances.

Still smiling at the thought of Malka and Oscar's blossoming romance, Miriam had to skirt around the other guests crowded around a radiant Rivka and slightly overwhelmed Avrum. Hugging them both, she said, "I am so happy for you. And now, Rivka, you will not only be my dearest friend, you will be a part of my family."

Rivka felt her eyes mist and pulled Miriam aside to talk. "All my life I have dreamed of having a family of my own," she said in a low voice. "Now that I am so close to seeing my dream come true, I am afraid of losing it. I have never had anything in my life as wonderful as Avrum."

Miriam stared at her friend. "How can you be thinking that way on such a wonderful day? Look around the room. It's filled with people who love you. Your father, all of my family, and most of all, Avrum. There is nothing he wouldn't do for you."

"I know. That's what makes it even scarier for me. I am so afraid this kind of happiness is not meant to last."

Sadie slipped into the kitchen to help her sister bring the brunch dishes to the table. "Everything looks delicious. When did you have time to prepare all of this?"

"Sonia and Ira did most of the work last night." Malka began to rear-range the plates the on the table. "Oscar came by to help, too," she added, averting her eyes.

Sadie found it amusing that her sister was being so coy about Oscar. "He is the loveliest man. When Meyer was injured I don't think we would have survived the ordeal without him. I am so glad that you and Oscar have found each other."

"After Lazar died, the last thing I wanted was a man in my life. But this man is a *mensch*, all the things Lazar never was. He is so kindhearted and considerate. You should see him with Rebecca and Esther. Even the older children adore him. I'm not sure how serious this is, and I know he's much older than me, but I am always happy when I am around him."

"I hope it is serious. There is no finer man out there than Oscar Gershunoff."

"Then I am not foolish to be thinking about love at this stage of my life?"

Sadie felt her throat tighten. "Malka, it's never too late to be loved and happy."

Miriam and Jacob stepped out into the afternoon sun, grateful the morning's breeze had not deserted them. "It was such a wonderful party," said Jacob, squinting in the bright sunshine. "It's too bad your father and mother had to leave early."

"Papa just tires easily, and I think all the noise bothered him. I could tell just looking at him that he had a headache. He'll lie down for a while and feel better."

Jacob put his hand on Miriam's elbow and guided her past a group of rough-looking boys milling about on a street corner. When one of the older boys whistled and leered at Miriam, Jacob whirled and stepped toward the offender. Cowering like a frightened puppy, the pimply-faced teen scampered away, his friends following him.

Expecting Miriam to be indignant, Jacob was surprised to find her smiling at him. "What's so amusing?"

"You," she laughed. "I like you in this role."

"What role is that?"

"You know, my protector. My knight in shining armor."

"Oh, that role," answered Jacob, sweeping his hat from his head and taking an exaggerated bow. Miriam's laughter enveloped him, its smoothness reminding him of flowing honey. Suddenly, the thought of ending their day together was unbearable. "Can you stay out a little later?" he asked. "I was hoping we could walk a little more, maybe stop by Chumsky's for coffee. I am just not ready for the day to end."

"Neither am I," said Miriam, pleasure pouring over her at the prospect of spending more time with Jacob. "I didn't know how long we would stay at my aunt's, so I told Mama I might be out a little later. I just have to be home by dinner."

They walked slowly, taking in the sounds of the street and the smells of cooking meals wafting from the open tenement windows. Children played on the stoops of buildings, their bare arms and legs growing pink under the brilliant sun. Mothers pushed baby carriages and laundry hung between buildings, rippling with the light breeze in a ghost-like waltz. They passed an ice cream vendor and opted for cones instead of coffee at Chumsky's. Sitting on a bench in Washington Square, they laughed as the melting ice cream dripped over the cones onto their hands.

"You've got a chocolate spot on your cheek," said Jacob, wiping the dab of ice cream from Miriam's face. His hand lingered for a moment. He started to speak and then hesitated before finding his voice. "I watched Avrum and Rivka today and seeing how happy they were and how happy their families were for them made me realize how much I want that for us." His eyes met hers, and he took her hand.

Miriam gasped and her pulse beat wildly in her throat. "Are you saying what I think you're saying?"

Jacob rubbed his forehead and frowned. "I am not doing a very good job of this. What I am trying to say is I love you and I cannot imagine my life without you. I am asking you to marry me. Will you wait for me to finish law school next year and be my wife?"

Her eyes shining with tears, Miriam flew into his arms. "Yes," she whispered into his ear. "I love you. If you asked, I would wait for you forever."

"I promise I will be a good husband." He paused, suddenly looking sheepish. "There is one thing, though. I should ask your father for permission to marry you."

Miriam tried to picture Jacob facing her father and smiled. "I think we can wait a bit longer to tell my family. Let's let Rivka and Avrum enjoy all the attention for a little longer."

Jacob sighed in relief. "Good. I have to admit I am still a little afraid of your father. When it comes to you, he can be very intimidating."

Miriam pursed her lips into a fake pout. "There goes your knight-in-shining-armor image."

Miriam sat in her bed, her arms wrapped tightly around her knees, listening to the late-night hum of the city streets. Despite telling Jacob they could wait, she longed to tell her parents about Jacob's proposal. Jacob did not need to worry about her father giving his approval. Although he would not admit it to her, Miriam heard him tell her mother that Jacob was a hard worker and that Miriam had chosen "a fine young man." A smile crossed her face. No, he wouldn't object to their marriage.

A parade of memories from the afternoon flooded her mind, her thoughts and feelings making it impossible to sleep. They'd walked for hours talking about their future. Jacob would finish law school in a year and continue to work for the ILGWU as an attorney. She would leave the Triangle factory and go back to school to study teaching. They would have a large family. Jacob promised they would take care of her parents and someday buy a house far from the tenements. Holding hands, they watched the sun as it began its slow descent toward the western horizon, neither one wanting to lose the magic of the afternoon. Recalling his arms around her waist and the warmth of Jacob's lips on hers when they said goodbye, Miriam was startled by the stirrings of overpowering desire.

CHAPTER 54

Saturday, December 31, 1910

"Hurry," said Rivka as they gathered their things at the end of the day. "I don't want to have to rush to get ready for tonight. It always makes me mad that we work a full day on Saturdays when the other factories work half days. But this Saturday is New Year's Eve and that makes me really mad to still be here at five o'clock."

"I can tell," said Miriam, grabbing her coat and stuffing her hair into her hat without bothering to see if it was on straight. "Let's take the trolley. It will get us home faster," she said as the other workers rushed passed them. "What time is Avrum picking you up?"

"He's coming over around six-thirty."

"There's plenty of time. Jacob is coming over at seven, and we don't have to meet Angie and Gino and Ambra and her boyfriend, Joseph, at the restaurant until eight o'clock."

Rivka's expression turned coy and she lowered her voice. "Yes, but my father isn't going to be home, so Avrum and I will have time to … you know."

"Do you mean you and Avrum are …?"

"Do you mean you and Jacob aren't?"

Stunned, her mouth agape, Miriam shook her head.

Rivka began to blink rapidly, heat rising to her face. "Oh, God, Miriam, I'm sorry. It's none of my business what you and Jacob do. Or don't do," she added, suddenly overcome by a fit of the giggles. Clapping her hand over her mouth to stifle her nervous laughter, she made snorting sounds instead. "You should see the look on your face," she said, gasping for breath.

"My face? You're the one who is as red as my mother's borscht." Laughing as hard as Rivka, she tugged her friend down the hall to the freight elevator.

Jacob arrived home later than he had planned and rushed to iron his last clean shirt. Inspecting his black suit and satisfied that it was without wrinkles, he sprinted down to the hall bathroom for a quick shave. Regretting he'd neglected to get his hair cut, he used a generous dab of pomade to keep his stubborn locks in place. He combed his hair straight back and surveyed the shiny, slicked-down results in the mirror. Not bad, he thought as he trimmed his mustache and slapped on aftershave. Miriam didn't expect him until seven o'clock, but his plan was to get to her apartment early.

A few blocks away, Miriam tried on and discarded several shirtwaists. She wished she had a fancy dress to wear for such a special occasion, but her wardrobe offered only skirts and blouses, and her dark-gray suit would have to do. Finally deciding on a shirtwaist her mother had embroidered with a floral design across the bodice, she pinned her mother's blue brooch to the top of its high neck. She was putting the finishing touches on her hair, when she thought she heard Jacob's voice in the other room. Nestling a tortoise shell comb into her upsweep, she added a bit of rouge to her cheeks and lips and slipped her arms into her suit jacket. One day, she thought, I will welcome the New Year in a dress covered in beads and rhinestones.

Sitting before Miriam's father, Jacob was so nervous he could feel his Adam's apple bobbing up and down like a boat adrift in a wild sea. Despite an hour spent rehearsing in front of the mirror, he forgot everything he wanted to say under Meyer's steady gaze.

"Mr. Raisky," said Jacob plunging in, his voice so unsteady he had to clear his throat and start over. "Mr. Raisky, I think you know how much I care about Miriam." He sat forward, unconsciously wiping his sweating hands on his pants. "Sir, I love her very much. I know I don't have much to offer her now, but I will be done with law school in less than a year and I will be able to provide for her. All I want is to make her happy. I know

we will have to wait a while, but I am asking for your permission to marry Miriam."

Meyer stroked his beard, his stern demeanor softening slowly. His lips
curled in a half smile, but he still did not speak. Jacob felt beads of perspiration trickling down his chest and sweat pooling under his arms. In the kitch-
en, Sadie dropped the pot she was washing, a small cry escaping her lips.

Almost as if the clattering of the pot helped Meyer reach a decision, a
wide smile creased his face. "My boy, Sadie and I were wondering what was
taking you so long. Jacob, you are a good man. We do know how much you
care for Miriam and how much she cares for you. You have my blessing for
this marriage. All I ask is that you be a good husband to my daughter."

"Mr. Raisky, I promise I will spend my life taking care of Miriam. That
is, if she will let me."

Meyer's smile broadened. "Ah, I see you know my strong-willed daughter well. And Sadie," he boomed, "you can stop hiding in the kitchen. I
know you've been listening to everything we said."

Laughing and crying at the same time, Sadie hugged Jacob just as Miriam stepped out of the bedroom. Confused, she stood gawking at the beaming faces of Jacob and her parents. "Is someone going to tell me what's going
on?" she asked when Sadie hugged her.

"Jacob just asked if he could marry you," answered Meyer, his face unreadable.

Inhaling sharply, Miriam looked quickly at Jacob and then back at her
father. "And?"

"And I said yes." Meyer opened his arms and Miriam stepped into them,
allowing herself to be cradled in the comfort of his embrace. The familiar
smell of his pipe tobacco and the feel of his arms around her carried her back
to Kishinev when they were still a happy family of four. She would soon be
Jacob's wife, but at this moment, she was still Papa's little girl, loved and
safe in his arms. "Thank you, Papa," she whispered.

Taking her face in his hands, Meyer kissed her cheeks. "Just be happy."

Walking to the restaurant, Jacob's arm looped protectively through hers,
Miriam was giddy with happiness. "You know, by tomorrow morning my
mother will have told my aunt, and everyone will know we are engaged. I
just wish you had warned me you were going to talk to my father. That was

quite a scene I walked into."

Jacob bowed his head in contrition. "I know I should have told you my plans, but to be honest, until the words were actually out of my mouth, I wasn't sure I would muster the courage to face your father and ask for his blessing. He turned out to be a big softy, but he gave me a moment of sheer terror when I thought he was going to say no."

Miriam set her mouth in mock sympathy. "My poor knight in shining armor. I hope I am worth it."

"You are," said Jacob, reaching into his vest pocket. Taking her left hand in his, he slipped a gold ring with a tiny ruby embedded in the setting onto her finger. "This was my mother's engagement ring. My parents were happy their whole life together. It's what I want for us."

Miriam's eyes were swimming with tears. Before she could speak, Jacob pulled her close and kissed her.

"Hey you, that's my cousin you are accosting in the middle of the street." Avrum stood with his hands on his hips, Rivka looking impish beside him. "What kind of shenanigans are you carrying on with my baby cousin?" Avrum tried to keep his expression stern even as his cheeks dimpled, and a smile began to steal across his face.

"Stop grinning at us, you big ape. Miriam may be your cousin, but she is also my future wife."

Seconds of silence were followed by whoops of joy that made people turn and stare. "This lucky dog is marrying my cousin," exclaimed Avrum to a passerby who tipped his hat and wished the couple many years of happiness.

They were still laughing when they entered the neighborhood restaurant chosen as much for its good food as for the prices that fit the budgets of the young couples. Angie, Ambra, and their dates were already seated at a table and waved them over.

"I'm so glad you are here," said Angie. "It's getting busy and people keep trying to take the four empty chairs from our table. Gino almost got into a fight with that guy over there." Angie discreetly pointed at a heavily built man with protruding teeth and a pushed-in face smeared with beer foam that made him look like a rabid bulldog. Wiping his lips with his sleeve, the big man looked over at them, his eyes narrowed into slits.

Jacob nodded his way and sucked in his breath. "He looks like he eats little children whole for breakfast. I can't believe you stood up to him."

Gino shook his head. "I just saw a hand going for a chair and stopped him. When I looked up and saw the size of the guy I thought I was a dead man. He just stared at me for a minute and then walked away. I nearly wet my pants. First thing tomorrow I am going to church to light a candle!"

"Amen to that," said Jacob, pulling out one of the contested chairs for Miriam. "Your reward for placing yourself in peril, my friend, is that you have the honor of sitting next to my beautiful wife-to-be."

Avrum and Rivka peered over their menus waiting for the others to react. Angie, who had been chatting with Ambra, stopped mid-sentence and gaped at Jacob. "Did you just say 'wife-to-be?'"

Looking like a man who had just found a pot of gold, Jacob winked and took Miriam's hand. "I did."

Angie's eyes widened as Jacob's words began to sink in. "*Dio mio.* I am so happy for you both. So much love is happening. First Rivka and Avrum. Now Miriam and Jacob. Gino, are you getting any ideas?"

Grinning playfully, he put his arm around Angie. "Oh, I am, my *bellissima*. I am going to have the waiter bring a bottle of wine so we can toast the happy couples."

Their stomachs filled with good food and fueled by wine-induced good cheer, the four couples stepped out of the restaurant onto a snow-dusted sidewalk. Falling flurries glistened in the glow cast by the streetlights and a gust of wind sent the tiny flakes pirouetting through the frosty air.

Jacob checked his pocket watch. "We're supposed to meet my roommate Max and Ida in front of the Times Building in about an hour. That should give us plenty of time to make it over to Times Square."

"Max and Ida? Are they getting married too?" asked Angie, glowering at Gino.

Jacob felt an instant tenderness toward Gino. Angie was going to wear him down. He was sure of it. "Not that I know of. I introduced them about a month ago, and they've gone out together a few times."

Angie sniffed and wagged her finger at her beleaguered boyfriend. "Good thing for you, Gino." Gino pulled his hat low on his head and shrugged down deeper into his coat.

As they approached Times Square, the dazzling electric signs that illuminated the restaurants and theater marquees from Broadway to streets west were ablaze in the night sky. Thousands of people—many already tooting horns and shouting "Happy New Year"—were crowding the Square to wait for the midnight drop of the wooden and metal ball from the flag pole on top of the New York Times Tower.

Overwhelmed by the sheer number of people on the streets, Miriam felt a rise of panic as merrymakers jostling their way into Times Square engulfed her. A sudden whooshing sound roared in her ears. Her face grew hot, her skin clammy. She began to shake uncontrollably. Her knees buckled as if without skeletal support and she felt herself being swallowed by the crowd. Pinpricks of bright light exploded behind her eyes and then everything went black. Lost in bottomless darkness, she heard muffled voices calling her name and felt the tug of strong hands pulling her back. Disoriented, she tried to sit up as the frightened faces of her friends slowly came into focus. "What happened?" she asked, still dazed.

Jacob put his arm around her and helped her to her feet. "You fainted. Are you all right?"

Miriam leaned against Jacob to steady herself and let the cold air clear her head. "I'm okay. I wasn't expecting so many people packed into one place. I felt like I was being crushed and couldn't breathe. I just need a moment to catch my breath. I'll be fine."

Jacob looked unconvinced. "Maybe we should call it a night, and I'll take you home."

Miriam looked imploringly at Jacob. "I am fine. Really. It's my old fear of being in confined places. I'm more embarrassed than anything else. Please let's stay."

"Are you sure you will be alright?"

Placing her arm in his, Miriam smiled. "I am. Let's go find Max and Ida."

Keeping a wary eye on Miriam, they slowly made their way through the mass of humanity pouring into Times Square. The flurries turned to large flakes, and with the midnight hour near, the crowd grew raucous. Dancing and shouting, the throng became an enormous pulsating creature moving at will. Jacob held tightly to Miriam while the others led the way. When they finally reached the Times Building, they gawked at the chaos all around them, giving up any hope of finding Max and Ida in the tumultuous current of people.

"We'll never find them in this mess," yelled Avrum above the roar of the crowd. "And get a load of the jerk standing on the lamp post waving his hat."

Jacob turned in the direction Avrum was pointing and burst into laughter. "That jerk is Max! Stay here, and I'll go get him and Ida."

When Jacob returned with the couple, they were swept into a tangle of hugs and handshakes. "We thought you'd given up on finding us," said Max, pulling the collar of his coat tight around his neck.

Miriam reached over to adjust Max's partially tucked in scarf. "If you hadn't climbed that lamp post, we'd still be looking for you."

Jacob's roommate turned to Ida, a satisfied grin plastered across his face. "And you said I looked like an idiot!"

Ida's eyes crinkled at the corners, her distinctive throaty laugh—somewhere between a bray and a guffaw—rose above the din. "I'll admit it proved effective, and I am very glad we were found. I would have hated to have missed welcoming in the New Year without my friends and fellow strikers," she said, flashing a smile that quickly turned to a look of consternation. "Wait. Someone is missing," she said, looking around. "Where's Osna?"

Rivka frowned. "She came down with a cough the beginning of this week. Her parents wouldn't let her come tonight because of the cold."

Ida made a clucking sound with her tongue." I hope she gets better. "I'm sure working in the awful conditions at the Triangle doesn't help."

"Probably true, and spoken like a true sister of the union," broke in Gino, "but let's agree there will be no discussing the Triangle tonight. I don't want to think about that place, let alone talk about it."

Gino's last words were drowned out by the raucous screaming of the crowd chanting "1911." Looking skyward, they saw that the light bulb-encrusted ball was aglow and making its descent down the Times flag pole. Its landing ignited the tens of thousands of people gathered in Times Square, their shouts and whistles so loud they swallowed the sounds of the horns and cow bells ushering in the New Year.

Amid the roar and revelry, Jacob circled his arms around Miriam and held her close. His kiss was gentle at first and then became charged with an intensity that sent an explosion of desire surging through her body. Responding with a hunger she had repressed for so long, Miriam's lips parted in feverish urgency and she pressed her body to his. His hands caressed her neck and Miriam moaned low in her throat. When she finally retreated from his arms she was trembling.

Breathing hard, Jacob pulled her close again, her head resting against his chest. "I think that 1911 is going to be the best year of my life," he murmured.

CHAPTER 55

Sunday, March 19, 1911

Miriam and Sadie were waiting anxiously outside the bedroom door. "Papa, hurry up, we're going to be late to the party!" cried Miriam in exasperation.

Meyer came bursting out of the bedroom, his shirt collar open, his tie dangling around his neck. "I don't understand why Rivka and Avrum got married in such a hurry and without the family. A week ago, they weren't even talking about a wedding. Now it's one, two, three they're married."

Sadie looked at him and arched her eyebrows. It took a moment before he let out a long sigh. "Ach, why didn't you tell me?"

Because, thought Miriam, we were hoping it wasn't true. Rivka had come to Miriam two weeks earlier to confide she thought she was pregnant. When she missed her second period and began feeling nauseous, she could no longer ignore the signs. Her advice to Miriam: "There is no such thing as a safe time."

"I hope you don't think less of Rivka," said Sadie, reaching up to help Meyer with his necktie. "And don't say anything about the pregnancy. I am not sure how many people know."

"No, of course I don't think less of her—and don't worry, I would never say anything. I just worry about how Avrum will support Rivka, a baby, and Malka and the kids."

Miriam watched her father stoop so Sadie could adjust his shirt collar.

Her heart warmed at the tenderness of the simple act and the way Sadie touched his cheek when she finished tying his necktie. When he straightened up, Miriam was startled to see how loose the collar was around his neck; a heartbreaking reminder of how much weight he'd lost in the years since his accident.

"These things happen. I am just surprised that they weren't more careful," said Sadie, looking directly at Miriam.

Miriam's mouth went dry. It was as if her mother had found a way to enter her mind. Although she and Jacob had not been intimate, it was only because they had not had the opportunity. On the one occasion they'd been alone in Jacob's apartment, Rivka had just confided in Miriam about her suspicions, and the very idea of a pregnancy had put a distinct damper on their ardor.

"Mama! You have nothing to worry about," retorted Miriam, trying to sound as indignant as possible.

"Good. Now let's get going, or we will miss the whole party."

Avrum and Rivka met them at the door and were immediately showered in hugs and kisses. "*Mazel tov*, my boy," said Meyer, wrapping his arms around his nephew. "You are a lucky man to have such a beautiful bride," he added, spreading his arms to embrace Rivka.

Miriam looked on as Rivka hugged her father, fearful that despite his assurances, he would blurt out something inappropriate about her pregnancy. When he kissed Rivka on the cheek and welcomed her to the family, she felt a sudden rush of shame for doubting him.

Disentangled from Meyer's arms, Rivka waited for the others to go into the front room to show Miriam the thin gold band that encircled her finger. "It's official," she said with a shy smile.

Miriam squeezed her hand. "I am so happy for you and Avrum."

Rivka peered into the front room. "I wish everyone felt the same way."

Miriam followed Rivka's glance as if expecting to see someone standing there. "Who's not happy for you?"

"My father, for one. He may actually have to find a job now that he can't count on my pay envelope every week. Plus, he's mad we were married by a justice of the peace instead of by a rabbi in the synagogue. I haven't told him about the baby, but he's not stupid. He just keeps glaring at Avrum."

"And my aunt and cousins?"

"Avrum's mother has been really sweet. I am pretty sure she's figured out I'm pregnant. She said we can have the little room your parents slept in when you stayed here, but I know it's going to be a hardship for all of them when the baby comes. Rebecca and Esther are very excited that we got married, but I can tell Ira and Sonia don't know how to feel."

Rivka's face fell, and she clenched her jaw to keep the tears from flowing. "I just feel like I let everyone down, including Avrum. He has so many plans for expanding the deli, and now he's going to have to put them off for who knows how long. I will work as long as I can, but at some point, my salary will go away at least for a little while. It's not that I don't want the baby, but I wish it hadn't happened now."

"Rivka, you haven't let anyone down. Your baby will bring so much joy to this family, and Avrum does not look like a disappointed deli owner to me," said Miriam, pointing at her cousin sharing a laugh with Meyer and Oscar.

"I hope you are right," said Rivka, placing a protective hand across her stomach. "I won't be able to hide the pregnancy too much longer, but I'd rather not tell the girls at the factory that we're married. When I am at work, I'm going to wear my ring on a chain tucked into my blouse."

"I'll do whatever you want. But you have nothing to be ashamed of."

Rivka's eyes began to blink. "Does Jacob know?"

Miriam nodded. "He'll be here as soon as he finishes his studies. I hope it was all right that I told him."

Rivka looked down, twisting the shiny ring on her finger. "It's okay. If you hadn't told him I'm sure Avrum would have. But please ask him not to say anything to anyone."

The despair on Rivka's face broke Miriam's heart. "Rivka, you are the sister I never had. My family loves you like a daughter. Jacob loves you. Your friends love you. But most important, Avrum loves you. Please don't let these feelings ruin the joy of your marriage. You'll see. Everything is going to be fine."

Her shoulders heaving, Rivka whimpered, "I am so scared."

CHAPTER 56

Saturday Morning, March 25, 1911
Miriam

Miriam awoke gasping for breath, her face wet with tears. Disoriented and frightened, it took her a moment to reassure herself she was safe in her own bed, and that it was all a bad dream. She trembled at its memory, shaking her head to dislodge the images from her thoughts to no avail. When she closed her eyes, Eli still stood at the mouth of a long tunnel, beckoning her to follow him. He cried out to her to run and then scampered into the darkness. She could hear him calling her name, but no matter how fast she ran, she could not keep up with him. She tried to tell him to wait, but no words left her mouth. The tunnel narrowed and grew hot. Her heart was pounding, and her lungs constricted, making it impossible to breathe. Her steps grew heavy and she was trudging through mounds of slimy, foul-smelling mud that sucked at her feet. A whoosh of hot air fanned her face and an arc of light pierced the blackness. Eli stood silently, his hand reaching for hers. She stepped forward and watched in horror as a wall of flames came toward her. The last thing she heard was Eli screaming her name.

Covered in sweat, Miriam stumbled into the kitchen and threw cold water on her face, its icy sting reassuring her that she was awake. "It wasn't real," she said out loud, trying to calm her wildly thumping heart.

"What's not real?"

Miriam spun around in terror, her body sagging in relief when she saw

Meyer standing there in his robe, rubbing the sleep from his eyes. "Papa! You frightened me."

"Are you all right? You were making strange noises in your sleep."

"I'm sorry if I woke you. I just had a bad dream."

"From what I heard, it must have been a terrible dream."

"It's okay. It was just a silly nightmare. Guess my imagination was working overtime."

"You know, when I was a boy, my mother hung a horseshoe in my bedroom to keep nightmares away."

Miriam smiled at the old Jewish superstition. "Did it help?"

"Not at all, but I never told my mother. And we don't have a horseshoe anyway."

"Probably a good thing, because I don't have a bedroom!" Laughing, Miriam hugged her father and felt instantly better. "I should get dressed for work."

"I thought we'd have breakfast together."

"I'm sorry, Papa, I don't have time. I'll eat a roll on my way to the trolley. And don't forget, I am having dinner with Jacob tonight and will be home a little later. We'll come back in time for all of us to have tea."

Meyer's mood, mercurial as ever, turned dark. "I hate that you have to go to the factory on *Shabbat*," he snapped. "It's a holy day. You should not be working. And don't bother to cut your evening short on my account." Without another word he turned and stomped into the bedroom like a petulant child.

Miriam stared at the closed door and sighed. This nightmare is real, and it will never end, she thought.

Rivka

In the cave-like blackness of the curtained alcove that served as their bedroom, Rivka waited for the nausea to pass. Her morning sickness occurred in the early hours of the day, and as long as she could leave for work before the smells of breakfast filled the apartment, she was able to keep her stomach from heaving its contents. She worried about how much longer she would be able to hide her pregnancy at work. It was getting harder to keep to only one bathroom break a day. Soon it would be impossible. Yesterday she barely made it to the toilet in time, and the urge to go was becoming stronger and more frequent. She knew some of the women wore layers of diapers and just urinated when they had to. She wondered how desperate she would have to be to wet herself. Just the thought of it made her shiver, and she snuggled against Avrum, his body radiating comforting heat.

Instantly awake, Avrum pulled her closer and nuzzled her neck. "Are you all right? Do you feel sick?"

"It's not too bad. I think the worst of it is over."

Avrum threw his arm over her and lightly touched her breasts. "You know, it's very quiet in the apartment, and that means no one is up yet. Are you sure you feel okay?" His lips brushed her neck and travelled slowly to her throat.

She shuddered as his hands caressed her body. "I'm sure," she whispered, her voice thick with desire. Pushing her hips against his, Rivka gasped at how quickly he was aroused. With a fevered urgency, she pulled up her nightgown. His lips moved gently down her body, his tongue dancing deliciously on her skin. Her hands raked his hair, her need for him becoming desperate. His mouth covered hers and just when her hunger for him seemed unbearable, he was inside her.

Afterward, sated with pleasure, Rivka forced herself to leave Avrum's arms. "It's not fair that I have to go to work and you get to close the deli because it's *Shabbat*."

Avrum stifled a yawn and patted her side of the bed. "Don't go. Stay home with me."

Rivka sighed. "I wish I could. Go back to sleep. I'll see you tonight." She bent to kiss him one more time, but he was already asleep. She smiled and whispered, "I love you."

Ambra

Her mother would not stop banging on the door. "Ambra, you are going to be late for work. Come eat your breakfast now."

Ambra cringed. God, she thought, her voice makes me wish I didn't have ears. It's like the sound of screeching trolley brakes, only worse. "I'll be right there," she yelled back. "I just have to finish ironing my dress for tonight."

Tonight. Ambra's aunts, uncles, and cousins were coming to celebrate her engagement to Joseph. She worried her shy husband-to-be would be

intimidated by the exuberance of her boisterous relatives. She was especially concerned about her uncle Salvatore, who liked to show off his strength
by challenging newcomers to the family to arm wrestle. Skinny Joseph did
not stand a chance against her muscular uncle.

"Ambra, your breakfast is on the table!" This time it was her father's voice
resounding through the bedroom door. When Papa yelled, she knew she'd
better listen. Leaving the iron to cool, Ambra scurried into the kitchen.

"It's about time," grumbled her mother. "I have been cooking and cleaning for days for your party, the least you could do is be on time for breakfast."

Ambra took a bite of her buttered roll and chewed furiously. "Mama, I
needed to iron my dress. I worked late last night, and I won't have time to
do it when I get home today."

Her father smacked his hand on the table spilling his cup of coffee. "*Bas-
ta*! When your mama talks, you listen, not talk back."

"I wasn't talking back. I was trying to explain why I was late for breakfast. And if I don't leave now I will be late for work. I am sorry, Mama. I am
just nervous about tonight. I really do appreciate everything you've done."
Grabbing what was left of her roll, Ambra kissed her parents goodbye and
headed for the door.

Her mother followed her down the hall. "Don't forget your coat," she
said, her voice only slightly less piercing when she didn't yell.

Angie

Angie sat at the table, the bowl of oatmeal before her untouched. Her
mother wasn't helping her foul mood, babbling about what a nice boy Joseph was, what a beautiful ring he had given Ambra and how happy she was
for her niece. Plucking Angie's nerves even more, her brother Marco was
smacking his lips and making loud slurping noises with each sip of his coffee.

"Can you please stop doing that?" she snarled. "It's disgusting and annoying."

"Ah, look who is in a bad mood. I don't suppose it has anything to do
with the party tonight? After all, Ambra and Joseph are engaged, while little Angie here is still waiting for Gino to find his balls and ask her to marry him."

The slap came so fast Marco never saw it coming. "Ma! What's that for?" he yelped, holding his cheek, stunned by its force.

"You will not use such language in this house. Now tell your sister you're sorry. And mean it!"

No one, not even her burly big brother, dared to cross their mother. His face bearing the red imprint of his mother's hand, a chastened Marco apologized to Angie. "I'm sorry. I shouldn't have said that."

It was hard for Angie to gloat over Marco's humiliation when deep down she knew he was right. She was fuming that Ambra and Joseph were engaged after dating for ten months, when she and Gino had been together for almost two years. She had been a fool to think he would ever want to get married. She was tired of waiting for him. She would tell him they were done tonight.

Osna

It was her first day back at the Triangle after a long absence. Osna stood outside the Asch Building waiting for Miriam and Rivka to arrive, trying to ignore the morning chill. She took a deep breath and relished the cool air that filled her lungs.

The cough that had kept Osna from joining her friends on New Year's Eve had worsened in the days that followed. Bouts of spasmodic coughing wracked her small body and left her weak from the effort. Fearing tuberculosis and desperate to get her away from the chill and foul air of the tenements, Osna's parents sent her to stay with her aunt and uncle on their farm in upstate New York. Under their loving care, Osna spent her days in the sunshine breathing the clean, crisp air of the Catskill Mountains.

With a steady diet of fresh food from the farm and the exercise she got keeping up with her young cousins, Osna grew stronger, her sickly pallor transformed to a healthy glow. Six weeks after her arrival, she was well enough to return to the city. Her departure from the farm was filled with mixed emotions. She would miss her aunt and uncle and would be forever grateful for their care, but she was eager to go home. She missed her parents terribly. She also knew that without her wages they were struggling just to pay the rent.

A sudden gust of wind whipped around the corner, sending dirt and debris swirling in the gutter. Cold and about to give up on Rivka and Miriam, Osna spied her friends, their heads bent against the wind, hurrying toward her. "I am being glad you arrive," she said as they hurried into the Greene Street entrance. "I am starting to be freezing out there."

Putting her arm around Osna to keep her warm, Miriam took the red scarf Sadie had knitted for her from her neck and wrapped it around Osna's. "You have no idea how much I missed you while you were away. We all did. It's so good to have you back and feeling better."

"I am missing you too. To me, today am a good day."

CHAPTER 57

Saturday, March 25, 1911, 4:40 p.m.
The Ninth Floor

From the way Salutsky kept looking at his pocket watch, Miriam could tell they were nearing the end of the day. It could not come soon enough, she mused, as she eyed the menacing foreman pacing in front of the table of workers. He had been in a bad mood all afternoon, fining the girls for coming back late from their bathroom or lunch breaks or for talking while working. When the girl sitting next to Rivka sewed the end of a sleeve together, he called her a stupid bitch and fired her. Too frightened to move, the sobbing girl cowered at her sewing machine until Salutsky threatened to yank her out of her chair if she did not leave.

When the bell finally signaled the day was over, Miriam watched Rivka bolt to the bathroom near the changing area. "I'll put your work away and meet you at the elevator," she called out to her friend.

The Eighth Floor

On the floor below, the sound of the bell sent workers on the main cutting floor scurrying to store their tools and shut down their machines.

"Time for a smoke," declared one of the cutters. Ignoring the Triangle's no-smoking policy, others joined him and lit cigarettes as they cleared their work, flicking their matches on the floor, unmindful of the scrap bins at their feet.

Eager to leave the factory, the eighth-floor seamstresses dodged the stacks of basted material and the baskets filled with scraps that littered the floor. Standing in line to retrieve their pay envelopes, they chatted about their Saturday night plans and filed into the narrow hall on the Greene Street side where they waited to have their handbags searched by the foreman.

Near the front of the line, sixteen-year-old Henya Stein sniffed the air and tapped her younger sister Bessie on the shoulder. "Do you smell smoke?"

Wiping her runny nose with a wrinkled handkerchief, Bessie shook her cold-clogged head and stepped forward to have her belongings inspected.

On the Washington Place side, the cutters were frantically throwing pails of water on a fire in a bin of rags where a tossed cigarette had landed. The floor manager grabbed a hose stored in the stairwell and screamed in anger when no water came out of the rusted nozzle.

The fire came to life in an instant, the half-full pails of water no match for its fury. Fiery fingers curled around the patterns hanging over the long tables and licked the oily residue on the floor, erupting into balls of flame. The wooden tables and stacks of material fed the hungry beast, its flames leaping to the ceiling, scorching a pathway to the ninth and tenth floors.

Cries of "Fire!" sent waves of terror throughout the eighth floor. Screaming in fear, people rushed toward the stairwell exit on the Washington Place side of the building. Choking on the thick black smoke that engulfed the room, they pounded on the locked door. Frantic workers piled up in front of the bolted portal, clawing at each other to reach the exit. When a manager found a key, a flood of crazed men and women surged onto the stairs, clogging the stairwell. Others broke windows and ran to the building's only fire escape. Just before he fled, a supervisor called the tenth floor to alert them of the blaze.

Nearly trampled in the rush to the door, Henya Stein grabbed Bessie's hand and shoved her way to the elevators on the Washington Place side. Fear gripped her heart like a vise when the elevator travelled past them on its way to the tenth floor. All around her men and women gave in to their terror. Some stood frozen in fear. Some begged God to save them, while others cried and called out for their mothers.

Fear turned to hysteria as the lung-choking smoke grew thicker and the fire fiercer, snapping at the workers' clothes and singeing their hair. Suddenly, the elevator stopped. When the door opened the terrified workers pushed and shoved their way into the car. Nearly knocked to the ground, Henya lost her grip on Bessie's hand. Reaching for her sister and screaming "Bessie!" she was swept into the elevator by the flood of workers behind her.

On the street below, coughing and gasping for air, Henya waited for Bessie, praying that she had gotten on another elevator. Suddenly the crowd that had gathered began to shout and pointed skyward. Looking up, Henya saw Bessie balancing on an eighth-floor ledge, shouting for help. Tendrils of flame shot out the window behind her. In seconds, Bessie's skirt was on fire, her dark hair smoldering. As hundreds of people wailed in horror, the screaming fourteen-year-old flung herself off the ledge, seeming to float above them for a brief moment before plummeting to the sidewalk in a cloak of flames.

The Tenth Floor

When the phone rang on the executive level, the clerical workers, salesmen, and designers on the tenth floor were preparing to leave to for the day. Co-owner Max Blanck rushed to clear his desk, while two of his daughters and their French governess sat in his office waiting to be taken on a promised shopping trip.

"Papa, please hurry," whined twelve-year-old Henrietta. We've been waiting forever."

"Forever," chimed in five-year-old Mildred, squirming on the governess' lap, her lips puckering into what Blanck knew was about to become a temper tantrum.

Pulling on his coat, he was hurrying to leave when screams from the street sent him racing to the front windows. Smoke was rising from the floors below, fire spitting out of the windows. Throwing open the door to his office, he nearly knocked over his secretary, white with fear.

"Oh, God! Mr. Blanck, there's a fire on the eighth floor and it's spreading fast. We've called for the elevators, but everyone is rushing to the stairs."

Pushing his daughters and their governess back into his office, Blanck tried to bring order out of the chaos before him. The scramble to the stairwell proved futile: When the rear door to the stairs was opened, a rush of heat and smoke drove the workers back. As the first elevator arrived, workers crammed into the lift, straining the car's capacity. A second trip took more workers to street level, but the smoke and flames in the elevator shaft made it too dangerous to make additional trips. Thick black smoke poured into the tenth floor, the heat searing the workers' lungs. Led by Isaac Harris, the remaining people—including Blanck, his daughters and the governess—groped their way through a smoky room filled with shirtwaist samples and onto a stairway that led to the roof.

Within minutes of their departure, the fire broke through to the tenth floor. Left on the desk where the panic-stricken secretary had dropped it, was the phone's receiver. No warning call had been made to the ninth floor.

The Ninth Floor

Miriam worked quickly to clear her area. Jacob would be at Chumsky's Diner in a few minutes, and she didn't want to keep him waiting. It had been a long, grueling day, made worse by Salutsky's tirades. Even now, he was glaring at the girls as they shut down their sewing machines and made plans for their day off.

"Hurry up," he brayed, tapping his pocket watch. "I want to get out of here tonight."

"He am being really mean today," whispered Osna as she passed Miriam on her way to get her things in the dressing room. Stopping suddenly, she tapped her head. "*Oy*, I still am having your scarf."

"That's all right. It will keep you warm. You can give it back to me on Monday."

"You being sure?"

"I'm sure." Miriam hugged her small friend. "I don't want you to get sick again."

"We should be waiting for you?"

"No, you go ahead. Rivka is in the bathroom and I told her I would meet her at the elevators."

Moving down the aisle to Rivka's machine, Miriam faltered when she saw Salutsky standing over the empty chair.

"Where is she?" bellowed Salutsky, his hands balled into fists. "If that bitch left without turning off her machine and cleaning up, she doesn't have to bother to come in on Monday. She's...." Salutsky's mouth gaped open, fear etching his face.

Miriam looked behind her and screamed. Flames and black smoke were curling in through an open window. Salutsky yelled "Fire!" and the terrified girls still at their machines pushed their way down narrow aisles packed with baskets of scraps, loose fabric and their fellow workers. Windows started to crack and break. Bursts of incoming air intensified the blaze. The flames rose and snaked their way across the ceiling and down the walls to the floor forming a river of fire. Devouring everything in its path, it roared like an angry demon, spitting and sizzling and sending showers of sparks to spread its evil.

Salutsky shoved Miriam to the floor and pushed past anyone who got in his way. Scrambling to her feet, Miriam looked for the nearest exit. A curtain of flames blocked her way to the Greene Street side. *Rivka! Oh my God, where is Rivka?* Miriam tried to make her way to the bathroom but was driven back by a wall of suffocating heat and flames. *Please, God, keep her safe.* The black smoke grew heavier, stinging her eyes and making it difficult to see. The oaky smell of burnt wood filled Miriam's nostrils. She began to choke and could feel her heart slamming against her ribs.

Pandemonium was all around her. An older woman had fallen in an aisle and was being trampled by workers climbing over her to escape the blaze. A screaming girl ran past Miriam, the edge of her skirt on fire. Men and women thwarted by the locked Washington Place door were piling up in front of the elevators, stampeding into the open doors as soon as the car stopped. Facing an agonizing death in the flames, some of the girls jumped into the elevator shaft trying to slide down the cable or hoping to land on the top of the elevator, only to plunge down the smoky shaft.

Shaking with fear, Miriam pushed her way forward to the Washington Place side of the room. Suddenly, Eli's voice was in her head. *Don't panic. Keep calm. Don't lose control. Think about Mama and Papa and Jacob. Miri, you have to survive. If you can't go down, go up.*

Startled, Miriam looked up, expecting to see Eli standing there. Instead she spied Salutsky charging up the stairs next to the passenger elevators. *If you can't go down, go up.* Miriam could almost feel Eli's hands propelling her forward. Pulling her skirt up over her head to shield her face, she raced through the ribbons of scarlet flames toward the stairs.

Barely making it to the bathroom on time, Rivka sat on the toilet and sighed in relief bordering on exquisite pleasure as she emptied her full bladder.

She laughed at how such a simple thing could make her feel so happy. An insistent banging on the bathroom door and shouting she could not make out interrupted her reverie. When the banging would not stop, she angrily yanked the door open, yelping in pain when her hand touched the hot handle. Before her was a maelstrom of fire, its flames swelling and rising, undulating like a stormy sea.

Rooted by fear, Rivka heard her name and suddenly a hand pulled her against the wall alongside the bathroom door. Startled and frightened, it took her a second to find her voice. "Osna! How did you know I was here? Oh, God, the fire is everywhere!"

"Miriam. She say you am here. We better to be finding a way out."

The roar of the blaze was deafening. A phalanx of red flames inched its way toward them. Rivka stood riveted in terror, staring into the growing inferno. Osna tugged at Rivka's sleeve. "Rivka, please we am needing to be moving," she said at the very moment an ember landed on her skirt and ignited. Forgetting her fear, Rivka began slapping at the smoldering material and grabbed Osna's hand, her eyes darting around the room in search of a safe exit.

"Come on, Angie," implored Ambra, standing at the lockers in the dressing room. "We need to get out of here. I want to have some time to get ready for the party tonight."

Angie scowled like a spoiled child. She was desperate for a reason to avoid going, dreading her relatives' humiliating questions about when she and Gino were going to get engaged. Just thinking about Gino made her stomach ball up in anger.

"Angie, *Dio mio!*"

"I'm coming," she snapped through clenched teeth.

"Angie, the factory is on fire!"

Standing in the doorway of the dressing room, Ambra began to scream. The fire was spreading quickly, acrid smoke stinging her throat and searing her lungs. Scenes of horror played out in front of her: A cutter ran past her holding his burnt and blackened arm, frantically looking for his sister. A seamstress slipped in machine oil puddling on the floor. Unable to get up before the swift-moving fire sipped the grease, she was engulfed in flames. The sickening smell of burning flesh mingled with the stink of the fire.

Ambra grabbed Angie and pointed at the elevators on the Washington Place side. Appearing suddenly through the murky haze of smoke, Osna and Rivka rushed to catch up with them.

"We were hoping Miriam was with you," sputtered Rivka, her breathing coming in short bursts. "I was supposed to meet her at the elevators."

Osna looked about anxiously, her eyes tracking the blaze as it advanced toward the Greene Street stairs. Before she could call out a warning, a jet of flames jumped to a barrel of machine oil stored in the hallway. The thundering explosion of oil and fire drove them back. Red and yellow flames and hot oil rained down on the panic-crazed crowd, setting workers ablaze and blocking the entrance to the stairwell. Screams of agony mixed with shrieks of terror. The crowd charged the front elevators in a frenzy of fear.

Knocked to the ground by the explosion, Rivka felt a hand pulling her upwards from the tangle of people lying on the floor. Blood dripping down her face, she groped blindly at her rescuer.

Osna seized Rivka's wildly flailing hands. "Rivka, get up or we am trapped!"

Ignoring the hammering pain in her head, Rivka grabbed Osna's arm and together with Ambra and Angie, pushed her way toward the elevators.

CHAPTER 58

The fire department and police arrived within minutes of the blaze's discovery. By now the street was clogged with thousands of onlookers screaming and turning their faces away from the atrocity of young women leaping to their deaths, crashing limp and broken to the pavement like rag dolls.

Hopes for rescue turned to utter despair when it was discovered the fire engine's ladders only reached the sixth floor, the fire hoses to the seventh. The safety nets spread out to catch the jumping workers quickly proved to be useless. The force of so many men and women jumping at once ripped the nets from the hands of the rescuers while the impact of others leaping from the top floors tore gaping holes in the nets. The efforts of the firemen to fight the blaze from the ground and rescue the workers were futile. Now the police were moving the crowd back, so they would not be injured by the falling bodies.

Miriam stumbled blindly out of the suffocating stairwell, her face blackened with soot, her eyebrows and hair singed. Her right arm was blistered and throbbing with pain. Seized by a paroxysm of coughing, she gulped in air desperately trying to clear her lungs. Her vision blurred by the smoke, it took Miriam a moment to realize she was on the roof.

The top three floors of the Asch Building were now a roaring furnace. Tongue-like flames flicked out the windows and red-hot embers caught in an updraft rained down on the roof. Miriam stared in terror as small fires erupted all around her. *Oh God, did I come this far to be trapped on the roof?* Tears burned in her eyes and she covered her ears to drown out the screams of the men and women leaping from the floors below.

Eli's voice, more urgent than before, rose above the din and filled her thoughts: *Stay calm. Get your bearings. Think, Miri, think!*

Miriam scanned the roof for a way to escape. Movement in the windows on the top floor of the building across the way caught her eye. Yelling and waving their arms, several students from the New York University Law School were lowering a ladder across the courtyard that separated the two buildings. As soon as it reached the factory roof, a young man scrambled across the ladder and secured it so that it spanned the courtyard to the university, one story higher. "Women first!" he shouted.

Eli's words echoing in her ears, Miriam dashed to the ladder, already surrounded by the others who had sought refuge on the roof. Hysteria was all around her as fear of the fire was replaced by the terror of crossing the smoke-filled courtyard on the precarious ladder.

Despite the cold wind, Miriam was covered in sweat. When it was her turn to leave the roof, she could feel the blood pulsing furiously through her body. Shaking so hard her teeth rattled, Miriam balked at mounting the ladder.

"Come on, miss. We are running out of time," urged the student. "Just don't look down and you'll be fine."

Blocking out the pain in her arm, Miriam grasped the sides of the ladder. Taking a deep breath, she placed her foot on the first rung. *I'm so scared. Eli, please stay with me.* One hand after the other, one foot after the other, Miriam slowly crossed the ladder above the smoky courtyard. *Stay calm. Don't look down.* Plumes of dark smoke rose from the chasm below. Miriam's eyes felt gritty. The air grew heavy and her lungs felt like they were going to burst. Time seemed to come to a halt. The university building appeared to be so far away. *Think of Mama and Papa and Jacob. You're almost there. You can do this.* She felt Eli's hand on her shoulder, steadying her.

"I can do this!" screamed Miriam, willing her body onto the final rungs of the ladder. Hands were grabbing her and pulling her through a window to safety. Faces and voices were all around her.

"Are you hurt?"

"You're safe now."

"Don't cry, miss."

"Miriam!"

Her breathing was shallow, and pinpricks of light flickered like fireflies in her eyes. "Eli?" she murmured, and crumpled into the arms of Jacob's roommate, Max.

Desperate to find Angie, Gino volunteered to take the passenger elevator to the ninth floor. His first two runs brought passengers screaming in pain and terror to safety, but Angie was not among them. Now as he guided his elevator to the ninth floor for the third time, he feared it would be his last trip. On each of his previous trips, the weight of workers jumping onto the top of the elevator nearly knocked the car of its guide rails making the descent more perilous.

The elevator rumbled to a stop. When Gino opened the doors, he was certain he had traveled to the depths of purgatory. The ninth floor was an inferno. Everywhere he looked people were human torches, their shrieks of agony unlike any sound he'd ever heard. A crush of pushing and shoving people stormed into the car, screaming as the fire nibbled at the edges of their clothes and nipped at their shoes. "Go down! Go down!" they cried and fought to reach the controls as Gino made one last attempt to scan the room for Angie. In the clamor of his hysterical passengers and the roar of the fire, he did not hear Angie shouting his name.

"Gino!" howled Angie in raw anguish, pushing through the panicked mass just as the elevator doors slammed shut. Pounding on the doors until her knuckles bled, she was shoved aside by three men who pried open the doors to the elevator shaft. Angie looked down into the smoky abyss. Locking eyes with Ambra, she mouthed, "Save yourself."

"No!" screamed Ambra, lunging to stop her cousin from jumping.

Angie turned and hurled herself into the fiery shaft, her hands finding the elevator cables. The scorching heat of the twisted wires seared her palms and jolts of excruciating pain shot up her arms. Angie could feel herself slipping, the wires tearing at her burnt flesh. Below her, the elevator continued its descent. Calling out Gino's name, Angie let go of the cables and closed her eyes. The impact of her body hitting the elevator roof rocked the car, unleashing panic inside.

Rivka wrapped her arms around Ambra and pulled her back to keep her from following Angie into the elevator shaft. Crazed by grief and fear, Ambra broke free and darted through the flames to the opposite side of the building. She ripped her burning skirt from her body and gritting her teeth against the pain in her blistered legs, she clambered through an open window onto the factory's single fire escape.

Straining under the weight of so many fleeing workers, the sole emergency staircase groaned in protest when Amber stepped onto the narrow ladder. She clung to the rungs with all her strength as the metal fire escape began to twist from the heat of the blaze. Minutes ago, she was willing to follow Angie to a certain death in the elevator shaft. Now she was desperate to survive. "I will live. I will marry Joseph. I will give Mama and Papa grandchildren," she vowed, lowering herself down the ladder.

Another girl stepped onto the fire escape and it began to shift and vibrate under Ambra's feet. Just as it felt as if it had steadied, a deafening crack echoed off the buildings surrounding the factory. The flimsy drop ladder shuddered and tore away from the factory, hurdling twenty screaming girls to the pavement, their arms flailing as if they thought they could fly, their burning and broken bodies thudding grotesquely against the cold sidewalk.

Rivka and Osna quickly lost sight of Ambra in the thick smoke that wrapped the ninth floor in a mantle of black. When the blood-curdling sound of the fire escape pulling away from the building pierced the air, they knew their last hope for escape was gone. Rivka looked at Osna and squeezed her hand. Tears welled in the tiny girl's eyes and she nodded. "I don't want to be burned alive," she whimpered in Yiddish. "How will Mama and Papa recognize my body?" Rivka took her hand and led her away.

The fire was raging, consuming the long wooden work tables, the bins of flammable material and the two hundred fifty men and women on the ninth floor. With the blaze swirling around them in a menacing ballet, Rivka and Osna fought their way through the flames and falling debris to the windows on the Washington Place side. Osna's weakened lungs quickly filled with smoke and she faltered, her breathing becoming labored. Rivka put her arm around her and half carried, half dragged her friend to the windows, weaving through flames that flicked at them like a serpent's tongue.

Reaching the windows, they stared in disbelief at the scene unfolding before them. Girl after girl climbed through the window onto the ledge. Some hesitated before jumping into the nothingness that awaited them; most leaped wordlessly as the flames rose through the window and urged them on. Louie, the chief cutter, gently lifted a crying girl who wrapped her arms around his neck. With tears in his eyes he carried her to the window and kissed her. Holding her away from the building, he let her drop and without hesitation, followed her in death.

Moving as though in a trance, Rivka pulled Osna through the window to the ledge. Standing on the narrow sill, Rivka's thoughts flew to Avrum and the life they would have had together. She touched her stomach and mourned the child that would never be. She pictured a little boy with Avrum's dark, curly hair and dimpled cheeks. She fingered the wedding band still hanging on its chain and hoped Avrum would know how much she loved him.

Osna was crying, babbling in Yiddish about her parents and being back in Russia again. Rivka pulled her close and spoke to her softly. "We are going to do this together. It will be over quickly. Just hold on to me."

Osna blinked away her tears and tying Miriam's red scarf tightly around her neck, she tucked the ends inside her shirtwaist. Her blue eyes flat and dull, she put her arms around Rivka. Talons of flames curled around them, setting their clothes on fire. The two women jumped and formed a single silhouette against the setting sun. Their flaming skirts billowed and flapped as they fell, setting fire to their hair. The crowd bellowed its anguish as Rivka and Osna, still clinging to each other, crashed through a glass segment of the sidewalk and came to rest in the basement of the Asch Building.

The street was littered with broken and burned bodies. The smell of burnt flesh filled the air. One after another the workers climbed onto the ledge and chose death on the sidewalk over death in the inferno of the Triangle Shirtwaist Factory. Each thump of a body drew screams of horror from the onlookers. As the bodies piled up, women fainted and men cried out in torment. Crazed by the carnage on the street, family members tried to break free of the police cordon in a desperate attempt to find a loved one. The torrent of water flowing from the fire hoses into the gutter ran red with blood.

The girls of the Triangle kept jumping out of the windows of the Asch Building.

CHAPTER 59

Jacob arrived early at Chumsky's and took a seat at their favorite table by the window. He patted his coat pocket to assure himself that the tickets were still there and smiled picturing Miriam's surprised look when he told her he was taking her to see the new Jacob Adler play.

"You have a rather silly grin on your face, my young friend."

Feeling foolish, Jacob pulled out a chair for the restaurant owner to join him. "I probably always look silly when I am thinking about Miriam. We are going to a play after dinner, only she doesn't know it yet."

The sound of horse-drawn fire engines clopping down the street caught their attention. Looking out the window, they were stunned by the towering plumes of black smoke spiraling up from the direction of the Asch Building.

Jacob could feel his heart sink. "Oh my God, Miriam!"

Returning from the stable where he stored his pushcart, Oscar was nearly knocked over by a man running blindly down the street. "Watch where you're going," scolded Oscar.

Still running, the man cried out, "The Triangle factory is on fire. My daughter is in there. The girls are being burned alive!"

Within minutes, Oscar was banging on the door of Meyer and Sadie's apartment. "Where's Miriam?" he demanded as soon as Meyer let him in.

Confused, Meyer stammered, "She's with Jacob. He came by to tell us he was taking her to a play after dinner. Why? What's wrong?"

Struggling to catch his breath, Oscar looked over Meyer's shoulder at Sadie's worried face. "What time were they meeting?"

"She was going to meet him right after work, about five o'clock or so. Oscar, what's going on?"

Oscar felt the cold grip of fear around his heart. "Meyer, there's a fire at the factory. It's bad."

Staggering as if she had been struck, Sadie held on to Meyer to steady herself. "She must be with Jacob. She has to be safe...."

An explosion of sound behind them made them jump as Avrum burst through the door. His eyes darted around the apartment. "Is Rivka here? Did she come home with Miriam?"

Sadie pressed her hand to her throat and began to cry. "Please, God, not both of them," she sobbed.

The color drained from Avrum's face. "I'm going to the factory. I told Ira if I wasn't back in an hour to bring Mama here."

"I'm going with you. Oscar, please stay with Sadie in case Miriam is on her way home." Meyer held Sadie for a moment and kissed her. "We will find both girls and bring them home."

Miriam opened her eyes and drew in a sharp breath. Her lungs burned and the pain in her arm was unrelenting. "She's coming to," someone shouted from what seemed to her to be far away. She strained to focus on the familiar face peering down at her. *"Eli?"*

"Miriam, it's Max. Can you hear me?"

Disoriented and her head throbbing, Miriam fixed her gaze on Max and waited for the blurry lines around his face to disappear. "Max," she rasped. "Where am I?"

"You're in the law school. You came across on the ladder to escape the fire."

The fire. Miriam's breath quickened, and she began to rock back and forth. "Oh, God. Did Rivka and the others make it out?"

Max reached out to calm her. "I only know they weren't among the workers that climbed across from the roof. Hopefully, they got out another way."

Miriam began to sob. "Please take me home. My parents will be so worried. And Jacob. I was supposed to meet him at Chumsky's."

"Let's get your arm looked at first. I'll send word to your parents and Jacob."

"Please," she begged, "I want to go home."

"Miriam, your arm looks bad. I think you need to see a doctor."

Miriam clasped Max's hand. "I need to see Jacob and my parents. Please."

Max sighed. "I'll send Murray to tell Jacob you're all right. I'll take you home."

Only then did Miriam give in to the darkness.

Following Max's urgent instructions to get to Chumsky's as fast as possible, Murray pushed his way through the cordoned-off street and sprinted the two blocks to the restaurant. "I'm looking for Jacob Zadkin. Is he here?" he asked, bending over, his hands on his knees, trying to catch his breath.

Chumsky shook his head. "You just missed him. We saw the smoke, and he ran off to the Triangle factory."

"If he comes back, tell him Miriam is safe. Max is taking her home," said Murray, still breathing hard.

"Thank God," muttered the old man, as he watched Murray race back to the factory.

Terror and adrenaline propelled Jacob beyond his physical limits. His lungs burning, his heart beating so hard he could hear his blood thrumming in his ears, he barreled past other pedestrians swarming toward the Asch Building. Shocked at first by the massive crowd surrounding the factory, he plowed through the throng and hurled himself against the police cordon.

"My fiancée is in there! Let me in," he screamed, grabbing a police officer.

An old man pulled him back by the shoulders and held tight as Jacob struggled to free himself. "You can't go in there, son," he said looking up.

Jacob followed his gaze. Transfixed in horror, he watched as a young girl, her skirt ablaze, tumbled head first off a crumbling ledge and slammed with a bone-crushing thud onto the pavement.

CHAPTER 60

After carrying their fire hoses up the stairs to reach the fire, the firefighters had the blaze contained thirty minutes after receiving the first call. When they entered the top three floors of the Asch Building, they were stunned to find the walls and floors intact. It was the twisted metal, smoldering ashes, and charred bodies piled up in front of the elevators and locked doors that told the tale of the raging fire that roared through the Triangle factory.

While a group of firefighters searched the basement for survivors, another group began the harrowing task of bringing out the charred bodies of the men and women who perished on the top floors. Wrapped in shrouds, the victims were lowered to street level as other rescuers hung out of windows to keep the bodies from striking the side of the building. Placing the blackened bodies side-by-side on the sidewalk below, hardened policemen—some who had harassed, beaten, and arrested these very same women during the garment workers' strike just months before—wept.

As word of the fire spread throughout the Lower East Side, the crowd ringing the Asch Building grew larger. Families desperate to find their loved ones wailed in despair and begged to be allowed to view the bodies as they were brought down to street level. Heart-rending cries in Yiddish, Italian, and English cut the air as firefighters doused still-burning remains and the police kept relatives behind barriers while they tagged and covered the lifeless bodies.

Thwarted at every attempt to breach the police cordon, Avrum and

Meyer stood helpless in the midst of the chaos. His head throbbing, Meyer covered his ears to block out the keening all around him. With each body lowered to the ground, he was tormented by the memory of his last words to Miriam that morning.

"I fought with Miriam before she left for work."

Lost in his own thoughts, and praying that Rivka was not among the bodies being lowered to the street, Avrum leaned toward his uncle. "What did you say?"

"I fought with Miriam before she left for work. I was angry with her for working on *Shabbat* and for going to dinner with Jacob afterward instead of coming home." His face contorted in grief and shame, he began to cry. "Oh, God, what if those were my last words to her?"

Miriam was lost in an ocean of terrifying thoughts and images. *Flames everywhere. Where's Rivka? My sleeve is on fire. No, I can't get on the ladder. Don't look down. Eli?*

She began to thrash, pulling at the cloth covering her throbbing arm. A cool hand touched her cheek and pale-yellow light seeped through her closed lids. A voice buzzed in her ears. Her eyes fluttered open and closed again, and she could feel herself slipping back into the dark sea. The voice grew louder, calling her name. She forced her eyes open, and blinking against the sudden light, looked up into her mother's face.

Miriam bolted upright, her words tumbling one after another, her voice rising in hysteria. "Mama! I thought I would never see you and Papa again. The fire spread so quickly, and I was so scared. My arm caught fire. I have to let Jacob know I'm okay. But I couldn't find Rivka. She went to the bathroom, and there was so much fire."

Sadie's body stiffened, and Miriam suddenly became aware of Malka crying softly in the kitchen, Ira and Oscar at her side, their faces grim.

"Mama?" Looking from her aunt to her mother, Miriam began to sob.

"We don't know if Rivka made it out. When we didn't know what happened to both of you, Papa and Avrum went to the factory to look for you and Rivka and haven't returned. Jacob's friend Max brought you home and then went out to find Jacob."

Miriam buried her face in her hands. "I shouldn't have gone to the tenth floor without her. If anything has happened to her, I will never forgive myself."

Sadie took her child in her arms, grateful to God for bringing her home. "Rivka is a strong woman, and I have faith that she found a way to be safe," said Sadie, despite her growing fears.

Day turned to night, the temperature dropped, and rescuers were still lowering bodies from the top floors of the factory. Corralled behind the cordoned-off area, distraught families grew angry and anxious as they watched the charred remains placed into coffins and loaded onto patrol wagons to be transported to a temporary morgue for identification. When word of their destination spread, a wave of heartbroken families flowed onto the streets leading to a covered pier on East Twenty-Sixth Street.

Unwilling to believe Miriam was among the dead, Jacob pushed and shoved his way through the throng to the perimeter of the barricade. Reaching the front of the crowd, he tapped a patrolman on the back. "Officer, do you know if anyone got out alive?"

The policeman turned, and Jacob found himself looking up at the soot-covered face of Officer Boyle.

Boyle studied Jacob, uncertain at first, and then a flash of recognition crossed his face. "I remember you. You helped the strikers." The big patrolman lowered his head for a moment and rubbed his jaw. "I heard they brought a girl up from the basement. They found her on a heap of bodies on top of the elevator. She was in pretty bad shape, but alive. They took her to St. Vincent's Hospital."

Jacob's body slumped. "Thanks, Boyle," he said, turning to leave.

"Wait," said Boyle, putting his hand on Jacob's shoulder. "I also heard about fifty girls and a few men got to the roof and crawled across a ladder to the law school."

"The law school?" Jacob's eyes lit with hope.

Boyle nodded. "I hope you find her." The big officer sucked in his breath and then extended his hand. "And tell her I'm sorry."

Jacob looked at Boyle's outstretched hand and shook it. "I will."

Moving with the crush of people streaming toward the makeshift morgue, Meyer stumbled and would have fallen if Avrum had not grabbed his arm.

"Uncle, are you all right? Do you need to rest?"

Meyer shook his head and leaned on Avrum to steady himself. He would not admit the anxiety and hours of waiting for word of survivors had exhausted him. Tortured by his last words to Miriam, a headache pounded in his temples and his stomach threatened to heave what little it contained. Fear of what he was going to find at the pier had him teetering on the edge of madness.

"I'm fine. Just tired. Avrum, what if ...."

His nephew cut him off. "When we see for ourselves that they are not there, we will know that they are safe at home."

When the elevator doors opened, the color drained from Jacob's face. The halls of the law school were empty, the classrooms dark. He stepped off the lift, his footsteps echoing off the walls of the hallway. "Is anyone here?" he called, hoping to find someone with news of Miriam.

"Jacob, is that you?" answered a tall, round figure standing in the doorway of the men's room wiping his hands.

"Professor Lang?"

"My God, Jacob, Max has been looking all over for you. She's safe! Miriam is safe, my boy."

Jacob stared blankly at the portly instructor grinning back at him.

"Did you hear me? Jacob, Miriam is alive!"

Relief flowed through Jacob's body like a bolt of electricity. He grabbed the big man and hugged him. "Thank God. Where is she?"

"Max borrowed my car and took her home," said Lang, awkwardly patting Jacob's back while trying to extricate himself from his arms.

"I love you, Professor Lang," Jacob shouted to the crimson-faced instructor as he sprinted to the elevator.

Meyer and Avrum joined the long line that had already formed outside the temporary morgue. Shuffling slowly into the entrance, they could hear grief-stricken family members wailing and calling the names of their loved ones. Meyer grasped Avrum's arm and began to shake as weeping family members were led from the covered building.

Avrum put his arm around his uncle's shoulders. "Are you sure you can do this?"

Meyer gestured toward the morgue and continued walking. Stepping into the building, he staggered back, overcome by the grisly nightmare before him. An eerie glow appeared above the coffins as police officers held lanterns over the bodies to help families identify their loved ones. An elderly man began to scream and had to be restrained from throwing himself on one of the coffins. A woman fainted at the sight of bodies burned beyond recognition. A young girl shrieked "Mama!" after recognizing the pair of shoes her mother had just purchased and fell into the arms of a patrolman. The smell of smoke mingled with the unmistakable smell of death.

Avrum tightened his grip on his uncle and they joined the procession of desperate families slowly walking past the numbered coffins. The tragedy of the fire unfolded before them in the broken bodies and unseeing eyes of those spared by the flames and the charred and unrecognizable faces of the victims who died in the blaze.

Meyer stopped at a body so badly burned it barely looked human, and his spirit broke. "Where was God when this happened? She is someone's child! How will she ever be identified and put to rest?"

Battling his own fears, Avrum urged Meyer forward. "Come, Uncle, we are almost at the end, and then we can go home where Rivka and Miriam are waiting for us."

Meyer wiped away his tears with the back of his hand and followed Avrum down the last few rows of rough wooden coffins. The bodies before them were the last to arrive. Taken from the basement and the ninth floor, most were horribly burned, their faces a mass of scorched flesh.

Walking a few steps ahead of Meyer, Avrum studied each of the blackened bodies, turning each time to assure Meyer they needed to keep looking. "Not this one either," he said, blowing out a sigh of relief and moving on to the next body. Getting no response from Meyer, he turned to find his uncle reaching into one of the coffins. Recoiling as if he had been bitten, Meyer cried out in unbearable anguish. "It's Miriam! Oh God, it's Miriam!" he sobbed. His knees gave way and he slid to the floor.

Covering his nose and mouth with the top of his shirt, Avrum leaned down and studied the charred body. "Uncle, this could be anyone. How do you know it's Miriam?"

"This," he cried, holding up the remnant of a red scarf. "Sadie made this for her. See, it has an 'M' embroidered on the corner."

Avrum sank down beside Meyer and buried his face in his hands. Weeping for his cousin, he prayed he would still find Rivka alive.

CHAPTER 61

It had been hours since Avrum and Meyer set out for the Triangle factory. Tormented that Meyer did not know Miriam was safe at home, Sadie
paced the confines of the small apartment, pausing to gaze at her daughter
asleep at last. At Miriam's bedside since he arrived, Jacob dozed in a chair,
still holding her hand.

"It is taking too long. They should be back by now," said Malka. "Ira,
go help Sonia take care of Rebecca and Esther, and then get some rest. And
stop by Rivka's father's apartment. Tell him Avrum is still looking for her."

"Mama, I want to stay."

Malka's face grew stern. "Go. I'll come home as soon as we know
something."

Ira looked at Oscar. "You'll make sure she gets home okay?"

"Of course. You go. Sonia must be out of her mind with worry."

Ira kissed his mother and aunt. "Mama, I don't know what Avrum will
do if Rivka didn't survive."

It was well after midnight when Sadie heard the sound of footsteps trudging up the stairs. "They're here," she said, shaking Malka and Oscar awake.

Meyer stopped in front of the apartment. "How do I tell Sadie that Miriam is never coming home again?"

Avrum studied his uncle's face creased with despair and took a deep
breath. "I think she will know."

The door flew open. "Thank God, you're back," said Sadie. "Rivka?"

Avrum shook his head and unable to meet her eyes, pushed passed Sadie into the apartment.

"She's gone. Our beautiful daughter is gone," wept Meyer.

"No, Meyer, no. She's safe. She escaped the fire. She's here."

Meyer stared at Sadie, not seeing, not hearing. His hand trembling, he held up the burn-scarred scrap of red scarf. "I found this...."

Sadie took his face in her hands. "Meyer, look at me. She is alive. Come see for yourself," she said, leading him into the apartment.

Roused by the noise, Miriam was in Meyer's arms as soon as he stepped into the apartment. "Papa, I heard your voice and I thought I was still dreaming."

Meyer clutched Miriam. "I thought you were dead," he sobbed. "I found this on a body and I thought it was you."

Miriam pulled away from Meyer's arms, her eyes fixed on the burnt piece of scarf in his hand. Her breathing became harsh and uneven; her skin turned pale and clammy. Near collapse, she began to sway. "Oh God, no. Please no," she moaned, her fingers digging into her cheeks. "It's Osna! I gave her my scarf to keep her warm." Her eyes widened suddenly, and she grabbed Avrum's arm. "Osna was going to meet Rivka. Please tell me Rivka got out," she implored, hiccupping between sobs like a small child.

"She wasn't in the morgue at the pier. I was hoping she was here," he said, looking at his mother, his lips trembling as he fought to hold back tears. Malka reached for him, offering the comfort of her arms but at a loss for words that would ease his pain.

Jacob touched Avrum's shoulder. "She might have been injured and taken to a hospital. I know they were bringing survivors to St. Vincent's. I'll go with you to look for her."

A flicker of hope crossed Avrum's face. He put his arm around Miriam. "I'm glad you're safe." He kissed her forehead and signaled to Jacob he was ready to go.

After Avrum and Jacob left, and Miriam had accepted a small glass of schnapps from Meyer to help her sleep, Sadie brought cups of coffee and rolls to the table. "I think it's going to be a long night."

"Ira is right, you know," said Malka. "Avrum will be destroyed if Rivka is dead."

The scene confronting Avrum and Jacob at St. Vincent's Hospital looked like it had been carved from the pits of hell. Doctors and nurses moved frantically among the broken and badly burned victims that continued to arrive in ambulances and carts. Screaming patients with bones protruding from their limbs and charred flesh hanging from their bodies lined the halls. The wailing of relatives and the cries of agony came together in a crescendo of bedlam.

Unnerved by the chaos and carnage, Avrum and Jacob steeled themselves for what they had to do. Walking slowly past the victims, they peered into faces contorted in pain and ravaged by the fire, losing hope of finding Rivka with each step they took.

Avrum pointed at the staircase leading to the wards. "Maybe she's up there." Wading through the crowd, they approached the lobby desk and asked if Rivka had been admitted.

The harried clerk looked at them in disbelief. "Look around. There's so many, we can't keep track of them," she snapped.

"Please," pleaded Avrum. "I can't find my wife. She' pregnant. Just check your list. Rivka Abkin. Please."

Eyeing the line of people standing behind them, the clerk passed a stack of papers to Avrum. "Here. I hope you find her."

With Jacob peering over his shoulder, Avrum ran his finger down the list of patients and failing to find Rivka's name, looked again.

"Stop," cried Jacob, pointing to a name. "Angie is here! She's on the second floor."

Taking the stairs two at a time, they could hear the cries of family members huddled around the beds of loved ones before they entered the first ward. Satisfied that Angie was not there, they moved on to the next ward, where they spotted Gino standing off by himself. Angie's parents were sitting by her bed. Her mother held a rosary, her lips moving in silent prayer.

Calling Gino's name softly, Jacob approached his friend. "How is she?"

Surprised by Jacob's sudden appearance, Gino's eyes clouded in confusion. "Jacob? Avrum? How did you know Angie was here?"

"We're looking for Rivka and saw that Angie had been admitted. How is she?"

Gino took in a long breath. "Not good. Her hands are badly burned, and her right leg is broken. They found her on top of an elevator. My elevator!"

he said, his voice quavering. "She cracked a couple of ribs, too. The doctor said the only reason she is alive is that she landed on the other bodies that had fallen onto the elevator. They've got her sedated because of the pain."

"Gino, I'm so sorry," said Avrum. He cleared his throat and asked, "Did Angie say anything about seeing Rivka?"

"Not that I know of." He reached into his coat pocket "All Angie wanted was for us to get engaged. I finally saved enough money to buy this." In his hand was a ring with a tiny diamond. "I was going to ask her to marry me tonight after Ambra's party."

Avrum breathed in the cold air and watched the first rays of peach-colored light play across the sky. "This is the last one," he said, dropping to sit on the steps of Bellevue Hospital. "She's dead. I know she is. I'm going back to the morgue."

Jacob put his hand on Avrum's shoulder. "You've been up all night. We can go back to the pier tomorrow morning, first thing. You need to go home and get some sleep. When was the last time you had something to eat?"

Avrum's face was set in grief. "I have to find her. I'm going back to the morgue." Rising from the steps, he began walking in the direction of the Twenty-Sixth Street pier.

"Damn it," muttered Jacob, hastening to catch up with him.

With Jacob at his side, Avrum once again walked among the dead looking for Rivka. Joining the line of distraught families, he searched the burnt and grotesquely contorted faces of the mothers, sisters, wives, and daughters waiting to be identified by their families. Just ahead of them, a police officer held a lantern over a coffin for an elderly couple looking for their child.

"It's not her," said the father, shaking his head. "Our Minnie did not wear a chain with a ring."

Avrum froze. "What? Did you say a chain and a ring?"

"Yes. See, there around her neck," said the old man, pointing at a bit of gold, his rheumy eyes filled with sorrow.

Before Jacob could stop him, Avrum stumbled to the coffin and stared mutely at Rivka's remains, her wedding band and chain barely visible under the burnt scraps of her blouse. He began to tremble, his chest heaving, his lungs begging for air. No matter how much he thought he had prepared himself for this moment, every fiber of his body felt as if it was tearing apart. His brain battled with the sight of Rivka's burnt body and the images of her radiant and smiling face when she left him in the morning. Shattered by the loss of his wife and the child he would never hold, he collapsed at the foot of the coffin, his soul-searing howl echoing throughout the covered pier.

CHAPTER 62

Six days after the fire all but seven of the one hundred forty-six victims—
mostly young women—had been identified. A pall of grief hung over
the neighborhoods of the Lower East Side and for days following the blaze,
funeral processions flowed down the eerily quiet streets. Families too poor
to hire carriages walked slowly behind horse-drawn hearses in the cold and
rain, their lamentations cutting like knives into the hearts of neighbors who
stood with their heads bowed as they passed by.

The clopping of horses' hooves as hearses made their way down Hester
Street intensified Miriam's grief; each procession an unwanted reminder of
the friends she'd lost. Osna was the first to be laid to rest. After sorting out
her misidentified remains, Jacob and the ILGWU arranged for the Hebrew
Free Burial Association to help with her funeral. Her parents held tightly to
each other as the rabbi intoned the prayer for the dead for their only child,
and Miriam wept for the loss of her tiny friend with the big heart and live-
ly blue eyes.

Ambra's funeral followed two days later. Jacob accompanied her to
Calvary Cemetery where Ambra was buried surrounded by her large family. The priest talked of her devotion to her family and her love for Joseph.
Joseph stood rigid, his eyes puffy and red-rimmed. Miriam recognized the
look and knew he had no more tears left to cry.

The next day they buried Rivka. The sky was gray, spitting occasional
cold rain on the mourners as the procession wound its way to the cemetery.

Walking with Jacob and her parents behind the hearse carrying Rivka's coffin, Miriam stared at Avrum's back, his shoulders rising and falling with his silent sobs.

"I was supposed to meet her," said Miriam, her voice so flat and low Jacob had to bend toward her to hear her. "I should have tried harder to find her. I never should have left the ninth floor without her."

Jacob drew in a long breath and blew it out. "Miriam, please don't blame yourself. From all reports, the fire moved so fast it is a miracle anyone survived."

Miriam looked away, a heavy weight crushing her chest. *But I did survive, and Rivka and her baby are dead.*

When the procession halted in front of one of several newly dug graves, Avrum stopped the workers from removing the coffin from the hearse. Waving off Malka as she stepped toward him, he ran his hand along the plain pine box, his face cloaked in despair. Sliding his wedding band from his finger, Avrum lifted the cover a fraction and slipped the ring into the coffin before joining the group at the grave.

Miriam watched the rabbi approach as the coffin was carried to the gravesite. Shoulders bowed and walking slowly, his drawn face was a testament to the toll presiding over the funerals of so many Triangle victims had taken. Acknowledging Meyer and Oscar with a nod, he spoke quietly with Avrum and Rivka's father before beginning the service.

Miriam tried to focus on the rabbi's words, but his voice grew fainter as memories of Rivka flooded her thoughts. She closed her eyes and pictured Rivka's sweet face and deep brown eyes and remembered so clearly the day they'd met in Miss Jacobs' English class. Rivka had been so shy and frightened and resistant to her offer to help her learn the language. Miriam recalled how quickly their friendship deepened and how her parents had come to think of Rivka as part of the family, thrilled when her marriage to Avrum made it official. She looked out at the rows of marble headstones that dotted the grounds and began to shake. *Rivka, I am so sorry. I should have waited for you.*

The sound of dirt hitting the coffin jolted Miriam back to reality. Avrum placed the spade in the mound of soil for Rivka's father and then one by one, the mourners cast shovelfuls of earth onto Rivka's coffin and withdrew. Still unwilling to say her final goodbye, Miriam lingered with Avrum.

"I can't believe she is gone." Avrum's voice was raw. "She made me happier than I ever dreamed I could be. We had so many plans for our life and the baby." He began to cry. "I don't know what I will do without her." A thick fog of grief coiled around him.

Unable to find the words to console him, Miriam took Avrum's hand and led him away from Rivka's grave.

After Rivka's funeral, Jacob left to attend another. Stopping at Miriam's apartment at the end of the day, he gratefully accepted the slice of challah and bowl of hot soup Sadie placed before him. "Thank you. This smells so good, and I haven't eaten all day."

Miriam sat with him while he ate, alarmed by his haggard appearance. She could see the long days he spent helping the families of fire victims arrange for their funerals were destroying him. "You don't look well. Can't Ida handle things for a day so you can get some rest?"

"She is working just as hard as I am. There are so many funerals. And it's not just the burials. Local 25 is working with the Red Cross and the Women's Trade Union League to raise money for the families that have no source of income now."

Jacob paused for a moment and his voice grew hard. "Today I helped a family bury their fourteen-year-old daughter and then when I got to the office I heard that Harris and Blanck have reopened the business in another loft building. Families are still burying their loved ones and they have already moved on. It makes me sick. I honestly believe their only remorse is for the inventory they lost."

Miriam was shocked. "Even they can't be that heartless. Who will work for them?"

"Salutsky, for one. Ida heard he escaped with Harris and Blanck. She said one of his eyebrows was burnt off. God forgive me, but that gives me immense pleasure."

Miriam smiled for the first time since the fire.

CHAPTER 63

April 5, 1911

"Miriam, I don't want you to go. It is pouring out there and you will catch pneumonia."

"Papa, please. I have to go. The unions worked hard to organize the funeral procession for the unidentified victims. As a survivor, I owe them the respect of mourning for them."

"You can mourn them in your dry apartment," said Sadie, the set of her jaw revealing her anger.

"Mama, I want to do this for Rivka. For Osna and Ambra, too."

The hard lines on Sadie's face disappeared, and seeing her chance, Miriam quickly added, "I promise I won't walk all the way to cemetery."

Meyer and Sadie exchanged glances that said they knew they were beaten.

Crossing his arms over his chest, Meyer let out a long sigh. "Make sure you wear warm clothes and comfortable shoes. And don't forget to take an umbrella."

Walking beside Ida, Miriam joined the one hundred twenty thousand garment industry workers, Triangle survivors, and union members who marched behind the flower-laden coffin drawn by six white horses covered in black netting. Wearing black arm bands and carrying banners proclaiming: "We Mourn Our Loss," a phalanx of marchers walked in silence through the rain-drenched city.

The downtown streets were lined with working- and middle-class men and women, many dressed in mourner's black. Alerted to the march by leaflets printed in Yiddish, Italian, and English, workers emptied out of the city's lofts and factories and joined the crowd of three hundred fifty thousand that stood in the driving rain to pay their respects as the silent procession went by.

Miriam nudged Ida and pointed to the black bunting hanging from the government buildings and the people waving handkerchiefs out the windows. "After everything we went through during the strike, I never thought the city would honor the victims this way. And who would have believed so many people would come out in the pouring rain?"

Ida looked up and wiped the rain from her face. "Unfortunately, it took the deaths of one hundred forty-six workers to make the politicians and the public acknowledge the abuses of the sweatshops."

"Do you think things will be different now? Better?"

Ida fixed her gaze on the hearse bearing the empty coffin. "God, I hope so."

Despite her umbrella, Miriam's clothes were drenched, and her shoes made sloshing noises with every step she took. Entering the apartment fully prepared for her parents' anger, she was surprised to find Avrum sitting with them at the kitchen table. Looking at their somber faces, Miriam felt a chill of fear. "Has something happened?"

Sadie regarded Miriam's appearance and scowled. "Nothing has happened. Go put on some dry clothes and join us."

Miriam peeled off her wet clothes and changed as quickly as she could. Emerging from her parents' bedroom, she was relieved to see a cup of tea waiting for her on the table. Sipping the hot brew, she was grateful for the warmth that radiated through her body. When no one spoke, she finally asked, "Is someone going to tell me what's going on?"

As if on cue, Sadie and Meyer rose from the table. "We are going to leave you two alone. Avrum has something he wants to talk to you about."

"Me? Why me?"

Avrum stroked the dark beard that had grown during his week-long mourning period. "Because I know you have been eating yourself up with guilt over Rivka's death and I want you to stop. No one—and I mean no one—blames you for her death."

Miriam looked away. "As soon as the end-of-day bell rang, Rivka ran to the bathroom. When I realized the building was on fire, I went to find her, but there was a barrier of flames between us. I should have tried harder to get to her. I never should have left the ninth floor without her." Her face sagged, and her body began to shake so hard she had to hold onto the table to steady herself. "I am so sorry," she sobbed.

"You have nothing to be sorry for. Thank God, you got out. Please, for me, stop blaming yourself. I can see it in your eyes every time you are around me and I can't bear it."

"I miss Rivka every day. You lost so much. I cannot even begin to imagine how you feel."

Avrum stared at the empty cup in front of him. "I feel lost and empty. And I am not going to lie. I can't even think about life without her. But it's not your fault. And if you had managed to get to Rivka and you both died, your parents would be sitting *shiva* for another child."

Miriam's breath caught in her throat, Eli's voice coming back to her: *Think about Mama and Papa and Jacob. You have to survive.*

"You brought Rivka into my life and gave me the gift of happiness. No matter what else happens, I will always have my time with her to cherish," said Avrum. "Choose to remember Rivka in life and not in death. Marry Jacob, raise a family, and live your life. Rivka loved you like a sister, and it's what she would have wanted for you. It's what I want for you."

Miriam met Avrum's steady gaze. His eyes were without luster, his sorrow so naked it pierced her heart. She knew he had ignored his own pain to come here and ease hers. "Thank you," she said, squeezing his hand.

April 11, 1911

Miriam entered Chumsky's Diner and was greeted warmly by the smiling owner. "Miriam!" he exclaimed. "I have missed you. You are feeling well, yes? How is your arm? Jacob said it was burned in the fire."

"I am doing well," she said, as happy to see Mr. Chumsky as he was to see her. "My arm has stopped aching and is healing."

"Ach, good news. We were so worried about you. Jacob was frantic." He looked over Miriam's shoulder. "And where is the good man?"

"He should be here soon. He's downtown waiting to hear if the grand jury voted to indict Harris and Blanck. The district attorney is charging them with knowingly locking doors that would have allowed the workers to escape from the fire."

"They should throw both of those bums in jail and let them rot there," said Chumsky, showing Miriam to the table by the window.

"Unfortunately, it appears they've learned nothing from the fire. Jacob heard that conditions in the building they moved into are just as bad as they were at the Triangle. Doors are locked and an exit to a fire escape is blocked by a row of sewing machines. And there are no sprinklers."

The old man shook his head. "We can only hope the city will put a stop to their way of doing business before there is another tragedy."

"They may have taken the first step today," said Jacob, coming up behind them. "The grand jury indicted Harris and Blanck on charges of first- and second-degree manslaughter."

"Finally," said Miriam. "Does that mean they're in jail?"

"Not yet," said Jacob, removing his hat and coat and taking a seat opposite Miriam. "They have a hot-shot lawyer representing them. They are free after paying twenty-five thousand dollars bail each. Their lawyer argued to have the trial set for December and won."

Miriam made no attempt to hide her frustration. "I can't believe they are free to go about their lives when so many families are mourning their loved ones. So much suffering, and they are going back to their families in their fancy townhouses. It's not right."

"I agree, but I have had enough of those two today. Let's order. I'm starving," said Jacob, turning to Mr. Chumsky. "What's good tonight?"

"I will bring you my chicken soup to start you off. Some say it's the best in the city. Of course the 'some' are my wife and children," said Chumsky, rolling his eyes skyward.

Walking back to Miriam's apartment after dinner, they stopped before the Washington Square Arch.

"I used to love the park," said Miriam gazing up at the arch. "Now it will always remind me of the fire. It frightens me, because I need to go back to work. We are running out of money. Mama's contract work has slowed down, and the money Papa makes from his job at the synagogue doesn't go very far. All I know how to do is sew, and that means going back to a sweat-shop."

"I know you've always wanted to go to school to become a teacher, but for now would you consider working for the ILGWU? Your skills at help-ing organize the strike did not go unnoticed at the union."

Miriam grew thoughtful. She'd been having nightmares about return-ing to work in a factory and dreaded the day she would have to go back. "Do you think there would be a place for me?"

"I will see what I can do. We are certainly busy enough to need more staff."

"I don't want you to jeopardize your position by asking for a favor."

"I think I will be doing them a favor."

CHAPTER 64

Miriam spent her first week at the ILGWU working with the relief committee providing aid to the families of fire victims. Each day she faced a line of mourners whose grief was magnified by sudden financial hardships and the task of arranging for the burial of their loved ones. Parents wept as they talked about the sons and daughters they'd lost; spouses anguished for their husbands and wives. All railed against the greed and indifference of the Triangle owners.

"I leave work exhausted, but it is so satisfying to help the families," Miriam told her parents as they sat down for dinner. "With the funds raised by the ILGWU and the Red Cross, we've been able to help pay some overdue first-of-the-month rents for the families who depended on their loved ones' wages. We've also found doctors who agreed not to charge a fee to treat injured workers. Sadly, we're still arranging for more burials," she said, her voice tapering off.

"I worry that being around so much despair is not good for you," said Meyer, tucking his napkin into the front of his shirt.

"I was worried, too, but when the families leave I know that in some way—no matter how small—I've done something to help lessen the difficulties of moving on, and that's a very good feeling."

Sadie eyed her daughter. "And what about you? Are you moving on?"

Miriam leaned back in her chair. "The fire will always be a part of my life. And I will always wonder if Rivka would still be alive if I hadn't left the ninth floor without her. But after working with the families, I see how grief and regret rob you of all other feelings."

Sadie bowed her head slightly and exhaled as if she had been holding her breath.

A lump began to form in Miriam's throat. "I talked to Angie's parents today. They were in to see about getting a doctor for her. She's home from the hospital but still needs a lot of care. Her hands were so badly burned they are afraid she may never have full use of them. Listening to Mr. and Mrs. Galissi and other families made me realize how fortunate I was to escape the fire and how grateful I am that you weren't the ones burying another child."

Wiping his eyes with his napkin, Meyer asked Miriam to pass the potatoes.

Jacob chatted with Ira while Avrum waited on a customer. Surprised but pleased to see him, Avrum came from behind the counter and shook Jacob's hand. "Hope you don't mind a little pastrami brine with your handshake."

"That's okay, though I will probably crave a pastrami sandwich for the rest of the afternoon," joked Jacob.

The corner of Avrum's mouth ticked up in a near smile. "Then I will make you one before your leave. What brings you by? Is everything all right with Miriam and my aunt and uncle?"

"Everyone is fine. Miriam told me you talked to her, and I wanted to thank you. Whatever you said made a difference. She seems more like herself again. She's working at the union now, and that has helped, too."

"I'm glad she is doing better." Avrum watched the last of the customers exit the store. "We're not too busy now. Do you have time to sit for a while?"

"Of course."

Removing his apron, Avrum left Ira to man the counter.

Jacob followed Avrum to a small closed-off area at the back of the deli, inhaling the heady aromas of the barrels of pickles and jars of spices lining the wall.

"My office," said Avrum, pointing to a battered desk with a thin wedge of wood positioned under one leg to keep it from wobbling. Jacob perched on a wooden crate as Avrum sank into an old upholstered chair, its stuffing poking out like wayward tufts of hair.

"Well, it is cozy." Jacob shifted on the crate trying to get comfortable. He looked at Avrum expectantly. "How are you doing?"

"I have trouble sleeping, so the nights are long." He grew silent, a far-away look on his face. "I feel so empty without her. We had so many plans for our life together. She was finally feeling happy about the baby. We even started picking out names and talked about getting an apartment of our own." His shoulders hunched, and he seemed to shrink before Jacob's eyes.

"I cannot even imagine what you are going through."

Avrum blinked at Jacob as if he had forgotten he was there. He fidgeted with the buttons of his sweater, taking a few seconds to collect himself. When he spoke, he was once again in control of his thoughts.

"I hope you never do." He reached across the scarred desk and adjusted a pile of papers. "You graduate soon, don't you?"

Jacob nodded. "In a few weeks."

"Have you set a date for the wedding?"

"Not yet. Why?" stammered Jacob, taken aback by Avrum's question.

"Because I am thinking of going away, and I don't want to miss it."

"I don't understand. Why are you going away?"

"It's just too hard to stay. People mean well and try to make me feel better, but sometimes it just makes it worse. They say things like 'You have your whole life ahead of you' or 'You'll find someone else.' But I don't want to find anyone else. I want Rivka. I think I am having a good day, and then something reminds me of her and I am lost. I'm not saying I'm going away forever. I just need some time alone. I've thought a lot about this. Oscar looks after Mama better than I ever did, and Esther and Rebecca adore him. Ira can run the deli, and Sonia can help if necessary. They managed perfectly well during the week I sat *shiva*."

"But where will you go?"

"One of our customers told me his son works on a coastal freighter that hauls iron ore up and down the Great Lakes. He said they need cooks." He lifted his shoulders in a half-shrug. "I can cook."

"Are you sure about this?"

"I am. It will be something new. Totally different from my life here."

Jacob's expression dulled, and his mind churned, trying to find the right thing to say to Avrum.

"From the look on your face, I can tell you don't think I am doing the right thing."

"I understand everything you are saying, but I am worried about you being alone and away from the people who love you."

Avrum met Jacob's gaze. "I could not be more alone than I am right now."

CHAPTER 65

"Miriam, you have to stand straight, or I won't get the hem right," complained Sadie through teeth clenched around half a dozen pins.

"It feels like I have been standing for hours. I told you I was perfectly happy to get married in one of my suits."

"Nonsense. You will get married in a proper wedding dress. Other than the hem, it's finished. Now step back so you can see the whole dress in the mirror."

Miriam gaped at her reflection, awestruck by what she saw. With Malka's help Sadie had turned a bolt of white lawn fabric and a few yards of shadow lace into wedding dress of simple beauty. Miriam fingered the lace-trimmed bodice and ran her hands down the empire waist, pleased with how it hugged her body. She turned to admire the flared ankle-length skirt, grateful for the long sleeves that hid the raised scars on her arm.

"Mama, thank you. It's beautiful" said Miriam, hugging her mother.

Sadie stood back, her hands clasped across her chest, tears brimming in her eyes. "And you will be a beautiful bride."

Sunday, June 25, 1911

"It's a lovely day for a wedding," said Sadie, pinning a tulle veil trimmed with shadow lace to Miriam's hair. She bent and kissed her daughter, inhaling Miriam's scent just as she did when she had been an infant snuggled contentedly in her arms. The sweet smell unleashed a kaleidoscope of memories, images of Miriam as a child so vivid that they took her breath away.

Blinking away her tears, Sadie took a thin gold bracelet from the pocket of her skirt and slipped it onto Miriam's arm. "This was your great-grandmother Tessie's. She gave it to my mother when she married my father, and my mother gave it to me the day I married Papa. Now I am giving it to you."

Miriam recognized the bracelet as one of the cherished pieces of jewelry Sadie had sewn into the hem of her coat when they came to America. "It's beautiful, Mama. Thank you."

Sadie looked deep into Miriam's eyes. "I only hope you know the same joy it has seen through three generations of happy marriages."

Miriam hugged her mother, clinging to her as if for the last time. "I love you."

Sadie touched Miriam's face. "I love you too," she said, kissing Miriam once more before she turned toward the door. "It's almost time. I'd better go see if Malka and Oscar and the children have arrived."

Sitting alone in the tiny room off the synagogue sanctuary, Miriam's head felt heavy, her thoughts disjointed, tumbling one on top of the other: Will Mama and Papa be able to manage without my wages? I miss Eli and Yuri. Rivka should be here. Osna and Ambra too. I am starting my life with Jacob, but Avrum will be gone in two days, leaving the only life he has ever known behind. She covered her face with her hands, guilt and regret pressing on her chest like an iron fist. I don't deserve this happiness.

"Miri, we all want you to be happy."

Miriam flinched, her eyes darting around the room. "Eli?"

"I'm here, Miri. We're all here. Be happy."

Behind her, the door opened. Bolting from her chair, Miriam whirled around and nearly knocked Meyer over.

"Miriam! Are you all right? You look frightened."

Miriam slid into her father's embrace, finding solace in the familiar feel of his arms. "I'm okay. Just a little nervous," she said, peering over his shoulder to be sure they were alone.

Meyer stepped back and held her hands, his eyes wet. "You look so beautiful."

Miriam held his hand to her cheek. "I love you, Papa."

"Of course you do," he said, smiling so broadly Miriam laughed. "Come—everyone is here, and Jacob is getting very impatient to see his bride."

They stepped out into the back of the sanctuary, where Sadie waited with a small bouquet of white roses. Meyer lowered Miriam's veil, and she took her place between her parents.

Standing nervously before the *chuppah*—the canopy formed from a tallis stretched over four poles held by Oscar, Avrum, Max and Ira—Jacob gasped and covered his mouth when he saw Miriam, sending ripples of laughter through the small group of guests, Mr. Chumsky's chuckles booming over the others'.

Miriam could feel her face flush under her veil as she gazed at Jacob, his handsome face beaming back at her. She heard the murmurs of delight as she passed the pew where Ida and Malka and the girls sat, laughing when Esther called out to her and waved. Miriam's eyes welled when she saw Angie sitting with Gino, her hands twisted inward by ropey burn scars, her cane resting against the pew.

As they neared the *chuppah*, Jacob stepped down and reached for Miriam's hand.

"Take good care of her," said Meyer, placing Miriam's hand in Jacob's.

"I promise I will," said Jacob, his eyes fastened on Miriam.

A shaft of light shone through the synagogue's stained-glass window, and looking up, Miriam felt a contentment she thought she would never feel again. Smiling radiantly, she joined Jacob under the *chuppah*.

Even years later, whenever Miriam recalled her wedding day, she could not be sure if she imagined seeing them or if they were really there. But on nights when sleep was elusive, when Jacob's steady breathing was the only sound, and Rachel and Etan slept peacefully in the next room dreaming the dreams of the innocent, their faces would appear to her just as they had the moment Jacob took her hand. Eli, his unruly hair curling around his forehead. Yuri, so handsome and happy. Osna and Ambra, their arms linked. Rivka, her beautiful face smiling back at her. "I am happy," Miriam would whisper into the night, and gentle sleep would come.

EPILOGUE

On December 4, 1911, Triangle Shirtwaist co-owners Isaac Harris and Max Blanck entered a New York City courtroom for the start of their trial for first- and second-degree manslaughter. The central issue put before the jury was whether the two men knew the ninth-floor Washington Place door was locked at the time of the fire.

During the trial, the prosecution produced more than one hundred witnesses—many of them teenage Triangle workers—who testified that flames blocked the way to the Greene Street entrance. Recounting their frantic attempts to gain access to the ninth-floor stairs, the witnesses all testified the Washington Place door was locked.

The defense attorney introduced fifty-two witnesses—some Triangle executives and relatives of the owners—who testified that the Washington Place door was unlocked and that a key was attached to the door by a string. In his cross-examination of the prosecution witnesses, the opposing attorney's questions were designed to discredit their testimony by portraying the young women as uneducated, unintelligent immigrants.

On December 27, 1911, after twenty-three days of testimony, it took the jury less than two hours to find Harris and Blanck not guilty. Though jury members believed the door had been locked at the time of the fire, they were not convinced the co-owners were aware that it was.

In March 1914, Blanck and Harris settled twenty-three civil suits brought by families of the fire victims, paying seventy-five dollars for each life lost. The co-owners collected enough insurance money to make a profit of four hundred forty-five dollars for each worker who perished in the fire.

The aftermath of the Triangle tragedy was far-reaching. Public outrage over the fire led to the creation of the Factory Investigation Committee, which launched an examination into the safety and working conditions in New York factories. From 1911 to 1914, thirty-six new laws reforming the New York state labor code were passed. The Bureau of Fire Protection was formed to implement and enforce stricter workplace safety regulations. The administration of Franklin D. Roosevelt enacted federal reforms to ensure workers' safety.

The Triangle Shirtwaist Factory closed in 1918. Their reputation tarnished by the 1911 tragedy, Harris and Blanck were never able to achieve pre-fire profits.

ACKNOWLEDGMENTS

A lthough *Ashes* is a work of fiction, the Kishinev pogrom, the 1910 garment workers' general strike, and the Triangle Factory fire are real
events. I have made every effort to portray these events accurately and
to do justice to the memory of the 146 men and women who perished
in the Triangle Shirtwaist Factory fire. I am particularly indebted to Ed-
ward H. Judge's *Easter in Kishinev: Anatomy of a Pogrom*, New York University Press, 1992, and Jo Ann E. Argersinger's *The Triangle Fire: A Brief
History with Documents*, Bedford/St. Martin's, 2016. Their invaluable information helped me bring these historical moments to the page. I am also
grateful for the help and information I received from the Kheel Center for
Labor Management and Documentation and Archives at Cornell University's ILR School (https://trianglefire.ilr.cornell.edu); the Lower East Side
Tenement Museum (https://tenement.org); the Jewish Virtual Library
(https://www.jewishvirtuallibrary.org/); and PBS' *American Experience:
Triangle Fire* (https://www.pbs.org/wgbh/americanexperience/films/tri-
angle/). Conversations attributed to historical characters are the products
of my imagination and any historical or geographical errors are my own.

 Ashes would be a lesser story were it not for the indispensable insights
of Kim Lazarovich. Many thanks for your encouragement and your note of
support; both inspired me every day. Special gratitude to Bernice Cozewith
for telling me what I needed to hear and for helping to make *Ashes* a better
book.

Ashes would never have happened without the loving support of my family. To my daughter Jenna, my son Jamie, and my son-in-law Kyle, mountains of love and an abundance of gratitude for your constant encouragement and love. Thanks to my grandchildren, Jack, Kate, and Sam, for believing in me and cheering me on. You are my enduring joy. Much love and appreciation to my brother Kenny for always being there for me. To my husband George, all my love and thanks for his unwavering faith in me, for his pep talks when I was ready to abandon my writing, and for his incomparable IT skills. I have been grateful for you since the day we met.

And finally, this book honors the memory of my parents and grandparents. I felt your presence and saw your faces throughout this journey.